little black dress
· IT'S A GIRL THING ·

Dear Little Black Dress Reader,

Thanks for picking up this Little Black Dress book, one of the great new titles from our series of fun, page-turning romance novels. Lucky you — you're about to have a fantastic romantic read that we know you won't be able to put down!

Why don't you make your Little Black Dress experience even better by logging on to

www.littleblackdressbooks.com

where you can:

- ♥ Enter our **monthly competitions** to win **gorgeous** prizes
- ♥ Get **hot-off-the-press** news about our latest titles
- ♥ Read **exclusive** preview chapters both from your **favourite** authors and from brilliant new writing talent
- ♥ Buy **up-and-coming** books online
- ♥ Sign up for an essential slice of romance via our **fortnightly email** newsletter

We love nothing more than to curl up and indulge in an addictive romance, and so we're delighted to welcome you into the Little Black Dress club!

With love from,

The

Five interesting things about Lucy Broadbent:

1. When I'm not writing novels, I'm a freelance journalist and my work is published in *The Times*, the *Independent*, *Daily Mail*, *Marie Claire*, *Glamour* and *Cosmopolitan*, among many others.

2. I live in an old 1930s building in West Hollywood where Tom Cruise once lived before he was famous.

3. I wake every morning with three men in my bed – my husband, who's meant to be there – and our two lads, who are not.

4. I moved to LA to work some years ago, but ended up staying when I met my husband.

5. I miss Britain a lot – especially my family, Marks and Spencer's, British telly and the rain.

By Lucy Broadbent

What's Love Got to Do With It?
A Hollywood Affair

A Hollywood Affair

Lucy Broadbent

little
black
dress

First published in 2009 by
LITTLE BLACK DRESS
An imprint of HEADLINE PUBLISHING GROUP

A LITTLE BLACK DRESS paperback

1

Cataloguing in Publication Data is available from the British Library

ISBN 978 0 7553 4524 3

Typeset in Transit511BT by Avon DataSet Ltd,
Bidford-on-Avon, Warwickshire

Printed and bound in Great Britain by
Clays Ltd, St Ives plc

Headline's policy is to use papers that are natural, renewable and
recyclable products and made from wood grown in sustainable forests.
The logging and manufacturing processes are expected to conform to the
environmental regulations of the country of origin.

HEADLINE PUBLISHING GROUP
An Hachette UK Company
338 Euston Road
London NW1 3BH

www.littleblackdressbooks.com
www.headline.co.uk
www.hachette.co.uk

Acknowledgements

Special thanks to Robin La Borwit, Sean Macaulay, Catherine Cobain, Leah Woodburn, Sara Porter, Helen Norris, Laura Sampson, Karolina Sutton, my wonderful husband, and all the offspring of celebrities who I have met and interviewed over the years and who gave me the idea for this book.

Sex was never meant to be this unnatural. I've got so many pillows stuffed under my rear end that blood is racing to my head. I feel like an Olympic gymnast, frozen mid-flight in a back-flip. I'm flat on my back, pelvis mid-air, and for twenty minutes I am not allowed to move. This was the doctor's advice, and my husband takes anything the doctor says very seriously. He is standing guard over me, in a way I suspect the military on a mission in Iraq might be impressed by. I wriggle – not out of contrition, but because my neck is jarring.

'Uh-uh,' he chides, shaking his head. 'Honey, you've got to stay still.'

'But you've piled up too many pillows,' I plead. 'My neck is hurting.'

He carefully removes a couple, changing the geometric angle of my upper body to something less likely to leave me with a permanent old-woman stoop. 'How's that?'

'Well, I've been more comfortable in the dentist's chair.'

Adam adjusts the pillows again, and ignores all further complaints. 'Now, you've got to relax. You've got to think about s-s-s-sperm,' he stutters, pulling the bedsheets and our giant red comforter around me. 'Imagine them fighting their way up the pike. Imagine them punching through to the ovum. Punch. Kick. Punch—'

'Is this what they call dirty sex?' I interrupt.

'Only if you're doing it right,' he quips, with a smirk that reminds me of times when sex had a little more frisson to it. 'Now take a deep breath in . . .' He sucks in his breath, filling out his mostly hairless chest and making a face like a puffer fish. 'And out . . .' He exhales theatrically. 'You've got to relax into the vision. You've got to make it happen in your mind.'

I close my eyes, take a deep breath and focus my mind on sperm. If sex is such a natural phenomenon, how come there are so many manuals on how to do it? I wonder. But that is beside the point. Right now, I must focus on sperm. Sperm look like tadpoles. Tadpoles turn into frogs. Frogs can be found in pet shops. I remember a sign I saw in a pet shop that read: 'All our pets are flushable.' True story. A smile spreads, and I'm tempted to share it with Adam, but I know he won't appreciate any tales of the U-bend just now. He is a man who takes on challenges with devotion and earnestness. And he views our current challenge – procreation – with all the seriousness of a banker reviewing debt.

He lingers by the bedside table, surveying the neatness of the bedcovers and considering what else he can do to help. If there was anything, Adam would do it. If waving pompoms and wearing a cheerleader skirt would help, he'd be in one. If standing on his head would help, he'd do it. Although he thinks *I* should be doing that. But I've told him I'm not going that far. You've got to draw the line somewhere.

'Go, boys, go,' he eventually calls, actually putting his head under the covers and addressing my belly button. 'These are going to be the ones, honey. I just know they are,' he says, re-emerging and mercifully now talking to my face. 'I can feel it. There's special magic gone into these ones . . .' He smiles sweetly at me, and strokes my shoulder. 'I think one of these is going to cut the mustard.'

For his sake, I hope one does too. A baby would make Adam feel so much more secure.

'I'll set the clock for twenty minutes,' he says, and begins to fumble with the buttons on the alarm.

'It's okay. I can watch for twenty minutes,' I say, waving him away.

'The devil's in the detail, Pearl.'

'It's okay. I won't cheat.'

'I'll set the clock,' he says firmly, and I let him, because when he's in the bathroom I'll turn it off anyway. Men just need to think they're in control.

Aware that he hasn't got any further excuses to hang around and stand guard, Adam takes his patrol to the full-length window and tugs the velvet curtains open to let the morning light spill into the bedroom. It's only seven a.m., but already the sun is bright enough to make the palm trees shimmer as they catch the light outside our window. Still naked, Adam surveys the view of our garden and the Los Angeles skyline beyond. It would be hard for anyone to see in – our house sits on a hillside, overlooking a high bougainvillea hedge at the end of our lawn, several trees, and the city way, way below. We sometimes have coyotes and deer passing across our land, but never any neighbours. Still, it doesn't seem right to stand at a window brazenly naked. My mother is Catholic, after all.

Eventually he disappears into the bathroom, leaving me to contemplate his swimmers, a small spider who is diligently weaving a cobweb overhead, and the reality of the day ahead, which is weighing me down like a pair of concrete boots.

I used to always be able to sleep no matter what lay ahead the next day, immune to nerves or the flotsam my brain would throw at me during the night. But these days I lie awake and worry, wrestling with fears and a frenzied state of exhaustion in the dark. With today pending in my mind's in-tray, it was never going to be a good night. But my therapist tells me it's best not to dwell. And I *must* think about sperm.

When did sex get to be so dull? I wonder. It was never that passionate in the first place with Adam. He's not that sort. He's kind and adoring, but not the sex-in-an-elevator type. Rather like Rachel in *Friends*, the most adventurous place we've ever had sex is the bottom of the bed. And when we first embarked on romance, he actually asked me how I liked my sex, rather like a waiter taking an order for steak. Rare, medium or well done. I half expected him to produce his notebook and take notes. Anything other than back to back, I told him. Maybe I should have been more specific.

Adam wanted to know because he felt it was important to get it right, which is cute in its own way. It shows a certain willingness. But taking orders for sex is a bit like shopping for clothes on the internet – it looks like just the perfect dress when you order it, but by the time it arrives you've already been to the party you had it in mind for, and now you fancy something different. Not to mention it's never quite as good in reality as it is in the picture.

Adam is a man who likes to get everything right. When a purchase is to be made, consumer magazines are consulted, options are weighed, stores visited, and only when he's convinced does he get out his credit card. Which would be all right if he was buying a car, but when it's only a roll of toilet paper at the supermarket ... I sometimes tease him about how much research and consideration must have gone into choosing me for a wife, but Adam says that some things you just know and no research is necessary. He knew from the minute we met.

The shower taps squeak as Adam turns them off. There's a restful silence after the water stops, then the click of the shower door opening and the thunderous and conscientious rubbing of towel against flesh. Now will come the ten-minute shave, the patting of aftershave, two precise minutes of electric toothbrush buzzing and then the combing of gel through his thick, tufty hair. After three years of marriage, the routine is strangely comforting to me. Precision is what Adam likes best, and if he missed just one second off his teeth-cleaning regime, I'd feel unnerved.

'I'm pitching a script today,' he tells me as he re-emerges from the bathroom and begins a search through his closet for clothes. I run an eye over the body I've come to be so familiar with. He is not a tall man, nor a big build, but he's fit. Three mornings of power yoga a week have produced the long, curved lines of muscle definition in his arms and torso. His hair is slicked back with gel, making it darker than its normal mousy brown. And his hazel eyes are yet to be shrouded by the armour of his dark-rimmed glasses, which transform him from the safe, loving person who shares the bed with me into the scriptwriter who battles with the politics of film-making every day. He's not a handsome man in a traditional sense, but beauty comes from within, and Adam is kind. It's one of the reasons I love him.

'It's g-g-g-going to be a b-b-big meeting,' he continues, picking out a pair of Gucci pants. Adam sometimes has a stutter. He's battled to overcome it all his life, and it usually only shows when he's nervous.

'Well, I'm sure you'll do well,' I say soothingly.

A loud thump from Thackeray's bedroom disturbs us. It's Thackeray's feet hitting the ground as he gets out of bed. He pad-pad-pads across the hardwood floor to my side and sleepily climbs into the bed. My gorgeous five year old. His toes are icy cold – one of the hazards of always kicking the bedclothes off – and I wrap him in my highly prized 1,500-thread-count Bloomingdale sheets, with his little head nestling in the crook of my arm.

During the day he barely stops – a human dynamo who has no time for cuddles – but in the morning and at bedtime, there's a brief chance to breathe in his smell, feel the softness of his warm cheek and smother him in abundant maternal love.

'Is it a school day today?' he asks, sitting up beside me and breaking into a smile that could only have come from his father's DNA – engaging, captivating, bewitching, the kind that I know will get him whatever he wants in life. Sometimes Thackeray looks so much like his father, it's almost as if I didn't have a hand in his birth at all. The dark eyes that can tell me his mood without him even needing to speak, the mop of auburn hair that he hates me cutting, the long limbs that I know are going to make him tall. God, he's beautiful.

'Yup, sure is.'

'When's it gonna be Saturday?' he whines.

'Today it's Wednesday, then comes Thursday, then it's Friday. Then it's Saturday.'

'But that's so long.' He pouts, and then notices my strange position. 'Mommy, why are you lying like that?' he asks.

'I'm practising being a human bridge for your train set,' I tell him.

'Cool,' he announces, as if it's perfectly natural and logical that I would want to practise such a thing.

Adam plants a kiss on Thackeray's forehead. 'Morning, buddy,' he says. 'Sleep well?'

It takes a special man to take on another man's child and raise him as his own. It's another of the reasons why I love Adam. Thackeray needed a father and Adam stepped up, consulting child behavioural books and *Best Toy* magazine as he went. And somehow that makes it even more heartbreaking that we haven't been able to conceive a child together ourselves. I want to give Adam that. He's been so kind to us.

We started trying for a baby not long after we got married. It was Adam's idea. 'It's the right thing to do,' he told me, and I knew it probably was. At first it didn't seem to matter that no baby ever came, but the more you're deprived of something, the more you want it, and now trying is part of the narrative of our life together. Every month we go through the motions of making love, but when sex is for its real biological purpose, it's about as romantic as an accountant's spreadsheet.

Sometimes I even secretly prefer the monthly visits to the doctor's medical office, where Adam disappears into a cubicle to magically produce his finest into a Petri dish. Then an hour later, after his sperm are spun through a special scientific kind of washing machine that is meant to make the little darlings more potent, rather than just plain dizzy, they are squirted inside me with the scientific equivalent of a turkey baster. It's clinical, soulless, but at least it gives me an opportunity to say to the doctor, 'How was it for you?'

I'm too young to be infertile, according to the doctors. I'm only twenty-five, after all. They think our problem lies in the mobility of Adam's sperm and the concentration of his semen, which means (and yes, we actually paid money for this advice), the more frequently we have sex, the better our chances. Also the use of this special sperm washing machine will help.

It's all just a question of timing – precise timing, a language that Adam speaks, metered out usually by the Cartier Ballon Bleu on his wrist, which took no fewer than ten shopping trips and three months' internet research to purchase. It can take approximately twenty minutes for a sperm to make it to a woman's uterus, where we hope an egg lies in wait, which is why Adam likes me to lie like this for twenty precise minutes after sex, pelvis raised to help them on their way. I've no idea if it helps, but I get a nice lie-in, which is fine on the weekend, but today is a work day, and not just any work day. It's a day I've been mentally playing out in my head for more than four years now. Today is a day that has my heart pounding like bad seventies disco music.

So after Adam has taken Thackeray downstairs for waffles and cereal, I sneak out of bed. What's a few minutes between sperm, after all? I scurry quietly to the bathroom, avoiding the squeaky floorboard in the middle of the bedroom, and then to my closet. What to wear? A killer suit, for sure. But the Donna Karan with the above-the-knee skirt or the Armani with pants? Or what about the Missoni double-breasted? Or the Alexander McQueen jumpsuit? I falter briefly. Sexy or bank worker? Defiant red or blend-into-the-scenery black? The look I am after is Carrie Bradshaw Kicks Ass. I choose the red Donna Karan with the above-the-knee skirt.

Now the shoes. I pick out a pair of Stuart Weitzman stilettos – spiky, mean, and high enough to change my view. The stiletto was named after the Italian knife favoured by assassins. How apt for a day like today. As a short person, I have always gone for heels. They change everything – they give height, authority, and a certain steeliness. They elevate the butt, sculpt the calves, elongate the thighs. It's just such a shame that they hurt your feet so much.

I dress quickly and survey the completed look. Today I am confident, strong, resilient. I am a desirable woman. I've got five thousand dollars' worth of therapy behind me. I can do this. But what's with the dark circles under my eyes? I lean in closer to the mirror. How did they get there? I pull the skin taut and experiment with a few facial expressions to banish the shadows. They don't seem to show if I scrunch up my nose, but this is not an ideal look for a day in the office. I pull out my make-up and work quickly. Concealer, foundation, fawn eyeshadow, more foundation, a little blush, mascara, eyeliner, more mascara, a bit more foundation, and some bright red lipstick to match the suit. Too much? Nah. Not for today.

'You look nice,' Adam proclaims as I teeter into the kitchen. Snowy, our white cockatiel, whistles at me from her cage by the window and Thackeray asks me why I've got red lips.

'It's only lipstick,' I tell him. 'You've seen me wear it before.'

'But they're so red,' he marvels. 'Like blood. Is lipstick made from blood?'

Thackeray is developing a frightening interest in all things biological. I caught him trying to dissect the neighbour's cat in the garden last week with a kitchen knife. Poor Pickles didn't even have the dignity of anaesthetic.

'No, it's just make-up. No blood,' I reassure. Thackeray looks disappointed.

'Not secretly running for office?' says Adam, who has returned to his task of stacking plates in the dishwasher. We have a maid who will do this, but Adam is an obsessive tidier.

'Just thought I'd dress up a bit today, that's all,' I say, doing my best to sound casual. 'There's a meeting on.'

I feel a stab of conscience. I don't like telling lies. And it's not that I have. I'm just wearing a suit to work. People do it all the time. It's just a suit, for goodness' sake.

'Well, you look great.'

'It's just a suit.'

I catch sight of the clock, which is seconds off 7.45 a.m. 'Got to go, I'm going to be late.' I grab a banana from the fruit bowl, and reach across the table to kiss Thackeray goodbye.

'Mummy, are you picking me up from school today?' he asks, always a master at keeping me glued to him.

'Sure am, sugar. Daddy's taking you, and I'm bringing you home. Is that OK?'

He nods. I kiss him again, then wipe the lipstick mark off his cheek, and blow one to Adam.

'Love you,' he calls after me.

Luckily, it usually only takes me fifteen minutes to get to work – as long as it's not a Thursday, when the traffic gods send us the garbage truck to test karmic patience and block our road. Our house is in Bel Air – not far from a house that Elizabeth Taylor once owned, and another that Ronald Reagan died in. To call it an expensive neighbourhood would be like describing LA as simply big. And you know, of course, that LA is super, mega, double-whammy, triple-XL, blow-your-mind enormous. It can take you three days just to get across it – and that's without traffic. When people buy houses in Bel Air, they're not worrying if they can afford the cleaner's hours to get round all of the bedrooms. That is, if they can even remember how many bedrooms they have.

We've always been able to remember how many bedrooms we've got, since there are only four. And we haven't a pool, but we do have a double garage, hot tub and, most importantly, the 90077 zip code, which matters a great deal. Call me a snob, I don't mind. LA wasn't built without snobs, just as Rome wasn't built in a day.

My boss's mansion has got the 90210 zip code, which some people think is better, but I say what's the difference? It's either grand cru or vintage champagne. Both are good. He's also got ten bedrooms, or is it twelve? I've forgotten. That's as well as the home cinema, basement massage parlour, spa, arcade games room, basketball court, tennis court, swimming pools, and grounds that are big enough to show up on maps. Those are big differences. Taking care of them all is part of my job. I'm his PA. And my office is just off the vast hallway.

*

Having made it to work on time, this is where I now cower. Despite all the affirmations of confidence and strength inside my head, the message that I'm a beautiful, desirable, intelligent woman doesn't appear to be reaching my hands, which are shaking like mini-earthquakes. Come on, you can do this, I tell myself. I try to make the coffee (decaffeinated, naturally), but am forced to abandon the mission when the waves inside the coffee pot reach tsunami proportions. I am feeling the way I used to as a little girl in the doctor's waiting room, terrified in the knowledge that the pain and lingering hurt of an injection is a certainty in my future.

I try reading today's *Variety* magazine, which is sitting on my desk – Julia Roberts has turned down millions to do a new movie because she wants to be a stay-at-home mom – but all I can think of is the buzzer from the front gates, and Brett Ellis's Ferrari pulling up at the front of the house. I practise being cool inside my head. I can do cool. I'm good at that. I'll be so frosty, the windows will ice up. I'll be Medusa and turn Brett Ellis to stone. I'll be Poison Ivy and turn him into a tree. I'll be Roxie Hart and murder him at an unsuspecting hour.

The buzzer goes. 'Hello. Can I help you?' I say politely.

The familiarity of the voice over the intercom shocks me. It's the same as it always was – warm, velvety, soft. Somehow, after all this time, I expected it to be different. Meaner, perhaps, harsher. It's easy to create demons, I realise, with the distance of time.

'It's Brett Ellis,' says my ex-husband. I press the button to let him drive his car up to the house.

2

I realised for the first time that my parents weren't the same as other kids' when I was four years old. We were at Mortons in Beverly Hills. The five of us were together, which in itself was noteworthy. We were rarely together as a family – not even at Christmas or Thanksgiving. Mum was wearing a big hat – a wide-brimmed straw creation that must have been fashionable at the time. Also sunglasses, big, black and shiny, that would slide down her nose. And bright pink lips that matched her nails. She smelled strongly of perfume and cigarette smoke. I remember also a yellow flowery sundress that showed off her shoulders and a bony collarbone. As always, she was groomed to perfection. My childhood is metered in outfits I can remember her wearing – Chanel, Givenchy, Lacroix, Fendi. There wasn't a designer name missing from the party that went on behind the closed doors of her closet every day. Dad would have been in his usual jeans, T-shirt, leather jacket maybe. Nothing noteworthy. But that was not his role. He was always low-key, hand in hand with a spectacular bird of paradise. He liked it that way.

That day, Lydia, my older half-sister by eight years, had pulled rank and insisted on sitting next to Dad. Ashley, who was five, wanted to sit on the other side of him. There was almost a scene. But I'd been placated with the promise of ice cream if I didn't cause a fuss.

It was then, with a basket of bread rolls obscuring my sightline of anything on the table because the chair was low and they didn't have a booster seat for me to sit on, that I became aware that people were looking over at us. The other diners would pretend that they weren't, but I could see them surreptitiously glancing over menus and whispering. Or they'd pretend they were just looking casually around the room, yet their gazes, all too obviously, kept returning to us.

Then I heard a woman at the next table saying, 'Isn't that Gavin Sash over there?' She was asking the waiter! Why would the waiter know who my dad was? And how did she know his name? Did she know my name?

'How come that lady knows you, Daddy?' I asked him.

'I don't know, sweetheart,' he said lamely.

'Because your daddy is famous,' Mum interjected from behind her dark glasses.

Even as a four year old, with scant understanding of emotion, I could see the pride with which she said it. 'Everyone knows your daddy,' she added.

'What, everyone in this restaurant?'

'Probably.' She nodded with a satisfied smile. 'Probably in all of America.'

'Probably all the world,' Lydia chimed in like a smartass, relishing the opportunity of showing off her twelve-year-old knowledge.

'But I don't want everyone to know him,' I stammered. The news upset me. I felt the wound of jealousy. It was bad enough having to share Daddy with Lydia and Ashley, let alone everyone else in the restaurant, let alone everyone else in the world. Who were all these people that had a claim on him? 'He's MY daddy,' I shouted. 'They can't know him. I won't let them.'

I caused quite a disturbance in the restaurant – the sight of Gavin Sash placating a tantruming child was enough to lift the veil off all pretence at politeness, and now people stared at us quite openly. In the end, I got to sit on Dad's knee – a supreme victory over Lydia and Ashley – but the jealousy was a long way off subsiding.

Strangely, I didn't feel the same stab of resentment when Lydia chose this moment to break it to me that Mum was famous too. 'Your mummy's a model. That means people photograph her because she's so beautiful,' she explained patiently, slyly, cat-like, making quite sure I'd understood. Tantrums from me always made Lydia look good. 'That means everyone knows who she is too.'

My placatory ice-cream sundae was too delicious to spoil with more tears, but somehow I'd always known Mum wasn't mine anyway. She was always too far out of reach. It wasn't Mum who woke us up in the mornings, it was Betty, our nanny. It wasn't Mum who took me to the park, it was Betty. It wasn't Mum who cuddled me when I fell and hurt my knee. Betty, I knew, was mine.

But even though Dad wasn't around much, he was still mine too. And I was his. He had told me as much. There was something between us that was always special. 'Who's Daddy's Pearl?' he'd ask.

'I am,' I'd say. 'And who's Pearl's big daddy?'

'I am, silly!' he'd laugh.

No need to say it. I know I am a chicken. Hiding inside my office, with Brett out there in the hall, practically on the other side of the door, wasn't quite what I had in mind this morning when I got dressed. I'm ashamed of myself. But I can't go out there. I can't.

'How ya doin', Maria?' I hear Brett say chirpily.

'Same shit. Different day,' she replies.

In a moment of impressive cowardice, I asked Maria, the housekeeper, to let Brett in. Showing clients into Stephen's office is my job. But I just couldn't do it.

'You're looking younger than ever,' I hear him tell her. He always could lay on the charm if he wanted to. 'Where's the big boss?'

'In his office,' says Maria. 'Step this way?'

I hear his footsteps stop by a David Hockney that's hung on the west wall. That means he is only a few metres from me now. If I put my nose to the crack in the door, I bet I could even smell him. Wonder if he still wears L'Homme aftershave. He'll be squinting at the picture now, creasing up his eyes with the air of an art dealer. He always liked to think he knew about art. Eventually I hear his footsteps on the stone floor disappear into Stephen's office, and then the false bonhomie and back-slapping as the two men greet.

'Can you get us some coffee?' I hear Stephen ask

Maria. Then the door closes and the voices become a low burble.

I let out a sigh. Pathetic. That's what I am. Pathetic.

I never thought I'd go back to work after Thackeray was born. But when he started school last year, I needed something to fill the hours. 'You must always have an upcoming album,' Dad used to say, speaking figuratively for a personal project. He always insisted we had to make our own way, just as he had. Adam was encouraging too about going back to work. He knew that too many hours on my own risked a bill from Fred Segal, my favourite place to shop. Working for Stephen is not the most ambitious of jobs. It's mundane largely, but I enjoy reading the movie scripts. There are a lot that pass over my desk.

I was Stephen's PA for two years before I got pregnant with Thackeray. In Stephen Shawe's world that was a record – most of his PAs quit after a month because being bad-tempered comes as naturally to him as it does to camels. He owns the biggest talent agency in LA, and likes to think that that puts him up there with Oprah Winfrey and the President in terms of power. But difficult people are my speciality – I've lived with enough of them – and when I heard Stephen was hiring, I called him up, laying out my terms for returning to my old job. Two mornings off a month for my charity lunches, and I had to be out of there before three p.m. to pick up Thackeray from school. No exceptions. Not that Stephen ever remembers.

What I hadn't thought through properly when I took on the job again was that Brett Ellis is one of Stephen's biggest clients. In the back of my mind I knew, of course. It was me who introduced the two of them in the first place. But Stephen's clients rarely come up to his house, so I thought it wouldn't matter. Stephen's other PA, Frank, deals with most of them up on the ninth floor of

Shawe Towers. Brett's getting the special treatment today.

It's also pretty unusual for Brett to even be in LA. Since going from B roles to A-list blockbusters, he's worked on all his films back-to-back. He's quite the star these days, and goes from one location to another, one film shoot on to the next. Bumping into him has never been an issue. Until now.

After ten minutes the door to Stephen's office opens. 'Pearl, bring in the file of Brett's reviews, wouldchya?' he calls.

The file is on my desk. I steady my hand, but there are vibrators that come less agitated, and somehow all the newspaper cuttings in the file spill on to the floor. Come on, you can do this, I tell myself. You're beautiful, confident and intelligent. Stride purposefully, and walk the walk. I take a deep breath, pick up the cuttings, and stride.

Over the six years since we split, I've indulged in so many fantasies involving revenge and the murder of Brett Ellis, I'm surprised I've not been locked up. I am aware that they are all ridiculous. But betrayal is an ugly business. Losing a partner to death leaves you only with sorrow and happy memories. Losing a partner who cheats on you turns happy memories into sour ones; it bequeaths a mistrust of all relationships and absconds with your sanity, leaving a dark, seething anger that keeps you awake at night. It's like a raging disease that comes alive with insomnia. There have been many nocturnal misdeeds committed in my mind. But sanity, not to mention my therapist, dictates the need to accept and move on. And in the mornings, I always do.

Brett is Thackeray's father. My marriage to him barely made it past lunchtime. 'Rock Royalty Wedding Hits The Rocks', ran the headline. 'Actor Brett Ellis Divorces Gavin Sash's Daughter.' I'm always Gavin Sash's daughter, by the way. Always the daughter of rock's greatest living legend. Never Pearl Sash, a person in my own right, never Pearl Sash, someone who is worthy of her own name.

I wish I could say I never read the articles about Brett, but it's like trying to not rubberneck when you see a car accident on the side of the road. You know you shouldn't look, and you always wish you hadn't, but you do. It's the lies that drive me crazy. 'Fame doesn't interest me. I care about good roles,' he told some sucker from *Vanity Fair*. Oh, yeah. And I'm Lindsay Lohan.

And then there's our marriage. That really gets me going. 'It was an amicable split,' Brett always tells the press. 'We mutually agreed to go our separate ways.' Funny how I can't remember mutually agreeing to him climbing into bed with Conzuela Martin on a movie set in Hawaii whilst my belly was so big I needed a forklift truck to get around, waiting for the arrival of our son.

I haven't spoken to Brett since finding him in bed in his trailer, lustily entwined around his co-star. It was a piece of off-camera action that defines Hollywood clichés. Funnily enough, I don't remember his face as I walked in on him, but I do remember the look of embarrassment on the crew's. The stage manager had even tried to steer me away, asking me if I'd like to wait in the catering unit while he fetched Brett. Everyone knew what was going on. Even I knew, deep down. The *National Enquirer* had been running stories about the two of them for months, but I needed to see it with my own eyes to believe it.

The memory of it still makes me flinch. The sudden urge to be sick, the panic, the mental chaos, the lurch in my stomach, my entrails turning to jellied eels. They all still reappear from time to time.

'Ah, Pearl,' Brett said, trying hard to keep order in his voice as I walked in. The blonde scrabbled to find a bedsheet and cover herself. 'Darling,' he added, filling the void with tenderness and concern.

I wanted to scream, but no sound came out. Confusion and pain zapped through my brain, short-circuiting common sense and the ability to even move. I don't know how long I stood there, with the walls of the trailer closing in on me like a bad dream. What did all this mean? What was this woman doing in my husband's bed? Why was she here?

'Nice to meet you,' I think I heard her say, as she pushed past me in the trailer doorway, disappearing down the steps wearing only the bedsheet.

Eventually I summoned up enough fury to pull my wedding and engagement rings off my finger and throw them at him, screaming, 'You piece of shit!' It's hard to be original when your life is falling around you.

'Darling, don't make a fuss,' he warned. Was that a hint of menace in his voice? 'It's so like you to make a fuss,' he added.

'What?'

'It was nothing, darling. Nothing,' he carried on. 'This is the movie business.'

As if I needed reminding. Eventually I turned tail and fled. I couldn't bear talking to him, still lying there in that trailer bed. I fled all the way back to LA. And two days later, he called saying that his 'nothing' was in fact true love, and he was going to move in with Conzuela. A month later, Thackeray was born.

I'd never thought I was the divorcing kind. Like there's such a person anyway. But I'd really thought Brett was my soulmate. All marriages have their hiccups, and for a while – all right, a way longer while than it should have been – I harboured hopes that Brett would abandon Conzuela and come back to me. Hadn't he said 'She was nothing'? or was it 'It was nothing'? I couldn't remember, but for a long while I thought perhaps he was right.

Perhaps I did make too much of a fuss. Maybe if I'd turned a blind eye, Conzuela would have disappeared and Thackeray would have had a father. Brett had wanted to do the right thing when we discovered I was pregnant, and we'd got married. For a long time, I even felt guilty. Imagine that. Me guilty for what *he* did. I thought perhaps it was all my fault. And I'd have taken him back too. I longed for him to come back.

But he never did, and eventually, anger overtook self-deception, and acceptance overtook the pain. I divorced him the following year. He didn't contest. Didn't even want custody of Thackeray. I could have gone after him for money. Girlfriends told me I should, but I just wanted to cut loose. And besides, Adam had already rescued me by then.

But it's not easy to forget someone when you still see their face all the time – on the covers of magazines, on the sides of buildings, buses, park benches. I can be sitting in traffic and suddenly Brett's face comes leering at me from the side of a bus, advertising his latest movie. It's really unnerving. Just as you think you've exorcised an unhappy chapter from your life, you pick up a newspaper and there's that familiar face again, smiling away as if nothing had ever happened. Brett's career trajectory has been nothing if not meteoric, and in Hollywood, that gives him a big presence.

It also now means he can pick and choose what roles he takes. And recently he's got really picky. So picky that Stephen's set up this meeting to try to persuade him to take one of the parts he's been offered. Brett hasn't signed a contract for a new movie for over six months, and he's been turning down so much that Stephen is now losing sleep over the loss of his twenty per cent. Worst case of an inflated ego Stephen says he's ever seen.

I march – beautifully, confidently and intelligently – into Stephen's office. I ignore Brett completely. Well done, girl, I tell myself. But out of the corner of my eye, I catch his face. There's a smile spreading across it. A genuine smile. This is a shock. For some reason, I anticipated hostility.

'Pearl,' he says slowly, relishing every letter. I try to read meaning into his intonation. Does this mean he's pleased to see me? Well, does it? But this is a dangerous game when just the tone of his voice carries resonance on the playback button inside my head.

'Hello, Brett,' I say as coolly as I can, although not nearly as icily as I practised.

'You look . . . you look . . .' He looks me up and down. 'You look beautiful.'

'Thanks,' I say with forced nonchalance, and hand Stephen the file.

'Tell me, how are you?' he says, all concern in his eyes. He's just putting it on, I tell myself. I've seen it all before.

'I'm fine,' I say flatly. Coldly. Harshly. I can do mean, I know I can.

Stephen is now muttering to himself at his desk and rifling through the file, uninterested in the significance of this meeting. Stephen's thoughts revolve around money and bank balances.

'Pearl, where are the reviews for *The Good Guys*, the really bad ones?' he asks. I find them for him in the file with just a small degree of personal satisfaction. I know what's coming.

'Yeah, these are the ones,' he says. 'Take a seat, Pearl. I'd like your input on this.' I pull up a chair, and he begins to read aloud. ' "A catastrophe of bad acting – Brett Ellis is a one-dimensional actor who overacts like a hambone. His performances are so dire that his movies should be called endurance tests . . ." '

Whilst Stephen is reading, I take stock of Brett's face. Eyes still dark and expressive. I can see the hurt of the bad review. He flinches at its harshness. He looks almost sad, haunted even. There are a few more lines around the eyes than there used to be. Dark circles too, and a seriousness about him that wasn't there before. The hair is still dark, unruly and so thick that I know he keeps a stylist on payroll to do daily battle with it. The jawline still chiselled and angular – no jowls: a lean diet and personal trainer make sure of that. The mouth, too big for his face, an imperfection perhaps, but the feature that makes him stand out from the rest. A breathtakingly handsome man, a man who defines movie-star good looks – but flawed because he's aware of it.

'Stop!' Brett runs his hands through his hair, paces over to the window and sighs a deep, long sigh. I feel the pull of physical attraction, like a fridge magnet pulling me towards the freezer section, but I know not to go there now. He carries an iced-up 'Hazardous Goods' label with him now.

'Stop with the reviews,' he repeats. 'You don't need to do this. What are you trying to tell me?'

'I'm trying to tell you that you can't keep turning down roles. You're not that good an actor that you can afford to.'

This, I am aware, is Stephen at his most cruel. Brett isn't that bad an actor. In fact, we had to search hard to find any bad reviews about him at all. But Stephen pushes his clients hard. And he knows their insecurities. If an actor thinks he's got time to rest, then Stephen's not making money. And nothing makes an actor work harder than thinking he's not good enough.

'Stephen, I've had five hit films in less than four years. I'm entitled to some breathing space.'

'Define "hit",' says Stephen, unmoved. 'One good opening weekend at the box office doesn't make it a hit. Really, you're not as hot as you think you are. Is he, Pearl?' He looks across at me. 'You tell him, Pearl. Tell him he stinks.'

Like most actors, Brett was always insecure about his

acting. To be told that he's not that good by his agent will be crushing for him. I know this. To hear it from me as well will be a painful, lingering kick in his side. It's my moment to hurt him where I can. I think hard of a cruel barb.

'Well, I wouldn't say he stinks,' my mouth says before my brains have caught up with it. God, what's the matter with me?

'I'm a box-office star,' says Brett matter-of-factly. 'People love my movies . . . But I need a rest. If I do another film, it's got to have integrity.'

I stifle a gasp. Brett contemplating integrity? I almost want to laugh. I can't imagine he even knows the meaning of the word. When he was clawing his way up past bit parts and crowd scenes, there wasn't a role he wouldn't trip up another actor to get himself, nor a contact he wouldn't sleep with. Ambition has no room for integrity.

Stephen is equally shocked, but for different reasons.

'What do you mean, "if" you do another film?' He is struggling to contain his temper.

'If I do another movie,' Brett repeats slowly.

'I'm busting my balls to get you good scripts to look at and you're telling me what? You're telling me you're giving up?'

'No, I'm telling you I need a good role. I want a part that has a message behind it. Not some mindless violent action schlop. I'm sick of action films.'

Brett made his name doing action films, but he's done some thrillers too, one of which even got him a Golden Globe. I'd have thought he'd have been satisfied with that. It gave him the high profile he craved.

'Artistic indie films have no budget,' Stephen says flatly. 'You know that, don't you?'

'So I take a pay cut . . .' Brett pauses. I can't believe I'd ever hear him say those words. 'Look, if you can't deliver, then I need to find a different agent.'

There's a momentary silence. This is Stephen's worst fear – and the reason, I realise, why he is inviting Brett here, rather than to his office. He chews on his lower lip nervously. Ordinarily Stephen would be telling Brett to take a hike – he only has a limited patience with difficult people – but Brett is a big client, and to lose him would be a public humiliation, not to mention costly.

'OK,' he says with a heavy sigh. 'You're probably right, you probably do need a rest. You're certainly not seeing straight. Let me see what Uncle Stephen can do for you.'

'I'm serious, Stephen,' Brett snarls at him, with frown lines running deep in his forehead.

'Take it easy. I'll do the best I can,' says Stephen, looking troubled. 'Pearl will show you out,' and he signals to me.

Brett doesn't speak as I lead him through the hallway, past the Louis XV gilded chairs, the Basquiat orginals, the giant crystal chandelier. I hear his footsteps behind me as my heels stalk the floorboards. I hope he's taking in my fabulously toned fifty-squats-a-day butt and realising what he's missed. Without a word, I show him out of the front door, where a motorbike is parked on the driveway. A motorbike? What happened to the Ferrari? Having done all that is required of me, I turn to walk back inside the house. He doesn't deserve a goodbye or a smile.

'Hey, Pearl,' he calls after me. 'It's nice to see you.'

This would be my moment to keep on walking; my time to ignore his over-pandered ego and get what small revenge I can muster from the iciness of a turned back and a cold shoulder. It's what I long to do. It's what I've practised doing so many times. But something, habit perhaps, good manners even, compels me to turn.

He is standing by his bike, helmet in hand, and looking straight at me. His face shows tenderness, and I feel the familiar pang of sadness for what was lost and gone before.

'I'm sorry,' he says flatly. This is so uncharacteristic, I think briefly that I must have misheard. Once he became famous, Brett Ellis never said sorry. His stock phrase was 'I'm sorry that you're upset'. Not 'Sorry for what I did' or 'I'm sorry I hurt your feelings', but 'I'm sorry that you've taken this the wrong way and chosen to be upset'. There's a difference.

He says it again. And I say nothing, because what can I say? Does he think 'I'm sorry' is going to fix a ripped-apart marriage, a broken heart, all that time on my own with a small baby? I feel a surge of anger well up inside.

'I miss you,' he adds quietly, and from the look in his eyes, he could easily mean it. But then Brett is an actor, I remind myself.

I march back into the house and slam the front door.

Back in my office, I begin the search for a packet of Marlboro Lights that I've got hidden in the bottom drawer of a filing cabinet somewhere, buried beneath a pile of actors' contracts. I gave up smoking years ago, but these are desperate times. Something's got to be done to calm the madwoman within. I find the packet, but it's crushed and empty, alongside a crumpled box of Hershey's chocolate kisses. There are six left. I stuff all of them in my mouth at once.

'Pearl, get me a lunch set up with Barry over at New Look Pictures today,' says Stephen, making me jump. He's leaning against the door frame of my office like a detective on watch duty. How long's he been there?

'Bu . . . ya . . . ga . . . a . . .' I begin to speak, but feel a river of chocolate dribbling down my chin.

'What *have* you got in your mouth, Pearl? Listen, I want Brett in a New Look blockbuster before the end of the month. Get me a list of all their new projects, and his last contract. How much did he make on his last film?'

'F . . . fixteeeen munion,' I say, waving an outstretched

palm three times, and attempting to swallow the chocolate. Stephen knows precisely what Brett made on his last movie anyway. It's ingrained in his heart, as is what all his other big clients make, but he finds the repetition of figures reassuring. He recites his list of further demands.

'Better make it Spagos for lunch with Barry, wouldchya?' he finishes. 'Second thoughts, the Polo Lounge.' He disappears from view and I hear his steps retreat. Stop. Then return.

'Make that Spagos.'

Stephen is a bellicose brain pain with a PhD in personal ambition. He is a short, fat Hollywood player, right down to the receding hairline, private jet and Swiss bank account. For him, putting together a movie deal for one of his big A-list stars is not so much a negotiation as an inspired work of art. He will nuture it, worry it, obsess over it, abandon it and then finally move in for the killer brushstroke that seals it. And he's good at it. Twenty years as Hollywood's top agent has put him in the Forbes 100 wealthiest people in the world. It's also made him one of the greediest and most impatient.

There was a time when I was frightened of Stephen – all that barking and changing his mind. But I've learned not to react to it. Swallowing the last of the chocolate, I call Stacy, Barry Finemann's assisant at New Look. 'Yes,' says the voice impatiently. Like everyone in the movie business, Stacy thinks she's more important than she actually is.

'It's Pearl here.'

'Hi, Pearl.' I hear her voice soften instantly. 'How can I help you?'

Stephen actually owns a share of New Look Pictures himself. This is one of the oldest and biggest studios in Hollywood. It's so big it even has its own record label, coincidentally the one my dad was first signed to.

Stephen is what they call a sleeping partner. He doesn't get involved in any of the day-to-day running of the movie studio. No one knows that he's even involved. But he always channels his clients towards New Look Pictures if he can. This is entirely to New Look's advantage, because they get first look at some of the top names.

It's also to Stephen's advantage, because by sending his best clients their way, he not only gets his twenty per cent from whatever his clients get paid, but on top of that he gets a share in the profits that the film makes too. It's called double-dipping. It's corrupt, immoral, and strictly illegal. But that's Hollywood for you.

Stacy and I set up Stephen's lunch, but then a thought occurs to me.

'Say, Stacy. Hasn't New Look got a period costume drama coming up?'

'Yeah. We're working on a script for *Northanger Abbey* right now.'

'The Jane Austen novel?'

'Yeah, the female market loves a costume drama. Not to mention—'

'Not to mention you don't have to buy the rights,' I interrupt her. Ever wondered why Jane Austen is so popular in the twenty-first century? Because the poor woman wrote her books nearly two hundred years ago, and production companies don't have to pay anything for the rights.

'Got a male lead attached?'

'Not yet. Got anyone in mind?'

'Might have.'

I put the phone down, lean back in my chair. Seeing Brett, I realise, has summoned a Vegas-style salad bar of emotions inside my head – sadness, anger, regret, hatred, fondness. Fondness? What? Are you out of your mind? I need a minute to steady myself. There's a large window by the desk in my office and I can see all the way to the bottom of the garden, where some bamboo bushes hide the perimeter of the estate. I allow myself to gaze out. There's a wind blowing, bending the palm trees over as they fight the gusts. People always imagine that southern California is warm all year round, but the mornings and evenings can be bitterly cold in the winter. We're still in January, and the winds often sweep up from the San Bernadino mountains or come in from the Pacific Ocean bringing mists or crisp, cold air with them. Today has a chill that is poking fun at the low sun in the sky.

A gardener is trying to fix the broken pump on a water fountain, just by the patio, that is meant to send water cascading over stone urns. Without the fountain running, the deep green pond the water is meant to flow into looks serene – far more natural. I can see the carp taking giant gulps of air from the surface with their curious mouths. But Stephen can't bear anything in his house to not function properly, so the pump must be fixed. And that's my job – maintaining the domestic status quo. If one of Stephen's cars breaks down, I get the handyman to run it to the garage. If the nanny is sick, I arrange the replacement. If the housekeeper hasn't done her job, I sort it out. If Stephen loses the remote control to one of his ten televisions, which he does almost every week, I reach for the box where I keep all my spares and replace it.

You couldn't call it a fulfilling job, but I'm not sure I was cut out for grand ambition. I'm a domestic pacifier, a smoother of the path. It's a natural position for me. I'm a Pisces – nurturing is what we do. It was my role as Brett's wife too. He would curse and swear when life didn't run smoothly, when he was overlooked for auditions or didn't get the role he wanted, and I would do what I could to fix it. When you're the daughter of someone famous in Hollywood, and you happen to work for Stephen Shawe, you can sometimes pull a few strings. You can get producers to return your calls, you can call up old friends for favours, you can get into the right parties. Trouble is, you never get paid or thanked for services rendered when you're the wife. I feel a shiver pass down my spine. Thank God I'm not married to him any more.

Brett was artistic and creative once, qualities I was raised to admire. He was writing poetry and love songs when I first met him. But as his success grew, his softness was replaced with an edge. His T-shirts with idealistic slogans preaching love and tolerance disappeared in favour of a made-to-measure Hollywood image. The long shaggy hair got cut and slicked back. The guitar soon gathered dust, as did his poetry books. His romantic ideas about peace and harmony were replaced with a BlackBerry, an agent, some weightlifter's muscles, and a role in an action movie. Ambition had got its grip.

'But this is for us,' he told me when I asked him about the transformation. 'Besides, we all evolve. You've got to move with the times. We've got to keep pushing forward.'

Well, he pushed forward all right. Right into the arms of Conzuela Martin. I feel the familiar surge of anger pumping through my veins. All other sentiments from my emotional salad bar are erased with a big plate of anger. My fists are clenched, I realise – so strongly that my nails are cutting into the palm of my hand. I close my eyes, breathe deep, unclench the fists, and imagine myself on a Caribbean beach like my therapist taught me to do. I am beautiful, intelligent, successful, and I have a loving husband and child, I tell myself as I have been taught. I have no need for anger. Anger is destructive. I have no need for anger.

The intercom hisses into life. 'Pearl, get in here.'

Inside Stephen's office, he's attempting to putt a golf ball across a million-dollar Persian carpet into a plastic tray with a built-in golf hole. He misses. 'Shit! That was your fault, Pearl. You put me off.'

'And you were doing so well up until then,' I say. The best way to handle Stephen is with a certain amount of contempt.

He retreats to his desk – a solid wood affair the size of a small swimming pool, with a gilt-embossed leather top. An unused Apple laptop takes up a fraction of its space. Stephen doesn't understand computers and refuses to spend the time learning to understand them. What he understands better is awards, and on shelves all around him are trophies won for films that he's had a hand in.

'Barry is out of the office today, but you're booked in for lunch with him tomorrow at Spagos,' I say, dumping the pile of scripts he wanted on to his desk.

'Polo Lounge. I told you the Polo Lounge, Pearl,' he yells. Stephen is a master at turning up the volume. 'What's the matter with you?'

'Actually, Stephen, you told me Spagos,' I say calmly and smile sweetly.

Ignoring further protests, I run through a list of Stephen's other engagements during the week, and remind him that he has a lunch today at the commissary on the Warner Brothers lot. Also Craig, his son, has a soccer match after school this afternoon, and he's hoping Stephen is going to show up.

Stephen smiles to himself. He has four kids, all displayed in silver frames on his desk – the closest he usually gets to them. He also currently has no wife – a position vacated by two previous occupants – so another part of my job is to coordinate his home life with his work.

'OK, Pearl,' he says, omitting the thank-you that I believe is usually present in polite society, but that is rarely heard within these walls. 'And I think you better make me an appointment at Dr Schreibner's.'

'Any special time?'

'As soon as possible. I'm very worried.'

I don't ask him about what, because it's always best not to. Stephen is a hypochondriac – he spends more time in Dr Schreibner's office than his own.

'Yeah. I got this pain in my chest. Lung cancer, do you think?' he asks seriously.

'Definitely,' I say with a smile.

'You think?'

'No, of course not. You only had a medical last week.'

'But they may have missed something.'

'Well, I'll make the appointment for you.' I turn to leave, but find myself hesitating at the door of his office. It's a bit of an out-there proposition, but hey, why not?

'Stephen. I was thinking about Brett Ellis. Have you thought of a costume drama for him?'

Stephen drops his golf ball and lets out an explosion of laughter. That got his mind off his chest pains. 'Tell you what? You stick to being the PA. I'll stick to being the agent.' He throws back his head and laughs again, so I can see all the fillings in his molars.

'Well, if you're just going to laugh . . .'

'Okay. Okay. Hit me with it.'

The truth is, Stephen respects my suggestions about movies. I have a knack for it. I don't know why. Perhaps because I just happen to like going to the movies. Anyway, I know he won't be able to resist hearing what I have to say.

'Do you know how much *Pride and Prejudice* made?'

Stephen grunts, sits down at his desk and starts fiddling with his computer, pretending to only half listen. The computer isn't even turned on.

'Thirty-eight million dollars. Do you know how much *Sense and Sensibility* made?'

Stephen grunts again.

'Forty-three million. Want to know who's making the next big Jane Austen movie?'

Stephen looks up.

'New Look Pictures. They're about to make *Northanger Abbey*, and the most desirable, biggest female fantasy role of next year will be Henry Tilney.'

'Who?'

'He's the hero of *Northanger Abbey*. It's different enough to entice Brett – didn't he say he wanted a role with integrity? But this is also likely to be big.'

Stephen smirks to himself. 'OK, I'll think about it.'

I turn to walk out of the door.

'It *was* the Polo Lounge I asked for, by the way,' he calls after me like a small child, eager to have the last word.

'Was it, Stephen? Then I'm sorry I made the mistake.'

I realise now that Dad was probably wired for most of my childhood. But we kids just thought his games were wild. He'd jump into the pool with all his clothes on, and we'd all follow in after him. He'd get out the vacuum cleaner and hoover the garden. He'd pull the lampshades off the lamps and make us wear them as hats. He'd turn up the stereo in the house and we'd all bounce on the sofas. Life with him was a series of high jinks.

There was also an unpredictability about him that was sometimes a bit unnerving. And there were plenty of times he'd lock himself away in his study and refuse to talk to us.

But these moments were easy to overlook, because when he was with us he had a way of making each of us feel special. I didn't know the word charisma then, but Dad had it in spades. He made us want to be with him all the time, because we never knew what he was going to do next. Spontaneity and rebellion coursed through his veins. 'Come on, let's have a game of poker,' he'd say when Betty was supposed to be getting us ready for bed. 'Let's give God a few laughs.' And he'd try to teach us kids to gamble with candy, which he'd end up eating by throwing it high into the air and catching it with his mouth.

Sometimes he'd come charging into our bedrooms in

the middle of the night and wake us up. It was always after he'd been away. Said he couldn't wait until the morning for hugs. Then we'd all go downstairs for a midnight feast and he'd produce gifts for us – dolls from Japan, fans from Spain, marbles from Italy.

Other times he'd even take us on his motorbike. Mum didn't approve, and I don't think Betty did either. It always caused fights over who was to be the lucky one. But boy what a treat it was to be picked – shirts flapping in the wind as we sped along Sunset, the warm Californian sun on our faces. And then we'd take a right turn along the Pacific Coast Highway and race against pelicans skimming the surf and smell the ocean, which reached out to infinity. Once in Malibu, the mighty roar of the motorbike would cease and we'd race on to the sand and throw ourselves into the waves.

I loved my dad. I guess that's what made it so hard to have to share him. In 1990, Dad's fan club had over five million fans. He'd sold more than fifty million albums, and during his world tours he sang to an estimated 1.2 million people. That's a whole heap of other people to have to share with.

5

At 6.29 p.m. precisely, when Adam treads steadily up the stairs – Adam rarely races anywhere, because he is never, ever late – he finds me in a Dolce and Gabbana silk dressing gown and some rather elaborate La Perla underwear. Talk about Hello Boys. My puppies are plumped, pushed and positioned to perfection in this bra, because this evening, sex has been scheduled. That's right. Scheduled. That's half an hour after the babysitter has arrived for Thackeray, and an hour before we are due to leave for the Children's Hospital benefit dinner.

'Will an hour be enough time for sex and for you to get ready?' Adam asked as we planned the event over the phone earlier in the day. The doctor had confirmed I was ovulating, and I half suspected Adam was writing it in his diary at the office. Would he have written the actual word 'Sex', and would his secretary see it? I wondered. I shuddered at the thought.

'Sure, an hour is plenty,' I reassured him.

'We've got to keep trying,' he said, perhaps sensing reluctance on my part.

'I know we have, honey. I'm up for it. You know I am.'

'Great, I'll see you this evening then.'

Now I prepare myself for Adam's advances, because even in the face of perfunctory sex, there's no harm in spicing things up a bit. I remove the dressing gown, revealing what lies beneath, and position myself on the bed in the kind of sex-siren pose that even Marilyn Monroe could have learned from, but Adam is absorbed in removing his clothes.

'Ready?' he says, walking over to the mirror and unbuttoning his shirt.

'Ready,' I say, running a hand temptingly up my thigh, but Adam is still lining up the creases in his pants. He picks a piece of fluff off the waistband. He inspects the pants for other pieces of fluff. He lays them on a chair. He removes his shirt. He folds his shirt. He places it on the chair. He removes his underpants. He folds them too. Yes, even his underpants. He removes his socks. He lines the socks up and then turns the top of one of them over the other. (Adam hates odd socks.) He places them on the chair too – on top of the underpants. The socks roll to the floor. He picks them up and places them under the underpants. He surveys the neatness. Adam is nothing if not fastidious. Finally he turns to the bed.

'Right then. Let's get these off, shall we?' he says in a practical voice – the kind I use when I'm undressing Thackeray and getting him ready for bed. He tugs, businesslike, at my underwear.

'But honey . . .' I say, sounding just a little put out. Even the sheep in Australia get more of a warm-up than this.

'Well, we want to make the dinner on time, don't we?' he says, with reason in his voice. How stupid of me not to mention foreplay when Adam was taking my order for sex.

Lying under Adam with my eyes closed, my mind is now a montage of lists. Shopping lists, to-do lists, guest lists, check lists. I'm not ashamed to admit this. All women do it, don't they? We're jugglers, and what is sex if not thinking time? I am on the committee for tonight's benefit dinner and there has been a lot of planning in the last few weeks. There's been the seating plan, the florists, the vintners, the caterers, the hotel administrators, the goodie bags. I run through the lists in my mind, hoping I've remembered everything. Adam pants on, on top of me.

I like being involved in charity fund-raising. I'm on quite a few committees. I'm aware that it's kind of what the Beverly Hills set do, and that I'm a good thirty years younger than the facelift-and-pearls platoon who dominate the charity scene, but it's kind of fun. There are always lots of parties.

I take a sideways peek at the clock. It's 6.46 p.m. Adam is still banging away. I fake an orgasm – simply a practical measure in view of the time. It works. Inspired by my performance, Adam climaxes. Our alarm clock now reads 6.48 p.m. in bright red numbers. Perfect. I still have forty minutes to get ready. I race to get out of bed.

'Uh-uh,' Adam scolds. 'What about lying still for twenty minutes?'

'But honey, I've got to get ready. Tonight is a big night,' I plead.

'But this is important too. We know the egg is being released around now, and every time we do this, we stand a chance. We've got to give it our best shot.'

I relent with a big sigh, looking forward to the three days hence when the egg is sure to have gone its own way, passing beyond the point of fertilisation possibilities, scheduling nightmares and further sex.

Adam puts the pillows into place beneath me and I reach for my daily fix. *This Side of Heaven* is on the bedside table. Now we're talking. *Travio pulled Perdita to his muscular chest and looked fervently into her eyes. She could feel his heart pounding beneath his open shirt, as if it were about to explode. They'd waited too long for this moment. Outside, the African sun was disappearing behind an acacia tree, and they could hear the distant roar of lions in the bush. His hands pulled at her skirt and in seconds were sliding between her legs . . .*

'How did your meeting go today?' Adam calls from the bathroom.

'Fine,' I say. I read on, caught up instantly in the drama. God, I love romance novels. *His soft, tender fingers lingered at the tops of her thighs, then suddenly, as if overcome by a supernatural force, prised their way past her underwear.*

'What was it about?' Adam calls.

She felt his warm mouth on top of hers, and gave in to her desires. Her knees felt so weak, she could barely stand up.

'What was it about?' Adam calls again.

Travio could wait no longer. He picked her up, carried her through a gap in the mosquito net, laid her on the bed, and—

'Honey, are you listening?'

'Sorry, sweetheart. What did you say?'

'I said, what was your meeting about?'

'Oh, one of Stephen's clients wants more money,' I say casually, sucked abruptly back into the real world, where a sperm count overrides a knee wobble.

'Which one?'

'Which what?'

'Which client?'

'Oh, no one you'd know,' I say absent-mindedly, part of me still entwined in an African sunset. And then I realise what I've just done. I've lied.

Forty-nine precise minutes later, Adam opens the door of the limousine for me – such a sweet gesture. It's something he's always done, and reminds me every time that chivalry is not dead. Men ought to be chivalrous, I think. But does holding a car door open for your wife still count as chivalry when you're complaining at her at the same time?

'I don't know why you can't be on time anywhere, Pearl,' he protests as I carefully climb in, conscious of the tight black Stella McCartney dress I've squeezed myself into. It's a size six and cost a fortune. There's something so fabulous about wearing a good name. The cut, the line, the secret thrill of being able to say it's a Stella McCartney, or a Balenciaga, or a Valentino.

Adam climbs in after me and I check myself in a mirror from my bag: lipstick – not smudged; eyeliner – not quite equal on both eyes, but it'll do; Tiffany diamond drop earrings which sparkle luminescently, a diamond choker, equally stunning. Both were gifts from Adam. Harry Winstons, of course. Then I check him: he looks so serious in his black tuxedo – it's a new one he bought from Armani – bow tie tied to precision, shoes shined, and a handkerchief in his top pocket folded like a piece of origami.

'I mean, you're always running late,' he drones on.

'We're only a few minutes late.'

'We're nineteen minutes late.'

Sometimes reasoning with Adam is as painful as watching a Joe Eszterhas movie.

'And why are we going in a limo? Limos are really passé,' he adds.

'Really? It's never been a problem before,' I tell him. This is not a stretch limo he's talking about, you understand. That really would be poor taste. Only tourists and girls on prom nights use stretch limousines. This is a regular black limo.

'It makes us look behind the times,' he argues, as the chauffer drives us down the hill towards the Hilton, where the benefit dinner is to take place. 'Now that everyone is so eco-conscious, we need to get a Prius. The hybrid is the new status car, you know that, don't you?'

'Right,' I say, and quietly laugh to myself, thinking of

all the research Adam will now devote to this. 'What colour do you think we should have?'

'I shall have to research it,' he says thoughtfully. 'Can you order some consumer magazines?'

'Sure.' I smile. 'How did the meeting go?'

'Terrible,' he sighs. Adam is always this way after a meeting. He's a great guy, don't get me wrong, but he can be a little needy sometimes. Rather like a small kid, he needs constant reassurance that he's doing fine. It's the artistic temperament.

'Which script did you pitch?' I ask. There are always several.

'*Made Up*,' he says.

'Is that *Rocky* with mascara?'

'That's the one.' Movie studios like to have a catchphrase they understand. This one's about the make-up artist who wins the big competition.

All movies start with the pitch. A pitch is a story idea told by an eager writer to a world-weary, tired, cynical studio exec in a gust of witty salesmanship. Usually the poor writer has got about twelve seconds. This especially isn't easy if you've got a stutter.

To get the idea over in twelve seconds means these peculiar movie hybrids emerge. 'It's *Jaws* set in outer space' was the line for *Alien*. 'It's *Die Hard* on a ship' (*Under Siege*). 'It's *Rocky* in ballet slippers' (*Billy Elliot*). Adam's big movie break was 'It's *The Merchant of Venice* on a bus.' A bit classier than your usual hybrid. It made $100 million in its opening weekend at the box office and Adam instantly became a player. So much so that Universal gave him his own office over on the lot last year. They call him in on jobs all the time. This means his computer usually gets more face time than I do.

'Well, what did they say?'

'They asked who I saw for the lead role.'

'Well then, they must have been interested. What else did they ask?'

'They asked me about the character development. What the girl's aspirations were, how I saw the finish of the film, who I'd like for a director.'

'Well, how could that have been terrible?'

'I don't know. They didn't seem to jump up and down.'

'When has a producer ever jumped up and down? Did they ask you to deliver a treatment?'

'Yes.'

'Well then, they liked it.'

The clipped front lawns of the Beverly Flats speed past us. I put my hand on his knee, and the deep red of my manicured nails stands out against the black of his pants. 'Thanks for coming tonight,' I offer calmly. Both he and I know that he wouldn't stay away from these events if he was paid to, but I think it's nice to honor propriety in married life. He is coming to support my work, and it's important to recognise that.

The truth is that Adam is entranced with Hollywood. He pretends he isn't, but I can see how much of a buzz he gets out of meeting Steven Spielberg at parties – he went on about it for weeks, the last time they met at a fund-raiser. And when Dreamworks flew him to New York on the company's private jet after he'd sold his first script, heck, he was like a small boy at a candy store. And then there was the time he met George Clooney for the first time to discuss his script, and the actor asked him for a ride home because his car was at the garage and Adam was heading his way. Adam was so nervous with Clooney alongside him in the passenger seat, he reversed into a wall before they'd even got out of the parking lot.

Although Adam grew up in LA, he didn't grow up like I did. His dad was a doctor, his mum was a home-maker. They lived in a regular two-bedroom house in Culver City, and Adam had to do shifts as a waiter to pay to go to college and study screenwriting. I'm proud of what he's achieved. When he sold his first movie script, he took a 25,000-foot hike up the mountain that's Hollywood's social strata. Five scripts later, he earns more than most of the actors who star in his films, but he's still impressed by fame.

'Who's going to be there tonight?' he asks as we speed through the dusk. The sunset is especially pretty tonight.

'Well, Ashley of course.' That's my brother. 'And Jasmin from the studio, and Lizzie and Bella, and—'

'I mean who *else* is going to be there?'

What he means is what big names.

'Danny DeVito said he was coming,' I say. This will impress Adam. A producer who makes films *and* a recognised actor. 'James Brooks and Ron Howard.' Also big-time producers who Adam already knows and will want to make sure he gets face time with. 'Scarlett Johansson, Debra Messing, Pamela Anderson . . .' Adam's eyes glaze over slightly. 'Oh, and did I say Will Smith?' Adam loves Will Smith. But then so does everyone else in Hollywood.

We pull into the Hilton and join a line of Priuses waiting to disgorge their contents on to a red carpet.

'See, what did I tell you?' Adam says in a told-you-so voice. Not that I remember ever disagreeing with him.

Red carpets take a little bit of getting used to. There's the flash of the paparazzi cameras, the screams from fans, the staccato thump of helicopters overhead, the cordoned-off crowds. No one is interested when Adam and I step on to the carpet and make our way into the hotel. The fans are all waiting for Will Smith, who is three cars behind us. But still there's the pressure of being under scrutiny by a crowd. It's quite terrifying. I'm always convinced I'll trip over my heels or find my Stella McCartney has somehow become tucked into my underwear.

Charity benefit evenings are a key element to the scene in Hollywood. With wealth comes the need to be philanthropic, and with fame (not always the same thing) comes the need to be seen to be philanthropic (also not the same thing.) Tonight's benefit is for a children's hospital.

For the event to get the most amount of publicity, you have to invite celebrities. This is a mixed blessing, because they're the ones who linger on the red carpet, blocking the entrance as they make sure the paparazzi catch their best sides. They're the ones whose assistants call five times to check who else is going to be there before they accept the invitation, who ask for a discount, who cancel at the last minute and can they have their money back?

Of course, they're not all like that – none that were coming tonight had – but you'd be amazed how many are.

Coincidentally, Stephen arrives in the car right behind ours. His Prius, wouldn't you know? We brave the flashbulbs together to reach the entrance. I made Stephen take a table for ten tonight. He takes a bit of cajoling every year, but it's good business to be seen at events like these, not to mention tax deductible. He's brought a date with him too – a blonde I've never met before, who towers over him by at least a foot. We smile politely at each other. She's a wannabe probably, judging by the sequinned miniskirt. (It's gowns only at an event like this, but a wannabe wouldn't be aware of the protocol.) Stephen's a magnate for wannabes, because of what he can do for them.

The four of us make it through the hotel foyer and into the ballroom, where a waiter offers us champagne in glasses with long, graceful stems, and we hear the distant screams outside as Will Smith plays to the crowd. In here, the threads of dozens of separate conversations fill the room, bouncing off the modern chandeliers and then disappearing into the thick taupe carpeting. The tables, dressed in their white tablecloths, silver cutlery and floral centrepieces, sit empty still, arranged carefully around the dance floor, while the high-gloss crowd mills in the reception area.

'Well done, Pearl,' Stephen says amiably, as I notice the podium is currently bereft of its band. I hope they're going to show up. Stephen can be pleasant sometimes, and I confess it's nice to hear his praise. There's a lot of work that goes into putting on an event like this. 'Looks like you got a good turnout tonight. A few hundred, I'd say.' We survey the crowd, which sparkles like Disneyland fairdust. Diamonds and sequins flash at every turn.

'How's tricks?' Stephen turns to Adam.

'G-g-g-good,' Adam says, closing his eyes briefly in a gesture that only I know is designed to abate the stutter. I feel a wave of affection for him. He's battled so hard to fight it.

'A-a-and this is?' Adam reaches out to shake hands with the blonde and waits for Stephen to make the introduction, but Stephen has forgotten her name. I can't believe him sometimes.

'Let me give you a clue. It begins with the letter M . . .' she says, still smiling sweetly at Stephen.

He struggles, and then remembers. 'That's it. This is Michelle.'

'Actually it's Madeleine,' she says. 'People call me Maddi.'

We smile cordially some more in the way that you do at these events, and I'd like to move on, but Stephen hasn't seen the rest of his party.

'So what did you think about the meeting with Brett today?' he says casually. I swallow hard on my champagne. 'Not sure it went especially well, are you?'

I knew there was a good reason to always tell the truth. So that you don't get yourself into a mess like this.

I look quickly across at Adam to see if he's listening, but fortunately there's a loud scream from the fans outside. I don't think he heard. And then Lizzie bounces up, her long curly red hair waving behind her, like Botticelli's *Venus* being blown to the shore by the wind gods.

'There you are, Pearl, I've been looking everywhere for you,' she trills, brushing past Stephen and engulfing me in Chloé perfume and the reassurance of female companionship as she kisses me on both cheeks. 'Pearl, I've got to talk to you.' She looks wound up, like a jack-in-the-box about to spring.

'Honey, do you mind?' I ask Adam. He waves his hand in consent dismissively. He's seen someone in the crowd he wants to talk to anyway. Stephen's moved on too. 'Let's go to the bar,' begs Lizzie, and grabs my hand.

Lizzie is my oldest friend from school. We've known each other since we were seven. On the first day we met she told me she was a tiger trainer and worked in the circus. At once I recognised in her someone who knew how to have fun. Our common ground was both having famous fathers. Her dad is Charles Sugarman, the tough action guy who did all those cop movies in the seventies. There were a few of us with famous parents at school, but the other kids weren't as wild as Lizzie and me. The minute we met, we instantly saw in each other the need for irreverent indulgence and inspired mayhem.

We were horrible kids. But because our dads were famous, everyone wanted to be our friends. So we thought we were really something. We thought we were princesses, royalty, special. And in truth, we were royalty of a kind. The rest of the world doesn't officially recognise Hollywood's royal family. There aren't any state dinners or family holidays in Balmoral. But Hollywood revolves around celebrity like no other place on earth – and there is a social strata to Tinseltown that puts up as good a pretension of nobility as anything Princes William and

Harry can muster. It's an elite group who enjoy privilege, fame and social advantage. Being the daughters of famous people put Lizzie and me on the Hollywood map, just by nature of our birth. Even our teachers treated us differently – not obviously, but in subtle ways that manipulative little girls can pick up on and use to their advantage. See, that's what LA is like – if your dad's a celebrity, everyone wants to kiss your ass.

It takes a while for Lizzie and me to make it to the bar, avoiding waiters holding trays of canapés, and the dazzling array of high society. 'God, the place is crawling with Twinkies,' she says as we fight our way through the crowd. Twinkies are what Lizzie and I call the Barbie Dolls. You know who I mean. The straight-haired blondes with no cellulite, stomachs or personality – usually found in toothpaste commercials and often with names ending with the letter 'i', like Mandi, Sandi, Brandi or Tiffani. We came up with the name at school, when we were both eating Twinkies, which is a kind of golden sponge cake that also happens to be blonde and over-the-top sweet. There are several of them clustered near the bar. Lizzie and I find a space away from them.

'Guess what? Tony Rinaldi has offered me a role in his latest film,' she announces, unable to contain a small squeal of excitement, as we settle on some bar stools.

'And you're pleased about this?' I say cautiously, noticing how Lizzie's red Halston dress almost clashes with her red hair and freckles, but somehow makes her look all the more beautiful. Lizzie is beautiful, but not in a Hollywood Twinkie way. She has too many freckles. Not to mention all the red hair, and green eyes that are just so mesmerising.

'Why wouldn't I be?'

'Because he makes porn movies,' I say in a hushed tone. I really don't want anyone here overhearing this. It's not that I'm a prude, but did I mention my mother is Catholic?

'For sure they're porn, but they're classy porn,' Lizzie says loudly. She's never been one to care what anyone else thinks. 'Do you know how difficult it is to be asked to do one of Tony Rinaldi's films? Do you know how many girls would just die to be in one of his movies?'

'But only Twinkies and Valley girls,' I say, referring to the great LA divide, those that live over the hill in the Valley, where there are cheaper rents.

'Not just Valley girls.' She sighs like I don't know anything.

'But porn, Lizzie? You don't need to do porn.'

'Don't be such a Joanie, Pearl. There's nothing wrong with porn. There frickin' isn't. Everyone's doing it. There's just one problem . . .' She takes a gulp of champagne.

'What?'

'He says I need a bit of cosmetic surgery first.'

'Cosmetic surgery? Are you out of your mind? You're only twenty-five. You don't need cosmetic surgery.'

'Not on my face, silly.' She bites her lip in an attempt to contain a smirk.

'Where?'

'Down there.' She points to her groin, and lets out another squeal of excitement.

'Gross!'

'A designer vagina.' She winks at me. Lizzie always enjoys the shock value. Half the time, I'm sure that's why she does these things. I refuse to rise to it.

'And how would he know what you've got down there anyway?' I ask.

She grins knowingly.

'Jesus, Lizzie. You don't have to sleep with every director, you know. There are other ways. Is that why you need cosmetic surgery? Because you've worn it out?'

She hoots with laughter. 'Oh, don't be disapproving, Pearl,' she pleads. 'I thought you'd be happy for me. This is a starring role.'

'For your woo-woo . . .'

Lizzie gazes down into her drink despondently. The champagne bubbles are creeping up the inside of the glass. It's hard to tell if she's genuinely saddened by my reaction, or is just acting it out. She's always been a terrible ham.

'Lizzie, you don't need to be doing porn movies, or having any kind of cosmetic surgery,' I say gently. 'You're a gorgeous, intelligent woman. You've got great acting skills. A good role is sure to be around the corner. Don't blow everything by doing porn.'

She looks really crushed. Her adult acting career, which so far has amounted to two commercials for Coco Pops, one for haemorrhoid cream, and bit parts in three comedies, has always been a source of disappointment to her.

'But I'm tired of not being "quite right for the part".' She pulls a face and mimicks the voice of a million stern casting directors who always seem to overlook her. 'It's a bummer taking rejection all the time.'

Fame is the most addictive drug in the world, and Lizzie is hooked. She wants attention. Doesn't matter if it's giving sex tips on an internet radio show, doesn't matter if it's a *Playboy* spread – and she's done both. She wants fame at any cost. She never eats, never misses a PR event or an audition. And now that addiction has led her to porn. I suppose it was always just a matter of time.

'I know it's difficult, Lizzie,' I say kindly. 'Look, let's talk about this tomorrow. Why don't we go out and have a long chat. It's kind of hard to talk properly here. And I've sat you next to Cameron Valentin at our table. You know who he is, don't you?'

She looks blank.

'He's the director of *Motherless Daughters*.'

A smile of recognition spreads across her face. 'Awesome,' she mutters.

I see Adam beckoning to me across the ballroom. The rest of the crowd is now settling at their tables. 'Come on, we've got to sit down.'

I've sat Lizzie next to Cameron Valentin in the hope that he might do something for her, either professionally or personally. In Hollywood, the two are intertwined. Not only is his film turning into a box-office success, but he's single too. Also at the table are Martin and Daisy McConnell, a husband-and-wife producing team – both in their thirties – who have made several of Adam's films; Jasmin Lee, who is a script-reader (she actually gets paid to do nothing but read scripts all day); and, next to her, Ashley, my darling, darling brother.

Ashley is an entertainment lawyer at Maxwell, Zucker and Sash and obsessed with work, which is why he never has time for dating, and why I've sat him next to Jasmin. I love matchmaking, and Ashley looks so handsome tonight in his tux. He's more confident these days, now that he's lost some weight. Ashley and I have always been close – it was a case of having to be. We had parents who came and went in our lives like the tide.

Next to Ashley are Bella and Jamie Shawe. Bella is this British 'bird', as she calls herself, and, along with Lizzie, is my BFF. She used to be nanny to Stephen's three youngest kids – that is, until she met Jamie, Stephen's eldest son, and ran off to Vegas and got married to him. Caused quite a scene – Stephen wouldn't talk to either of them for over a year. He always fancied Bella for himself, but being the retard that he is, never actually told her. But he's pretty much forgiven them both now, and there are times when they even act like a real family.

Bella is a blonde. Curvy, tall, slim, but with the kind of face you'd expect to find in an old Dutch Master's painting perhaps, thus ensuring that she could never be a Twinkie. Her complexion is always pale and flawless, with cheekbones to die for. She is wearing vintage couture tonight that's just so gorgeous I could weep. 'Where'd you get the dress?' I lean behind Adam to ask her.

'Lily et Cie on Beverly. It's an old Valentino.'

'No . . .' I feel a shiver of awe spread down my spine. 'But they're so rare.'

Bella smiles coolly. When she'd just arrived in LA from England, I taught her how to dress in Hollywood and the importance of designer names. Now she's beating me at my own game, and knows it. 'You should go in there. There's all kinds of famous dresses – dresses that Elizabeth Taylor once wore. J.Lo shops there, and Demi Moore.'

'How much?' I demand. Adam monitors how much I spend on clothes, like a Mormon in a mission. Must have cost a fortune.

'Too much,' she says with a wink, and taps the side of her nose. Bella can be so annoying sometimes.

Around the table, everyone else is talking movies. That's what people talk about round here. Which films are performing well at the box office, which ones are winning prizes, which directors are geniuses, which directors are assholes. There are plenty of both. Hollywood is like high school, where everyone knows everyone – and even if they don't, they pretend they do. And everyone has an opinion and everyone loves to dish the dirt. Except to people's faces, that is.

'I see *Motherless Daughters* is doing really well,' Jamie offers to Cameron. A safe opening gambit.

'Yes, a great movie,' everyone chimes in. Even Ashley, who I seem to recall telling me what a load of crap it was only last week.

'So moving.'

'So inspiring.'

'Really fantastic.'

See, that's what you do in Hollywood – you congratulate each other. The film might be a piece of junk, but you have to make nice to anyone involved in it. Cameron holds up his hands and bows his head in a gesture that implies modesty.

'That's because it had a great script,' says Jasmin, who I'm sure I can recall pouring forth her criticisms of it to Adam one evening, long before the film got made.

Jasmin must be in her thirties, but is wearing a dress that ages her terribly. Perhaps I should offer to take her shopping. She also closes her eyelids as she speaks, bringing attention, I notice, to huge clumps of mascara on her lashes. Eeeeuuwww. She's a sweet girl, gentle-mannered, bookish even. She'd be a great date for Ashley, but I'd simply have to give her a makeover.

'It's like I always say, if you've got a good script, you've got yourself a good movie. Period,' she adds to nods around the table.

'Never heard such c-c-c-crap,' says Adam abruptly. So abruptly, I am shocked. His cheeks look flushed. Adam is sometimes cranky with me, but never this tactless in public. 'P-p-p-p-plenty of good scripts get turned into bad movies.' His stutter is back in serious style too – I wonder what's rattling him.

'Oh, but very rarely,' says Jasmin coolly, closing her eyes again. Ooh, that mascara has to go.

'Nonsense. All the t-t-t-time . . .' Adam begins to spout a list of films. It is really so unlike him to be so confrontational. 'Good scripts get b-b-b-brutalised by b-b-b-bad directors . . .'

There's a long, uneasy silence. God, this is so embarrassing. Finally conversation moves on. Lizzie is going great guns with Cameron Valentin. I hear her tell him that relatively speaking the barnacle has the biggest penis of all creatures on the planet. She's so crass sometimes. Ashley gallantly rescues Jasmin from social Siberia and the two of them embark on a critique of Sona – safer ground, since Sona is a restaurant. And then I hear Bella asking Adam what he thinks about *The Obscure*. It's a horror film that's just come out.

'Didn't like it,' says Adam sharply.

'Really? I'd have thought it was right up your street,' says Bella, in her usual polite British way of making light. 'Sustaining storyline, good character development, gorgeous music. I loved the music. Didn't you love the music?'

'I thought it was a piece of sh-sh-sh-shit,' Adam says crossly, emphatically enough to kill the conversation.

'Sorry I asked,' says Bella, giving me a look across the table that I know means, what's up with him?

I have no idea. What *is* up with him? And then I see what's up with him. Brett Ellis is standing at the bar, staring at our table. I feel a rush of colour to my own cheeks. What the heck is he doing here?

At the age of nine, I discovered the full advantage of what it meant to have famous parents. It was called room service. We were in the Plaza Hotel in New York. Dad was singing at Madison Square Gardens, part of a world tour that had kept him from us for months. And so we'd flown across with Betty to join him and arrived at the Royal Terrace Suite on the twentieth floor, where we were to stay for a week.

Unfortunately, he and Mum weren't around when Ashley and I charged through the door expecting to find hugs waiting for us. Lydia dragged herself in after us. She was a difficult teenager, and reluctant to be here. But Mum and Dad were out somewhere. Then Betty disappeared too, telling us to watch TV and be quiet while she went to find her room. But that left us alone, and there was nothing on TV, nor was there anything else to play with except for the telephone.

Ashley picked it up. 'Room service, can we have three ice-cream sundaes straight away. The Royal Terrace Suite.' I don't think he expected anyone to actually listen to him; he'd just seen it done on the movies. But no sooner had he put the phone back on the hook than there was a knock on the door and three ice-cream sundaes miraculously appeared. It was just like magic.

Now Lydia wanted to do it too. 'Room service, can we

have a bottle of champagne.' She paused to think of the most outrageous thing she could imagine, while Ashley and I tried to contain our giggles. 'And some tequila slammers.'

A triumph. We squealed with laughter. My turn. 'Room service, we'd like pizza. Lots of pizza and some hamburgers, and hot dogs and pretzels, and can we have some marshmallows to toast?'

This was inspired genius. There were a number of candles set up around the suite. It wouldn't be hard to toast marshmallows on them. The food arrived – vast silver platters of it. We tucked in. We lit candles and toasted marshmallows, dripping wax and melted sugar on the carpet. We opened champagne and drank from the bottle, spilling that on the carpet too. We knew how it was done. We'd seen Dad party a million times. We burped. We farted. We ate some more. We threw French fries at each other. We threw pizzas out of the window like frisbees and watched them landing on 58th Street way below. We threw hot dogs out of the window, watching them sail through the air on to passers-by beneath, who looked up confounded. We drank more champagne. Ashley threw up – also on the carpet. We called room service for more food, intent on a gambling game to guess how long it would take for the order to arrive. Then Mum and Dad walked through the door.

The look of fury on Mum's face warned us instantly to run. Lydia and I took a leap into a nearby closet. But poor Ashley was too drunk to make it. From inside the closet we heard Mum slap his face.

Both my parents had always thought of themselves as strict disciplinarians. They somehow felt that administering punishments would make up for the vagaries of a showbiz lifestyle, as if a firm hand would compensate for them never being there. I can't now remember the punishment we got, but I do recall the incident as the time when I felt most abandoned by them. They didn't understand. We were just waiting for them to come back to us.

The light in southern California is unlike anywhere else. It's why they make movies here. And it's especially beautiful in the spring, when the sun never reaches its full height in the sky and its lower position casts long shadows and softening colours. I love the mornings best, when the sun swathes everything in pink and the palm trees almost sparkle. I like to sit up in bed, sipping coffee (preferably caffeinated, but I am really trying to give it up), and survey the morning skies.

But there is no time for my ritual this morning. Nor is there any sex – scheduled or otherwise. Adam is still angry with me. He didn't speak to me all the way home, and we slept in the bed avoiding each other's limbs, both of us retreating to our own sides. Adam is out of bed and downstairs before I even wake.

'Please, Adam, I didn't know Brett was going to be there.' I catch him in the kitchen, still in my nightgown. 'I had no idea.'

'Then why did you lie to me?' he asks. So he did hear Stephen after all. Oh, God! His face looks pained. His mouth is turned down curiously at the edges. 'He was the one at the meeting you got yourself all gussied up for, but you didn't tell me.'

'Because I didn't want to worry you.'

'That's a joke,' he says scornfully.

I reach out to stroke his face, but he brushes me aside.

'Truly,' I say. 'Look, I should have told you he turned up at Stephen's yesterday, and you're right, I *did* know he was coming, but sometimes we have to face our demons in our own way. I didn't want to see him, believe me. But I had to face him. Sooner or later, one way or another, I was always going to bump into him, and I didn't want to make it into a big deal. If I told you I was going to meet him, it would have made it a big deal. For you and for me.'

'Well, it's an even bigger deal now.'

'I see that. Look, I know I did it all wrong. I'm sorry.' I sigh. Thackeray calls from the top of the stairs. 'Mummy, where are you?'

'I'm here, darling. Just coming.'

'I mean, I'd have liked to have been there for you,' Adam says, speaking more calmly now. 'I'd like to have been supportive, protective. You could have allowed me that. Instead I'm the last one in on the deal.'

'What deal? There's no deal. Sweetheart, I'm sorry I handled it all wrong. I saw him up at Stephen's house because he had a meeting there. That's all there was to it. And I had no idea he'd be turning up at the dinner last night. He certainly wasn't on the guest list, or maybe I'd have thought twice about going. Let's just forget about it, shall we?'

Adam looks unconvinced.

'Look, he's not a man who means anything to me now,' I say, wrapping my arms around his neck and pulling him close to me. 'You're the one I love.' I kiss him.

'You're sure about that?'

'Yes, quite sure.'

'Only sometimes I think you've never got over him.'

'Come on, let's not let him ruin our day. You know you are the man for me.'

Adam smiles and lets me kiss him.

*

There's a stack of mail on my desk and Stephen is singing when I get to work. This suggests two things: firstly that being an agent, not a singer, was a good career move, and secondly that he must have got lucky last night. Madeleine or whatever her name was will doubtless now be put forward for the next female bit part that comes flying on to Stephen's desk.

'You're ten minutes late,' he announces as I turn on my computer, and his rotund figure appears in the doorway of my office. I'm not. It's eight a.m. precisely – one of the advantages of having a precision-obsessed husband is that I'm usually on time in the mornings. But there's no sense in arguing about it.

'Am I? Sorry,' I say defiantly.

'Yes, well there's a lot to be done. First thing, I need you to advertise for a new housekeeper.'

'A new housekeeper,' I repeat matter-of-factly. I write it down on a notepad. Few things surprise me when it comes to Stephen. No demand is too outrageous. He once even handed me his shoes covered in dog mess and asked me to take care of them. (I did. Put them straight in the trashcan.) But replacing Maria is a surprise. She's worked here for as long as I can remember.

'Has Maria quit?'

'No, I fired her.' I do not ask why. I will find out in time. 'And get me some coffee, wouldchya?' He disappears back into the hall, and returns moments later. 'And change these flowers in the hall. They look as old as I feel.'

'Actually they were fresh yesterday, Stephen.'

'Well, you can tell the florists they look like shit.'

In the hall is an arrangement the size of a small Amazonian jungle that is replaced every week at a cost of a thousand dollars. It does not look old.

'And send one of Michelle's pictures over to New Look, wouldchya?'

'Michelle?'

'You know. The babe I was with last night.' He smiles wistfully. God, he's revolting.

'Do you mean Madeleine?'

'Yeah, that's the one. New Look have got a comedy coming up called . . .' He scratches his head. 'What was it called?'

I say nothing and settle myself comfortably. This could take some time.

'You know, the one about the chick with the dog . . . Oh, come on, Pearl, you know the one. The pitch was paws with a cause.'

'*Dog Knows*?'

'Yeah, that's the one. Get a picture over to them. They're looking for a cute girl for the second lead.'

'Sure. And will you let me send over one of Lizzie's pictures too?'

'Lizzie who?'

'Lizzie my friend. You know, Lizzie Sugarman. Charles Sugarman's daughter. She was in *Family Connections*.' Recognition spreads across Stephen's face.

'Yeah, and I've told you before, if I wanted your friend Lizzie as one of my client's, I'd sign her. She's a has-been. No deal.'

Stephen harrumphs back to his office and I sigh. Periodically I try for Lizzie. She's a friend and she's not untalented, but sometimes having a famous father puts you at a disadvantage. Everyone thinks you can't be talented in your own right.

I set about my tasks, the first of which is to find Maria. Maria has two children still living in Guatemala who she hasn't seen for four years. She sends all her money home to her family who are raising them. Life must have been hard for her to take that option, I think to myself as I climb the stairs. I don't know how I would cope not being able to see Thackeray. She's sobbing upstairs in her room.

'What happened?'

'Ee tell me I st . . . st . . . steal hees money,' she sobs into a tissue. Her thick accent isn't easy to understand at the best of times, but it's even harder through tears.

'What money?'

'I don't know. I no steal hees money.'

'Of course you didn't,' I pacify, sitting down next to her on the bed. The pictures of her children smile happily in a photo on her dressing table. They look adorable. 'But tell me, what money does he think you stole?'

'Ee say I take two hundred dollar from hees office. But I no go in hees office.'

A light bulb goes on inside my head. Stephen is such an idiot sometimes. 'Don't worry, Maria, I know exactly where the money is,' I tell her calmly. 'Dry your tears and go back to work.'

'But ee say I fired.'

'You're not fired.' I smile. 'He's crazy. I'll sort it out.'

'Thank you, Miss Pearl. Thank you.' She's pitifully grateful.

Well, that's easy. I take Stephen his coffee along with the two hundred dollars he gave me yesterday to put in the petty cash box. He's on the phone.

'Well, of course they're not going to want you in the picture if you're pregnant,' he yells at someone. 'You'll be too fat.'

I put the money on the desk in front of him, on top of the files he wanted. Stephen's brow furrows in perplexity.

'You gave it to me, remember?' I whisper to him.

'No, they won't hold up filming while you have a baby,' he carries on.

'For petty cash,' I hiss. Recognition dawns. He hits the top of his head with the palm of his hand, and smiles.

'Well, we're all disappointed,' he shouts. 'You're not the only one this is going to cost. Have you thought of terminating the pregnancy?'

I can't believe I heard Stephen say that. Back in my office, I search through a pile of Twinkie photos that are stacked up on the floor. Every Twinkie in town sends Stephen her photo, hopeful for her big break. Searching for Madeleine's picture in this stack is not going to be easy. Stephen can't remember her last name (he couldn't even remember her first), and I can't remember her face. All Twinkies look the same. It's like they fall off a production line of glamour Identikits. The real joke is that most directors wouldn't touch these women. Except for their own personal pleasure. The really successful actresses in Hollywood aren't picture-perfect. They have flaws. It's how you remember them. Look at Julia Roberts. Her mouth is far too wide for her face. Look at Sandra Bullock with her mushed nose. Keira Knightley's chin is way too prominent. Hilary Swank has the square jaw thing going on. Sarah Jessica Parker has a hooter that takes up her whole face. I'm not being mean. They're all beautiful in their own way. And that's the key. They're not all trying to look the same.

The pile goes on. I can't see Madeleine's picture anywhere amongst this lot. I'll have another look later. Instead, I slip one of Lizzie's pictures and a résumé into an envelope. *Thought this kid might interest you for* Dog Knows, I scrawl, mimicking Stephen's handwriting, on one of his personal compliment slips. You never know, they might like her. It's all a crap-shoot anyway.

Now I weigh up whether to start on the mail, begin paying Stephen's household bills, peruse one of the scripts on my desk, or grab a few pages of *This Side of Heaven*, which is beckoning at me from my bag. No contest.

Perdita's breath was taken away by Travio's love-making. The noises of an African night filtered through the window – the chirruping of cicadas, the whoop of a far-off hyena, a lonely Scops-owl. She knew in her heart she could never go back to her husband now. This was love like she had never known before. Whatever it was going to cost her, she was going to have to pay the price . . .

The phone rings. I pick it up absent-mindedly. I'd like to go to Africa – the scenery, the animals, the sunsets, Meryl Streep, Robert Redford. *Out of Africa* is one of my favourite films.

'Pearl.' I recognise Brett's voice instantly. It's a deeply resonant sound that carries a kind of warmth, no matter what he is saying. For a split second, I feel like I have stepped back in time and feel the old lurch of joy. He used to always make me feel special.

'Brett,' I say as officiously and icily as I can. 'Stephen's on the phone right now. Would you like to hold?'

'I haven't called for Stephen. I wanted to talk to you.'

'I have nothing to say to you.'

'Of course you haven't. Why would you? But I'm sorry—'

'Brett, I haven't time for this,' I interrupt. 'If you need to speak to Stephen, I suggest you try him at his office.' I hurl the phone back in its stand and find my hands are shaking. Outside, the gardener is back at work on the pond's pump. He's hammering a pipe and I feel an overwhelming urge to ask if I can do the job for him.

The phone rings again.

'Pearl, don't hang up,' Brett says quickly. 'I want to see Thackeray.'

This winds me. It's as unexpected as a paparazzo's flashbulb. I didn't even know he knew our son's name. And he's never, ever acknowledged him as his own.

I'm so stunned I can't think of anything to say, although the word 'Why?' seems to be escaping, unbidden, from my lips.

'Because I know he's my son, and I know I've done wrong by him, and by you, and I want to redress the balance.'

The balance? This is too much. He thinks he can call up and redress the balance? Normal service is suddenly returned to my lips. 'No you can't fucking see him,' I rant. All my maternal protective feelings come rushing at me headlong.

'You don't need to give me an answer now. Just think about it, would you?' he says calmly.

'Leave us alone.'

'Please think about it.'

'My answer is no.'

There's silence on the line. And then Brett delivers his *coup de grâce*. 'Wouldn't you like him to know who his real father is?'

'No, I wouldn't. His father is a cheat,' I say and hang up the phone. The gardener is still hammering. The clanging of metal on metal echoes everywhere, leaving no escape from its disturbance. There were often times when I was on my own after Thackeray was born and I felt the world was closing in on me. That same feeling returns. Sometimes life is such a battlefield, and really, I'm not the warring kind. I'm a Pisces. I'm a mellow chick from California. I'm not equipped to deal with it.

After work, I collect Thackeray from school and head to Dad's. I often call in on him in the afternoons with Thackeray. The warm afternoon sun has won its victory over the earlier chill of the day, and its brightness is bouncing off the other cars on the road, sending shards of white light into my eyes. So many cars! LA has so many cars.

But the car gives me a chance to collect my thoughts. I am unnerved by Brett's reappearance. Stupid understatement. I am completely floored by it. Adam and I ignored him at the party last night. But once we knew he was there, it was like having the rumbling sound of faraway thunder threatening to disturb a garden party – a deathly presence hanging over us that made us feel awkward and uncertain. Adam is aware of how much I loved Brett once. I always knew we'd have to deal with him being back in LA at some stage – LA is, despite its size, a very small town when you're involved in the film industry – but Brett was out of town for so long, I'd managed to convince myself it might never be an issue.

The truth is, it always bothered me that Thackeray would never know his real father. It was one of the things that upset me the most. I'd hold him in my arms after he was born – my tiny little boy with the big brown eyes – and I'd tell him how sorry I was that his daddy had left us. Boys need daddys. I promised him I'd play football with him when he was bigger. I promised him I'd teach him how to shave and drink beer and tell fart jokes, but I knew – we both knew – it wouldn't be the same as having a real dad around. We both knew it wouldn't be the same as being around the person who'd had a hand in your creation. I've always struggled to get over the guilt.

But to have Brett play a part in his life now? To have him upset everything after all this time? I tremble at the thought of him even coming near my baby. He's done too much damage. After Brett left, I couldn't eat, I couldn't sleep, I couldn't leave my apartment. I wouldn't even wash. The world was a very dark, not to mention smelly, place. I've rebuilt my life now and I have to think what is best for all of us – what is best for Adam, for Thackeray and for me. The right thing is to not let him see him. I know that.

I'm holding the steering wheel with clenched fists as Thackeray's voice drags me away from my thoughts.

'What's inside your leg, Mummy?' he asks from his car seat in the back.

'Bones,' I say. Thackeray's interest in all things squeamish seems to know no bounds.

'Anything else?'

'Muscles, veins, tendons, ligaments . . .'

'And blood?'

'Oh, yes, lots of blood.'

'If I cut my leg open, will I see it?'

I pull into Dad's driveway, making a mental note to make sure there are no sharp instruments lying around at home. Lullabelle and Perdy, Dad's two black Labradors, come rushing out to greet us as I unstrap Thackeray from his car seat. They lick his face and he squeals with delight.

I love coming here. It's where I grew up. The house was built in the thirties from creamy stone, with lead-panelled windows, a thick oak front door and wisteria doing its best to envelop it in nature. *Architectural Digest* described it once as one of the most beautiful mansions in LA. They called it gothic baronial, which I didn't especially like. Made it sound spooky, which it isn't. But it *is* beautiful. Flowerbeds and soft grass fill the front garden, with a white fence separating our world from the world beyond, and out the back, tall eucalyptus trees and foliage giving the impression of being in the countryside. There's a pool, a paddock to the side where I used to keep a pony, and a big patio that catches the sun, where Dad has always loved hosting barbecues.

'Hi,' I call through the front door, but I hear voices out by the pool. Thackeray and I wander through, followed by the dogs.

'Alreet, our kid?' says Dad, looking up and accepting a kiss on his stubbly cheek. A lot of his Geordie accent has been swallowed up by an American one after all the years he's been here. But he's always been so proud of growing up in Newcastle upon Tyne that he hangs on to lots of words still. He's reading some legal papers on a sunlounger in the shade of a garden umbrella and ignoring Casey, who is two years old and tottering dangerously close to the edge of the pool.

'Watch out, Casey, come over here, sweetheart,' I say, grabbing his sticky hand and steering him towards some toys. 'Are you meant to be watching him, Dad?'

'Yes, he is,' says Heather, coming out of the house wearing a bikini, with a sarong tied around her tiny waist. 'I only left him for two seconds.'

Heather is my stepmother, and has the look my dad always goes for. Blond, tall, slender – she did a bit of modelling at one time. Definitely a Twinkie. Mum and Dad split when I was eleven. Ashley and I secretly laughed about Heather when we first met her, because she so patently isn't the sharpest knife in the drawer. 'Oh, I love California. I love all the lakes,' she cooed on first introduction. (California, by the way, has many things – mountains, beaches, farmland, desert. What it is not noted for is its lakes. But Heather is from Minnesota, where they do have a lot of lakes, and perhaps she was confused.) She's not who I'd necessarily choose for Dad. But we both make an effort to get on with each other. You have to when you've got a dysfunctional family like mine.

Dad has had four wives. Heather is Casey's mum, and she has another child due in nine months' time. She announced that she was pregnant only last week. She also has a kid from a previous marriage – Joely, who's fifteen. Heather replaced Kimberly, who never had any kids with dad. And it was Kimberly who replaced my mum. Before her was Jodie, who is Lydia's mum. It gets kind of complicated and I've got more step-siblings than most people have pets. This isn't necessarily an easy situation. Do we fight? Like hell we do.

It's funny how you can see a type, after four marriages. My mum was the only brunette Dad ever fell for. I joke with Dad (although only when we're on our own) that it's only a matter of time before he trades Heather in for a younger model, and he always jokes back that there won't be a fifth Mrs Sash because he can't afford the maintenance, but I don't believe him. He might be fifty-seven, but there's life in him still.

'That's a good colour on you,' I tell Heather, as she lowers herself on to a sunlounger. Her bikini is bright yellow, but it works.

'Do you like it? I got it at Macy's.'

We chit-chat while the kids play and Dad reads his papers. I notice how tired he is looking. Years of drug abuse do little for the skin's complexion, but he's paler than usual. He'd hate it if he knew. His hair should probably be grey by now, but he has it dyed a mousy brown. There's Botox fighting off the wrinkles too. It's hard to grow old gracefully when you used to be a rock star, and Dad has fought it all the way.

'What's up, Dad? You look tired,' I venture.

'Lawyers,' he grunts, without looking up. 'Fucking lawyers.'

I've never really understood Dad's business – songwriting and artists' royalties is a world of its own, with its own special rules and definitions, and as long as I can remember, Dad's always been battling over something or other. Money that the record company haven't paid him, advances that they're demanding back. Licensing deals that they haven't disclosed.

'I thought they were meant to be on your side,' I say.

'Not when they work for someone else.' He sighs heavily and removes his reading glasses. 'These people are such assholes.'

'I'm sure it'll be all right,' I say gently, keen to make him feel better. I move round and begin to massage his shoulders. Dad loves being massaged. 'It's not worth getting stressed about.'

But Dad can't relax. 'Everything's not always all right, Pearl.' He snaps abruptly at me, and then stomps inside muttering, 'Sometimes it's fucking shite.'

Heather and I exchange glances. I hate it when Dad gets like this. Even though he's been going to Alcoholics Anonymous for ten years now, he's still unpredictable sometimes.

'He'll get over it,' says Heather wisely, as she rearranges herself on the sunlounger. 'He's been doing a lot of paperwork recently. It makes him tetchy.'

I settle in a chair next to her.

'How was the benefit dinner last night?' she asks.

'It went well, I think. No brawls or bar fights anyway.'

'That's 'cause your daddy wasn't there,' she laughs. Dad's too old now for bar brawls. But when he was a young man, he had a reputation for getting into trouble. He was always in scuffles. It's become part of our family folklore now and we always like to tease him about it.

'Perhaps that's what he needs. A good old-fashioned fisticuffs. It would probably do him good,' I say, as a joke obviously. But I'm forgetting that Heather takes everything literally.

'Oh, I don't think a fight would do him any good at all,' she says earnestly.

'It was just a joke, Heather. A figure of speech,' I soothe.

'Oh, really?' She looks confused, and flashes me an uncertain smile.

It can't be easy being the fourth Mrs Sash. There's always all that history ahead of you. She met Dad after one his concerts. She was one of the groupies and somehow got herself into one of the after-concert parties.

I don't know all the details of how they got it together. I don't *want* to know. Suffice to say, there's a reason why people talk about sex, drugs and rock and roll. And Dad was already a drug-free zone by then.

'How's Casey doing?' I ask, moving on to safer ground.

'Oh, he's just fine. Aren't you, sugar?' It's funny how some women feel obliged to raise their voice twenty octaves and revert to baby-speak when they have children. I told Adam when he married me that if I ever showed similar tendencies he was to shoot me.

'And what about itty-biddy Thacky?'

Only Heather calls him this, and I've always resisted telling her how much I loathe it. Diplomacy is important to family life – well, certainly in ours, anyhow.

'Apart from a preoccupation with sado-masochism, he's fine.'

Heather looks confused again – long words have always stumped her. Thackeray sends a toy car coursing down my leg, accompanied by zooming noises. 'By the way,' she adds. 'There's a package for Thacky by the front door. It arrived by courier earlier. I almost forgot to mention it.'

'For me, for me?' says Thackeray, wide-eyed at the prospect, and races into the house immediately to find it.

The box is enormous. Thackeray and I struggle to carry it out to the patio. It takes us ten minutes, and two trips to the kitchen for scissors that work, to get into it. Inside is a motorised toy car that really goes. It has a little battery-powered engine, like a Prius. I wonder if Adam would like one.

Inside the box is a note. I read it, curious to know who it's from. Thackeray's birthday isn't for months. *To Thackeray, just the start on what I hope to make up to you. With love from your father, who you will get to know*.

What? Now he's sending gifts? I feel fury surge

through my veins, like a Class A drug. Unstoppable and consuming.

'Got any cigarettes?' I ask Heather.

'No, honey,' she twitters. 'What's up?'

Fortunately, Thackeray can't read and he's not interested in who it's from. He's off doing laps around the garden.

Madison Square Gardens heaved. I had never seen so many people before in my life. They jostled and pushed, swayed and merged into a giant organism that swallowed up individuals into the mass. This many people? All here to see my dad? I couldn't believe it.

I looked down on them all from a box, like a nine-year-old princess becoming aware of her subjects. I had never been to one of Dad's concerts before, and although I knew he was famous – the word was bandied around all the time – I hadn't fully realised what that meant. Tonight was a treat. It had been Dad's idea.

'Do all of these people really know my dad?' I asked Mum, leaning dangerously over the guard rail to survey the scene. It really was an astonishing sight.

'Uh-huh.'

'But how?'

'They buy his records,' she explained with a distinct lack of interest, picking up a copy of *Vogue* she had been carrying in her bag. She was dressed, as ever, like a fashion plate, in a pink pantsuit, dark glasses, and miles of noisy gold chains dangling from her neck. She leaned back in her chair, positioned towards the back of the box, where her sightline of the stage couldn't have been good. She flipped the pages of her magazine and claimed the music was making her tired. Everything made Mum tired

– dinner times, breakfast times, birthday parties, other kids, us kids, Dad being away on tour, Dad being home. She was an impenetrable universe sometimes and it was hard to know what it was that she liked. Mostly she seemed to like us out of the way.

She liked fashion a lot too. I used to go through her magazines sometimes, and cut out catwalk photos to give her as presents. Sometimes she'd actually fold up the cutting and put it in her purse. 'You're getting quite an eye,' she'd tell me, and my little chest would heave with pride.

But she was as impenetrable as ever this evening.

'Why do they buy Dad's records?' I persisted.

'I don't know,' she said absently, her nose wrinkled as she examined an editorial shot close up. 'They see him on TV.'

'And they come here because they love him?'

'They come here because he inspires them.'

'What does inspire mean?'

'It means he takes them to a different place.'

'What kind of different place?'

She let out a sigh. 'Just watch and you'll see.'

The drums and guitars began their staccato thump, and Dad emerged through thick smoke on stage. He didn't look like Dad at first – his eyes had black lines of make-up around them, and he was wearing silver trousers. Silver trousers? Well, it was the nineties. He looked like an astronaut making a lunar landing. But then I recognised his familiar step – he walked with a little bounce, as if on tiptoes, as if life was always good. The audience screamed. I put my hands to my ears. I'd never heard anything like it before.

Giant video screens zoomed in on Dad's face, where beads of sweat began to pour and make his hair wet. I longed to wipe them away for him. I longed for him to look up at me and wave.

'Daddy!' I called out, waving frantically. Lydia and Ashley joined in shouting too. But he didn't look up. Didn't he know we were here?

We knew all Dad's songs by heart, but it was different seeing him pour his soul into a microphone on stage. Mum was right, the songs were transporting. While electric guitars whined, his deep, gravelly voice resonated across the arena. He sang about love and heartache, sweetness and longing – none of them groundbreaking subjects, I realise now, but the delivery took us all to an otherworldly place where his voice soothed and caressed us. He lulled us into reverie. Boy, did I love my dad.

F red Segal is an ivy-covered boutique on the corner of
Melrose and Crescent Heights that is a labyrinth of
what is truly cool and hip in LA. Chip and Pepper Jeans,
C&C California, Blue Cult, Jet, Juicy – they're all here
and a billion more names. How I love this place. How I
love the smell of its fresh leather, the new clothes, the
tissue-filled handbags. I love the sound of heels on its
hardwood floors, the clink of coat hangers on the rails, the
burble of shop assistants, the tinkle of necklaces. I love
how the assistants smile sweetly and direct you to new
brands, fresh collections, innovative lines. Just the thrill
of a new line is enough to send a shiver down my spine.
I admit I'm a fashion junkie. But who could not
appreciate the array of designers here, the colours, the
textures, the downright hipness?

And once you've done your worst on a credit card,
there's a salon to get your nails done and a café to sip a
cappuccino. I can't think why anyone ever shops
anywhere else. Tonight it doesn't close until nine, and
with Thackeray ensconced with a babysitter (Adam
always works late), I meet Lizzie and Bella here.

Every woman should have girlfriends – she should
also have at least two Prada jackets in her wardrobe, and
a manicurist to call her own, but equally important are
girlfriends, and two is the absolute minimum. One who

you can laugh with, and one who's a shoulder to cry on. Lizzie is my oldest BFF, who drives me insane because she's so crazy but who I can't imagine life without because she's always been there. Bella is my practical BFF who's kind of tough on the outside, or likes to think she is. And I owe her one, because she was so kind to me when Brett left. It was Bella who got me to the doctor and suggested antidepressants. Bella who came visiting, jollying me along with little gifts and cheerful female companionship. She was the one who helped me through the divorce, and really pulled me back into the real world.

Lizzie is outrageous in her spending this evening – and that's coming from me, having bought two of the cutist Robert Rodriguez tops you've ever seen. 'Well, I've got to look good for Cameron,' she says, affronted by my astonishment at the sheer number of carrier bags she's arranging around the armchair in the café.

'Show me what you got?' she asks, peering into my carrier bags. 'Bitchin'. Want to see what I got?'

She pulls out her purchases, wrapping silk scarves around her neck, and holding up dresses and skirts to her slender frame.

That's why I love Lizzie. She totally understands why it's important to wear good clothes. And she's even more extravagant in her spending than I am, which always assuages any guilt I ever feel.

'Has Cameron called you?' I ask, pleased that my matchmaking has gone so well already.

'No, but he will.' Lizzie smiles slyly.

'How do you know?'

'I just know. We got on so well last night. Like I know he is the one . . .' She gestures wildly with her hands, accidentally hitting a guy behind her and spilling his coffee down his pants and on to the floor. Typical behaviour. She's often a klutz. 'Sorry, so sorry,' she says effusively, abandoning her shopping and racing to fetch napkins and falling to her knees to mop his pants and clean up. The guy looks delighted by the fuss she's making over him. Guys always fall for Lizzie.

'Bet you he's going to put me in his next frickin' movie,' she adds as she returns.

'Who, Cameron, or the guy you spilt coffee over?' asks Bella drily. 'Are you sure you couldn't have fitted in a blow job too while you were down there?'

'Why? Do you think he was a director?' Lizzie asks, looking round to see if he's still there.

Bella says nothing. She just rolls her eyes to the ceiling. She's become as fond of Lizzie as I have over the years, but she has that dry British wit, that is sometimes a little contemptuous. She's real, where Lizzie is impractical. Bella's parents died when she was young and it made her kind of cynical. She ended up in a whole load of foster homes, but being Bella, she wasn't going to let that hold her back. She saw this ad to work as a nanny in Hollywood and got the job. That was at Stephen's, where I worked.

I remember meeting her for the first time. She was only eighteen, but she was so bold and feisty. 'Oh yes, my room is perfectly fine,' she told me breezily when she'd just arrived. It was one of the better rooms in Stephen's mansion, and she'd come straight from Britain. We both knew she'd never seen anything like it before in her life, but she wasn't going to admit as much, and I thought that was kinda ballsy.

And I liked her because she was so rude and dismissive of wannabes. Still is, and doesn't always hide her disdain for Lizzie's preoccupation. 'Why would anyone want to join the ranks of so many?' she often says. The irony is, she got offered a job as a model. No surprise, since she is so effortlessly beautiful. It's the cheekbones that do it. You could hang coat hangers off them. And now she's a TV presenter, and she's almost famous, not in an

A-list kind of way, but enough to get fan mail and make Lizzie ever so slightly envious of her. Especially since she wasn't even trying to find the spotlight, and poor Lizzie tries so, so hard to seek it out.

Lizzie's biggest problem is that not only was her dad famous, but when she was six, she was too. Her parents put her up for a sitcom and she got the part. For two years she was the precocious, wisecracking Isadora of *Family Connections*, who got good ratings. That is, until she grew too old for the part and got dumped off the stardom conveyor belt.

I used to be envious of Lizzie. I wished my parents would let me audition for TV shows. Lizzie missed heaps of school. But now I wonder what the heck her mum and dad were thinking. The career trajectory of the child star follows a certain and well-established path: drug addiction, almost inevitable alcohol addiction, an eating disorder, a stay in rehab, then if it's not a lifetime of being chased by photographers, it's an even worse fate – obscurity, like poor Lizzie. If you don't die young (River Phoenix), you'll grow up dysfunctional (Michael Jackson), your marriage will be doomed (Drew Barrymore, Macaulay Culkin), you'll have trouble making any relationship work (Tatum O'Neal, Liz Taylor) and your ego will become so huge you'll be a living nightmare (all of the above).

I've given up telling Lizzie that fame isn't all it's cracked up to be. The best I can hope for is to try to steer her clear of porn.

'Still doing the porn movie?' I ask fearfully.

'Oh, the porn,' Lizzie says casually. 'Actually I was never *that* serious about it.' She's always been fickle. 'Although I would still like a designer vagina,' she adds, far too loudly. 'Only eighteen thousand dollars.'

'And you could get all your directors to give it a rating out of ten,' snipes Bella, perhaps a little cruelly.

'Perhaps I could get them all to contribute to its cost too,' Lizzie adds eagerly, oblivious to Bella's tone. 'Or rent it out like a timeshare apartment.'

I stifle a giggle. But Bella's face looks stern. She doesn't quite seem herself this evening. It's always hard for anyone to compete with Lizzie, but she's not usually so harsh. I move the conversation along and tell them about Brett's phone call and his gift to Thackeray. I'm hoping they'll have some good advice. Bella in particular is usually smart at knowing what to do.

'Tell him he can't see Thackeray. You have sole custody,' she says, wholly certain in her words.

'Yes, but he *is* his real father,' I find myself saying.

'Makes no difference. Say no,' she says emphatically. 'He deserves nothing.'

'Would you *like* Thackeray to meet him?' Lizzie asks more sympathetically. She's always a softer touch than Bella.

'I don't really know. It's never come up before. But yes, I always wanted Thackeray to know his own dad.'

'Then maybe Thackeray *should* meet him,' says Lizzie.

'Pearl, do you want him back in your life?' Bella asks crossly.

'No, of course not.'

'Well then. You have to say no.'

'But what about the kid?' Lizzie argues. 'Doesn't he have any rights?' She has a point. 'Would Thackeray like to meet him?'

'I haven't asked him. Thackeray knows Adam isn't his real father, but what really scares me is that he will end up liking Brett and then Brett'll disappear like he did before. The last thing I want is Thackeray getting hurt.'

'Then don't let him see him,' Bella snaps. 'Brett's a jerk. It's quite simple. You're way better off without him.'

We sip our lattes in silence. We all know she's probably right.

'Why are men like cars?' says Lizzie, who is never known to let a silence last for long. 'Because they always pull out before checking if anyone else is coming.'

She throws back her head and laughs.

'It's always a mistake to laugh at your own jokes,' Bella quips, rather meanly. She's usually dry, but never mean.

'Is there anything the matter?' I ask.

'No,' she says abruptly. 'Do I look like something's the matter?'

'No, not all,' I say swiftly. Sorry I asked.

Then Bella sighs. 'Sorry. Didn't mean to bite your head off.' She sighs again and hesitates a second as if deciding whether to voice her worry or not. There's clearly something bothering her.

'Sorry. I think I'm turning into a grouch. You see, I've had this letter from an aunt,' she declares eventually. 'It's been really bothering me.'

'I didn't think you had any relatives,' I say, perhaps less than tactfully.

Bella was thirteen when her mum died from an aneurysm. Her dad committed suicide the following year, driving his car into a wall and leaving her nothing but debts. She ended up in the British foster-care system, passed from family to family, orphanage to orphanage, school to school.

'Aunt Livonia was my dad's sister,' Bella explains. 'If anything happened to Mum and Dad, she was supposed to take care of me. It's all there in the letter Dad left for me. But when my parents died, she wouldn't have anything to do with me.'

'Why?' asks Lizzie.

'I don't know. Everything was handled by the social services. And they don't tell you anything.'

'What does the letter say?' I ask.

'Just that she'd like to meet up. She's coming to LA.' Bella fidgets anxiously with her hands. Clearly this is a big deal for her.

'And do you want to meet up with her?' I ask carefully.

Bella says nothing. She almost looks like she's about to cry, and I've never, ever seen her do that before. 'I've always thought it would be nice to have some family,' she says joylessly at last. 'I've always craved it. You do, you know, if you're on your own . . .'

'Of course you do,' I say softly.

'But she was the one who abandoned me. Why didn't she take me in? I mean, why didn't she want me? It's something I've never understood. She knew I had no one else.'

I reach out to squeeze Bella's hand, and a small tear appears in one of her eyes and trickles down her flawless pale cheek. Lizzie passes her a tissue.

'Maybe she's coming to apologise for letting you down all those years ago,' Lizzie suggests.

'You never know what people's motives are,' I add.

'Maybe.' Bella sniffs.

'You won't know if you don't meet her,' Lizzie reasons.

'Yeah, I guess,' says Bella. She looks unconvinced. There's a vulnerability about her face now that is unfamiliar.

'You could always use it as an opportunity to scream and shout at her, if you felt like it,' Lizzie adds gleefully. Lizzie always loves an excuse for melodrama if there is an occasion.

'I guess.' Bella forces a laugh and wipes her eyes. 'It's just taken me a little by surprise. That's all.'

'You need to sleep on it,' Lizzie says kindly. 'Don't rush into anything.'

'Yes, give it some time,' I add. Sometimes, no matter how much you want to help a friend, it's hard knowing the right thing to say.

The store manager tells us it's nine o'clock and we have to leave because the shop's closing and haven't we noticed that the lights have gone out? So they have. When did that happen? Lizzie begs to be allowed to just have one last look in the accessory section, and somehow, because Lizzie is a persuasive force, she gets her way. Bella and I disappear to the parking lot.

'Don't stress out about it,' I tell her as we hug goodbye. 'It sounds like it might be what you've always wanted.'

She smiles, and I feel sorry for her as she gets into her car. My parents have never been perfect, but at least I *have* parents.

At three a.m. the phone rings. I force my consciousness back to the real world, away from dreams of Fred Segal, and reach blearily for the receiver on my bedside table. Our bedroom is dark, but there's a stream of light coming from the hallway outside our room where we keep a light on for Thackeray. It would take an earthquake to wake Adam – a big one at that. He is snoring heavily, the back of his head flat on the pillow, which is how he always sleeps, as if sunbathing in the dark. Covers neatly – no, precisely – pulled up across his chest, exactly where he likes them. Legs spread out like a starfish, leaving me only inches of the bed.

'Pearl, it's Heather,' blurts the voice down the line. There's an urgency to her tone that I can't remember ever hearing before. It can't be the Heather I know. Must be a wrong number.

'Heather who?'

'Heather Sash, who do you think?'

'What's the matter?'

'It's your dad . . .' Her voice disappears into a sob.

'What? What's the matter with him?'

'He's had a heart attack. At least, I . . . they . . . they think . . .'

'A heart attack!' I sit up sharply in the bed. This must surely be a wrong number. We don't have heart attacks in our family. At least, not since Grandad had his.

'The paramedics think it was a heart attack.'

'Where is he?'

'We're at Cedars. He's in the emergency room at the moment. They won't let me in.' She sobs again.

'Is he going to be all right?' I ask. A stupid question, I know, but I feel panic rising.

'I don't know,' she wails.

'I'll be right there.'

I dress quickly in the dark and wake Adam. I'm so shocked, I don't feel like I'm me any more, but someone else watching me throwing on clothes and moving around my house from on high. Is this what they call an out-of-body experience? I wonder.

'I must come with you,' Adam insists, now sitting bolt upright in the bed, once I've broken the news.

'No, no. You have to stay with Thackeray.'

'But I'm worried about you. You shouldn't have to go on your own, honey.'

'Heather will be there. And I need you to take care of Thackeray for me.' He looks unconvinced.

'Are you sure? Thackeray could come too.'

'No, no. Best to let him sleep.' I kiss Adam on the cheek. 'I must go. I'll call you.'

By the time I find Heather in the hospital, Dad is in an operating theatre and she's pacing up and down a waiting room, wearing sweatpants and an old sweater. Her face is blotchy and red. This is not a good look for her.

'Oh, Pearl.' She throws her arms around me in a way she never has before and jerks with each sob. We hold each other and I find I'm grateful for the warmth of her body and the solidarity of embrace. She's not that bad really.

'What did the doctors say?'

'No one's told me anything,' she says, blowing her nose into a tissue. She has the panicked look of a captured animal. 'They just rushed him into surgery. Told me to wait here. It's been nearly an hour.'

'Who's with Casey?'

'Joely's there.'

I lead her to a row of chairs and persuade her to sit down. There's no one else in the room, but there is a tank full of tropical fish. A stripy one keeps racing up and down the tank as if on speed.

'What happened?' I ask.

'He said his chest was hurting when he went to bed,' Heather whimpers. 'But he thought it was indigestion. Took some Rolaids and went to sleep. Next thing I know he's telling me to call an ambulance. Said there were knives in his chest.'

'You weren't . . . ?' I find myself struggling for the right words.

'Weren't what?'

It seems inappropriate to ask, but Heather is twenty years younger than my dad. 'Having sex,' I whisper.

'No, we weren't.' She smiles weakly and sniffs.

Thank God. No one enjoys thinking about their parents having sex.

'And did the paramedics say anything?'

'They said they needed to get him to hospital straight away. Said it was a heart attack most likely . . .' She begins sobbing again. 'He was throwing up by the time we reached the hospital.'

I feel the weight of the situation suddenly, like a jumbo jet crash-landing in the pit of my stomach, leaving panic, chaos and terror stirring in its wake. People die of heart attacks. Could my dad actually die? Surely this is all a mistake. I've never lived in a world without my dad in it. I can't begin to imagine it. He is such a big person –

not literally, but a big personality. Big people don't die, do they? They live for ever. They get a special big person life licence. He can't just die.

'He'll pull through this,' I tell Heather. I don't know why I'm so confident. But I am. Perhaps because I can't conceive of anything different. 'Dad's really strong. He always has been. He'll pull through.'

Heather nods pathetically. It's what we both want to believe.

There's a clock on the wall in the waiting room and the second hand moves interminably slowly. Nurses come and go, but not with any news. We take turns to fetch coffee from a vending machine down the hallway. Real coffee, with caffeine. And we discuss whether to phone my siblings. Should we wait until we have more news, or should they all be racing here now to catch his last moments? We stare at each other blankly, unsure what to do. We call Ashley, because he'd want to know; but Lydia? Lydia's a tough decision. She's lived in New York for the last five years, and hasn't spoken to Dad for longer than that. There was an argument and a falling-out between them. But she'd want to know, wouldn't she? Heather suggests we leave it till we hear more news.

The second hand moves slowly on. I feel jittery. Probably the onslaught of caffeine in a body that's been deprived of it since easily last week. The first streak of dawn is breaking through the darkened plate-glass windows when a doctor finally walks in.

'Mrs Sash?' he says, approaching us. He's an Asian man, wearing turquoise scrubs and rimless spectacles.

'Yes,' we both say immediately, leaping to our feet. He looks between us, momentarily confused.

'I'm Mrs Sash,' says Heather emphatically. 'This is his daughter.'

'Pearl Sisskind-Sash,' I say, holding out my hand. I

couldn't bear to part with my maiden name when I got married. I'd lived with it for too long. So I merged it with Adam's. It kind of works, I think.

'I'm Dr Kim.' He shakes our hands slowly. Just give us the news, I want to scream. Come on, I urge him silently.

'There's good news and there's bad,' he says, addressing Heather.

I feel a flood of relief. Good news must mean he's still alive.

'The good news is, he's still breathing. The heart has stabilised,' he continues in a tone reserved for undertakers and doctors with grave news. 'The bad news is that he has suffered a very extreme heart attack. We have given him a heart catheterisation.'

'A what?' asks Heather, looking bewildered and confused.

'This means that we threaded tubes through the femoral artery in the groin into the coronary arteries to identify the blockage. We've given him nitroglycerin to dilate the blood vessels and heparin to thin the blood. Then we performed angioplasty.'

'Angio what?' asks Heather. The doctor studies her face a second, weighing up her ability to take all this in, and then carries on, now addressing me instead.

'Angioplasty is when a balloon is placed at the blockage site to allow the blood and oxygen to pass through the heart. What we are concerned about now is how much damage the coronary attack has caused. When a heart attack occurs, part of the heart muscle dies and is ultimately replaced with scar tissue. This leaves the heart weaker. We will be transferring Mr Sash now to the coronary care unit, where we'll do further tests.'

'But he'll be all right, won't he?' I say cautiously.

The doctor says nothing.

'Will he?' I feel alarm rising in my own voice.

'The truth is that we can't say yet.'

'You can't say!' Heather sinks down on the chair and bawls into a tissue that is falling to pieces from overuse.

'But surely you must know,' I find myself pleading.

'We're going to be monitoring him very closely,' says Dr Kim in his aloof, professional, I-can't-get-too-involved voice. 'A heart attack is serious. Echocardiography will measure how badly damaged the heart is. And if there are multiple areas of blockage, he may require bypass surgery.'

Heather lets out another sob.

'Look,' Dr Kim drops his voice a key and shows just a fraction of sympathy in his face, 'Mr Sash is in the best place he could possibly be in the whole world. We have the very latest technology there is to help him.'

'And his chances? What are the chances he'll be fine?'

'I'm afraid we are just going to have to wait to see what the tests show,' he says impassively. 'Was Mr Sash a cocaine user?'

'No,' says Heather, at the same time that I say, 'Yes.'

'Not for a long time, though,' adds Heather.

'Yes, not for a long time,' I agree.

'There's a strong correlation between cocaine usage and heart attack,' says the doctor.

Great. It was kind of him to throw that in.

Clearly tired of two women's stupid questions, Dr Kim eventually disappears through the swing doors and Ashley arrives through some others. He stands, legs wide, as we fill him in on the news, and he nods, rubbing his hand on his chin, as if taking in a legal brief.

'We better call Lydia,' he says decisively. He always got on better with her than I did. 'She'd want to know.'

Heather and I nod lamely. He pulls out a cell phone from his pocket.

'What did she say?' I ask when he's finished talking. The last time any of us saw Lydia, she was wishing death upon Dad in a row that made family history. Part of me half expects her to be gloating because her wish has come true.

'She seemed pretty stunned.'

'Is she flying out?'

'She didn't say.'

I wrestle three dollar bills off Ashley for more coffee from the vending machine. Heather and I are all out. And then, finally, we're allowed to see Dad.

Absentee parenting wasn't so much a catchphrase as a way of life for us, and Mum and Dad weren't home at all that last summer I had in LA. So I often used to find myself perusing the contents of the safe in their bedroom. It had always been a source of fascination to us kids – the clicking and turning of wheels, the fact that it was hidden in a closet behind rows and rows of Mum's clothes on hangers. Dad had shown us how it worked once, and I'd memorised the code.

Inside the safe were rings and bracelets, earrings and baubles. I used to try them all on, teaming them up with clothes from a dressing-up box. There was one really chunky diamond necklace in the safe that Mum always wore for special occasions. It sparkled magnificently. I used to struggle with the catch to put it on, and study myself in the mirror. I was a princess decked out for a ball. I was a duchess receiving guests for tea. I was a movie star on the night of her premiere.

One afternoon the thought came into my head to borrow the big necklace. It would be fun to show it to Lizzie. She was a girl who appreciated these things. So I put everything else back, closed the safe, carefully returned Mum's clothes to their original position and wore the necklace to ride on my bicycle round to Lizzie's house.

Lizzie certainly appreciated it. 'Why don't you sell it?' she suggested helpfully, once I'd let her try it on. 'We'll spend the money in the toyshop, and maybe have enough left over for the movies. Pawnshops take shit like that, and give you money straight away. I've seen them. You might get a hundred dollars for a necklace.'

It seemed like an excellent plan. Mum and Dad had so much going on, they'd never notice.

As it turned out, we got five hundred dollars for it and couldn't believe our luck. We couldn't even carry all that we bought at the toyshop, and still there were wedges of bills in our pockets.

Selling the necklace remained a good idea for three weeks. Three glorious weeks of toyshops, ice-cream parlours and movies. Until Mum and Dad came home and happened to open the safe and discover its absence. The police were called. They'd think it was a burglar who took it, I told myself, as I stood at the bottom of the stairs listening to them talk to Mum and Dad in the bedroom.

'How many people know the code?' the sheriff asked.

'Only my wife and me,' my dad said.

'You sure?' said the sheriff. 'Only the safe hasn't been damaged at all. It would be unlike a thief to have left so many of the other jewels. How much would you say the necklace was worth?'

'Over a million dollars,' Mum said. A million dollars!

'Hmm . . . Someone might have cracked the safe just for that. But there's no evidence of a break-in. It looks to me like it was someone who knew the safe was there and knew the code. What about your staff? Did they know it was there?'

'No, I don't think so.'

'The kids?'

'Well, they know the safe is there.'

'Do they know the code?'

'I don't think so,' my dad said.

'It's worth asking them, sir. I've seen cases like this before.'

The three of us were summoned to the bedroom. I wondered if anyone else could hear my heart pounding as I walked upstairs. If it banged any louder it would give me away. Did we know anything about this? We all shook our heads innocently. Did we know the code? No we didn't. Of course we didn't – we were just kids. We were dismissed. I breathed a sigh of relief.

But then, as we were leaving, a different voice came from inside the closet. A fingerprint expert's voice. The size of the fingerprints were peculiarly small, he announced. Extraordinarily so. In fact, he'd put money on it that they were the fingerprints of a ten or eleven year old. I was called back. I was cross-examined. I was confused. I was tearful. I was in disgrace. I was SO in disgrace.

I cannot begin to describe my father's rage.

*P*erdita *was a good liar. It surprised her how easily treachery came. When Alex, her husband, returned from his hunting safari, she told him about the baboons who had raided their fruit trees, the army ants who were making ready for the rainy season, and how she'd been lonely waiting for his return. Travio had long since departed, leaving her with only memories of their lovemaking and aching for his caresses again. How was it possible for one man to make her feel so much? She knew she would have to tell Alex eventually. Their marriage was void now . . .*

My cell phone rings, disturbing my escape into the pages of *This Side of Heaven*. Fortunately, the book was in my bag when I raced to the hospital. I sent up a little prayer of thanks to the romance gods when I found it there. There's been a lot of waiting around. 'Is that Pearl Sash?' asks an abrupt voice. 'Stuart Wise from the *Daily Globe*. Can I ask how your dad's doing?'

'How did you get this number?' I feel outrage mounting. Dad's only been in hospital half a day, and already the press are phoning. How did they even know?

'Sorry to intrude at this time,' says the reporter, trotting off a line. He's not sorry at all.

'Please, I have nothing to say. Except do not use this number again,' I say sharply and cut him off. Jeepers, are we allowed no privacy?

A nurse makes me jump, as she silently arrives in Dad's room and starts fiddling with equipment. Dad's trussed up like a laboratory rat. Wires and tubes pour out of him. Lights flash on screens around him and a monitor is beeping in time with his heart on an electrocardiograph.

Once the doctors told us that there was really nothing we could do, Heather went home to get some rest, Ashley disappeared to his office, and I phoned both Adam and Stephen to tell them I would be staying here for when Dad woke up. Then I curled up in an ugly vinyl armchair in the corner of the room to take up my vigil.

It's a shock to see Dad this way. His face looks ashen grey and his chest hair, I notice, is white – quite a different colour to the dyed hair on his head. A respirator tube has been forced down his throat and his lower arms are strapped to the bed with belts.

'Is it really necessary to tie him down like that?' I ask the nurse.

'It's in case he wakes and tries to pull the respirator tube out,' she informs me. 'It's the natural reaction to try to pull it out, but the tube is making sure he can breathe.'

Dad seems to be oblivious to it anyway. His eyes are closed – peacefully, it seems – and the regularity of the respirator, which makes a steady rasping noise, is strangely soothing. When the nurse is gone, I hold Dad's pale and wrinkled hand in mine and tell him again that I love him. I've told him so often, he's probably sick of the sound of my voice by now.

The respirator whooshes on, the cardiograph beeps in time. Everything seems calm. So I retreat to *This Side of Heaven* again. Romance novels are good for times like these. I love the escapism, but also the celebration of love and the optimism. Not to mention all that passion. Wouldn't it be great if sex was as good in real life as it is in books?

Of course, real life isn't like that and real romance isn't just about passion. Real romance is about kindness and golden wedding anniversaries. Rather like fairy stories where princes and princesses meet each other, kiss and get married all in the same day, romance novels rarely get as far as checking into the old people's home. They rarely even go beyond the wedding day. But that's where real love starts.

Poor Dad never quite got the grasp of it. Given that he changed wives almost as frequently as he did hairstyles, it's hard to imagine that he understood the term commitment. Would he ever have known real love? I study the familiar features of his face – the crooked nose, broken in a fight in Newcastle, the determined chin, the deep-set eyes. On his arm is the tattoo – now faded – with Ashley and my names on it that he had done years ago. Dad's career was what Dad really loved. We all knew that. But he loved us kids in his own way. I've always known that too.

My phone rings again. 'Pearl, I need you to make me another doctor's appointment.' Stephen's voice blasts into my ear, disturbing my thoughts.

'Stephen, I told you I'm at Cedars. Dad's had a heart attack.'

'Yeah, but I've got this rash I'm worried about. I need you to call him for me.'

'Stephen, his number is in the book.'

'Which book?'

'The address book on your desk.'

'Do you think it could be measles?'

'I shouldn't think so . . . Syphilis more likely,' I add under my breath.

'What?'

'Nothing.'

'And I need some dandruff shampoo. Can you pick some up on your way round?'

'I'm not on my way round.' Jeepers. 'Have you looked in Maria's store cupboard?'

'What store cupboard?'

'The big closet on the landing outside your bedroom. Look in there. There's tons of bottles of your shampoo.'

'OK.' Click. The phone goes dead. Two seconds later, it rings again.

'Stephen, why don't you ask Maria?'

'Sorry?' says a confused voice. 'Pearl, it's Brett. I just heard the news.'

How did *he* know? And how did *he* get this number?

'Why are you calling me?' I say icily. He's the last person I want to talk to. Even less than Stephen.

'Stephen told me the news and gave me your number. Pearl, I want to help,' he says tenderly.

'There's nothing anyone can do to help.' I draw an audible breath, and realise the enormity of the words.

'Really?'

'Really.' I pluck a thread that is hanging loose from one of the sheets on Dad's bed.

'Is he going to be all right?'

'I don't know,' I whisper, and find myself wiping away tears for the first time. When I first heard the news, I was too shocked to cry. Now, for some reason – perhaps because it's Brett's voice on the line – my emotions seem to be cutting loose. I let out an unexpected sob, and accidentally drop the phone.

'Pearl ... Pearl ...' I hear Brett's detached, tinny voice contained within the earpiece of the phone on the shiny hospital floor. 'Pearl, are you all right? Pearl? Pearl? OK, I'm coming over.'

I pick the phone up off the floor. The back of it, holding in the battery, has broken off.

'No, don't ... Please ... I'm fine. I dropped the phone. It's just been a shock, that's all.' I sniff hard and try to regain composure.

'Of course it has, my darling. My poor Pearl. My poor, poor Pearl.'

It's been years since I've heard Brett call me 'my darling'. The familiarity is comforting. For a split second I feel a sensation of calm. Then ire returns. How dare he call me darling? I'm not his darling.

'Look, thanks for calling. But really there's nothing you can do,' I say briskly, pulling myself together and pushing my finger towards the call-end button.

'Pearl, we were happy together, weren't we?' The affection in his voice is seductive. The words a surprise. Why is he doing this?

There's a pregnant silence down the line, and then I find that my lips are whispering, 'Yes.'

'You had every right to be angry with me.'

Angry? Is my mother Catholic? That was only the tiniest fraction of all the emotions I battled against in order to regain my sanity.

When Thackeray was born, I sank into the kind of despair and depression that even Virginia Woolf might have been impressed by. Part of it was hormonal, the doctor told me, as she prescribed antidepressants. Most women get a little blue after a baby is born – the lack of sleep, the abrupt turnaround in their lives transforming them from independent creatures into slaves to a howling infant, the realisation that there's no going back and no option to escape the responsibility. An option that Brett clearly imagined he had.

But my depression was deepened a thousand-fold by Brett abandoning me. A darkness descended and cast a shadow that removed the light from everything. There was the sadness, the hurt, the humiliation, the loneliness, the feeling of worthlessness – all the usual suspects that accompany a broken heart were there. Not an ingredient missing from the line-up. A million times I cursed myself for being so foolish as to fall in love with him.

'Yes, I was angry,' I say calmly. My finger still hovers over the call-end button.

'I did wrong by you. I know I did,' he says slowly. 'I'm not expecting you to want to listen, but I know I made a terrible mistake.' He draws breath and I say nothing. There is nothing to say. 'Look, I know I hurt you, and I want you to know how sorry I am. I really am. I've changed, you know.'

I think of how many times I longed for him to come back to me with that line. He was always unreliable and a terrible flirt, but that was oddly part of his charm. Just like Dad, he had charisma – that indefinable quality that just made people want to be near to him. It was what made him a good actor. It was what made him worth having. He'd transgress terribly, forgetting birthdays, turning up late to meet me, flirting with my girlfriends, but then he'd look me in the eye, crack a joke and make me feel like I was the only person in the world that mattered. I never knew if he'd been unfaithful with others before Conzuela Martin. I didn't want to know.

'What is it you want?' I ask eventually, after a long silence.

'I want to make it up to you.'

I let out a laugh. He's got to be kidding.

'I think you're a bit late for that. And by the way, I'm married now – or did you imagine I was waiting for you to come back to me?' I hear a cruel sarcasm in my own voice. It's not usually my style.

'I know you're married, Pearl. But I've never stopped loving you.'

Was that the respirator suddenly gasping or me? I am shocked by the revelation.

'You must want something from me,' I say dispassionately. 'Might as well just come out and say it. I haven't got time to be played with.' Alarm bells are now clanging loudly inside my head, warning me away.

'I don't want anything,' he protests. 'I just needed to say I was sorry. Look, I didn't mean to make you angry. Just let me know if there is anything I can do to help. OK?' I am too stunned to say anything. 'OK?' he demands.

'OK,' I mumble and press the call-end button.

By the afternoon, Dad is awake and the respirator is removed. The faintest trace of colour returns to his cheeks and I know he's on the road to recovery because he's swearing at the nurses. I feel the tension in my shoulders release as he demands a sip of water, which the nurses won't let him have in case he vomits again.

'Dad, we were so worried,' I tell him.

'I was quite worried myself.' He smiles weakly. Heather returns, with her daughter Joely at her side, and the doctors say they are very pleased with his progress.

'Looks like he's through the woods,' one of them tells me. Relief spreads like a warm electric blanket.

'Now you're better, can you get me tickets for Miley Cyrus?' Joely demands straight away, waltzing up to his bedside.

'Joely!' I say, feeling instantly protective of Dad. 'He's just had a heart attack.'

'I can ask him if I want,' she snarls viciously at me. She's always been a brat.

'But he's sick. Give him a chance to get better.' I look across to Heather to intervene, but she won't catch my eye.

Joely turns back to Dad with a sugar-sweet voice. 'Only they say they're sold out, and you must be able to get me some, can't you? You must know someone who can get me some VIPs.'

Dad smiles benignly. 'I'll do what I can.'

Joely shoots me a triumphant look. Time to leave. Sharing Dad has never been easy.

'Will you promise to take care of yourself, Dad?' I kiss him goodbye on his bristly cheek. 'No chasing after the nurses.'

'What? Not even the blondes?' he asks with outrage. We've always shared jokes about blondes. Being a brunette, I feel it my duty.

'Not even the blondes.' I squeeze his hand and head for the door. 'I'll come back tomorrow.'

'Alreet, our kid,' he calls in a rasping voice.

'Alreet, our dad.'

There's a small handful of reporters and photographers waiting outside the gates to my house when I get home. I've sort of become accustomed to the lack of privacy and the secrecy necessary to lead a normal life over the years, but it's been a while since there was big-time interest in us. Dad stopped touring years ago, and without any whiff of a scandal to whet their interest, the press have pretty much left us alone. Rather like the church, the press appear at pivotal life moments – births, marriages and deaths. *Hello!* got the first photos of Casey after he was born, and would be sure to be offering big sums for the first pictures of his baby brother, not even born. They popped up when I got married to Adam too, offering us money for exclusive photos of the wedding, but we refused. I think the last time there was a big gaggle of reporters on our doorstep was when Dad started cheating on Kimberly and married Heather.

Still on a high from the good news about Dad, I wind down the window of the Mercedes and throw the dogs a bone. I tell them that Dad's had a heart attack but he's on the road to recovery, and they soak up the information gratefully. A female reporter asks me if I'll do a sit-down interview with her talking about the whole scare, but I refuse – why would I want to share my private drama with the rest of the world? I drive through our gates, leaving them all behind.

My home is always my sanctuary, but after a day like today, it's really special. I fall on to the Shabby Chic sofa in the living room, squashing the cushions and appreciating their luxury after the hospital. This room is my haven. I went for a fresh, spacious feel when I was decorating – lots of dark woods in the furniture, chosen, of course, from Barclay Butera on La Brea, but light walls and fabrics. I sometimes like to play games and imagine how a real-estate agent might describe the room.

The room has been tastefully decorated with a clear artistic eye, his notes might say. Yes, I'd really like that. *It has been arranged to make maximum visual use of the glass doors that open out on to the south-facing garden. The living is true Californian style, where the border between inside and out has been obscured. With the doors wide open, the living room becomes part of the garden, and the garden becomes part of the living room. And its owner is clearly an exponent of feng shui – vital for the positive flow of positive chi. The sofa is against the back wall to represent the Black Tortoise, the one-seater to the right to represent the White Tiger, the two-seater to the left for the Green Dragon, and the coffee table in front to symbolise the Phoenix. How wise the owner is to recognise the significance and importance of these essentials.* Oh yes, I'd love that. Adam just laughed when I told him this was how the room *had* to be.

'Come back to earth, Pearl,' he chided. 'You're away with the fairies.'

He doesn't get feng shui at all. And he didn't like the sofas I chose either, each covered in a beautiful pale green silk, with just a hint of a pattern in the grain of the fabric. 'How long do you think that silk's going to last with a kid in the house?' he demanded.

Adam can't help being an inflexible Scorpio. He is,

after all, the only man I know who keeps a record of his phone calls and then actually spends time checking them off against the bill; who knows precisely what's in his bank account at all times right down to the last cent (something I'm secretly impressed by); and who adheres to the speed limit, even if we're the only car on the road doing twenty mph. He can't help it. The stars define all of us.

But those qualities also make him trustworthy, loyal, safe. He's dependable like a favourite pair of jeans that aren't anything too fancy, but you adore them still and know you could never, ever throw them away. He cares about me. And unpredictability, for all its thrills and spills, gets old pretty quick in a relationship. I shudder at the thought of Brett's call. I learned that mistake a long time ago.

I kick off my shoes, relishing the cool silk of the cushions on my skin and realising suddenly how exhausted I am. Adam has been forced to take time out of work to collect Thackeray from school for me and he's playing with him in the garden with the new toy car. Ah, yes. The toy car. Adam's not going to be pleased about that. I'll just take five minutes to put my feet up, and then go and join them. But Thackeray has seen me.

'Mummy, Mummy.' He comes running at me with the force and speed of a jet on takeoff and throws his arms around me. 'Is Grandad better?'

'A little bit,' I tell him. 'I think he's going to be OK.'

Adam wants to know the news too. He brings me a cup of mint tea, and settles next to me while Thackeray disappears back into the garden, leaving me to show off the new language I have learned today – a hospital language that until this morning I was a mere novice in. Words like angioplasty, nitroglycerin and arteries trip off my tongue like I've been studying medicine all my life.

'And are *you* all right?' Adam asks. 'How are you feeling?'

'Tired. But I'm fine. The main thing is that Dad's OK.'

'Sure.' He rubs my feet, which I have balanced on his knees, and then I catch the uncomfortable look on his face. I know what's coming.

'Honey, will you mind if I go back to the office?'

'But it's nearly six o'clock,' I plead. Most people eat dinner round about now, but I can't remember a time when Adam was ever home to eat with us. If I have one complaint about my husband, it's that he never stops working. He is in his office before eight a.m., and never back before nine. Saturdays too. If he wasn't so loyal, I'd swear he was having an affair with someone.

'I've got to get this script done before the end of the week. I can be sued if I don't deliver on time.' He sighs. 'I'm sorry, honey. You'll be OK, won't you?'

Well, I usually am. So I smile and nod like a good wife should. Putting in the hours is what it takes to stay ahead in Hollywood, and Adam is blindly ambitious.

'But before I go . . .' He looks across at me with a pleading expression in his eye. 'Can you help me out with one thing? You see, I've got the guy telling the girl how much he loves her. And he's moving past first base. But the question is, does he hit a home run?'

This is not Adam's secret life as a swinger but a scene he's writing. He often asks my advice. He likes the female input. We've always dreamed up movie pitches together. It's what we do. From the minute I discovered books were more than something to throw at the cat, I've always loved stories. And I've always been fascinated by what Adam does.

'No. Of course he doesn't,' I tell him. 'You need another scene in there first. The guy's got to woo her some more. Girls need wooing. You need a romantic dating scene.'

Adam looks antsy. 'A romantic dating scene. Got any ideas?' Poor Adam. There weren't too many in our history.

He played it straight. It was movies followed by dinner all the way. 'How about the movies?' he suggests.

'Not original enough.' He misses the irony.

'Dinner?'

'Yeah, but you got to dress it up. What about both of them have a pedicure and they go home and he blows her mind by sucking her toes?'

'Women really like that stuff?'

'Sure they do. Want to try?' I wave my pedicured toes in his face, but he pushes them away. 'What about he buys her a cowboy hat and takes her square-dancing, or a breakfast picnic on top of Mount Hollywood? Or what about an ice-cream parlour?'

'I like the ice-cream parlour,' says Adam, now smiling. 'I can use my ice-cream joke. What's the best ice cream to go with a marital break-up?'

'Rocky Road,' I say.

'You knew!'

'Everyone knows that one.'

He gets to his feet and rearranges the creases on his pants. 'Thanks for the ideas. I'll be back before midnight.' Thackeray speeds past the window in his new car. 'Nice car, by the way. Where did you get it?'

Ah yes. The car. I take a deep breath.

'Brett sent it to him.'

'B-B-B . . . !' Adam sits down again. The stutter is back. 'And you let him have it?'

'Well, I didn't know it was from Brett until Thackeray had opened the box.'

'B-b-b-but why didn't you send it back?'

'Because Thackeray was there. He wanted it. What was I supposed to do?'

'You should have returned it to the sender saying thanks but n-n-n-no thanks.'

'Well I'm sorry I didn't,' I say abruptly. I don't mean for my voice to rise, but it's been a long day.

'So what are we m-m-m-meant to do now? Write him a thank-you note?' Adam's voice has risen too, and I hear anger in it.

'He wants to meet Thackeray,' I say quietly. There is no point in hiding it from him. Adam's face is contorted with apprehension. 'It's OK. I've told him he can't.'

'So you've spoken to him then?' he snarls.

'Yes, he called me.'

'He called you!' Adam explodes.

'He called me at Stephen's. Look, please don't be so defensive. I don't want him calling me any more than you do. And I hoped you'd be supportive. Helpful even. Tell me what's the right thing to do, because I don't know. Should we let him see Thackeray? He is his father.'

Adam sighs heavily, and raises his palms to the ceiling in a gesture that suggests defeat and despondency.

'My father?' Thackeray wanders back in from the garden, catching the tail end of my words.

Adam shoots me a despairing look, as if to say 'now look what you've done'.

Although Thackeray calls Adam Daddy, and Adam has always assumed that role, Thackeray has been told that he has another daddy out there somewhere. I never wanted to lie to him.

'Your father is right here,' I reassure. 'Go give him a hug, because I think he needs one.'

He obliges sweetly, and I watch Adam wrap his arms around him.

'Let's talk about this later,' Adam says, more calmly now. 'I better go.'

12

Boarding school was always the nuclear option. 'If you don't sharpen up your act, then it'll be school in England,' Dad had warned a million times.

Following the incident of the missing diamonds, he pressed the button. I was shipped out on a plane to Heathrow. Betty waved me off at LAX with tears in her eyes. Then it was ten hours with a sign around my neck that said 'Unaccompanied Minor', and a minibus to Buckinghamshire. I felt sick. Caused, for the first time, by something other than too many sweets: remorse.

'This will be your dormitory,' announced an overweight woman who had introduced herself as Matron at the entrance to Mandlewood Abbey Boarding School for Girls. 'You will unpack your suitcases and put your belongings in this chest of drawers here. This will be your bed.' She pointed at the bed, made up with white sheets and a khaki blanket. 'Bathroom is through there.' She gestured at a battered door on which carved graffiti had been gloss-painted over. 'You are expected down in the common room in thirty minutes, where you will meet the rest of the girls. They're playing hockey at the moment.' She gave a satisfied sigh. 'I'll leave you to it.'

I looked around the room. Six iron beds were crammed into the space like at a hospital, each with a chest of drawers by its side. On each of these the girls had positioned framed photos of their families. The beds were laden with cuddly toys – small markers of individuality among uniform beds. I had brought neither photos nor a teddy.

I sat on the bed, loneliness competing with weariness. Outside the window by my bed, the soft British sun was toasting the remaining leaves on the trees into September yellows and browns. I could see the playing fields down the hill, and girls in white shirts and navy shorts running around on them. It was four in the afternoon here, but midnight in LA, and I hadn't slept at all on the plane. I lay down and closed my eyes to stop the tears. I'd never felt so alone.

School in England was what made children great and good, according to Dad. It was where he was from. It was what had made him great and good. Trouble was, I wasn't great and good. By the time I turned eleven in sixth grade at Beverly Hills Elementary, I'd spent more time in detention than any other kid at school, apart from Lizzie. Homework was a chore that I considered beneath me. And as for turning up for class. I knew how to play truant, play electric guitar and do my own make-up, but actually doing schoolwork? It wasn't even a possibility.

Instead my greatest thrill was to pull down my underwear and do moonies at the tourists in the buses that passed our garden's picket fence with their commentary blaring, 'And this is Gavin Sash's mansion.' Ashley, Lizzie and I would lie in wait and burst out of the bushes with our butts in the air. It was raucous fun to see the shocked faces.

Running wild came naturally to me. Lizzie and I were Butch Cassidy and the Sundance Kid, and embarked on a glorious life of crime, which came with the full adrenaline rush of misdeed and transgression. We'd often run away, raiding strangers' handbags and even trying our hand at shoplifting.

Trouble was, there was no cavalry on our heels and no one ever caught us. I don't think anyone even noticed we were missing. Apart from detention at school, there was no punishment for our life of crime, no stern adult attention for our felonies. It was almost a relief when the diamond incident caught up with me.

'Wake up,' said a harsh voice with clipped vowels. I woke with a start from a deep sleep, disorientated about where I was. I must have dropped off in the dormitory. Girls' faces came into view. There were five of them, laughing and rifling through my still unpacked suitcase. One of them was wearing a floral shirt of mine over her school uniform. It was a fancy one from Elegant Child of Beverly Hills – even back then I understood the importance of good clothes. She was parading up and down the dormitory.

'Think I'll have this one,' she announced in her plummy British accent.

'Hey, get your hands off my stuff,' I shouted.

'Oooh, a Yank! Get your hands off my stuff.' She mimicked my drawl. The others laughed. 'I don't think so. I'm head of dorm, by the way. I take what I want. This is my fee to be kind to you.'

I struggled to my feet and was about to grab my things, but I was suddenly giddy from the jet lag, the lack of sleep, and the rude awakening. The girl pushed me roughly back on the bed. She was taller than me and had a long face, like a greyhound's. 'What's your name anyway?'

'Pearl Sash.'

'What's that? Gotta rash? Pearl Sash, gotta rash?'

The others began chanting it.

'Hey, I know who you are,' observed another girl. 'You're Gavin Sash's daughter, aren'tchya? I heard you were coming here.'

'What's it to you?' I spat back.

'Actually, it's nothing to me,' sneered the greyhound. 'Absolutely nothing. I'd never buy one of his records anyway. His music is horse manure.'

'Don't say that about my dad,' I screamed, realising as soon as I opened my mouth that I had risen to the bait. 'My dad's a legend.'

The girls hooted with laughter. 'Your dad stinks,' snarled another of the girls. 'And everyone knows the kids of famous people stink too.'

'You don't know what you're talking about,' I spat back.

'Don't expect any special treatment, Rashface, just 'cos Daddy's famous,' warned the greyhound. She helped herself to a pair of Guess jeans from my suitcase, which now had its contents spewed all over the floor. 'Mmm, these would be good too.' She held them against herself. 'We don't like girls with fancy airs and graces. And Daddy can't rescue you here.' Her voice growled maliciously. 'Listen, I'm going to be kind to you. Payment for these.' She held up the shirt and jeans and stared spitefully at me, bringing her face to within inches of mine.

'I'm going to give you some advice. Round here you're no one. Might as well forget your dad, because he's long forgotten you. You can forget Mum too, because she don't care. Wouldn't have sent you here if she did. Round here you're just one of us. You're not special. And like everyone else here, you're on your own.'

13

There's got to be something up with the moon. Or the good planets have mysteriously drifted away from Bel Air. Or maybe Mercury's in retrograde again, or perhaps my chakras need realignment, because nothing seems to be right this morning. Thackeray spills birdseed all over the kitchen floor while attempting to feed Snowy; Stephen hangs up on me when I phone to tell him I'll be late in because I want to stop off at the hospital on my way to see Dad; the toaster burns the toast; and Adam's left a note saying he's gone to work early because he's got so much on. On top of this, the maid phones to say she can't come in to clean this week; the peanut butter jar is empty, which means I have nothing to put in Thackeray's sandwich for lunch; and I can't find my car keys anywhere. If the cosmos is playing a joke on me, it's not a very funny one.

Adam is always cynical about karma and astrology and all those good things that explain the whys and wherefores of our existence. But then he's never been to Esalen, the famous holistic retreat at Big Sur, where you find yourself and come back and say 'Ta-da! Here I am!' And you can get in touch with your inner being and everybody hugs everybody and there are these great workshops for healing. He says that's way too touchy-feely for him and just because he was born in California doesn't mean that he has to start hugging strangers. I respect that. But if it weren't for the stars, those glorious heavenly bodies that align our tiny, distant lives, how else could any of us explain why it is that on some days just everything seems to go wrong?

I find the car keys hidden in a box of toy cars where Thackeray put them, and I'm racing out of the front door to get him to school when my cell phone rings again.

'Stuart Wise. The *Daily Globe*. I was very sorry to hear of your loss.'

'I thought I asked you not to use this number . . . Wait a minute. My what?'

'I was sorry to hear that your dad passed away. I wondered if you had any comment.'

I reach for the door frame. Did he just say that Dad had passed away? Surely he didn't say that. The hospital would have called me. And the doctor had said Dad was through the woods.

I grope for words but none come. Could it possibly be true? I cut him off and dial Heather immediately. My call goes straight to voicemail. Shit. I call Ashley. I get the engaged signal. Fuck. Thackeray is now whining at me to get off the phone. 'Mummy, come on. What about school?' I call the hospital and get a recorded announcement. If it's a medical emergency, I should hang up and dial 911. What? That's no fucking use to me. Eventually a human voice comes on the line.

'I'm phoning about Gavin Sash,' I say, trying to stay calm. 'Is he . . . dead?' The word itself is so awful. I can't believe I've just used it in connection with Dad. But this is a receptionist, and what does she know anyway?

'I'll try to connect you,' says the voice. Beethoven's Fifth plays in my ear. I never liked Beethoven. Thackeray tells me I'm mean because I'm ignoring him.

'Cardiology,' says a bright female voice.

'I'm phoning about Gavin Sash—'

'I'm afraid we can't take any more calls. This is a hospital, not a press department,' says the voice firmly.

'But I'm his daughter. I need to know if he's alive . . .' I feel the thud of certainty in my chest. If they've had that many calls from the press, I already have my answer. 'I can't get through to any of my family. I was there last night and I thought he was doing OK. Please can you tell me.'

Thackeray is now hitting me on the leg with his fists. I hear the woman heave a sigh. Her voice becomes gentle. 'He died at seven forty-five this morning. There was a second heart attack, and complications.' She pauses to let me take in the news. 'Honey, I believe your mum is still here.'

'She's my stepmum.' The correction is almost automatic, I've said it so many times over the years.

'Would you like me to put you through to her?'

'No, it's OK. Thank you.'

'I'm so sorry.'

I look at my watch. It's 8.25 a.m. He died only forty minutes ago – while I was getting breakfast. Couldn't he have hung on till I got there? Didn't he realise that I was on my way? Why didn't he wait for me? Where was my goodbye? Didn't you want to say goodbye to me, Daddy?

I sit down on the front doorstep and hug Thackeray, desperate for the warmth of his little body, the softness of his skin. 'Can we go now?' he whines and wriggles to be free of my embrace. I always thought there would be tears at a moment such as this. But none come. I feel as if a jolt of electricity has passed through my body, leaving my brain disabled somehow.

A bird is digging a worm out of a flowerbed, hopping up and down as it drags the creature into the sun. A breeze rustles the camellia bushes that line our drive – they're all in flower and their pinky reds dazzle against the dark leaves. A bee is zipping through the clover that we don't seem to be able to eradicate from our lawn. How strange that everything in the garden is still the same. A police siren wails in the distance and a helicopter passes overhead. I somehow imagined that the world would look different without Dad in it.

The phone rings again. My hands are trembling as I answer it.

'Pearl, it's Ashley. I'm afraid it's bad news.'

'I know.'

There's silence down the line and I fight a feeling of nausea. 'How come no one called me?' I manage to ask eventually.

'I just found out. Heather was with him. I guess she was too shocked to call.'

'At least he wasn't on his own . . .'

I hear Ashley sniff. It's years since I've heard him cry. 'Dad wouldn't have liked to have been on his own,' I add.

'Yes, that's true.'

The thought passes through my mind that perhaps I should still go to the hospital. It seems strangely logical. I got up this morning with the intention of going there. But now there's no point. There is no warm, pulsing, vibrant being who might ask, 'Alreet, our kid?' There's no grumpy old man who will tell me to stop talking nonsense. No dour-faced northerner to tell me to get my head out of the stars and back in the real world. Will his body even be in the same room still? They've probably moved him already. Where would they have put him? I feel a wave of alarm.

'Where will they put Dad?' I ask.

'I think they'll keep him in the morgue until we make the funeral arrangements. We could probably go see him if you want. I think I might. Do you want to meet me there?'

'I don't know.' My bones suddenly feel terribly heavy. So heavy, I can't imagine ever getting up from this doorstep again. 'Ashley, is he really dead?' I ask. It's a strange question, but somehow I feel like I need to be sure. Part of me hopes that perhaps it's all been a big joke.

'Yes, Pearl. I'm afraid he is,' he says slowly. 'Look, I think you should see him for yourself. It gives a sense of closure to see the body. Meet me at the hospital in half an hour.'

The line goes dead. But what about Thackeray? I heave myself up from the doorstep I have become rooted to and call Adam. His assistant says he's in a meeting. Typical. I call Bella. She comes round straight away. Girlfriends, you've got to love them.

The warmth has already gone from Dad's body by the time I get there. Without thinking, I bend over to kiss him on the forehead, and discover the coolness on my lips. His skin is grey and silk-like. He looks like a cocoon that a butterfly has escaped from. The party has clearly moved on.

'Bye, Daddy,' I say pathetically. I want to hold his hand, but its temperature alarms me. Instead I hold Ashley's, who stands next to me, fighting back tears.

'I love you, Dad,' I add, staring at the papery, fragile face that doesn't even look like him any more. 'I'm going to miss you. I really am.'

A tear finally breaks loose and rolls down my cheek on to the bedsheet. Another swiftly follows, leaving a circle of damp. If he were alive, Dad would wipe my tears and tell me to be brave. He'd say, 'Cheer up, our kid.' But he's not.

Back at home, I hear Bella talking to me, but not what she is saying. I see her mouth moving and words coming out, but none of it makes sense. Something about shock, or perhaps it was sock.

I don't know how I got back here. Did Ashley drive

me? Adam's here now too, and Lizzie. I pick out odd words that they speak – grief, or was it belief, or thief? Someone mentions healing, or was that ceiling or kneeling? It's another new language. The language of bereavement.

I see Bella on the phone. She's cancelling my appointments, she's making tea. She's breaking the news to Stephen and booking a nanny to take care of Thackeray.

I sit in the kitchen, staring at breakfast crumbs left on the table, and I am unable to speak. I'm looking at the world through a kaleidoscope – the pieces are there, but they keep shifting around and nothing is the same any more.

'I need to go to bed,' I say eventually, and dive into the darkness, leaving them all. I'll just stay here for ever.

Death is the ultimate leveller. It makes no difference what we've achieved with our lives or what we've become. Death still snatches us. There's no buying time – no matter how many albums you've sold, no matter how rich you are, no matter how much Botox you use to wipe away the visible years. I'd kind of imagined Dad was immortal – perhaps because he was loved by so many, perhaps because his songs are so timeless, or perhaps because everyone in California thinks they'll live for ever. Dad wasn't ready to go. I know that.

I know it by the corner of the page turned down on the book he was reading by his bed, by the 'personal best' tally he kept on the video games he'd hooked up to the TV, by the appointment with a songwriter he'd had lined up for next week, written in his diary. Why couldn't death have spared him until he'd written a few more songs, or met his next child, or said goodbye to me?

For five days, I am one of those zombies from *Scooby Doo* – lifeless, dazed and just a little bit scary. I hibernate at the house, unable to face the outside. Then Heather calls and asks me to help her go through Dad's papers and I seize the lifeline. Anything to feel closer to him. So now I'm sitting at the desk in Dad's office. But where to even begin?

I open a drawer and find a notebook filled with Newcastle United football results going back to 1983. There's a file with newspaper cuttings about the club too. Dad always followed them. He went to watch them play whenever he was in England. There's a copy of *Model Railroader* magazine – Dad loved model railways. There's an invitation to the Rock and Roll Hall of Fame dated 1994, there are bills that should have been paid, letters from lawyers, contracts from record companies, tax demands going back to the eighties – all muddled up. Organisation was never a strong point of his. This is going to take a long time to sort through.

I try to remember the last time I had a really good time with Dad. Last summer there was a cricket match underneath the Hollywood sign. He was a player for the Beverly Hills Cricket Club, a group of homesick British ex-pats who used to get together to play in the park. Dad hit a half-century. Thackeray and I went along to watch and Dad was so pleased with himself, he started dancing on the pitch like he used to do at his concerts. Even without the drugs, and ten years sober, he still had it. We all laughed till our stomachs ached.

I lean back in his chair and take in the Grammys gathering dust on his bookshelves, the World Music Awards, the football trophies he won as a 'wee laddie' – he was as proud of them as he was of his music awards. And all the framed photos – Dad on stage, Dad on his knees at the Hollywood Walk of Fame, Dad collecting awards, Dad crooning into a microphone, Dad with all his kids, Dad with Thackeray – he had trouble coming to terms with being a grandpa, but he was proud of his first grandson.

Oh Daddy, what am I going to do without you?

Heather wanders into the room and sits down in a leather chair opposite. Her face is heavily made up, and she has an expression of resolution and purpose. She was a bit aloof when I arrived – I opened my arms wide in an attempt to offer a hug, but she gestured it aside, not in a mean way, but with enough body language to show she wasn't interested. Grief takes us all in different ways.

'It's a nightmare, isn't it?' she says, casting her eyes over Dad's desk.

'That's one way to put it.'

'Thanks for helping out. I took one look and thought, let's do this another day.'

'How's Casey doing?' I ask her. It's going to be harder on him. He'll grow up without ever knowing Dad.

'He's confused. He doesn't really understand,' she says matter-of-factly.

'And how about you?' I ask.

'I'm . . . I'm . . .' For a second I think the face make-up is going to crack, and she's going to cry. I'm ready to offer another hug. I've been the recipient of so many of them in the past few days, and Heather probably feels terribly alone. I don't know if she has lots of girlfriends. But she pulls herself together. 'I'm fine,' she says, sitting as tall as she can in the chair and patting her cheek, as if to wipe away emotion and restore a more composed face.

'You know, I'd be happy to be a birthing partner when Junior comes along,' I offer, nodding at her belly. It occurs to me that she probably hasn't got anyone else.

'Thanks, but I'm OK,' she says in a voice that has a distinct air of the brush-off about it.

'Or I could take care of Casey.'

'I'll be fine,' she says emphatically.

Poor Heather. She must be hurting badly.

'I'm arranging an open funeral at the All Saints

Church in Beverly Hills,' she announces in a by-the-way manner, as she picks up some of the papers on the desk. What?

'Shouldn't it be a private ceremony?' I ask. 'Just family and close friends?' Must I share Dad even when he's dead?

'He'd want to say goodbye to everyone, including his fans,' she says calmly.

'He's dead. He's not saying goodbye to anyone,' I say, more sharply than I intend.

'Even so, that's what I'm arranging,' she says. Her tone offers no room for compromise. I've never heard her so forthright before.

'But don't I get a say in any of the arrangements? Couldn't we plan the funeral together? There's a sweet hymn that I'd love to include ...' Heather regards me with steely eyes and says nothing. 'He was my father,' I find myself pleading.

'And I'm his wife,' she says forcefully, staring back at me so intently that I feel obliged to stand up by the window and turn my back to her. Heavens, what vivid shade of grief has she become? Why's she so cold suddenly? I gaze out of the window, clutching one of the files from Dad's desk.

'I've chosen the hymns and my father has agreed to say the eulogy,' she adds shrilly.

'Your father!' I whirl around, and in doing so knock the file in my hands against the lamp on Dad's desk. Papers scatter theatrically and the glass lampshade smashes on the hardwood floor, sending one piece of glass flying into my leg and causing blood to pour. 'But your dad didn't even know him. What about Ashley? Shouldn't his oldest son be the one to read a eulogy?'

I pull the glass out and wipe the blood with a tissue from my bag.

'You're just upset,' Heather says calmly, and attempts

to help me pick up the larger pieces of glass off the floor.

'But Heather, we're his family too. For God's sake, we're more his family than yours.' I didn't mean it to sound so callous, but it's true.

Heather puts her hands on her hips. 'I hate to disillusion you, Pearl. But he divorced your mother years ago. He divorced Lydia's mother years before that. He divorced Kimberly. But he married me.'

'Yes, but . . .'

'I was the wife that he loved.' Heather is certain in her delivery. She pauses to draw breath. 'Of course your dad loved all of his children.' Her voice softens briefly. 'But Casey and I were his immediate family.' I find myself reeling at the sly implication that Ashley, Lydia and I were less immediate, less loved, less of his family. I cannot think of a thing to say. 'And he married into my family when he married me, which means it's perfectly natural that I should want my father to read the eulogy.'

I sit back down in Dad's desk chair again and stare at the broken glass. Even in the short period since my father's death, my landscape has changed so dramatically. This house is no longer my home. I can see that now. Even when Dad brought in new wives, it was still my home. He made sure that it always was. Without him, new territorial lines are being drawn up that I could never have anticipated.

Silence hangs in the air. I begin to sort Dad's papers into piles – tax documents here, accountant's letters here, old magazines in the trash. In spite of the awkward atmosphere in the room, I find it comforting to do it. I like organising things. Heather sifts through a pile of fan mail. Buried at the bottom of a drawer, I find some old letters in their envelopes tied with a ribbon, also a file marked 'Pearl', another that says 'Ashley' and another that says 'Lydia'.

I open the file with my name on. Inside are old school reports, some school photos with me grinning cheesily, a couple of home-made birthday cards I drew for him in crayon, and the letter I wrote to him from boarding school, all those years ago.

Dear Mom and Dad,
I just heard the news. I saw it in the papers. Please
don't get divorced. I'm sorry about the necklace. I
really am. And I promise I won't ever be bad ever
again. Please, please, please don't get divorced.
Love Pearl
PS Our team won the hockey cup this term.

'He was a terrible hoarder, your dad,' Heather says, making a conversational peace offering to break the silence. 'Never seen so much stuff.'

'Sorry.' I force myself back to the present from memories of the past. I think it was the hockey match where I scored.

'He was a terrible hoarder,' she repeats.

'Yes, he was a great collector,' I concede.

'I thought we'd put some of his old things into a memorabilia auction,' she adds, as she drops the fan letters in the trash one at a time, barely even reading them. 'It might raise some funds.'

'What sort of things?'

'Well, there's trunks of his old stage clothes upstairs, there's his trophies, his motorbike, his model railway . . .'

This is too much to bear. 'You can't do that,' I blurt out. 'I mean, Thackeray would love that railway. I'd love to keep his trophies. Surely his children and grandchildren should have some of his keepsakes.'

'Yes, well, we'll have to see about that,' she concedes, getting out of the chair. 'But it's no good for any of us hanging on to this stuff. We've all got to move on,' she mutters over her shoulder and leaves the room. Perdy and Lullabelle follow after her, with their tails and heads hanging low. I know they're missing him too.

Move on? How can I move on? I don't want to move on. Moving on means forgetting him. It means abandoning him. It means letting him slip into memories. I'm not ready to do that. I pack the contents of Dad's desk into boxes. And load them into the car.

'I'm going to take some of the papers home with me and sort them there,' I call through to Heather in the kitchen. I can't bear the atmosphere suddenly.

'Okay,' she calls back through the silence.

Should I go in to say goodbye? I wonder. I stand in the kitchen door. Her back is to me. She's feeding the dogs.

'Bye then,' I say hesitantly.

'Bye.' She doesn't even turn around.

14

British public schools are about as homely as prisons, according to Evelyn Waugh, whose books I used to read in the school library. Those, and every other novel I could find. He was right, of course. School was lonely, cruel and a million miles from home.

My escape was reading. And the school library had the added advantage of few bullies. They rarely troubled themselves with books. So that's where I would hang out, disappearing into the pages of novels and only reappearing back in the real world when the bell forced me out for lessons, bed and mealtimes.

There was also a fresh newspaper every day in the library. I'd comb it daily for news of Dad. It was one of the advantages of having a famous parent. I could still catch up on news of the family, even when they didn't write. I could read reviews of his concerts and albums and discover where his latest tour had taken him.

Unfortunately, the newspapers brought other types of news too.

Gavin Sash Splits from Wife Number Two, read the headline. *Rock star Gavin Sash and model Bonnie Banks have separated after twelve years of marriage. 'It's heart-breaking, but necessary for us,' said model Banks, from Hawaii, where she is currently staying. Gavin Sash is still residing in the family's Beverly Hills home and has been sighted with a mystery blonde. He was unavailable to comment.*

I didn't cry. I just stood there. There was a picture of Mum and Dad alongside the article – it was a recent one of them on the red carpet outside the Grammys. A tear had been drawn in down the centre of the picture to symbolise their separation.

Why hadn't anyone called me?

15

'Heather wants to sell everything?' exclaims Lizzie far too loudly, twisting her right arm over her head in an attempt to achieve a pose that I know she's getting wrong.

'Sssh . . .' says a Twinkie in front of us, wearing Lycra leggings that everyone can see her underwear through.

'But that's outrageous!' Lizzie continues, now in a whisper. 'She's got to let you keep some things.'

'Well, I hoped she would. But she says we all need to move on.'

'Bitch!'

'She's probably just having a hard time without Dad.'

'You know what your problem is, Pearl?' Lizzie looks at me from under her armpit. 'You don't switch on the bitch enough. It's time you put in some full-fat, triple-XL, industrial-sized meanness. Stand up to Heather. Why are you so damn nice to everyone?'

'I'm not.'

Lizzie blows a childish raspberry and the Twinkie shushes her again. 'Anyway, your dad must have written a will.'

'I guess.'

'Well then.'

With arms outstretched and legs wide, we move slowly – flowing, as instructed – into a pose that is

122

supposed to make us look like dragons, although orang-
utans seems more accurate. It's 2.30 p.m. at Crunch on
Sunset and we're in a qi gong class, a discipline that
might be ancient in China, but is absolutely the newest
and latest thing to do in Los Angeles. There's meant to be
silence, but Lizzie was insistent on coming with me. She
said she wanted to keep me company during this tricky
time, which is kind, although I suspect she really wants to
talk to me about her first date with Cameron Valentin.
Although he took his time, he did ask her out.

'Anyway, I expect your dad will have left you oodles of
dough,' Lizzie carries on. 'There's always a silver lining.'
She flashes a wicked smile. 'Think of all the things you
can spend it on.'

'Lizzie!' I reprimand her, but I know she's just trying
to be funny.

Jade, our instructor, looks at us sternly. 'As we are all
part of the universe, we are attracted to heaven and to
earth, and so we must achieve a balance between the
two,' she explains, contorting her body into a treelike
position. Chinese music tinkles in the background. 'The
energy field that draws matter to itself must have a
centre; thus we have the term centring. It is the state of
not being unbalanced.'

I breathe in and try to not be unbalanced. It has been
ten days since Dad died and I need to feel centred,
whatever that is. In that time, I have broken off the wing
mirror of the car, left my iPhone in a shop somewhere and
completely forgotten a hair appointment, which I never,
ever do. I need to feel centred. I concentrate hard. It
sounds nice, it sounds soothing, it sounds organised, it
sounds better than dreaming up revenge on Heather.

'Anyway, do you want to hear about my date with
Cameron or not?' Lizzie whispers.

'Not,' I whisper back with a smirk. It won't make any
difference what I say anyway.

'Meditation is entering the state of being in the centre and not being drawn away,' Jade drones on. Her voice is soporific. I concentrate hard on my centre. Where could that be? My heart perhaps? I think of my heart. Pumping. I think of Dad's heart. Not. Lizzie's date would be a lighter topic.

'Tell me later,' I whisper, as we bend our knees and flow into a new position. I must try to focus on this balancing business. The last ten days have been so unbalanced, I'm surprised the world hasn't toppled off its axis. There was the call to my mother. 'I heard on the radio,' she said flatly when I broke the news to her. 'Silly old man. Too much sex. That was his problem.'

I hoped that there might have been some kind words about him from her, but even dead, there was to be no reprieve. Dad was still a source of bitterness.

'I won't come to the funeral, Pearl, if that's what you're phoning for. I won't put myself in a line-up with all his other wives.'

I explained that she didn't have to. I was just phoning to keep her posted. Although I wished she would come. Even though we were never close, I still find myself craving her company sometimes. I don't know why.

A cactus would be easier to snuggle up to than my mother. When I was in my teens, she told me matter-of-factly that some women were natural mothers and some were not. She was sorry that she just wasn't the earth mother kind. It wasn't that she was Cruella de Vil; she just wasn't interested. It was as if she imagined motherhood ended at the delivery. You popped the child out, and then got on with your life as if nothing had happened. As a kid, you can't miss what you don't know. But as an adult, I sometimes wonder what I might have become with a mother's support to fall back on.

Mum is part Spanish – the neurotic Catholic part. This gave her the olive skin, the big brown eyes, hair the

colour of bitter chocolate, and the churchgoing disposition. Divorce is against her principles. At least it was
when she and Dad split up. 'Catholics don't believe in
divorce,' she repeated like a war cry when Dad took up
with Kimberly. It was a different story when she wanted
to marry him and he happened to be married to Jodie.
But then as the saying goes in Hollywood, 'If you don't
like my principles, don't worry. I have many others.'

She and Dad met on an airport stopover. He was en
route to Australia for a tour. She was off to a model shoot
in the Barrier Reef. But the plane got diverted to Hawaii,
and they had twenty-two hours to kill. Twenty-two hours
to get to know each other. They wrote to each other for a
whole year after that. Eventually they met up again and
married. Romantic, isn't it? I've often thought someone
should turn it into a movie script.

The heroine would have to be a little less fiery than
Mum, though. Whereas Dad seemed to relish being with
us, Mum resented the contact. And she yelled her disapproval often. She saw us as competition. The discovery
that we entranced our father and held his attention was
unbearable for her.

Mum and I became marginally closer as I grew older
and shared an interest in fashion. She fundamentally
understood fashion and could turn a dress that looked
dull on a hanger into a page-stopping creation. People
underestimate this as an ability. But it's a skill. It's an
awareness of design, of texture, of creativity. The best
times I ever had with Mum were shopping.

'Darling, take this into the changing room,' she'd say,
picking out a garish purple skirt. 'I want you to try it on
with this.' And she'd hand me a bright orange T-shirt, or
a psychedelic swirly blouse.

The shop assistants would reel and gasp at the
audacity of suggesting such a mix of colours and styles.
But obligingly I'd go into the changing room and put

them on. I had faith that Mum knew what she was doing. She'd appear in the changing room with necklaces and bangles and shoes that she'd scoured the store to find. And when it was all put together it always did work, and the shop assistants would reel and gasp some more at the brilliance of her foresight.

Shopping was what we had in common. But when Mum moved to Hawaii after she divorced Dad, that fragile whisper of rapport vanished. Dad got custody of us. She didn't want it. I was older by then too, and I suppose I resented her jealousy of Dad's love. We speak to each other on the phone sometimes, but there's never any warmth.

'Of course Jodie's not going to the funeral,' she said. Mum was always jealous of Jodie – not that any of us ever saw her. Although her jealousy was popcorn to what she felt about Kimberly.

'But I guess Kimberly will be there? May she burn in hell.' Kimberly's name was never said without the adjunct 'May she burn in hell'. I've almost come to think of it as her last name now.

'I don't know.'

'Why don't you know? And what about Heather? Another piece of work.' 'Piece of work' is Heather's last name. 'I don't doubt you've been talking to her?'

'Yes, of course I've spoken to her.' Somehow Mum has the knack of making me feel disloyal for talking to any of Dad's other wives.

'Well?'

'Well what?'

'Well what's happening with her?' Mum, I suspected, was getting a perverse pleasure from all this.

'I think she's as shocked as everyone. It's going to be hard for her.'

'Too right.' Yes, she was definitely enjoying this. 'Well I won't be coming, and that's final.'

'That's fine. You don't have to. I was just phoning to—'

'But I'll pray for his soul at Mass.'

'Well, that's nice of you.'

'More than he deserves. That scum.' Dad's last name? Yes, you've guessed it. 'He probably needs all the prayers he can get now.'

'Yes, Mum.'

'After his life.'

'Yes, Mum.'

Did I say I sometimes craved her company? Let me correct that.

'Well, I better go. I've got a workout booked at the gym. I don't want to be late.'

'Well ... bye then,' I said. Somehow you'd have thought, after all these years, I'd have got used to abrupt departures from Mum. But they always take me by surprise. For several seconds I was reluctant to hang up. The line remained open as I wrestled with the desire for maternal comfort, craving her sympathy and under-standing, and then suddenly her voice reappeared.

'You know, you were always your Dad's favourite,' she said unexpectedly.

'Pardon me?'

'Manuel sends his love,' she cooed breezily and the line went dead. Manuel, by the way, is her boyfriend. He's a personal trainer from Mexico, who speaks no English.

The rest of the week proceeded to other horrors – a siege of reporters, a tidal wave of administration, 103 messages on the answerphone – all expressed in the dialect of grief, the language I now speak so fluently: *We were so sorry to hear ... such a terrible loss ... He was a great man ...*

There were more territorial lines from Heather too, as she made her thumbprint on the funeral arrangements, and sackfuls of mail from people I don't even know.

Only Thackeray was easy. I'd dreaded telling him about his grandpa's death, but he took in the news with the kind of nonchalance that only someone who doesn't understand death's permanence can do.

I close my eyes and my arms sway as I hold a giant imaginary ball between my hands. Qi gong builds vitality and wards off evils. It balances mind and body, Jade tells us. I picture myself tightrope-walking and wonder if mine will ever be balanced again.

At the end of the class, we glug water from plastic bottles and Jade stands in the doorway bidding us a serene farewell. Lizzie pulls on a Juicy hoodie over her Liquid Blue T-shirt, I wrap a Sweaty Betty sweatshirt over mine and then we make our way down the escalators to Buzz Coffee in the plaza for lattes.

'OK then, spill the beans,' I say to Lizzie as we settle ourselves at a table outside. It's a respite to think about something else other than Dad.

'Well, he picked me up in a Jaguar.'

'Great.' What car a man picks a girl up in on a date is very important.

'I wore my Marc Jacobs.'

'Cool.'

'And then he took me to Il Campanile.'

'Great.' Where he takes her is also very important.

I take a sip of my latte and cling to the warmth of the cup with both hands. A sparrow has hopped on to the empty table next to us where someone has left some crumbs and is pecking at them diligently.

'He's quite a trip,' Lizzie carries on. 'He thinks he's a G . . . G . . . G . . . What was it again?' Her bright green eyes look skyward as she struggles to remember. Lizzie's dating stories are never straightforward. There was the British aristo who turned out to be a transvestite, the lawyer who used coupons to pay for the meal, the speeddater who took her to a gun range. And that was only last week.

'That's it. He thinks he's a Gammon.'

'Like the ham?' I question.

'No, that's just bad actors. A Gammon is an immortal spiritual being.'

'Right.' I nod earnestly.

'He believes that we all have many past lives and they can have an impact on our dreams. But only Gammons understand how.'

'Why only Gammons?'

'I don't know,' she says vaguely. 'But he's a cool guy. He sent me flowers the next day and he's invited me for brunch at his church up in Hollywood on Sunday.'

'That's great, Lizzie.' Not sure about the church thing. But maybe she's actually found someone suitable.

'I know. You wanna know what else?'

'What?'

'I didn't sleep with him either.' She pulls back her shoulders and thrusts out her well-proportioned chest, like a male bird out to impress a mate, and takes a sip of coffee. 'By the way, have you decided if you're going to let Thackeray see his father?'

'I'm thinking about it. He called me again.'

'Really?'

'He phoned to say he was sorry about Dad. But he also said something else . . .' I pause. Lizzie isn't the most discreet of friends, but if I told Bella, she'd be angry with me for talking to him. Bella has never liked Brett. 'I can trust you not to pass this on to anyone, can't I?'

'For sure.'

'Really?'

'You know you can rely on me.'

'Yeah, that's what I was worried about.' We both laugh. 'Well, he said he never stopped loving me.'

Lizzie puts her latte down on the table. 'For real?'

'For real. And I know I shouldn't even give it a second thought, but somehow—'

'Does he want to get back together?' Lizzie interrupts.

'I don't know.' A waitress shoos the sparrow away from the table, and wipes the crumbs on to the floor, where the bird continues his meal.

'Well, he wouldn't say that if he didn't,' Lizzie says observantly. 'Maybe you should give him another chance, Pearl. Perhaps he's changed.'

'That's what he said.'

'What, that he's changed? You know, you were always so good together.'

'But it's too late now for all that. I'm a married woman, remember?'

'Yeah, but Adam's such a dweeb.'

'Lizzie! I can't believe you said that,' I exclaim, reeling at her blatancy. I know Lizzie has never been one for subtleties, but to call him a dweeb . . .

'Well it's true. You were much more fun when you were with Brett.'

'Was I?'

'Yeah. Course you were. Remember when you and Brett jumped into the pool at the Sunset Tower?' She puts her hand over her mouth to contain a giggle.

The hotel was called the St James Club then. It was a dull party, spread out on the terrace beneath the art deco tower, right by the pool with its concrete palm trees overlooking the city below. Lizzie was there with Alex Hamilton. Alex was the son of Rex Hamilton, the famous actor. Brett and I hadn't been dating for long, and he made us laugh all evening. He'd been at an audition that day, and in the loudest voice possible, because he was several martinis down, he was telling us how he'd screwed up.

'You're full of shit,' I teased. 'Bet you get the part anyway.'

'Bet you I don't.'

'How much you want to bet?' I went on, because standing by the balcony was Jason Lime, the director of the film, who I happened to know, and Brett hadn't seen him there. Jason was smiling away like the Cheshire Cat, listening to Brett.

'Bottle of champagne,' Brett suggested.

'Nah. Too easy,' I said. 'If you get the part, you have to jump into the pool with all your clothes on.'

'You're on,' he said. 'Shame, because I won't find out till Monday.'

'Shame,' I said, 'because isn't that Jason Lime over there?'

And I walked up to Jason and, bold as brass, asked him if Brett had got the part. Straight out he said, 'Yes.' And before I even had a chance to say thank you and turn around, Brett grabbed my hand and pulled me into the pool with him. Then Lizzie pulled Alex in with her, just because she can't resist a scene, and the four of us wallowed there ordering drinks and watching our evening clothes billow up around us in the water, until the manager asked us to get out.

'You were totally way more fun with Brett,' Lizzie carries on.

I hadn't really thought about it before.

'And what about Wisconsin?'

I stifle a snigger. Wisconsin was a disaster. 'Let's have a weekend away, on the first plane we can get ourselves on out of LAX,' Brett suggested late one night. We were at a nightclub. Lizzie was dating Nat Brinkman that week, the heir to the Waldom Foods fortune.

'Sure.' Nat leapt at the idea, getting his chauffeur to bring the car straight away. 'It's got to be the first plane out, wherever it's going, right?'

'Right,' we all agreed.

In our minds, we all had visions of New York or Vegas

or Mexico City. Or perhaps even London. Certainly somewhere glamourous where we could keep on partying. As it happened, the first plane out of LAX that we could get tickets for was to Milwaukee, Wisconsin. We ended up on the edge of Lake Michigan in the middle of winter, wearing nothing but sleeveless dresses and T-shirts. There wasn't even a bar open.

'Tell me the last time you did anything impulsive and fun with Adam,' says Lizzie.

'The charity benefit evening,' I say.

'Oh, come on,' says Lizzie.

I'll admit she has a point. I guess I was more spontaneous then. Bolder possibly, too. I got more fearful of everything after Brett left. But heavens, look at the time. I've got to go or Thackeray will be the last kid left at the school. I say goodbye to Lizzie.

'Later,' she chimes.

I drive along Santa Monica Boulevard, because the traffic is sure to be less than on Sunset, and notice the bright shop windows decorated with pink and red Valentines. The Empty Vase florist has an enormous heart outside the shop made entirely from roses. Goodness, how did it get to be that time of year again?

I pass Trattoria Amici, where I had a Valentine's dinner with Adam last year. It was the same restaurant as the year before, and the year before that. The card, the roses and the chocolates are always the same too – always the White Chocolate Gift Box from Godiva, and always a floral card in which he writes 'For the girl I will always love'. I've never had the heart to tell him I don't actually like white chocolate. And invariably we race through dinner, as Adam fights valiantly to do the right thing by me and still meet a work deadline. He knows Valentine's Day is important to me, so we eat early and then he races back to his office. There's always some deadline or other.

Adam's a dweeb, Lizzie said. A dweeb! Well, yes, I suppose he can be a bit nerdy. He's predictable, certainly. And sure, there haven't been too many impulsive, let's-party-till-we-drop moments. But he's kind, and he loves me. He's a good man. What does Lizzie know anyway? Functional relationships are scarcely her speciality.

Adam was a friend of my brother Ashley at school. I can't even remember the first time we met – he was always just part of the scene. But how he and Ashley met is almost as much a part of our family history as Dad's fighting. Adam was a new kid and about to be beaten up by a gang of no-brain football jocks in the school's bathroom. Being of slight build, he really didn't stand too much of a chance. But then Ashley came into the bathroom. He actually wanted to use it. But he couldn't get through because there were so many jocks in the way. Ashley always jokes that he really wasn't interested in rescuing Adam. He just needed to pee. But he did anyway, and they've been friends ever since.

Any time I can remember being at home, Adam was round. He'd be up in Ashley's room and they'd both be playing air guitar to Metallica or Aerosmith. That progressed to Nirvana and the Smashing Pumpkins as time went on, and then to Korn and Limp Bizkit. Their musical taste never improved, but their friendship did. Ashley started at law school and Adam went to UCLA to study screenwriting. But they still stayed friends. Adam was part of the family by then. And I used to enjoy hearing about screenwriting school. Sometimes Adam would take me to the movies with him. They weren't dates. It was just two people who enjoyed the movies. We'd analyse the script, tear apart the plot lines, scrutinise the acting, study the direction. It was fun.

We even devised our own script together. Well, Adam wrote the script. I just gave him a few ideas. This was ages ago – before I even started dating Brett. We'd been to see *Vanity Fair*; you know, the Mira Nair version with Reece Witherspoon. It's all about a girl trying to marry into money. I said to Adam: 'Why not turn it around and have a guy trying to find himself the money in order to woo a woman who's rich.'

'Been done before,' he told me. '*Merchant of Venice*.'

'Why not modernise it then?' I said. 'Make it a romantic comedy. What about a penniless bus driver who falls in love with an heiress and has to come up with some cash in order to romance her?'

'Why would an heiress use a bus?' he demanded.

'Her car broke down.'

'And where's he going to find the money?'

'He robs a bank.'

'Wouldn't he get caught?'

'Yes, but it turns out the guy who owns the bank is the girl's father and he realises how much he must love her, so he doesn't press charges.'

'Not sure it's believable enough.'

'Doesn't matter if it's believable or not as long as it's got a happy ending. It's *got* to have a happy ending.'

'Why?'

'Because I like happy endings.'

'I'll think about it,' Adam said. Next thing I know, there's a bidding war between the studios and he's sold the script for over four million.

The point is, I always thought of Adam as a friend. I know it's kind of *When Harry Met Sally*, the movie where Meg Ryan fakes an orgasm in a restaurant, and the big question is can a man be friends with a woman without sex getting in the way. Well, being a girl, I always took the Meg Ryan view that yes, of course you can be friends with a guy without it having to be more. Just because you enjoy going to the movies together doesn't mean you want to date each other.

But then Bella pointed out that maybe I meant just a wee bit more to Adam than that.

'He's in love with you,' she said one day up at Stephen's. We always used to have lunch together in the garden.

'Are you crazy, girl?' I responded. These Brits are a bit nutty sometimes. It's because they drink warm beer and never see the sun. 'Of course he's not.'

'He is,' she insisted, nodding her head.

'He isn't,' I said, shaking mine.

'He is.' She nodded her head some more.

'He isn't.' And on we went until we both got neckache.

Anyway, I ignored her. Brits don't understand how romance works in America. Guys don't hang around like lovesick puppies here. They ask you out if they're interested. And anyway, I was in love with Brett.

But when Brett left, Bella had another go. Adam's still keen on you, she told me. He just hasn't had the nerve to ever say it to your face. Too afraid to spoil your friendship, she said. And hadn't I noticed that Adam had been paying money into my bank account? What? No, of course not. Who can be bothered to read their bank statements? It was to make sure I was OK, she said. Adam had told her himself. What? I mean, what kind of guy does that?

A devoted guy, she told me. A guy who was different to the heartbreakers I always picked. 'You've got a broken picker,' Bella said. 'You always pick the bad guy.' I stopped to think about that. Could she be right? Maybe there was a pattern. And maybe there really was a relationship to be had with Adam where I could feel secure and be happy. It wasn't a case of fireworks going off and lightning bolts striking. None of that heart-stopping stuff like when Brett and I got it together. But look where that got me.

Realisation dawned slowly and then pervaded all my horizons. We were friends. We'd known each other for ever. He was reliable, kind. He wouldn't rush off with another woman. And most importantly, he really cared about me and Thackeray. It would be a rebound relationship after Brett. I was aware of that. But it was a safe one. He wouldn't hurt me, like Brett had, and I had Thackeray to think of. He needed a father.

Needless to say, it was a strange conversation with Adam, after I had my epiphany. I only had Bella's insistence that Adam cared for me to go on. And I'd never, ever chased a man before in my life.

'Um, Adam, this is k-k-k-kinda hard.' I stuttered more than Adam that day. And I'd had to hang around a movie set for hours to get to see him.

'G-g-go ahead,' he stammered back. The pair of us sounded like broken records. (An accomplishment in the digital age.)

One of the guys from the catering truck brought over a couple of cups of coffee. We had the rest area to ourselves. Everyone else was still shooting.

'H-h-how do you think a person should tell a very good friend that they like them?' I tried.

'L-l-like them?' He looked up at me, and I could see my reflection in his glasses. I looked uncomfortable.

'Yeah. You know, like them. Like really like them.'

'I don't kn-kn-know. It's d-d-d . . .'

'Difficult?' I suggested. There's always the urge to finish Adam's sentences for him.

'Dangerous,' he corrected me. 'Because it could hurt their f-f-f . . .'

'Feelings?'

'Friendship.'

'Really? You think?'

Adam stared at the catering table we were sitting at. There was a long pause. This was harder than I'd thought it might be.

'Have you g-g-got a s-s-s-s . . .'

'A secret?' I proffered.

'No, a cigarette.' He looked momentarily annoyed. I must stop finishing his sentences.

'Why don't you ask the catering guy?'

Adam returned a few minutes later, inhaling deeply. He used to smoke back then.

'Look, Bella told me something,' I said.

'Yeah?'

'Yeah.'

'Wh-wh-what did sh-sh-sh . . .'

Oh for God's sake, we could still be here at Christmas.

'She told me you were keen on me, and that's fine, because I think I'm keen on you too, and I think we could make a great couple together.' The words suddenly came crashing out, fast and furious, and I couldn't stop. 'And this is probably a bit of a shock for you after all this time, but we could make it work because we're friends, right? And we've always been friends, and that can make the best relationships, right? I mean, there's no reason why friends can't become more? Right?'

Adam said nothing. I took a gulp of air. He looked like a deer caught in the path of a careening, brakeless juggernaut. He didn't even move. He just blinked. The cigarette between his fingers burned unnoticed and the ash eventually fell on to the table. Oh God, I thought. Bella's got it wrong. The embarrassment will be so great, I might just have to shoot myself.

But eventually words came to his open mouth. 'You really have feelings for me too?' he asked. Strangely, the stutter had completely gone.

Too. He'd said 'too'. Hadn't he said 'too'? That implied the two of us, right? Could it be Bella *was* right?

'Yeah,' I said.

'Really?'

'Yeah.'

'I've always loved you,' he said suddenly, and I knew

it was true. His eyes were bright with excitement, his face lit up like a toothpaste ad.

'Why didn't you ever say?'

He looked into his coffee cup. 'Afraid, I guess.' Then he let out a nervous laugh. 'Not to mention, you were kind of hung up on Brett.'

'Well, I got that wrong, didn't I?'

We both laughed nervously and I wondered what I should say next. Awkwardness filled the space between us.

'Why did you put all that money in my account?' I asked.

'It was your share.'

'Don't be silly.'

'The movie was your idea. I just fleshed it out. You deserved a share of what they paid.'

'No, I didn't.'

'Yes, you did.'

'Uh-huh.' I shook my head.

'Are you going to be the kind of girlfriend who argues about everything?'

'You bet I am,' I said, and we both laughed stupidly, relieved that it was out in the open. He'd said the girlfriend word and neither of us had imploded.

Then he asked: 'Can I kiss you?'

The request shocked me. Not that it was inappropriate. It was the formality of asking. I thought a kiss would come more naturally.

'That's what boyfriends usually do,' I said. Now *I'd* said the boyfriend word.

Adam swung his legs over the bench he'd been sitting on and walked round the table to meet me. It was a tentative kiss at first. We were both so nervous. But it was also gentle and affectionate – no pyrotechnics in the sky, but we'd warm up to that. I felt treasured in his arms.

*

I'm falling asleep on the sofa when Adam walks in from work. It's gone ten p.m. I feel a twinge of irritation.

'I'm sorry I'm late, honey,' he says, kissing me on the cheek, and throwing himself on the sofa next to me. It's what he always says, because he always is.

'Did you eat?'

'No, I'm starving.'

'There's food laid out in the kitchen.' I always prepare food for two in the evenings and hope that he'll make it home to eat with me. But I've usually given into hunger long before he makes it back. He fetches a shrimp salad and two glasses of chilled white wine.

'Did you get the script done?' I ask.

Adam settles himself on the sofa next to me with a tray on his knees. He places his glass of wine on a coaster on the table next to him. He arranges the knife and fork on the tray exactly just so. Then he readjusts the coaster so that it is exactly perpendicular to the table's edge, and then he readjusts the knife and fork.

'Yes, finally.' He heaves a long sigh.

'Now you can relax. Perhaps we could have a real weekend together. Take two days, like most people.'

'Well, not quite, because now they want me to do the rewrites on *The Paperweight*.'

'*The Paperweight*.' This is a prestigious project, and to be asked to do the rewrites is a measure of how much Adam is valued. I feel a swell of pride for my husband, and angry with myself for being so churlish. Of course he had to work late all this week. It's not easy being a screenwriter. There's always competition snapping at your heels.

'When do you start?'

'Right away, I'm afraid.'

It's always right away. I feel the perimeter of disappointment.

'Lydia's coming back for the funeral,' I tell him,

moving the conversation along and sidestepping the issue I really want to talk to him about.

'Is she? That will add a few fireworks to the occasion.' He bites into a shrimp.

Adam and I often chat later than we should on the sofa together in the evenings. It's a good time of day and I look forward to it. Often he asks my advice on storylines, and we hammer out dialogue together. But tonight I've decided to take the bull by the horns. Adam's not going to like what I have to say, but we're all grown-ups here. I take a deep breath.

'Honey, I've been thinking about Thackeray.'

'He didn't hit another kid in school today, did he?'

'No, nothing like that. It's just I . . .' I hesitate, searching for the right words. 'It's just I'd like him to have the chance to meet Brett.'

Adam puts down his fork, which sends a clatter into the ensuing silence. He stares at me, mouth pursed. OK, we're not all grown-ups here.

'Look, it's just that my dad was so important to me. He was so much of who I am, and I'm not sure I ever realised or appreciated it properly before. I want Thackeray to know who his real father is.'

I pause, because Adam is looking at me like I've just confessed to a chainsaw massacre. 'Look, I've thought about it a lot,' I carry on, trying to keep my voice steady. 'When your parents are gone, they're gone. Thackeray has a right to know where his genes come from. Our parents untangle the cobwebs of who we are.'

Suddenly I feel tears well up again. I didn't intend there to be. But there have been so many this week, I could put myself forward for the *Guinness Book of Records*.

Adam's face softens a little. He searches my expression. He seems bewildered, which annoys me. Is it so extraordinary to value one's family? I'm not asking anything unreasonable. His cell phone rings in his jacket pocket and I watch him flinch. There's always another job, another call, another deadline.

'Please leave it, this is important,' I ask him.

He puts his plate on the floor and answers it anyway. 'Yup. Sh-sh-sh-sure. What now? . . . For when? They've got to be k-k-k-kidding . . . OK . . . Yeah, I'll be there.' He hangs up and turns to me, his face resolute. 'I've got to go back to the office. They want a new scene written for *The Paperweight* by the morning. The whole crew is on standby for it.'

'Can't we even talk to each other?' I plead. 'I don't know if you noticed, but my dad died and I haven't seen you all week.'

'I'm sorry.' His voice is softer now and his hand reaches across to my shoulder. He pulls me towards him and cradles me in his arms. 'I'm s-s-s-sorry, I know this is a difficult time for you, but I can't let them down. This is a big break for me.'

Success is a lure. The desire for it can envelop a person. It entices people with the promise of adulation, acknowledgement, influence, power. I've seen it all before.

16

After months of pleading, Dad finally conceded that I could come home from boarding school. I returned less sure of myself. Kimberly was fully established in our house. I was fifteen years old, mercilessly independent, but without a direction to take it in. I was also a remodelled version of the girl who had been sent away three years before – the arrogance had been replaced by insecurity, the conceit by confusion and a desperation to please. Part of me was always convinced that I was somehow responsible for my parents' divorce.

Lizzie threw a party for me at her house to celebrate my return.

'Wanna try some?' offered a biker with a red bandanna tied over his hair. He arranged a line of coke on a piece of paper on a coffee table, and offered me a rolled-up dollar bill to snort it with. Lizzie's parents were away, and she'd filled the place with hipsters, surfer dudes, biker guys, anyone she could find. Guns N' Roses was playing on the sound system. Lizzie was having her heavy rock period.

'Sure,' I said, snorting down the coke and knocking back a large slug of tequila from a bottle. I was game for anything.

'Gavin Sash's daughter, right?' asked the guy.

'Yeah.'

'Cool.' I offered him a slug from the bottle, which he

accepted. 'I like his records. Gavin Sash is a cool guy.'

I felt proud. I always did whenever anyone praised Dad. It was a kind of validation for me.

'He is a cool guy,' I agreed. 'He's got another album coming out next year.'

'Cool,' said the guy again. 'I'm Jeff, by the way.'

'Pearl.' We both took another slug.

'Must be kinda interesting to be the daughter of Gavin Sash? What's it like?'

People always asked me that. Such a dumb question. 'Umm . . . pretty normal.'

'Yeah?'

'Yeah.'

Jeff leant back into the sofa and smiled at me. He looked mellow. There was stubble on his chin and crow's feet around his eyes. The tattoos on his bare arms were mostly of flowers, and I liked that. Dad had flower tattoos on his arms too.

'You wanna go upstairs?' he asked. I knew the offer was to make out, and I was curious. A boarding school for girls gave little exposure to the opposite sex.

'Sure.'

Ten minutes later, I heard his voice downstairs boasting to his friends, 'You'll never guess who I just fucked. I fucked Gavin Sash's daughter.'

17

I have a good tip for de-stressing. You have to rub your hands together to generate a little heat with your palms, then you gently cup your hands over your eyes and concentrate on the warmth of your palms. Breathe deeply, in, out, in, out. When you take your hands away, you should feel a lot calmer. It usually works. The trouble with doing it at funerals is people think you're crying.

'Are you all right, honey?' Adam asks, sitting next to me.

'I'm just taking measures to stop myself from unleashing pain and suffering on Heather,' I say, in a sufficiently loud voice to ensure she will have heard in the front row.

It's Dad's funeral, a day I knew wasn't going to be a waltz in the park, but which is now shaping up to have all the ingredients of a bad reality show. Rather like those shows that follow controlling, domineering brides, they could do one on funerals and check out the attention-seeking widows.

I have just been ushered to row three in the church. That's right. The third row! The front row of the church, as I understand it, is where the family of the bereaved usually sit. It is, indeed, where the minister had told us we should sit, when I called him after Heather hadn't returned any of my calls asking about the funeral service. But Heather has other ideas. She is in the front row, with Casey and Joely. Next to Joely is Joely's father – Heather's ex. Can you believe that? She's actually bringing her ex to Dad's funeral. Next to him are Heather's parents. And then behind them, filling up another entire row, are Heather's other relations. In the front rows on the other side of the church, Heather has seated Dad's old band and a couple of his managers. Lydia, Ashley and I were told by security guards where we could sit. I almost felt we were lucky to get those, because the place is packed.

Breathe deep, I told Ashley and Lydia. Dad knows we love him, no matter where we sit. But it isn't easy. Earlier in the morning, I also learned what Heather has had engraved on the headstone for Dad's grave. 'In Loving Memory of Gavin Sash. Rock Legend. Adored husband of Heather and loving father to Joely and Casey.' And then, in smaller letters: 'Also Lydia, Ashley and Pearl.'

Dad would have hated that. Not the fact that Lydia, Ashley and I have been sidelined – shrunk in importance to a smaller font size, displaced in a graphical line-up by a daughter who wasn't even his – though that stung bitterly when Heather showed me the template. It was calling him a rock legend. Dad was never fond of the title, or of self-importance. I even remember him joking about what he wanted for an epitaph. 'Gavin Sash has died. Good career move', he dreamed up one Christmas. There were others he liked too: 'At Last I Get Top Billing', or 'Stiff At Last'. Or Frank Sinatra's, which reads 'The Best is Yet To Come'. Did Heather ever really understand my dad? I wonder. I tried to argue with her over the gravestone, but she was vehement.

The funeral gets under way with 'Dear Lord and Father of Mankind'. It was one of Dad's favourites. At least Heather got that right. 'Forgive our foolish ways,' we sing, and I try to forgive Heather.

My cell phone vibrates in my bag. I look briefly at the number. It's Stephen. Doesn't he ever let up? I ignore it and sing louder. It vibrates again. I ignore it. It vibrates again. For God's sake.

'What is it?' I whisper.

'I've lost my spectacles.'

'Ask Maria to look for them.'

'She's out.'

'Then look for them yourself.'

'I have.'

'Have you looked in the drawer of your desk?'

'No.'

'Then look there.'

Silence.

'Yes, got 'em. And on your way over, could you pick up some—'

'Stephen, I'm at my dad's funeral,' I interrupt him. 'I'm not coming in today,' I say with finality and hit the call-end button.

Dear God, please save me from murdering Stephen. I take a deep breath and smooth out the skirt of my Max Azria suit. Adam sings quietly on my left. I hook my hand under his arm and he squeezes it close to his body – a little gesture that implies so much. This isn't an especially happy day for him either. I got my period this morning, so no babies this month. We hugged over breakfast and he said we just had to be positive and keep on trying, but I knew he was disappointed.

On my other side, Ashley is singing louder than all of us. I catch him wiping a tear away with the back of his hand, and long to give him a hug. Beyond him is Lydia. No tears from her. That defiant chin hasn't changed at all. But she's grown more beautiful since I last saw her. She looks a little less angry perhaps. Her wide, startled eyes show less hurt, her expression has become less indignant. She looks across at me, and I feel a warmth towards her that I haven't felt in years – the solidarity of a shared past, the bond of a common grief. Will her grief be greater than mine for missing out on all those years with Dad? I expect it might be.

'Where's Thackeray?' she mouths.

'With a babysitter,' I whisper back. 'She'll bring him to the house after the service.'

'I'm dying to meet him.' She smiles. Lydia fell out with Dad when he married Heather. There was a terrible scene and some name-calling and expletives I should think I shall go to hell for even recalling in a church. Somehow Lydia took Dad's serial marriages as a personal slight. Where Ashley and I accepted that this was the way he was, Lydia felt she needed to challenge it. Lydia is the sort who challenges everything – probably because she's an Aries. She struggled and seethed when my mum replaced hers as a child, and then when a third and finally a fourth wife came along, it was all she could do to contain the rage. The hurt simmered constantly beneath a fragile teenage veneer, exploding violently from time to time. Somehow she took Dad's infidelity as a disloyalty and betrayal to her. I think we all suffered from having to share him in one way or another, but Lydia seemed to suffer the most.

Unfortunately Heather was around when Lydia launched into her usual tirade with Dad over the news of their engagement, and the name-calling spiralled out of control. It didn't help that Heather refused to have Lydia at her wedding and promised to divorce Dad if he had Lydia's name tattooed on his arm when he announced he wanted all his kids' names inked on his biceps. Deep down, Lydia is probably the most like Dad of all of us – hot-headed and proud.

She left for New York the night of the big row. I thought she'd get over it. Every family has its scraps. But one Thanksgiving gathering without her rolled into another and another, and now it's been more than five years. Ashley sees her sometimes when he goes to New York, and sometimes – rarely – I speak to her on the phone. But she's always refused to come back to LA. She's got her own jewellery design business now and I'd like to hope she's not so angry with Dad any more. She's here anyway.

I look around the church. There are plenty of faces I recognise, dragging up memories. There are roadies from old tours, guitarists, drummers, managers, producers. It's odd to see so many flamboyant characters looking so sombre. Then there are the cousins from Newcastle, Dad's sister from London, and Betty, our old nanny. Oh, sweet Betty. I haven't seen her for ages. 'Thank you for coming,' I mouth at her and blow her a kiss as I catch her eye across the pews.

Strangely, I don't feel that sad today. An overload of emotions perhaps, the joy at seeing so many old faces, the irritation with Heather. They all seem to overcome the sadness. Whatever it is, I'm glad.

The minister leads us all through prayers, there are more hymns, and a truly awful eulogy from Heather's father, during which I have to fight back giggles when he talks about sobering thoughts. Was that a deliberate joke? I wonder. I'll swear I hear guffaws from the back. Then finally we are allowed to escape into the bright California sunshine outside, face the glare of the paparazzi, and breathe in fresh air instead of the fusty, musty smell of incense.

After the service, Dad is buried at the Westwood Memorial Park, where he'll have Marilyn Monroe and Natalie Wood for company. A blonde and a brunette. He'd probably be happy with that. Only close family go to the burial. And then we all head back to Dad's house, the house where I grew up, where Heather has caterers running amok.

Dad would have truly loved it. Isn't that what they always say about funerals? There's almost a festive atmosphere here, with waiters serving wine and little pastry hors d'oeuvres on the patio. There must be nearly two hundred people here. I greet cousins, old friends, business acquaintances, and I bump into Betty among the crowd. She hugs me tight, and I notice how old she is looking. She must be pushing sixty-five now. Her hair is completely white.

'You're going to miss him.' She sniffs, I think for my benefit. 'You always loved him more than he deserved, my sweet little Pearl.' We find a seat together. 'How is your mother?'

'She's doing fine.'

'She wouldn't come to keep you company?' Betty asks, only too well aware of the dynamics of our family.

'No. I think it would be too difficult for her,' I say, and Betty sighs. I don't think she ever really approved of either of my parents.

'Are you taking care of yourself?' she asks. I nod. 'It takes a long time to get over loss. You must be kind to yourself.'

I promise her I will.

'And is that your husband playing with Thackeray?' She points towards the bottom of the garden, where Thackeray is now kicking a football with someone whose back is turned to me.

'No, I don't know who that is. But Adam's here somewhere.' I wave a hand in the direction of the crowd.

'Thank you for the pictures you sent me of Thackeray, by the way. What a handsome boy he is.'

'Yes, he's going to break hearts,' I say with pride, watching Thackeray race for the ball. His curly dark hair waves wildly as he runs. Then suddenly my heart lurches down to my feet. There's a mop of curly dark hair that's waving wildly on the guy he's playing football with too.

He turns, and I catch sight of Brett's face. What's he doing here?

'What do you think you're doing?' I call, unable to contain my rage, as I march towards them at the bottom of the garden.

Brett and Thackeray look up with the same expression of bewilderment. God, they're so alike, it almost takes my breath away. I have never seen the two of them side by side before, and Thackeray is almost an exact replica of his father.

'We were playing soccer, Mummy,' Thackeray explains innocently. 'What's wrong with that?'

I don't want a big scene in front of him, so I am forced to stop in my tracks and tell him that there's nothing wrong with that.

'This guy's cool. He can do tricks,' Thackeray tells me. 'Like this.'

Fortunately Thackeray's attempt at a soccer trick sends the ball flying into the bushes and he is forced to disappear into them to find it. 'You might have asked me if it was OK,' I hiss at Brett.

'I did,' he says flatly.

'And I didn't give you my answer. What are you even doing here?' I grit my teeth hard in an effort to contain my temper. If I was a man, I'd be tempted to hit him. Instead, I tell myself to breathe deep.

'Hold on there. Don't get so angry. I didn't come here to meet Thackeray,' he says calmly.

'What did you come for then?'

'I came because it was your dad's funeral. He *was* my father-in-law, remember?' He stares at the bush, where Thackeray's butt is sticking out. 'Maybe I shouldn't have. But I loved him. You know I did.'

I'm forced to acknowledge that he's speaking the truth, because the pair of them did get on. They say that girls marry men who remind them of their fathers, and there *was* common ground. They both shared a love of music, creativity, humour, silliness, and of course, the soccer field. They bonded on that the minute they met.

'Look, I wasn't even going to come back here after the church. I just wanted to pay my respects, but Heather saw me in the crowd and told me I should. I didn't even know Thackeray was going to be here,' he continues. 'I'm sorry if I've overstepped the mark.'

Thackeray re-emerges from the bushes with leaves in his hair and I feel the heat slowly disappear from my cheeks. 'Come on,' he calls to Brett, kicking the ball straight at him.

'Am I allowed to play?' Brett asks as he catches the ball. 'I'll leave if you want. Perhaps I should.' He stares at me with his big movie-star eyes, the kind of look that used to make me melt.

'Oh please, Mummy,' Thackeray whines.

I hesitate. But there's no point in turning this into a big drama.

'Fine,' I say, and head back to the house, where Lydia informs me that Adam has just stormed off. Shit. It already is a big drama.

'Problems?' she asks.

'Kinda. Got all day and I'll tell you about them,' I say, as a joke.

But she looks at her watch earnestly – a beautifully designed modern one made from twisted metals. 'Sure, I've got all day,' she announces. 'Flight's not until nine p.m. I'm catching the red-eye. Shall I fetch us some wine?'

We curl up on the swing seat, like we used to do when we were kids, from where I can keep an eye on Thackeray and his new soccer coach. Lydia knows about my marriage to Brett and subsequent divorce, but we've spoken so rarely over the years, she missed out on the details. I've forgotten what a good listener she is.

'Shame! He's cute. And good with kids too,' she announces when I've finished, casting her cobalt-blue eyes over Brett, and now understanding – as best as anyone can – why Adam has stormed off.

'He was a great guy when I met him. But he changed when he got famous. Dr Jekyll became Mr Hyde . . . or is it the other way round? I can't remember.'

Lydia pulls out a packet of Marlboro Lights from her bag and offers me a cigarette. I take one, light it, but inhale only once before stubbing it out again. It was such a battle to quit. I don't want to start again.

'Sounds like you really loved him too.'

'I got over it,' I say, taking a sip of wine and washing away the taste of nicotine.

'You don't tell it like you are.'

'Believe me. I'm over it.'

A waiter offers us a platter of satay chicken, which we both refuse.

'I don't think fame did much for Dad either,' Lydia laments, exhaling a trail of smoke.

'But he didn't turn into a monster like Brett. He didn't leave his wife when she was pregnant.' For some reason, I've always felt the need to defend Dad.

'No, he left her when their kid was six instead,' she says flatly. 'And that was only his first wife.'

She's right, of course. She sucks hard on the cigarette, and silence hangs between us. Not an uncomfortable one. This is the first time I can ever remember seeing Lydia so relaxed. Her clothes look good on her too. She always used to dress like she was trying too hard, but today she's in a simple dark pantsuit and white shirt that show off her, rather than the clothes.

'I think fame does something bad to good people,' she continues, as we watch Brett playing chase with Thackeray, who is tearing around the garden. 'Dad would have been the first to admit to that, if he hadn't been so damaged by it. He was so caught up in himself, he had no time for us.'

'But he loved us,' I say, defending him as always.

'Did he?' The old bitterness creeps back into her voice, and I see her features stiffen slightly.

'I know he did,' I say forcefully. I would so like her to believe it.

'Dad didn't know how to love anyone but himself.'

I say nothing, because I've had this argument too often with Lydia before. Overhead the eucalyptus trees rustle as a light breeze blows through their branches, sending down a strong aroma.

'Anyway, it looks like this guy wants to be involved now.' She points down the garden at Brett, who is showing Thackeray how to tackle properly.

I sigh. Actually I have no idea what Brett really wants. His reappearance has been so unexpected.

'You haven't told me about your life in New York. Have you got someone?' I ask, changing the subject.

She smiles.

'No. No guy. A nice cat called Theo.' She grinds the cigarette stub into a flowerbed. 'And the jewellery business. That keeps me busy.'

'I saw some of your designs in *InStyle* magazine.' She nods modestly. 'Everyone's wearing them.'

'Yeah, the stars give them a good profile. I had Gwyneth Paltrow in the store the other day. Here.' She tugs at some long earrings that are dangling from her ears, sporting skulls and crossbones in fine crystals. 'Have these.'

'Are these your design?' She nods again, and I see how proud she is of them. 'And the watch?'

'Yup.'

'They're beautiful. I never even knew you were so artistic.'

She stares at me for a second, as if trying to pass on

some secret message. 'It's taken me a long time to know who and what I am.' She's about to say more, but Brett is marching up the garden holding Thackeray's hand. 'Now, do I get a turn to play with my nephew or not?' she asks me brightly, as we both get up from the swing seat. 'Because,' she adds to me in a quieter voice, 'it looks like you've got some unfinished business here.'

She bends low so that her eyes are the same level as Thackeray's, and introduces herself to him. 'I need a guide to show me round the garden,' she tells him. 'Would you be my guide?'

'He's such a sweet kid,' Brett tells me, as they disappear. 'You've done a real good job raising him, Pearl.'

Now it's my turn to feel proud. Being a mother isn't as easy as it looks in the books. I smile half-heartedly and sip from my wine glass, hoping to look nonchalant.

'Thank you,' he adds.

'Meaning what exactly?' I say, suddenly feeling the rage return. 'Thank you for taking on the responsibility while you were off—' I stop myself.

'Thank you for being such a great mother and thank you for letting me meet him,' he says calmly. 'It's meant a lot to me.' He pauses. 'More than you could ever imagine,' he eventually adds, spitting out the words with such feeling that I turn to study him.

He's staring into the distance with a pained, faraway expression, and for the first time, I suspect that something has happened to him. I can't say what, but I can see there *is* a real change about him that I wouldn't even know how to begin to put into words. Somehow, the conceit I remember so vividly from before has gone.

'Why?' I ask.

'Why what?' He looks at me.

'Why, after all this time, are you suddenly keen to be involved with Thackeray?'

'I don't expect you to understand,' he says quietly.

'How could you? I can't even expect you to forgive, after what I did.'

Silence hangs. I feel uneasy. Thackeray and Lydia are lost from view, and the party is thinning out.

'I brought you something,' he says cautiously, and searches in his trouser pockets. There's a hesitancy about him now. He's not as sure of himself as he used to be. 'Here,' he says eventually and hands me a small box.

I recognise the ring inside instantly. It's a delicate band with a line of seven diamonds. It was my engagement ring, which I threw at him when I found him in bed with Conzuela Martin.

'I don't know if it's the right thing to do, but I want you to have it. It was yours,' he says quietly. I hold the box in my hands, but I'm lost for words. 'I never found the wedding band,' he adds. 'Not that you'd want that back, I suppose.'

'I've got another one now,' I remind him, and show him the rings on my finger, including the big dazzler that Adam gave me.

'Of course you have.' He looks forlorn.

'I can't keep this,' I say, closing the box and handing it back. 'It wouldn't be right.'

'Save it for Thackeray then.'

The sound of someone yelling goodbye comes from the driveway, where guests are disappearing. I falter.

'Please?' he adds. 'It would mean a lot to me.'

'I can't.'

'Yes you can. You can if it's for Thackeray.'

I waver. 'OK, I'll keep it for him,' I say, and put the box in my pocket.

'I better go,' he offers, and then hesitates again, as if contemplating whether to kiss me, and for the teeniest, teeniest millisecond of a millisecond I want to throw my arms around him and kiss him back. It would be like nothing had ever happened. But what am I thinking of?

Turn and leave. Turn and leave, a voice tells me inside my head.

'Well, bye then,' I say coldly and head back into the house. What was I thinking?

18

When I was sixteen, I won a short-story competition. I was at Beverly Hills High. It was a regional competition and my story was printed in the local paper. It was the first time I'd ever won anything, first time I'd achieved anything at school, and Dad made a big fuss about it. He took me out to dinner, told me how proud he was of me, and showed the story to all his friends. Dad always encouraged creative inventiveness.

Then I got a call from a reporter. They'd seen the story too, and would I like to give an interview? Well, of course I would. Dad always gave interviews when he had a new album out. I was so excited to talk about my work.

The reporter came to the house and I led her through to the patio, where I'd laid out some iced tea. She was younger than she sounded on the phone, and wore a short skirt and heels. 'Is your dad home?' she asked as she peered, way too obviously, into rooms.

'No, he's out,' I said vaguely. I never knew where he was.

'So what's it like growing up with famous parents?' she asked, pulling out a tape recorder and notebook from a huge shoulder bag. Not that question again.

'Um, pretty normal,' I answered.

'Would you say you were spoilt?'

'Not especially. Dad's pretty strict.'

'In what way?' she asked in a nasal whine. She had a way of asking questions that made her sound like she was a horse whinnying.

'Oh, you know, likes us to be polite, doing chores and stuff. We have to be home by ten p.m.'

'Was it difficult for you when your parents divorced?'

'Kinda.'

'In what way?' Definitely a horse whinnying.

'Well, in the way it is for most kids ... but I guess it's better for Mum and Dad now. There's less fighting anyway.'

'Did they fight a lot?' She looked at me earnestly and whinnied again. 'In what way?'

'Well ... I think they sort of competed with each other. They were both so successful, they kinda ...' I stopped myself. 'It's kinda hard to describe.'

'Was it because of your dad doing drugs?'

The woman was getting on my nerves now. 'Look, I thought you wanted to talk to me about my story, not my dad.'

'Of course, of course ...' She seemed momentarily flustered. 'I just needed a bit of background. You know, some filler. So tell me, how did you get the idea for the story?'

It was then that I realised she wasn't interested in me or my story at all. It was all about Dad. Stupid of me to not realise sooner.

'Offside,' Stephen roars at me. 'That ball was offside.'

'No it wasn't,' I shout back.

'Yes it was. We'll take a penalty kick.'

'No you won't. I'm the referee and I say the ball was fine. Continue play.'

Stephen rolls his eyes to the cloudless sky overhead and lollops down the lawn with his round belly swaying from side to side like a pendulum as he goes. I sometimes wonder if my job could get any stranger. We are on the lawn outside Stephen's house, with a makeshift soccer pitch marked out with items of clothing at the four corners, and some foldaway children's-size goals. Stephen is making one of his periodic attempts at being a good father. On one team there is Craig, his awkward and rather self-conscious fifteen year old, and Logan who, although only eight, is clearly destined to be great on the soccer field. On the other team are Stephen and Marcie, his precocious fashion-plate of a twelve year old, who is making her disdain for the sport clearly known.

I have been called in as referee, because, as always, Stephen likes everything to be done properly, and even though there is enough mail on my desk to start my own post office, he was insistent. I made the mistake once of telling him I used to watch videotapes with Dad of Newcastle FC's most glorious moments, so now he thinks

I am an expert on soccer rules. And compared to him, I probably am.

Given that Stephen is as short as I am and must weigh nearly 250lb, he's quite a sight on the soccer pitch, especially because he's wearing a pair of bright yellow shorts. He makes an attempt at kicking the ball at the goal and misses, and I see the annoyance on his face. Craig now has his chance, and the lanky teenager comes gracefully up the pitch, dribbling the ball as he goes. He passes to Logan, who has astutely placed himself where he needs to be, and he scores the goal.

'Five – nil,' I shout.

'Damn,' Stephen mutters. 'Come on, Marcie, you're not trying hard enough.'

'But Daddy . . .' she whines.

'But Daddy nothing,' he shouts back.

'Stephen, they're only kids,' I call to him, which is possibly dangerous ground, given his short temper. 'It's meant to be fun, remember?' He harrumphs like a small child himself, and they play on.

I started back at work after the funeral. One of the universal truths about bereavement is that no matter how much you miss someone, no matter how much you long for the ache to disappear, the world carries on mercilessly. And when you've got a five year old, it possibly spins even faster. There's still a bathtime to do every night, a cockatiel that needs to be fed, a dishwasher to be filled and then emptied. I could have let a nanny take over, but routine is comfort. Thackeray is comfort. And going to work, even if it does mean making sure Stephen doesn't cheat on his own kids in a game of soccer, is probably good for me.

Today's going to be jam-packed, which is good for keeping me from mooching and feeling sad. And Adam is taking me to dinner tonight. Restaurant guides have been consulted, phone calls made, the babysitter is booked, and we are going to sample the delights of Comme Ca, rated as Hollywood's hottest new eatery.

I've barely seen Adam since the funeral. Every night there are new scenes that have to be written up for *The Paperweight*. I tell him it's bad chi to have no harmony between work and home life. He tells me I'm a California space cadet. But he did, at least, apologise for storming off at the funeral. Eventually. First of all there had to be the stony silence when I got home. Adam's big on being passive-aggressive. Then came the hand-wringing, the accusation of disloyalty, the 'I'm a better father than Brett's ever been', and finally, when I eventually convinced him that I wasn't running off and having sex with Brett in the bushes at my own dad's funeral, the acknowledgement that maybe he'd overreacted. I forgave him, of course. It's not an easy situation for any of us. So tonight, we will down a few apple martinis, toy with some appetisers, bump into a few familiar faces and Adam will fill me in on all the gossip at the studio, which I love to hear.

It's twelve – nil by the time the kids are begging their dad to stop play. He concedes, showing off with a final big kick that sends the ball flying into the branches of a tree.

'I can get that down,' he says gallantly, and starts climbing the tree. He's out of his mind. It's not an especially big tree – a Chinese elm with lots of low branches – and the ball's not particularly high, but underneath, the ground has been left uncultivated and a number of cacti have made it their home.

'Why don't I get it, Dad?' says Craig, which might be a better idea.

'No, I'll be fine,' he says, chest heaving with male prowess and reaching out to dislodge the ball. And then slowly, almost cartoon style, the branch on which Stephen is standing bends, buckles, and delivers him, cruelly, straight into the cacti.

*

Did I wonder if my job could get any more surreal? I am now looking at the unpleasant sight of Stephen's bare ass, from which I am removing cactus spikes. Gag me with a spoon, why don't you?

'Jesus, Stephen, I expect a good bonus for this,' I tell him. He grunts and howls like a baby.

'By the way, I want you to get Brett back in here,' he announces between howls. 'Barry and I came up with a real good idea. We're going to offer him the lead role in the new Jane Austen.'

'But that was my—'

'They're making *Northanger Abbey*, you know. It's the perfect role for Brett. Dark and smouldering, soft and sensitive, and a real break from what he's done before.'

'But—'

'I think it'll be real good for him. Set up a meeting, wouldchya?'

I am tempted to pound the cactus spikes back.

'And better call the doctor's office too,' he adds.

'What for?'

'Tetanus shot. These could be deadly.'

I wish. I recoil to the sanity of my office and catch up with the mail on my desk.

There's always a lot of it. Stephen generally spends enough to support the American economy, so there are always plenty of bills, and when he chooses to spend a day at home, rather than his office, it means a courier will bring up another batch of mail from his office in town too. I reach for my coffee. There's a bill from his lawyer, the maintenance contract for his office building, which needs renewing, the sign-off papers to pay the staff monthly salaries, three invitations to take out new credit cards, fifteen more to social events, and a bunch of advertisements for household improvements. I sort them into piles, according to priority, and toss the junk mail.

And then I find some medical bills in the batch of papers that have come up from the office. How odd. They shouldn't be here. It's not an agent's job to take on their client's medical bills. I cast my eye over the papers. Turns out they have been paid by the production company who made Brett's last film and they want reimbursement. I read the bills, which carry Brett's name. They're for emergency therapy. A stomach pump procedure. Hospitalisation. A stay in rehab.

Jeepers. What happened? I saw a change in Brett – the demand for no more movies, the humbler disposition. Could this have anything to do with it? There was nothing in the press. I'd have seen it. And Stephen's never mentioned anything.

Anyway, it's none of my business. Except that rather like a line of clothes at Fred Segal that you know you can't afford but you can't stop thinking about, thoughts about Brett keep popping into my brain. I've tried to think of other things – the summer collection at Barney's, the shoes at Christian Louboutin, Thackeray's goldfish, Adam's screenplays, anything. But ever since the funeral I've found myself thinking about Brett – in a way that I really don't want to. There was that moment when his arm brushed mine – an innocent second that did not deserve the hours it has played out in my head. There was the smell of the soap powder his shirt had been washed in. The look of contrition on his face. Was it real? Physical attraction is a dangerous instrument – it engineers fantasies that play tricks on you. And I cannot afford to fall under his spell again.

But he seemed different – more like his old self, long before he became famous. There was an evening, not long after we first started dating, when he bought a picnic and tickets to the Hollywood Bowl. It was Tchaikovsky's 1812 Overture and there were fireworks for the grand finale. 'Did you know Tchaikovsky wrote his first piece of music for his mother?' he said. 'She died when he was fourteen, and so he wrote her a waltz.'

'She never heard it?'

'No. Isn't that heartbreaking? She would never have known what a genius her son was. And he was a genius.'

I nodded enthusiastically, not that I knew anything about Tchaikovsky. I'd never even been to a classical concert before.

'What wouldn't I give to have talent like that,' Brett marvelled.

He was deferential back then. Humbler. But by the time he was on to his third movie, he was so cocksure of himself that there wasn't anyone who was better than him. Not even Tchaikovsky.

Seeing Brett so unpresuming reminded me of those early days. And hadn't he been genuinely pleased to meet Thackeray too? How I used to hope for him to turn up and admire this beautiful baby that we'd created between us. I wanted him to share in the joy of each stage of Thackeray's development – his first smile, the day he started crawling, his first words, which happened to be da-da. Having a child on your own is rather like sitting down to a delicious meal in a fabulous restaurant on your own. The child is a wonderful experience in its own right, but the occasion is so much enhanced when there are two of you to enjoy it.

But there's no point in dwelling on these things now. I have my life back. And I have Adam, who I love. If Brett has incurred medical bills, well, it's not my problem. I can't be thinking about this stuff. I put the bills in an envelope to forward on to him and check his address on Stephen's client base on the computer. 'New Address Pending' it blinks back at me. What, he moved? I was going to have to call him anyway, because Stephen wants a meeting set up.

'Wotcha,' says Bella chirpily, popping her head around

the door of my office. I've been so absorbed, I forgot she was coming. And bringing her aunt too. Bella called last week to tell me her aunt had arrived in LA and they'd already met up. She felt she had to. But would I like to meet her too? I got the impression Bella wanted to show off her new life in LA, and that I was part of that. Stephen was too. By marrying Jamie, Stephen's oldest son, she got herself the freaky father-in-law, and I'm not sure why anyone would want to show him off.

'Busy?' she asks.

'You don't even want to know what I've been doing this morning,' I tell her. Ever since Bella was a nanny for Stephen's kids, she and I have always swapped Stephen stories. You needed to work for him to know how outrageous he could be.

'Do tell.' She kisses me on both cheeks and throws herself into the chair opposite my desk. She looks happy.

'Picking cactus spikes out of his ass.'

She lets out a howl of laughter. 'What, no hospital visit? Surely our little hypochondriac didn't miss a hospital trip.'

'Doctor's appointment this afternoon. Say, I thought you were bringing your aunt with you.'

'I have. She wanted to look round the garden.'

We both lean forward to see a woman in her forties looking into the pond outside my window. Unaware that we're watching her, she dips her hand in the fountain, which is finally working again, and seems to be relishing letting the water run through her fingers. She's wearing a floral dress and practical flat shoes, and looks agreeable enough – laughter lines around the eyes and a generous mouth. But this is the woman who turned Bella away when her father parents died. I already know I don't want to like her.

'How's it going?' I ask carefully.

'Great.' Bella's smile is wide. She pushes her long

blond hair behind her ears, and fixes me with her big blue eyes. She really is so beautiful. It's no wonder she ended up on TV.

'She's OK?' Somehow this wasn't what I was expecting.

'She's really nice. I thought it might be awkward ... you know, after all this time. But she's lovely, Pearl. Really lovely.' She stares wistfully at the woman outside. 'I can't tell you how great it feels to finally have family.' She knocks on the window so that her aunt looks up, and they wave joyously at each other. I've never seen Bella so ebullient. 'I know it probably sounds nutty, but having her around makes me feel complete somehow. Does that sound odd?'

'No, of course not,' I say obligingly.

'She's invited me for Christmas too. Imagine that, Pearl. After all this time, with no family, a family Christmas!' Bella looks triumphant, like she's just won an Oscar.

I long to ask her why her aunt abandoned her all that time ago, but I don't want to spoil her moment of happiness. 'That's great,' I say.

'And she's got loads of photos of Mum and Dad,' Bella carries on.

'You've seen them?'

'Well, no. They're all in England. But at least there are some. I can't even remember what Mum and Dad looked like now.'

Bella has an almost dreamy expression, which is just *so* unlike her. 'So where did you meet? Come on, Bella, I want all the details.'

'Well, she came to my house. I didn't want to meet anywhere public, where the paps might get us. And the minute I opened the door, she threw her arms around me.'

'Wasn't that a bit much? I mean, after all this time?'

'No, not at all. It sounds kind of corny, but it felt right. It felt like I was coming home, like being safe somehow. Do you know what I mean?'

I don't. But I nod anyway. 'And you've forgiven her?'

'There's no point in brooding on the past, Pearl. You were the one who always told me that sometimes you have to forgive and move on. It's one of the reasons I've agreed to give her the money.'

'What money?'

'She needs a bit of money,' Bella says carelessly.

'How much money?'

'She's been widowed, you see. And she's got three kids to support. My cousins! My family, Pearl.' Bella has gone all dreamy-eyed again.

'But you don't know anything about her!' I say, perhaps a little too stridently. Alarm bells are going off inside my head now.

'She's my dad's sister, Pearl. I feel responsible.'

'But Bella, she didn't give two figs about you when you lost your parents.'

'Two wrongs don't make a right. And you're the one who's always telling people that they need to do what is right in their heart.'

'Did she even say why she didn't take you in?'

'It's all water under the bridge now,' she says blindly.

Bella's always been so stoical about being without a family. Caustic even. Used to crack jokes about being better off without parents because she didn't carry any baggage. Not that anyone was ever taken in. But now her desire for family seems to be overriding all common sense. I can't believe what I'm hearing. Ironically, now that she has what she always craved, she seems to have lost her cynical, jaundiced reserve.

'How much does she want?' I ask again and take a sip of my coffee.

'Twenty grand.'

'Twenty thousand!' I nearly spit the coffee back out.

'Pounds.'

'But she's obviously only contacting you because she wants your money.' I feel mean saying it, but someone has to.

'I know it's hard for you to understand, but I want to help her. I really do. She says they're going to repossess her house.'

'But don't you think you should check out if her story is true?'

'Does it matter if it isn't?' she asks me, with a look that makes me feel unkind for even suggesting it. 'I've actually got a family, Pearl. A family! It's what I've always wanted.'

I find myself thinking about how much I'd pay to bring Dad back to life, or summon a family if I had none other.

'Can you afford to give her that much money?'

'I've got savings.'

It seems so unfair. When Bella arrived in Los Angeles, she didn't have two cents to rub together. She's never told me how much money she makes – she hates discussing money – but I know she's worth a bit. She and Jamie live in a fabulous house down on the beach in Malibu, which Bella bought herself. She presents a movie review slot on MTV, has modelling contracts, and makes guest appearances on chat shows. So she's got to have a bit stashed away, and that's regardless of what Jamie earns. But the point is, she worked hard for it all herself. Every penny.

'Look, why don't you give yourself some time to think it through?' I suggest. 'Go and visit her first. Get to know her a bit and then think about the money.'

'She says the debt collectors won't wait. She spent her last few hundred getting here because she felt it was rude to ask me in a letter after all that had gone before. She says I'm her last chance. You'd do the same, Pearl, I know you would.'

Would I? Would I be that desperate for a family? Would Thackeray be that desperate to know about his own real father one day?

'Want to come and meet her?' Bella is on her feet.

'Sure.'

I follow her into the garden, where her aunt is peering through the darkened windows of the guest house at the far side of the lawn.

'Aunt Livonia, this is Pearl,' Bella announces as we walk up.

She turns a little jumpily and we shake hands. I must try to be friendly. This woman clearly means so much to Bella.

'How are you enjoying the States?' I ask her.

'I'm having a lovely time,' she says and eyes me cautiously. 'Everything's so big. So much bigger than at home.'

For a woman who turned away an orphaned child, she looks quite benign. I study her face hard, searching for telltale clues – a tortured past, perhaps; a distant hurt. There must have been a reason. She's probably full of remorse now. I take in her pale English skin, the lines in her brow, mousy hair that's starting to grey, but there is no hint of regret or sadness. She is composed and surprisingly confident.

'And where is home for you?' I ask politely.

'Oh, a tiny town outside London. I'm sure you won't have heard of it,' she says breezily. She speaks like Judi Dench – lots of polished enunciation and rounded vowels.

'Try me. I used to go to school in England.'

'Oh, no one's ever heard of it,' she says vaguely. 'I say, aren't these roses beautiful, Bella?' She steps towards a flowerbed and sniffs at an open bloom.

'Yes, aren't they?' Bella replies, trotting after her like a dog at heel.

Eventually we go into the kitchen, where Maria has laid a table in the nook overlooking the garden and left an array of salads. Stephen waddles in briefly, oohing and aahing about his injured ass, and Bella makes the introductions, but he doesn't stay. Livonia tells us once more how impressed she is by the size of everything. Brits are always impressed by the size of everything in America. That, and the weather.

'Bella tells me you've got kids,' I say casually as we sip ice teas.

'Yes, three,' she trills.

'How old are they?'

She looks upwards to the ceiling, as if counting silently. 'They grow so fast, it's hard to keep track. How about you? Have you got kids?'

'Yeah. I've got a five year old, who's at school right now.' The gardener starts the engine of his mower outside, and Bella closes the doors to keep out the noise. 'Who's looking after them while you're away?'

'Oh, they went off to stay with an old friend of mine in Dorset.'

'They must be pleased to be missing school.'

'Yes . . .' She hesitates, and seems momentarily confused.

'Thackeray would love a chance to miss school.'

'Luckily it's half term for them,' she says, gathering confidence again.

We chat on for a while, discussing all the sights that LA offers the tourist – Hollywood's Walk of Fame, the Getty Museum, the Hollywood sign and, more crucial than all of that, Fred Segal and the Beverly Center for shopping. Bella promises her aunt she will show her all the sights. She offers her a room at her house too, instead of the cheap tourist hotel where she is staying. But Aunt Livonia declines the offer. I watch Bella hang on to her aunt's every word and see how happy she is. I am pleased for her. But there's something about Livonia that disturbs me. I just wish she wasn't asking for money. It seems so blatant.

After lunch, we make our goodbyes. The phone is ringing when I reach my desk. It's Adam. He's got to cancel tonight.

'There's drinks on the lot,' he says, sounding weary. 'I don't want to go, but I've got to.'

'Really?'

'Yeah. I really don't want to go.' Yes, you said that. 'But I think I've got to put in some face time. The CEO is going to be there, and Nick Hargraves and Ben Schmuley . . .' He rattles off more names that will be part of the studio's chain of command. 'I really don't want to go. You know how nervous I get at these things, but I think I ought to go. Don't you?'

Adam always wants my opinion. I suspect it eases his conscience.

'Yeah, I guess.'

'I'd much rather be with you. You know that, don't you?'

'Sure.'

'I'm sorry, honey. You'll be OK, won't you?'

I usually am. I might go shopping instead, since we've a babysitter booked. Success buys you nice things, but it sure comes at a price. This is the third time this month he's cancelled plans.

By the end of the afternoon, I've sorted the mail, paid the staff their wages, and booked six weeks of Gourmet Diet meals and a colonic for Stephen (don't ask). I've heard the latest from the dating front line – Lizzie has now been on three dates with Cameron Valentin, including a visit to his church, where she assures me her presence didn't make the holy water boil and sizzle – and I've ordered *The Green Car Guide* for Adam, marking the page where I noticed a convertible Prius. The first of its kind. I feel the satisfaction of completing tasks, and that makes me feel better. I often write lists just for the contentment of being able to mark a tick when jobs are done. It's a good feeling. There's just one last thing to do and then I'm finished for the day – those medical bills, waiting in their envelope for an address to send them to. I brace myself.

'Hello, Pearl.' Brett answers straight away.

'Hi.' I keep my voice briskly officious. 'Stephen would like to set up a meeting and I need your new address. I have some medical bills to pass on to you.'

'Ah, yes. I wondered when they would catch up with me. Do you want to send them here?'

'Wherever you want.' I keep my tone neutral.

'Nine seven two five Charleville Boulevard, Apartment 38. Beverly Hills, 90212.'

'You're living in an apartment?'

'Yeah.'

'What happened to your house?'

'It's a long story,' he sighs.

'Are you OK?' The words are out of my mouth before I've given it permission to start running away of its own accord.

'Yeah. I'm fine now.' He sighs again. 'It was great to see you,' he adds, more brightly.

'You too,' I say, without even thinking it through. Jeepers, what's the matter with me?

'And Thackeray. He's a great kid.'

'Brett, what happened?' my mouth asks. I didn't give it permission to. It just seems to have taken on a life of its own. I feel like a lemming jumping off a precipice. I know I shouldn't care.

There's silence a while, then he answers. 'I had a nervous breakdown.'

'A breakdown?' Brett's the last person I could ever imagine having a nervous breakdown. It was his confidence and self-assurance that was always his appeal.

'Yeah.' There's more silence. 'Look, there's no need for you to know all the gory details. Just send the bills over and I'll take care of them.' He's obviously embarrassed.

'I'm sorry,' I say gently.

'No need. I'm fine. I'm a lucky guy. I've been very lucky . . . and to have met my own son. That was just so great.'

It's odd how it seems to mean so much to him now.

'Is there anything I can do?' There goes my mouth again. It's like I have no control over the damn thing.

'Yeah. There is.' He pauses. 'Come back to me.'

I feel a lurch inside. He's got to be kidding, right? I have no idea how to respond. This time, even my mouth doesn't know.

'Brett, I'm married now. I have a husband who I love. You're too late,' it eventually says.

'Am I really?' he asks, so softly, so thoughtfully that there's the implication that he really thinks he stands a chance.

Yes, of course he's too late, I tell my mouth. And get it right this time.

'Yes, you're too late,' I say definitively and hang up, forgetting to set up his meeting with Stephen.

Damn.

I knew Jesse Wheaton had only asked me to the movies because my dad was Gavin Sash. But since pimples had landed on my face and multiplied like germ warfare, I was grateful for any advantage I could garner over other girls when it came to high-school dating. To ignore the fact would have been like not putting on make-up and making the most of myself. Jesse was a biker, and had been in detention more often than me, but I could see the look of awe on his face when I invited him back to my house after the movie and Dad was actually in.

'Thanks for bringing Pearl home,' Dad told him in our driveway.

'No trouble, Mr Sash,' he stammered. 'Say, do you think I could get your autograph?'

Guys were always interested in who my dad was, and seeing the value, I took to hyping it up, telling them what I knew they'd want to hear – news of Dad's latest album, Dad's tour plans, what Dad liked to eat for breakfast. People never seem to tire of celebrity news. In return, I was never short of dates. The problem was, I was never quite sure if guys ever liked *me* at all.

Not that the insecurity stopped me. Quite the opposite. By the time I was seventeen, there wasn't a drug I hadn't tried or a scene I hadn't tried to fit into. There was even a spell when Lizzie and I got involved in

. . . well, the papers called it a high-class call-girl ring. I didn't much care for them calling it that, because we never got paid for sex – it wasn't like that. But we got invited to the best parties that LA had to offer – movie stars, politicians, producers, and always mountains of coke. I mean, coke like you'd never seen. I mean, parties like you'd never believe. For a while we lived high on the hill of Hollywood Babylon, and sex was all just part of it.

And then one day I woke up in rehab. Everyone goes to rehab at some point in LA. Lizzie's been three times. In fact if you don't go during your teens, you begin to feel you're missing out. It was Heather – newly inaugurated into Kimberley's previous marital position – who'd taken me there. And I've always been grateful to her for that. It was six weeks of cold turkey and the awful realisation that I had lost my way. I had a famous father, but no identity of my own. I had good taste in shoes, but no idea what to do with my life.

Fortunately, Heather did. She signed me up for a secretarial class. Dull, I know. And it never occurred to me that perhaps I could have done something different or better. But I realised that I needed to do something. I needed to do something other than be the daughter of Gavin Sash.

See, that was really my problem. I felt like I was permanently at a party with one of those stick-on name tags pasted to my lapel telling everyone that I was Gavin Sash's daughter. 'Ah, so *you're* Gavin Sash's daughter,' complete strangers would say, like they were old friends of the family or something. And it wasn't that I wasn't proud of Dad, or that I didn't love him. I did. Way and beyond. I mean totally. But I didn't really know how to be me.

The secretarial class was my first step to being me. Heather thought she was just signing me up for something that would keep me away from the coke. But after rehab, I took to using a fake last name. It was kinda fun to keep changing it too. I had several different pseudonyms. Then I set about achieving sixty-three words a minute. I also learned that Excel is a computer program, not just something to try for, and that shorthand is very, very difficult. And slowly my world shifted. The following year, I started as Stephen's PA. Not the most exciting of jobs, but I won it on my own merit, and that meant more to me then than all the coke in Hollywood.

21

L aura Lippid, better known as 'the Michelangelo of
Metaphysics', lights a small white candle to remove
negative energy and symbolise the joining of conscious
minds. She closes her eyes and breathes deep. On the
walls of her consulting room in West Hollywood are
astrological star charts, a giant photo of the moon and
some Native American art. Laid out on a table in front of
me are crystals, which are glowing in the soft light.

'Your aura is your spiritual blueprint, your spiritual
signature, if you will. And by changing the quality of your
aura, you change the quality of your life,' she breathes.
'Now it's important that you relax to free up the energy
field.'

She stands me in front of a white wall, where I shake
out my shoulders, close my eyes and breathe deep too.
I've had my aura read many times before, of course, but
manipulating the power rays of spiritual enrichment can
also help with fertility. And it's that time of the month
again. That time when sex gets scheduled, 'trying'
becomes a catchphrase (yes, very trying) and Adam
comes home from work early.

So I'm thinking that an extra metaphysical push might
help a baby along. Adam doesn't have faith in any of this
stuff, but I figure it can't hurt.

I concentrate hard on making my aura shine by

thinking of colours radiating from my body. But the Michelangelo of Metaphysics is reeling with shock.

'Your aura is looking dark and grey,' she announces. 'I've never seen it so grey.' Normally my aura is bright and clear, which is an indication, according to Michelangelo, that I am spiritually advanced, which I always like to hear. 'Are you troubled? Unclear of your intentions?' she asks carefully.

Of course not. Although I did dream about Brett last night. It was so vivid, I woke up in shock to find Adam in the bed next to me. What was he doing there, snoring away in his sunbathing position in the bed, while I was wrapped in Brett's arms, with him doing unspeakably delicious things to my body, only seconds before? It took me a few seconds to whiz forward in time and realise that I was married to someone else.

'Can you set it straight for me?' I plead. I really don't want a grey aura. 'The thing is, my husband and I are trying for a baby, and I need to be fertile.'

'All things are possible,' she says soothingly, and waves her arms around me, as if warming her hands against a fire. 'You must think pure thoughts. Think of the pinks and whites of innocence.'

I think hard about pinks and whites. I think about babies. Little bundles wrapped in white blankets. I remember Thackeray wrapped in his. He was so adorable. He was the loudest baby in the hospital. I marvelled at his lungs. 'Must have got those from his father,' I joked with the nurse. Brett was always singing at the top of his voice. There was that afternoon when we went to the farmers' market on Fairfax to buy some vegetables, and there was a karaoke stage set up. Some old women were singing Frank Sinatra medleys. We stopped to listen. Next thing, Brett was on stage belting out 'Have I Told You Lately That I Love You?'. The Rod Stewart number. And he was directing it right at me in the crowd, wouldn't take his eyes off me, and all these old ladies were staring at me. He always had a way of turning the ordinary into the magical. And now he says, 'Come back to me.' I should be angry. I shouldn't give it any head space. I shouldn't even be thinking this stuff. *But he said, 'Come back to me.'*

'I'm seeing red now,' says the Michelangelo of Metaphysics, breaking my reverie. She's been massaging the air around my body for the last twenty minutes, while I . . . Heck, what was I thinking?

'Red is an indicator of both passion and fertility. I think this is a good sign,' she announces, looking pleased with herself.

Jeepers. What was I thinking? I must think loyal thoughts. Wifely thoughts. Devoted thoughts. Adam's a good man. He's kind, faithful, dependable, and I love him.

The photos on the wall of my gynaecologist's waiting room make me laugh. This is my next stop after my aura reading. Dr Greenblatt is running late, giving me time to contemplate his choice of wall decoration. Hollywood's obsession with fame takes some obscure turns sometimes. Supermarkets sell ham that claims to be 'Celebrity Healthy Ham', liquor marts post signs promising their beer is 'Star Endorsed', dry cleaners offer services that claim 'Celebrity Style' – even car mechanics have signs outside promising 'As Used by the Stars'. Now I'm looking at autographed photos of celebrities hammered to the wall in a gynaecologist's waiting room! I mean, come on. We see enough photos of female crotches in the rag mags without having to contemplate them at the doctor's office too. Dr Greenblatt, by the way, is known as the Feeler and Fumbler to the Stars.

Down my shirt I am clutching a long thin tube containing Adam's sperm. Yes, really. This is how they do it. He was sent into a cubicle an hour before to rustle up his best; then, once he'd delivered, he was allowed to go back to his beloved office, and I collected the product of his labours, now tidily placed in the tube, which must be kept at body temperature – hence the need to keep it down my shirt.

'I'm sorry the doctor's running late,' a nurse apologises through a hatch in the wall. 'But he won't be long now.'

'No worries.' I've got *This Side of Heaven* in my bag.

Perdita could live with the guilt no longer. It was destroying her. Every minute of the day she was consumed with thoughts of her lover, and her body ached to be with him again. She knew she had to leave her husband. Either that, or she would kill herself – the pain ran too deep.

'Mrs Sisskind-Sash?' the nurse calls.

I'm ushered into a room, shown the bed, told to remove my panties, and given a paper sheet to hide my modesty. I know the routine. Feet in the stirrups, a light up the woo-woo, and then the doctor delivers the contents of the tube directly into the feminine reaches where babies are currently fearing to tread. It takes no time at all.

'Sorry to hear about your dad,' says the doctor, talking into my private parts. 'Must have come as a shock.'

'It was,' I concede, staring at the ceiling. I used to think this such a strange circumstance to make conversation over, but I've got used to it now. 'We were all shocked.'

'How are you coping?'

'I'm fine,' I say automatically. 'A bit emotional, I suppose.'

'It's an emotional time,' he says sagely, and inserts a cold metal clamp where I don't believe cold metal clamps should naturally go. 'And probably more emotional for your family than most.'

'Grief is grief,' I say. I've never liked people to make exceptions for us, just because of who Dad was.

'Not sure that it's that simple for your sister, though,' he cautions, now inserting the tube.

'Lydia?' I didn't even know he knew Lydia.

'The article.'

'What article?'

'The article in the *Daily Globe*,' he says. 'Hold on, nearly finished here.' He feels and fumbles around some more. 'You haven't seen it? I thought you would have. Go, boys, go,' he calls as he finishes up. 'I'll get it for you. You can read it while you wait your twenty minutes.' After an intra-uterine insemination, which is what this is, I have to lie still for twenty minutes, same as regular sex. 'Though you've got to promise not to hit the roof,' he warns. 'It won't help those sperm if you start—'

'What the heck has she said?' I interrupt.

'You better read it.' He returns with the newspaper and then shuts the door.

The Father I Hardly Knew

Exclusive to the *Daily Globe*

All of us will think fondly of the aptly titled *Remember Me*, Gavin Sash's platinum-selling record that made him a global phenomenon. But not all the memories are sweet ones for Lydia Sash, Gavin's oldest daughter.

'Dad pretended I didn't exist for the first five years of my life,' says 33-year-old Lydia, talking for the first time since her father's death last month.

'I was a secret. A wife and daughter wouldn't enhance a sexy rock star's image. So Mum and I lived in a small house in Newcastle upon Tyne.

Dad was away touring, usually in the States. For the first few years, I didn't even realise I had a father.'

Once Sash's career was established, Lydia and her mother moved to Los Angeles to be with Sash, who had set up a home there. 'I remember it as a huge upheaval,' explains Lydia. 'And suddenly we were living with this guy who neither of us really knew.'

A year later Lydia's parents separated. Lydia's mother suffered a mental collapse and Gavin married his second wife, Bonnie Banks, who raised Lydia.

'The move to the US was hard on Mum. They had been separated for too long, I think. And Dad was famous by then. He wasn't the same person she remembered,' says Lydia, who now lives in New York and has launched her own jewellery line.

'The hardest part of growing up for me was getting over the knowledge that Dad publicly pretended that I didn't exist. I often used to feel it must have been because he was ashamed of me.

'I've come to terms with it now, and realise that wasn't true. But it's taken a long time.'

Sash's career skyrocketed in the years following the album *Remember Me*. He is listed as one of the most successful musicians and composers of our times, with sales of over 50 million albums. He also wrestled a well-documented drug addiction for more than a decade, eventually becoming sober in 1998.

'Over the years, I've forgiven him the drug use, the wild excesses, the long absences. I've even forgiven him for having four wives. When your dad is a celebrity, you come to recognise that this is all part of the terrain. But pretending I wasn't part of his life when I was little is still a hard one.

'He wrote songs about love and faith all the time. But he never really understood what the words meant.'

Oh, Lydia. But he did love you, I want to yell. In his own way he did. I know he wasn't perfect, and I know you came off the worst of all of us – you never let Dad forget about keeping you a secret in England. It came up in every row. But he did love us. And did you really have to make this so public?

However hard I search, I can't remember a time when there weren't periodic news reports about Dad. Most of the time the headlines made us laugh. There was 'Gavin Sash Parties at the Roxbury', which was funny because he hated the place; there was 'Gavin Sash in Headlong Motorcycle Collision' when his bike was in the garage for a service; and 'Gavin Sash Abandoned as a Child', which he was, if you count Grandma going away for the weekend when he was nine, and leaving Dad with Auntie Sue for the night.

Most of the time the blatant inaccuracy was a cause for mirth. You've got to remember that these are people whose primary employment perk is seeing their name wrapped around fish and chips, as Dad used to say. But Lydia's story is different. All our lives we've had the press snapping at our heels, presenting a warped parallel picture of our existence and tormenting us with requests for interviews and photos. It was an unsaid agreement between us that we never gave in to them.

I sit up angrily. Never mind twenty minutes of lying still. I can't possibly lie still. What was she thinking? I reach for my cell phone.

'What were you thinking, Lydia?' I ask her straight out.

'Ah, the *Globe* interview.' I hear her inhale on a cigarette down the phone line.

'Why, Lydia? Why was it necessary?'

'Because it's cheaper than therapy,' she says assertively.

'But he did love you. He did.'

'Dad loved himself. Not you. Not me. Not anyone.'

'That's not true. Look, I know it wasn't easy for you. I know you got the worst deal, but when he brought you over to LA it must have been because he wanted you to be with him. Why would he have done it otherwise?'

'Because my mother was yelling in his ear probably. Look, you think I haven't thought about all this myself? I've lived my whole life with the knowledge that my father didn't want me around. He didn't want any one of us around. We were just a nuisance to him. Believe me, there's a lot more I could have told the *Globe*, like how he drove my mum insane . . .'

'He didn't send her insane,' I argue. This has always been a contentious point. Things began to fall apart not long after Jodie and Lydia arrived in LA. No one really knows what went wrong. Dad never liked to talk about it. I doubt even Lydia knows. Whoever really understands a marriage, apart from the two people involved? Jodie ended up in a mental hospital for a while and then went back to England after they divorced. I think she's taken care of in a home there.

'Why do you always make excuses for Dad?' Lydia asks. 'You're always making excuses for everyone.'

Am I?

'It's just I don't want you to feel so bad. I'd like to make it better in some way.'

'There's nothing anyone can do. Anyway, I'm over it now. But you wanted to know why I talked to the *Daily Globe*. It's because I was sick of everyone hailing him as the great hero.'

I don't know what to say now. I feel like I don't know Lydia at all. And that makes me sad. Dad being dead makes me sad. The article makes me sad. Jodie's story makes me sad. Why does my family have to be so frickin' dysfunctional? Why can't we just be normal? Suddenly I have an overwhelming urge to cry. I hang up abruptly.

Now I'm standing in a doctor's office without any underwear and crying my eyes out.

'Everything all right?' asks a nurse who has put her head round the door after clearly hearing me blubbing.

'Do I look like I'm all right?' I yell.

I dress and offer apologies. I didn't mean to yell at her.

In the car, I feel an unfamiliar pounding in my chest, which I have every suspicion is my heart. Confrontation is always so ugly. I avoid it usually. I'm surprised at myself for even calling Lydia. But confrontation forces you to think. Dad wasn't perfect, but would he really have wanted to disown Lydia? I thought he loved her. Surely he would have tried to make it up to her? Were we all so dispensable? Was I a nuisance to his career too? Supposing Lydia was right. Perhaps I never knew Dad at all. I feel as if my world has had a seismic shift, and nothing is the same any more.

'Of course your dad loved you,' Adam says, when I pull the car over beneath a palm tree on Santa Monica Boulevard and call him, seeking reassurance. He's busy. I can hear it in his voice.

'No, but did he *really* love us? Lydia says we were all just a nuisance to him.'

'Of course you weren't a nuisance,' he says without even thinking.

'But maybe we were. Maybe—'

'Sweetheart, don't let this upset you. Why don't you go

and buy yourself something at Fred Segal? Take your mind off it.'

'But I need to know.'

'Look, don't get yourself wound up. Can we talk about this later? Only . . .'

Only he's got to go. Of course he's got to go. Adam's always got to go. I say goodbye.

But I don't know what to think, and I need to know what to think. I want to peer into my life and see clarity instead of mud. I call Ashley.

'Was Dad a real jerk?'

'No more than anyone else,' he says calmly.

'Have you seen the article in the *Globe*?'

'Yeah.' Ashley sighs.

'Why did Lydia do that?'

'I don't know.'

'She says Dad didn't love any of us.' Why is this so important to me? I wonder. 'He did, didn't he?'

Ashley pauses. A long pause. This is either because he's a lawyer and lawyers always take long pauses before they answer questions in order to add gravitas. Or it's because he's really thinking about the question. 'It was always hard to tell with him,' he says eventually.

This doesn't answer the question.

'He was a complicated man,' Ashley continues. 'I think he was probably plagued by his own self-doubt a lot of the time. He was ambitious, but also fearful of many things . . .'

'But he did love us, right?'

'Sure,' he says soothingly. But I can't tell if this is because he knows it's what I want to hear. 'Why does it matter so much? He's gone now.'

'It's just I couldn't bear it if he didn't really love us.' I feel a surge of tears again. 'And I miss him, Ash. I really miss him.' Now a torrent is unleashed.

'I know,' says Ashley. 'I miss him too.'

I grip the phone like a comfort blanket, but there's nothing Ashley can say. And after a while, just blubbing down the line seems silly.

At 3.10 p.m. I turn on to Alta Vista, the side street where Thackeray's school is located, and quickly check my make-up in the side mirror. My face looks like a collection of rubber tyres melted together – large red blotches have spread, likewise rivulets of black mascara. I wipe away the disorder and search my bag for some foundation as I'm driving. But what's this? A legion of paparazzi and reporters is waiting outside the school gates. Cameras begin flashing as I pull up.

'Can we get your reaction to your sister's story?' one reporter calls at me.

What? A TV crew moves in front of the hood of my car. Others dash round to the passenger side and peer in. I see one of them reach for the door handle and I press the automatic lock quickly.

'Can you tell us how you feel?' I hear a reporter call.

'Can you spare ten minutes for radio station KCWC?' someone else cries.

The car is swamped and I am panicked. I can't even get my door open. How am I ever going to get Thackeray?

'Please, can you move out of the way?' I shout through the closed window, signalling at them.

They do not budge. I grab my phone and call the school.

'I'm being swarmed by photographers outside your gates,' I tell the director, shouting above the noise outside the car.

'We left messages on your cell to warn you,' she replies.

'Is there a side door I can meet Thackeray at?'

'I'm afraid not. We only have the one entrance.'

'I'm going to have to make a dash for it then,' I tell her. 'Can someone help me at the door?'

'Sure,' she agrees. 'We'll be waiting.'

Nothing for it then. Got to be brave. I unlock the car door, push hard, and force my way out. The camera bulbs flash furiously as I step out.

'Pearl, can you tell us about your relationship with Lydia?'

'Do you have any other secret siblings?'

'Can you tell us how we can get hold of Jodie Sash?'

'Please, please. I just need to collect my son from school. I have nothing to say,' I plead. But they're crowding all around me, so close I can smell their breath. Someone's elbow is pushing against my side, and it's impossible to walk forward because a TV camera is blocking my way. 'Please can you just let me through?' I say more forcefully.

The crowd parts a little, and I take a step forward, but someone's foot is still in the way. Suddenly I'm nose down on the sidewalk, and my knee is hurting. All I can see in front of me are rows of feet, perilously close to my head. Shit. And where's my bag gone? I pull myself up on to my knees, fighting back fear. I see my bag being trampled on the sidewalk. The crowd has moved in closer now. I reach through the legs to grab its handle and cling on. I try to stand up, but it's difficult to breathe now. There's no air, only faces. Only questions. Only cameras. Only microphones. 'Give me some air,' I find myself pleading. I feel faint suddenly. The crowd presses in closer. God, this is scary. The faces are beginning to blur, the sounds to meld. I'm just wondering if I'm going to be trampled to death, and then I hear a familiar voice.

'Get out of the way,' I hear it say angrily. There's a murmur in the crowd.

'Get out of the way,' he shouts again, and all of a

sudden I'm being scooped up and carried through the crowd to the door of the school.

'Isn't that Brett Ellis?' I hear one of the reporters say, and the flashbulbs go into overdrive. 'Isn't that her ex?'

Inside the school, I catch my breath on a sofa in the reception and the school director offers me water and a Band-Aid for the gash on my knee.

'I'm so sorry,' I say to her. I feel responsible for all the fuss at her gates. The other mothers, here to collect their children, study me carefully. I never tell anyone who my dad is. After my teens, I made it my policy not to tell anyone.

'What have you done?' one of them asks me. 'Are you famous?'

'No. I just robbed a bank,' I tell her. This is so embarrassing.

The school director beckons us into the privacy of her office.

'Are you OK?' Brett asks with concern.

'Yes, I'll be fine.' I study the gash. It doesn't look as bad as it feels. 'Never thought I'd be so pleased to see you, though.' I find myself laughing from relief. 'I really wasn't expecting that.'

I introduce Brett to the school director as an old friend, leaving out the fact that he happens to be Thackeray's father, and Thackeray comes charging through the door. 'What happened to your leg?'

'Oh, I just fell over. It's nothing.'

'Oooh, blood,' he says, poring over the wound with fascination. 'Can I touch it?' Then he notices Brett. 'Hey, it's the soccer guy. Have you come to play soccer with me?'

'Maybe,' says Brett, clearly pleased that Thackeray has remembered him. 'Although we've got to figure out a way out of this mess first.' He peers through the blinds at the window. 'What's all the fuss about?' he asks me.

I tell him about Lydia's story in the papers.

'That was helpful of her. I'm sure you needed the press attention like a hole in the head.'

'I could do without it,' I concede.

'What was she thinking?' He sighs sympathetically. 'It'll all blow over, of course. These things usually do. But we need to get you both home safely.' He peers through the window again. 'Have you got a way out of the back?' he asks the school director, taking charge of the situation.

'No, there's only a front entrance. The children's play area is at the back,' she says.

'And beyond the play area?'

'It's surrounded by a wall, and beyond that is the garden belonging to the house on the other side.'

'Would you mind if I take a look?' he asks. She nods, and they both disappear into the play area.

'Why aren't we going home, Mummy?' says Thackeray.

'We are, sweetheart. We're just waiting for Brett.'

'Who's Brett?' He looks confused, and I realise he doesn't even know Brett's name.

'Brett's the soccer guy.' I survey the scene at the front of the school through the blinds. There seem to be more reporters there now. It's going to be a nightmare getting through them. And I know it will alarm Thackeray.

Brett returns with a plan, and I welcome someone else taking charge. It's a nice feeling to be taken care of. My car is to be abandoned at the front for now. The school director will get the janitor to drive it home for me later. Meantime, we are going to climb over the wall at the back, and go through the neighbour's house. The occupants have agreed to help, and they're calling a cab, which should be there in a few minutes.

I remember escapades like this with Dad when I was

little. There was more than one occasion when the only way he could leave a venue was shut in the trunk of his car. But that all seems like a long time ago now.

The wall at the back of the school is nearly twelve feet high, and covered in impenetrable, and spiky, bougainvillea. It towers over me and Thackeray.

'We can't get over that,' I tell Brett. He's out of his mind. 'Who do you think I am, Superwoman?'

'Do you trust me?' he asks with a wry smile on his face.

'Not in a million years,' I say flatly. And then I can't help but laugh.

'This is going to be a piece of cake,' he says, and disappears, returning a few minutes later holding one end of a ladder, while the bemused janitor is carrying the other. The ladder is placed against the wall, a giant canvas sheet is thrown over the top of the bougainvillea to cover the spikes, and from the other side of the wall I hear voices.

'Over here,' says Brett, who is now standing at the top of the ladder. 'Thank you so much for this. It's really super kind of you.'

'Glad to help,' comes a male voice from the other side.

'What are we doing, Mummy?' Thackeray asks.

'Looks like we're playing at army manoeuvres today,' I tell him. 'Going home a new route.'

'Cool,' he marvels excitedly.

'Do you think you can climb over that?' Brett asks Thackeray.

'Of course I can,' he says eagerly.

With Brett shadowing him close behind, Thackeray climbs over the wall, helped down on the other side by the kindly neighbours. I follow, cursing my choice of wardrobe. A short skirt.

'Don't you dare look up,' I tell Brett, who is below me on the ladder.

'Cross my heart,' he assures me with a wicked smile.

'Thank you so much,' I call back to the school's director, and a number of other mums who have gathered to hold the ladder and watch the show.

Finally we're in a cab and heading back to Bel Air, Thackeray on my knee because we haven't got a car seat, and without a single paparazzo in tow. The relief is overwhelming, and we both laugh riotously at the thought of all the paps still sitting out by my car waiting for us.

'I can just imagine their faces when they see the janitor get in my car,' I giggle.

'The victory was ours,' says Brett. 'They'll be sitting there for the rest of the day, scratching their heads.'

Thackeray winds the window down and thrusts his head out to feel the warm breeze. Then it hits me.

'What were you doing there anyway?' I ask Brett. He looks sheepish suddenly. Embarrassed possibly.

'Do you want the honest truth?'

'I should think so.'

'I don't want you to think I'm some weird stalker or anything, but I sometimes come to watch you pick up Thackeray from school. I like seeing him . . .' He pauses. 'And you.'

I feel a shiver of alarm. Weird stalker is right. He just stands there watching us? How dare he? The nerve of it. The sooner we get out of the car, the better. And then I shall call the police. But then I see the look on his face. He's watching Thackeray wave his hands in the breeze. He really seems to be interested.

'I like seeing his happy little face,' he adds. 'I like seeing him skip out of the gates, clutching his paintings and lunchbox. And you look so serene and in control. I think you've become even more beautiful with motherhood.'

Flattery won't get you anywhere, I think to myself.

The cab hugs the curves of Sunset Boulevard and speeds past the Pink Palace, the mansion once owned by Jayne Mansfield, famous for its heart-shaped swimming pool. Its thick green hedges look so pretty against the pink walls.

'Look, there's a good one.' Brett points to the licence plate of the car in front. It reads: 2FKNFST. 'Ten points to me.'

'No way. Eight points,' I tell him, and find myself laughing.

When we were married, we used to play a game when we were driving in the car. There's always a lot of driving in LA. Ten points for a really unusual licence plate, or vanity plate as they're called. Fewer points for less originality. Anyone can have a custom-made licence plate on their car, as long as no one else has got the same combination of letters and numbers. In our hall of fame was IPMS247 (clearly a female driver); L8ASUSL (obviously a male driver); DRTHVDR (*Star Wars* fan); UCOMPNS8 (clearly a lawyer) and BVRPLZR (you can work that one out for yourself).

It was a long-running game of ours. And I confess I still find myself looking for odd licence plates in the traffic even now. But I'm not going to start getting nostalgic now.

'I don't really get it,' I tell him.

'It means "too fucking fast",' he explains.

'Not the licence plate, silly. I mean you. When Thackeray was born, you weren't interested at all. And now?'

'I was an idiot,' he says, poker-faced. He is sitting sideways with his back to the car door so that he faces us. 'I know I can't expect to suddenly walk back into your lives. But . . .'

'Ssh.' I put a finger to my mouth to stop him. This is not right. Not in front of Thackeray.

The car pulls into Stone Canyon Road, with its high
hedges and ironwork gates. I give directions to the cab
driver as we wind through the labyrinth of high-end
properties and manicured garden borders, and then,
ahead of us, I see another crowd of photographers and
reporters outside our own electronic gates. I should have
known they'd be there too. Jesus. Won't they leave us
alone?

'Stop. Turn around. Quickly,' I shout at the cab driver.
'Look, we'll have to drop you off first,' I tell Brett, feeling
flustered. 'I can't have the paps taking pictures of you and
me together, driving into our house. Adam will go crazy.
Where's your car, by the way?' In all the commotion, I'd
forgotten he must have left a car at the school too.

'I rode my bike to the school. It'll still be there in the
morning,' he says calmly. He gives his address to the
driver and the car squeals off in a new direction.

'Mommy, I need the bathroom,' Thackeray whines, as the
cab pulls up outside Brett's apartment.

'Can't you hang on?' I beg. I really, really don't want to
go into Brett's apartment.

'He can use my bathroom,' Brett suggests helpfully.

'No, no. We're fine. Thackeray can wait.'

'I can't wait, Mommy.'

'Yes you can.'

'No I can't. I gotta go.'

'Well you can go on the sidewalk here.'

'But you told me only bums pee on the sidewalk.'

'Come on,' says Brett, laughing. 'Use the bathroom
upstairs. I won't bite, I promise.'

So I sigh and we climb the stairs up to his apartment
on the second floor. This really shouldn't be happening.
Brett fumbles with the lock and I brace myself for what I
might find. I don't want to meet his latest Twinkie and be
forced to admire her taste in home furnishings. I don't

want to see the notches on his bedpost, the pictures of his conquests, the line-up of his women. Do I really have to endure this?

But inside it's sparsely furnished and decidedly lacking any female touch at all. A bare sofa in the middle of the room, a table covered in papers by the window, books stacked up in the corners without a bookcase to keep them in, a couple of guitars on their stands, a TV, an old rug on the hardwood floor, and in the bedroom, which leads off the living room, I can see an unmade bed that doesn't even have a headboard, and clothes strewn on the floor.

It has to be said that the lack of a Twinkie is a great relief. Just the thought of having to make light conversation . . . But the apartment itself is so unlike anything I ever expected, I can't help but be curious. When Brett got the starring role in his third action adventure, he bought himself a house up on Mulholland, a piece of real estate that defied a rational price tag. It was after we'd gone our separate ways, but I remember reading about his collection of cars, his extravagant taste in household furnishings, and how he was a man to relish luxury. There'd been a spread in *Hello!* magazine showing him lounging by his pool. He was Mr Arrogance himself lying there in skin-tight white bathing trunks. Might as well have had a balloon coming from his mouth saying, 'Look what I've got, girls.' I remember tearing out the pages and throwing them at the wall. (OK, so the therapy sessions didn't sort out everything.) But the point was, he was surrounded by wealth. What happened to it all?

Then I notice the photos around the apartment. On the table by the window is our wedding-day photo, framed and prominent. I boxed up my wedding pictures years ago, and threw them into the furthest corner of our attic. This was the last place I was expecting to see one again. I look so happy in the picture, in a Vera Wang dress carefully arranged to hide the bump that became Thackeray. Brett is beaming at the camera, with his arm wrapped around me. We made up our own vows, promising to love each other 'through good times and bad, whether happy or sad'. What a joke that was.

Next to it on the table is a photo of Thackeray, also framed. It's one that has been cut from a magazine. I remember a paparazzo getting in our face last year on the beach when Dad came with us for a picnic. Dad has been cut out of the picture, but Thackeray looks adorable in a sun hat. And on the wall is a framed black-and-white print of Thackeray and me leaving his school. It's been enlarged so you can see the look of concentration on our faces as we march down the street. Brett must have taken it himself with a long lens. How odd that I never even noticed him there.

I stare at them dumbfounded, while Brett shows Thackeray where the bathroom is.

'It's a nice picture, isn't it?' he asks as he returns. I nod, unable to speak. 'Surprised?'

'You could say.'

'I told you I never stopped loving you,' he says gently. 'We were special, you and I. Two halves of the same soul.'

Then how come we're divorced? I want to say. How come you were in bed with Conzuela, how come you didn't come back to me? I feel the urge to shout at him. But clearly not enough, because all I can do is stand there. The movie *Dumb and Dumber* comes to mind, and I seem to be playing both parts. Thackeray wanders back in and demands food.

'Let's see what I've got in the refrigerator. Do you like hot dogs?' says Brett, leading him by the hand.

'Yeah!' Thackeray cries. 'Hot dogs. Hot dogs.'

'Can I give him one?' Brett asks.

'No, we've really got to go,' I tell him. This is so awkward. 'Come on, Thackeray.'

'But I'm hungry,' he whines.

'You can eat at home.'

'Just one hot dog?' he pleads.

'OK, just one. We'll take it with us in the cab.'

They disappear to the kitchen and I hear a microwave whir.

'Can I see what's on TV?' Thackeray asks Brett.

'No,' I call through to the kitchen, just as I hear Brett say, 'Yes.'

'No, really, we can't,' I repeat.

But Thackeray knows all about getting his way. He has already found the remote and is making himself comfortable on the sofa.

'We've really got to go,' I tell Brett, aware that I'm King Canute fighting back the tide. Brett is now pulling a bottle of chilled white wine from the fridge and pouring two glasses.

'Take a minute,' he insists. 'You've had a tough day. Sit down here and relax a few seconds. How's your knee?' He offers me a chair at his table by the window, clearing away the papers. I really shouldn't. Adam would have a meltdown if he knew.

A cool, soothing breeze blows through the window, making the white curtains billow. Outside a tree is bursting with pinky-white blossoms, and the window opens directly into its branches. On the street two dogs are barking at each other, and I see the cab driver lighting a cigarette while he waits for us.

'It feels like you're in a tree house up here,' I say, peering out of the window through the branches.

'That's what I thought. And I've even got a bird's nest,' says Brett. 'Look.' He points to a crevice in the trunk where some twigs have been woven together. 'Can you see, she's there.'

Two black eyes blink back. A tiny bird is watching us cautiously.

'Thackeray, have you seen this bird's nest?'

But he's too engrossed in the TV.

'We'll only stay a minute,' I say to the back of Thackeray's head, and take a big gulp of wine. It's icy cold and instantly calming. Brett pulls up a chair next to me.

'Thanks,' I say. 'I could use this. Sometimes I don't feel like myself any more. Ever since Dad died . . .'

'You've felt lost?'

'Yes.' Brett always did have an uncanny way of knowing what I was thinking.

'But your dad adored you. You know that, don't you?'

How does he know that's just what I want to hear?

'Did he really? Lydia doesn't seem to think so.'

'If you start doubting him, you'll drive yourself insane.' Brett looks at me, his eyes intense and loving, like they always used to be.

'But why is Lydia saying he never loved her? That can't be true, can it? You knew him.'

'Maybe it took him a little while to realise what he was missing out on.' Brett smiles, and the significance of the comment is not lost on me. 'Look, I can tell you that when you and I decided to get married, he made me aware in no uncertain terms how much he loved you.'

'He did?'

'Yeah.' Brett laughs uneasily. 'He took me aside and told me that if I broke your heart, he'd break my balls.'

We both laugh. Dad was always well intentioned.

'So tell me about him.'

'About Dad?'

'Yeah, tell me all the stories. Tell me everything you remember about him.'

'You really want to hear?'

'Of course.'

And strangely, I realise, that's exactly what I've been longing to do these last few weeks. I've just wanted to talk about Dad. I want to relive my stories about him and wallow in the memories. I want to bore someone endlessly about him. I want to talk about how he sat up all night with me as I came down off my first taste of acid, how he gave me a job as a tour assistant one summer when I had nothing else to do, how proud he was of my name tattooed on his arm.

'Does this sound like a dad who didn't love his daughter?' Brett asks eventually.

But I'm not done talking yet. It's like my mouth is on a race track and nothing is going to stop it. The stories keep coming – how Dad wanted me to be *his* bridesmaid when he married Kimberly (yes, unusual I know, but Dad liked to make up the rules to everything as he went along), how he knitted my dolly a sweater when he got measles, how he cried when he watched *Gone With the Wind* with me.

I drone on, but still there's more. It's like there's been a verbal blockage for the last month, and now it's all come spilling out. What am I to do about Heather, who's selling Dad's train set? Why has she turned so mean? Now I feel I can't go up to the house any more . . . and . . . and . . . and . . . I go on for some time.

Brett listens. To all of it. So intently, we're both surprised when the cab driver comes to the door and asks if we've forgotten about him. And we both laugh, because we have. 'We'll call another cab later,' Brett says, pulling a fifty-dollar note from his pocket for the driver and pointing at the sofa, where Thackeray has fallen asleep. All the excitement must have worn him out.

Brett fetches another bottle of wine from the fridge. God, have we drunk that first one already? Brett always was easy to talk to. I'd sort of forgotten, I suppose. And it feels so pleasant sitting here and talking. The gentle breeze, the cool wine, the rhythm of Thackeray's snoring. I feel like a coil that has released its tension suddenly.

'But I've done nothing but talk about me. Me. Me. Me.'

Brett laughs. It was a little joke we used to have about people who only ever talk about themselves. There's a lot of them in LA. 'Let's talk about me, me, me,' we'd say, impersonating culprits we knew.

'Not much to say about me, me, me,' he says, smiling.

'But why are you living here? What happened to your house?'

'I sold it,' he says carelessly. 'I didn't need it. It was too big for one person to rattle around in.'

'And what about Conzuela?' I ask cheekily, and suddenly I realise there's flirtation in my voice. Perhaps seeing the pictures of me around his apartment, and him living so humbly, has made feel safe. I realise the anger has gone.

'She was nothing. She never was. I was deluded.' He stares into his wine glass. 'Look, this is hard to explain, but something happened to me when I hit the big time. I got lost. You know the feeling?' He looks up at me, and I smile. 'I was overwhelmed by who I thought I was. I was this big-shot movie star who could do what he wanted, fuck who he wanted, behave how he wanted. I was hideous. I know I was.' He runs his hands through his dark hair and stares out of the window. 'It was like the normal rules of life no longer applied to me. My mum and dad tried to tell me. Do you remember they never made it to our wedding?'

I nod gravely. I remember how upset I was.

'I couldn't tell you, but we'd had a big row. They told me I wasn't anyone they recognised any more. Told me I needed to start behaving like an adult. I didn't listen to them.' He takes a sip of wine and a siren wails in the distance. 'I didn't listen to anyone.'

He pauses, and the siren gets closer. 'The worst thing that ever happened to me was winning that Golden Globe.'

I can't believe I'm hearing this. Short of an Oscar, it was all he ever wanted.

'It's true,' he says, seeing the shock on my face. 'Once you get an award, the job offers come in like an avalanche; that pushes up your fee higher than anything anyone could call reasonable. And all of a sudden you've got to live up to it all. I was in a state of paranoia, my whole worth as a human being judged by other people.'

He pauses again, and looks into his hands, watching his fingers lock and unlock. 'First of all everyone tells you how great you are. Managers, publicists, producers, directors, fans.' He pauses. 'Even Stephen. It's like there's a whole set of machinery designed specifically to tell you how fabulous you are, and after a while you start to believe it. After a while you think you're fucking God Almighty.' Anger has crept into his voice now. 'I was an arrogant fool, I know I was . . . And then you've got all the girls throwing themselves at you. You know there were others before Conzuela, don't you?'

I feel a stab, but say nothing. I suppose I knew. I just always hoped it wasn't true.

'There's no point in lying to you,' Brett continues. 'They didn't mean anything. But I couldn't stop myself. It was all part of this crazy, crazy world. I even forced myself on your friend Bella. Did she ever tell you?'

I nod again. We were at a party up in the hills. It was really crowded and I lost both Brett and Bella. Adam told me later he'd seen Brett try it on with Bella, and come off the worse. I'd always put it down to Brett having too much to drink that night.

'I was out of control. And I'm so ashamed now. Really ashamed. I became something I wasn't. You knew me before. I wasn't like that, was I?' His eyes implore me to concede that he wasn't, but I say nothing.

'All the time, the stardom machine carries on turning the thumbscrews,' he continues. 'The more famous you are, the more pressure they apply. The work schedule becomes hideous, the burden to perform gets heavier . . . the reviews, the scripts, deadlines, night shoots, day shoots, four a.m. wake-up calls . . .' He sounds exasperated. 'Suddenly you've got three attorneys, ten cars and a domestic staff that rivals the White House. I couldn't sleep for the pressure. Months went by without a single night's sleep.' He takes another sip of wine, and I notice his hands are trembling.

'Before I knew it, I was taking sleeping pills. I didn't mean to take an overdose, but the more sleeping pills you use, the more you need, and one night I forgot how many I'd taken. It was really that stupid. Next thing I know, I'm in hospital after a stomach-pumping. Luckily my assistant found me in time.'

He stares out into the blossoms of the tree and I see the pain etched into his face. Stillness hangs in the air, and without any conscious thought from me, my hand travels the distance between the two of us, into his. He grasps it tight, and clings on. God, how did that happen? Now I'm holding hands with him.

'Lying there in that bed, I realised what I'd become. I didn't have a real friend in the world, because I didn't deserve any. The only real friend I'd ever had was you, and look how I treated you.'

He looks down at my hand in his, and I can see that he means it. What a mess. There was always a part of me that wondered if I should have waited longer for him to come back to me. I should have. I really should have.

Outside the sun is setting, turning the sky into an ice-cream sundae swirl of pink and purple. People are coming home from work, marching briskly along the sidewalk. I wonder who they are walking home to. Does everyone else screw up their lives like this? Other people always look as if they have their lives in order, but no one really escapes their own dramas. Everyone has them.

Eventually Brett releases my hand and rubs his eyes, as if to summon a brighter outlook. 'So anyway, now I've made some changes,' he says brightly, and pours out the last of the second wine bottle. 'I sold my house. I never liked being on my own up there anyway. Got rid of the cars. Life is much simpler now, and I like it.' He pauses. 'All that excess, it was absurd. I didn't need the Persian carpets, the Rolex watches . . . you know I had fifty of them. Fifty!' He lets out a laugh. 'Fifty watches. I've only got one wrist. It was excessive beyond decency. The important things in life are people. People are what really matter, and if I don't do another movie again, I won't care.'

'Really?' It's almost impossible to believe. Brett worked so hard to get to the point where he could take the pick of the best roles in Hollywood.

'Really,' he says flatly. 'I know I've been a terrible father, and I know it's not as simple as just walking back into someone's life, but I want to make it up to Thackeray. I'm just blown away by him.'

We both look across at Thackeray, who's rolled on to his back with one leg hanging off the side of the sofa, as if he's just hurled himself at sleep.

'The point is, I want to win you back,' Brett says in a softer voice, and turns his gaze back to me. His eyes always were so inviting. He strokes my arm and I feel the hairs along it rise in anticipation. It's as if the movement itself is electrically charged, sending powerful messages to my brain that shouldn't be there. 'Kiss him,' tempt the electrical currents.

'But that's impossible,' I tell Brett and look away. 'I must go. Can you call another cab?' I stand up, and find my head spinning momentarily. Have I really drunk that much? Or is it Brett himself that has me reeling?

'Have I offended you?' he asks, leaping to his feet.

'No, but I can't do this,' I tell him.

'Of course not,' he says softly. 'I understand.'

'I'm married to Adam now. I can't come back to you. It wouldn't be fair.'

'I know,' Brett says gently. 'I'm sorry. I shouldn't have said anything.'

'No, you shouldn't,' I tell him, with irritation in my voice. But then he places one hand on my shoulder, and touches my cheek with his other, and I don't resist. A smarter woman would leave now, but for some reason I'm still standing there. I feel the warmth of his hand, the smoothness of his touch, the margins of desire.

'I'd forgotten how beautiful you are,' he marvels. 'Good, kind, honest, I knew all of those qualities. You always were a beacon. But you take my breath away.'

I stare into his face, feet frozen to the floor. He has the same expression he did on our wedding day – doting, solicitous, real. I really must leave. It's just a question of putting one foot in front of the other in the direction of the door. That's not so difficult, surely? But now he's cradling my cheeks in his hands and my heart is lurching in a way that it hasn't in years. Time to go, I tell myself. Just move those feet towards the door. But now he brushes a kiss against my neck, and I catch my breath. This can't happen. It really can't. All that time between us. It's been too long. 'Do you think I stand a chance?' he whispers.

'No,' I say feebly. But somehow my arms are wrapping themselves around his neck. Don't do it, I tell myself. But now I'm leaning into him, and something about it feels right. The drama of the day has disappeared, the emotion of losing Dad has gone, the confusion of life. Here, in Brett's arms, it feels as if the past never happened.

'I love you. I always have,' he says, kissing me forcefully, and I surrender to the feeling, encountering the blistering depths of passion and desire head on. A hand finds my breast and lingers there, sending me to an unworldly place. Then another is underneath my skirt, but all the time a voice inside my head yells, 'You must stop. You must stop. YOU MUST STOP.'

'This isn't right,' I say eventually and pull away. I almost make it to the door too. But Brett has my hand still.

'Come with me.' He beckons. 'It's private in here.' He leads me to the bedroom.

'Brett, I can't have sex with you,' I tell him. But we both know I don't mean it.

22

The first time I ever met Brett, he was yelling at another woman. It was right outside Yogatopia in Brentwood. I'd just finished a yoga class and was walking out to my car, parked on the street, with my yoga mat and water bottle in hand. I noticed this guy shouting at a girl on the sidewalk. He was a tall guy and quite good looking, but he was yelling.

'Don't you even realise what you've done?' he shouted at the top of his voice to the Twinkie, his arms waving with anger. 'You've fucking ruined everything, you heartless bitch.'

I'd have walked on and ignored the scene, but I caught sight of the girl's face out of the corner of my eye as I walked past, and she was cowering with fear.

'Don't hit me,' she pleaded, and I could see that the guy might. There was a ferociousness about him and his arms were all over the place.

In my mind there was nothing for it. It's what anyone would have done. 'If you lay a finger on her, I'm calling the police,' I told him boldly. It did the trick. The guy stopped in his tracks and turned round instantly in surprise. So much in surprise that one of his hands caught my water bottle and sent it flying to the sidewalk. Oh God, he's going to hit me now, I thought.

But his face was calmer. 'It's OK, that won't be

206

necessary. You don't understand,' he said.

'I understand completely,' I told him sternly. 'You can't hit women. You need to learn to control your anger. And cursing in the street too. It's not right.'

I was about to carry on, but then I noticed he was smiling. The Twinkie was smiling too.

'We were just acting,' he said. 'You know, practising our lines.' He pointed to a sign on the building next to Yogatopia. The Jack Mandell Acting School. Nightly Evening Classes. 'They send us out of the classroom to practise on the street . . . But look, I'm really sorry about your water. Can I buy you another?' I was lost for words. I felt so foolish. Of course it was an acting school. And I could see there were other couples on the street rehearsing the same lines too. It was so stupid of me. 'There's a coffee shop across the street. Let me buy you another,' he said.

'No, no. It's fine,' I replied, but he was insistent.

'Purleese,' he pleaded. 'It will be on my conscience all evening if I don't.' I could see he was the kind of man who knew how to persuade. His eyes were wide with enthusiasm and sensitivity. And there was something immediately likeable about him. So I agreed.

'That was a brave thing you did there,' he said as we crossed the street. He really was quite good looking. 'Are you always in the habit of tackling villains?'

'It's a dangerous job, but someone's got to do it,' I said, and he laughed, the kind of laugh that would make anyone who heard it want to be in on the joke too.

There was a poetry reading taking place in the coffee shop, and we both found ourselves drawn into it while we were waiting in the line to be served. A British guy who called himself Belowsky was reading his poem about falling through a Cheerio and surfing on a piece of frosty flake cereal. He was funny and we both laughed.

'He's good,' said the guy, while the audience applauded. 'I love poetry.'

'Me too,' I said.

He looked closely at my face, as if scrutinising my features. 'You wouldn't like to have a coffee and stay to hear some more, would you?'

I wasn't in the habit of going for coffee with guys I'd literally just met on the street. But there was something about him that I really liked. Not just his looks, although they really stood out. But he had a confidence about him, a self-assurance that made me feel safe. Besides, it was only a coffee – and the poet was on to his next poem.

'What about your class?' I whispered.

'It can keep,' he said dismissively, buying two cappuccinos, as well as a bottle of water.

'Come on, let's sit over here.' He guided us to a table. 'Besides, I'll probably learn more here than at acting school. Brett Ellis, by the way. Out-of-work actor. Will work for food.'

He smiled broadly with a mouth that looked too big for his face, and offered me a big hand to shake.

'Pearl Java,' I said, taking it. It was the first name that came into my head. A bit obvious, since it was written down the side of the coffee cup, but he didn't notice.

We were six months into our relationship before I ever told him my real last name. Brett was the first man who I was sure loved me for me.

23

The dictionary defines guilt as a feeling of culpability or remorse for some offence, crime or wrongdoing. It's that part of the human conscience that brings us before the judge inside our heads and convicts us for being so, so bad. I just wish the judge inside my head would pronounce execution and then I could be put out of my misery. Guilty? I'm beside myself.

But guilt is more than just an internal judge; there's the nagging jury too, who won't give me a night's sleep, and who have me looking anywhere to confess, anywhere that might provide forgiveness, a pat on the back, a hug to tell me I wasn't that bad, not really. But I was that bad, and there's no getting round it. If I was Catholic, like my mother, it would be so easy. What a marvellous service the confessional is. A few Hail Marys and all is forgiven. Buddhists chant sutra verses and bow before a Buddha image to seek repentance, but they also have to apologise to the person they have wronged, and I can't bring myself to do that. That would require a confession to Adam first, and that would hurt him too much.

How did Thackeray and I make it home after that evening with Brett? I don't even know. I've paced the house. I've prowled the garden. I've counted sheep right through the night until the alarm shrills its 6.40 a.m. wake-up call. I've gone through the motions of daily life

– as much as is possible with a horde of reporters in tow – but my every sense is numbed with shock, every thought consumed and every breath troubled. Adam never deserved this. How could I have done such a thing to him? I am despicable, treacherous, dishonest. And I'm going as crazy as Britney Spears.

So after two days, I take myself after work to the therapist, a place I thought I'd moved on from. There is nothing else for it. 'I'm an evil person. I can't bear myself,' I tell Dr Zolensky, with tears brimming in my eyes. 'I never wanted to hurt Adam. He's been so kind to me. How could I have been so cruel and deceitful?' Dr Zolensky offers me the tissue box, and writes pencil notes on a pad of paper. 'I was unfaithful. I can't believe I was unfaithful. Me. I'm not the unfaithful sort. It's just not who I am. I want to forget all about it, but I can't. I feel so bad.'

Dr Zolensky is a kind man. You can see it in his eyes. He never judges; sometimes he asks questions, but mostly he listens in a giant leather chair, grasping his beard in his hand, with his bald head cocked to one side. His office is in Beverly Hills, and is lined wall to wall with books. After Brett left me, I was here every week, and I never thought it would be possible to get any more books in, but I notice that several more piles have been stacked up in the corners since then.

'Do you still love him?' Zolensky asks.

'Who, Brett or Adam?'

'You tell me,' he says casually.

'I love Adam, my husband. I have to love my husband.'

'You have to?'

'Well, I am married to him. Of course I have to love him.'

'I see,' says Zolensky, running the end of his pencil through the bristles of his beard. Outside there's the whoosh of sprinklers turning on to water the grass verge at the front of his office. 'And what do you think was the impetus that made you have sex with your ex-husband?'

'I don't know,' I sigh. 'I've asked myself the same question a million times. I was emotional. There was Dad's death. The funeral. Lydia's article.'

'Lydia's article?'

I explain its significance in a day, a month, a life that seems to be spiralling out of control.

'Tell me about events leading up to your meeting with Brett,' he says, and so I begin with the article, the thought that Dad didn't love us, the tears, the paparazzi, Brett's calm apartment . . .

'I think I just got swept away with it all. It was such a mistake,' I finish.

'I see,' says the doctor again. I remember now that he always said 'I see' rather a lot. 'And how is the sex with your husband?'

'Is that even relevant?' I bristle. I don't like talking about sex very much.

'According to Sigmund Freud, sexual satisfaction leads to emotional contentment,' he says earnestly.

'Look, I was perfectly happy with Adam before Brett showed up. In fact, I thought I'd found my happy-ever-after, my own Hollywood ending,' I carry on. 'After everything I went through with Brett, I thought Adam was the answer to my prayers.'

I look across at Zolensky, who is as contemplative as ever. I know he can't magically make it all better, but perhaps he has an insight. He coughs, and takes a sip of water from a glass on a side table. The sprinkers stop outside the window, and the distant rumble of traffic resumes. 'Ultimately, Hollywood endings have a lot to answer for,' he says calmly. 'Ever since the Greeks, narrative structure has required an ending. Novels and movies all build to a certain place, there's a climax and then a denouement where everything gets tidily wrapped up. Life, unfortunately, doesn't work that way. Life isn't so structured and organised, and there's never the pay-off scene. Life is messy and ragged and confusing.'

'My life certainly is,' I can't resist saying.

He coughs again and looks sternly at me. 'The big problem for people living in Hollywood, and I see it all the time, is they really do think that there are Hollywood endings out there for them. You're not alone, Pearl. You wouldn't believe the number of producers and directors I get in here trying to live up to the same ideals that they put into their movies. It's a real problem for people who live here. They're all caught up in it, and they all fall into the same trap. You need to watch out for the Hollywood-endings trap, because life's not like that. But let's see if we can find some real-life clarity to your situation. Let me ask you about your husband. What was it that attracted you to him in the first place?'

'How do you mean?'

'Was it his looks, his sense of humour, his intellect, his demeanour?'

'Well . . .' I think hard. I want to be truthful. I mean, Adam is clever, but that wasn't it. And he's OK looking, but that wasn't it either. 'He's kind . . . and he was reliable.'

'I see,' says Zolensky.

'You see, we'd known each other for ages, and we were old friends. And I was on my own with Thackeray.'

'I see,' says Zolensky. 'So it was a convenient relationship?'

'I wouldn't like to call it that. You make it sound premeditated.'

'Was it?'

'No. I loved Adam.'

'And what about Brett?'

'Brett was a cheat,' I say, hoping to hear the old anger

in my voice return, but the words come out without the venom they used to. Being angry with Brett, I realise, somehow kept me sane. Without that fury, I feel I've lost an anchor.

'Yes, yes, we've established that,' says Zolensky. 'But before he was a cheat, what was it that attracted you to him?'

'Well, that was different,' I say, and suddenly I'm transported back to the poetry reading just after I met him. 'I don't suppose you'd let me take your number?' Brett asked. 'Only I don't meet too many women who appreciate a good stanza.'

'Or good rhythm either, I suppose?' I said flirtatiously, and he laughed.

He took me to a restaurant on Melrose on our first date. It had a shady patio area at the back and crayons set out on the tables so that customers could doodle on the paper tablecloths.

'See, we've got something in common,' he said, absent-mindedly drawing a picture of an elephant.

'What? We're both bad at drawing?' I teased. It was an awful drawing.

'No. We're both romantics.'

'How d'you figure?'

'Well, you like poetry.'

'That doesn't make me a romantic. I could be the most hard-bitten cynic you ever met.'

'Yeah, but you probably wouldn't be carrying a copy of *Love and Redemption* if you were.'

He pointed at my bag on the floor and we both laughed.

'And what makes you think you're a romantic?'

'You'll just have to wait to find out,' he said, with his wide, heart-melting smile. I knew even then that I was in love with him.

'It was like a seductive force that just drew us

together,' I explain to Zolensky. 'There wasn't a single component. He was handsome, yes, and he made me laugh, and he was romantic and fun to be with, and we got on together, but none of those things alone drew me to him. There was a chemistry that I don't even know how to put into words. Soulmates sounds so corny ... but I never understood what that meant until I met Brett.'

Zolensky says nothing. That's what therapists largely do. They ask you questions, and by answering them you're supposed to solve your own problem.

'Would you consider going back to Brett?' he asks eventually.

'No, I couldn't. I couldn't do that to Adam. It would break his heart. Besides ...' I pause, because there's a nagging feeling I realise I'm too terrified to even voice.

'Besides?'

'Besides, I'm scared it was all just a ploy. A cheap trick Brett set up to see if he could have me.'

'What makes you think that?'

'I think he just wanted to see if he could still have sex with me. Men play those kinds of games. Could it have all been just a calculated ploy?'

'You're feeling insecure because this is new terrain,' says Zolensky. 'And you're distrustful of him because of what he's done before, but that doesn't mean he's being dishonest now.'

'Yes, but maybe I'm the biggest joke in Hollywood. And Brett's just had the last laugh.'

The clock on the wall informs me I've been here over an hour. 'Look, it seems to me that you have three choices,' says Zolensky. 'One.' He holds up his index finger and smiles sympathetically. 'You tell your husband all that has passed, you get some therapy, and work on making it a better marriage. This is a strong possibility. Two.' He holds up another finger. 'You don't tell him, and learn to live with the secret. Others have done it before you. Or three. You consider a new life with your ex.'

I stare dumbfounded at him. I mean, it's obvious those are my choices, but only three! Couldn't there be some more we've overlooked? Isn't there some miraculous course of action that might reverse time? Or how about a remedy to at least quieten this turmoil inside my head?

'Sometimes things happen for a reason,' Zolensky says quietly. 'Maybe you should be asking yourself why.'

I'm asking myself why I'm even paying you, is what I want to say. I mean, what am I even doing here? It's not like you've helped. Stupid old man, with your sanctimonious options and scratchy beard. I mean, what is this? A game show? Ooh, let me see, which option shall I pick? Oh yes, let me pick option two. A lifetime of keeping secrets from my husband. Simple.

I don't wish Zolensky goodbye because I'm too angry. With him. With myself. With frickin' everyone.

Keeping secrets is an art. Unfortunately I'm not sure I have it down. At every turn, I feel I am about to be found out. The following day we're invited to Frank Golding's mansion in the hills. Frank is a big-time producer who likes Adam's work and is promising to put up the money to make one of his screenplays. Thackeray, contrary to his wishes, has to stay at home with a babysitter.

The party is on a terrace overlooking a swimming pool and skyline view. It's a gloriously clear late afternoon, and the little island of Catalina is visible beyond the Santa Monica Bay – a small lump of land in a deep blue horizon. A collection of people have gathered under a muslin awning that is shading the bar from the last of the day's rays. I recognise a couple of faces as they sip martinis – actresses and directors mostly.

It's an impressive house that has the feel of an extravagant Tuscan villa, lavishly decorated with exceptional taste – marble flooring, Italian furniture, gilt picture frames, and statues everywhere. 'Honey, isn't this beautiful?' Adam marvels as we arrive.

'Welcome to my humble home,' Frank greets us, and I smile. It's anything but humble. And I can't help but remember what Brett said about Hollywood excess. Because here it all is. Millions and millions of dollars of it – Byzantine statues, Bijar rugs, Renaissance art – and that's alongside the kitchen designed by Porsche, the infrared barbecue, the robotic faucet, the Sony theatre, the helium-filled floating fruit bowl. Brett was right, of course. There is no excuse for excess like this.

'We loved the script,' Frank says breezily. He's a slim man, grey-haired, but tanned and wearing a linen suit. 'Of course, we'll have a proper meeting, but I'd like to know who's your ideal for the female lead.'

Adam stammers and stutters as they discuss the possibilities. And I smile politely as a good wife is supposed to do, barely even listening. A waiter offers a plate of canapés. I take one and realise that I haven't eaten for days now. But then my ears prick up.

'We'd like Brett Ellis for the male lead,' Frank says bullishly. I catch the look of horror on Adam's face. 'Be good to see him in a different kind of role to the ones we usually see him in, and the girls love him, don't they?' Frank looks across at me for support, and suddenly I find there's colour rising up my neck, in my cheeks. Even my ears feel hot. I haven't blushed in years.

'I don't think he wants to do any movies at the moment,' I say, grasping for anything that might divert attention from the colour I fear my face is becoming.

'Really?' says Frank, genuinely surprised. He looks momentarily confused, but then his face breaks into a smile. 'Of course, you were married to him. I'd forgotten. So you must be in contact.'

'I think Pearl sees him all the time,' Adam says caustically. His eyes squint in fury.

'No I don't,' I say. 'I just work for his agent.'

'Ah,' says Frank. 'You'll be able to pull some strings for us then.'

'I can try.'

Overwhelmed and flustered, I make some excuse to escape to the bar, but later, we row all the way home. I've already told Adam that I met Brett at Thackeray's school that day. I had to tell him. There were reporters ready to spread the word faster than you can say 'internet'. I told him the whole story, without its ending of course, and he said he appreciated my honesty, which made me flinch. But he wasn't happy about it, particularly at the thought of Brett standing around outside Thackeray's school like a stalker. He wanted to contact the LAPD and take out a restraining order against him. I managed to talk him out of it, because hadn't Brett helped us? But it wasn't easy.

'How come B-B-B-B-Brett Ellis's name comes up in almost every conversation now?' he demands derisively, as we drive home along Mulholland, catching glimpses of the sprawling neighbourhoods of the Valley between the trees. The views from up here are always so impressive, and LA is so much prettier by night, with all the little lights twinkling, but Adam is not letting me enjoy them. 'That was embarrassing. H-h-h-humiliating.'

'But it wasn't my fault,' I say, trying to sound calm.

'And how come you know he doesn't want to do movies?'

'It's what he told Stephen. I was there in the meeting, remember? I told you I was.'

If Adam was a bull, he'd be pawing the ground, getting ready to charge.

'Look, let's just forget about it,' I suggest, and fix my eyes outside the car window.

'No, I won't forget about it. How can I forget about it? How can I ever f-f-f-forget about f-f-f-f'king Brett Ellis when every time I look up, he's there?'

Like a torrent that won't stop, Adam carries on raging about Brett all the way home. On and on, as we drive down the twists and turns of Coldwater Canyon, past its eucalyptus trees and oleander borders, on and on along the curves of Sunset with its tall hedges, on and on to Bel Air. Is it possible to smell infidelity on your wife's breath? I wonder. Can he see it in my pores, perhaps? 'Why are you so insecure about him?' I ask.

Adam doesn't speak and a rumbling schism opens between us.

'Because I think you've always loved him more than me,' he says eventually, as he stops our car in the driveway. The taut look of anger has disappeared from his face, replaced with what? An air of resignation, perhaps. He looks sad, and I can't bear that I've made him feel this way.

'I love you,' I tell him, wrapping my arms around his neck. 'This isn't necessary.'

He stares into his hands. 'I always feel I have the sword of Damocles hanging over me,' he says with a long sigh.

'Meaning?' Adam is so literary, I don't always know what he's talking about.

'It was a Greek legend. Dionysius hangs a sword over Damocles' head by a horsehair to show that there can be nothing happy for the person over whom some fear always looms.'

'But you have nothing to fear,' I tell Adam, and feel the spasm of guilt. 'I love *you*,' I tell him again. And I do really mean it. Adam's been such a good husband to me. I must exorcise Brett from my life completely. I must. It's the only way.

24

Valentine's Day begins as it always does in our house. In bed. Adam presents the White Chocolate Gift Box from Godiva, and the floral card that reads 'For the girl I will always love' and Thackeray bounces in to deliver a heart-shaped picture frame for us both that he's made in school. I give both of them books, a beautiful pop-up children's book for Thackeray, and Shakespeare's love sonnets for Adam, in which I've inscribed my own promises of undying love to him. My mission, I've decided, is to make Adam feel more loved. I need to show him it more. He needs to feel utterly, utterly loved and secure. It has been a week since the day I slept with Brett. A day that I have erased from my memory. It was a day that never even existed. I've forgotten it already. What was it we were talking about?

Ah, yes. Valentine's Day. Usually I love Valentine's Day. It's the idea of a day devoted to sweethearts and the celebration of love, the excuse to bestow gifts, and the fun of romance. In the early days, Brett would leave a trail of secret clues – internet messages, floral deliveries, balloon bouquets – all leading to an evening rendezvous. But we're not thinking about Brett. Heavens no. Today there's a meeting with lawyers about Dad's will, and I'm not especially looking forward to it, not least because Heather will be there. I haven't heard anything from her since the funeral, and I've been heartily pleased about that. Hopefully there won't be any great dramas today, but it's so awful to think of all Dad's worldly goods being divided up, and it's yet another reminder of the permanence of his departure. I don't think I shall ever get used to him not being around any more.

The offices of Bernstein, Gottlieb and Crutcher are on Canon Drive in Beverly Hills, sandwiched between an upmarket shoe shop and a restaurant with tables on the sidewalk. There's a brass sign on the brickwork outside the door and a fountain in the foyer. I find a parking meter right outside and thank the parking meter gods because I thought I was going to be late. I had to put in half a morning's work at Stephen's first – he only begrudgingly gave me the rest of the day off. Ashley arrives at the same time and we hug in the foyer.

'This shouldn't take too long, should it?' I ask him. Being a lawyer, he knows these kinds of things.

'Shouldn't think so. It's just a formality,' he says.

'Good, because I've promised I'll meet Lizzie and Bella for lunch later.'

'How are you coping?' he asks gently, as we're shown into Alexander Bernstein's office on the first floor. Ashley's not the most emotionally communicative person, but he's always been a protective older brother.

'All right, I suppose,' I say. 'Better than before. Sorry about bawling down the phone.'

'No worries.' He smiles.

'How about you?'

'I'm OK.' It's the most I'll get out of him probably.

Bernstein's office is an oak-panelled room with a thick, plush carpet and windows draped with dark blue velvet curtains. There's a big desk, several leather chairs arranged opposite, and all of it quite empty. I take a peek out of the window, and look down on to the restaurant below. A waitress is serving salads and white wine to a couple who are arguing with each other. I wonder what other couples argue about. Perhaps one of them is being unfaithful. Bound to be the guy. It's usually men who are unfaithful.

Heather disturbs my musings as she is shown into the office. She's wearing pastel pink sweatpants and a white T-shirt that look absurdly out of place in a lawyer's office. The first signs of the pregnancy are beginning to show. 'Hiya,' she says cheerfully, as if we're off on a picnic somewhere. Ashley and I smile politely and she manoeuvres herself into one of the leather chairs. Alexander Bernstein follows her in, introducing himself and shaking each of us by the hand.

'And will we see Miss Lydia Sash today?' he asks, settling himself behind the desk. He's a middle-aged guy, with close-cropped sandy hair, a short-sleeved shirt and an air of professional disinterest. Somehow I thought he'd be older. Ashley tells him that Lydia didn't want to fly back from New York again.

'Very good,' he says calmly. 'We will keep her informed. Then shall we begin?'

He opens a manila file on his desk.

'The reality is, there is no legal requirement for an official reading of a will after the death of the testator,' Bernstein explains. 'The only legal requirement is that the will must be filed with the county clerk's office in the county where the deceased lived. You can all have a copy of the will right here.' He gets up, walks importantly round his desk and personally hands us each a copy. His leather shoes are shiny and polished, like his face.

'But we need to have this gathering because the probate arrangements of the deceased are not straight-forward.' He returns to his seat and knits the fingers of each hand together, placing them carefully on the desk. 'You will see that the deceased intended to divide his estate between you all. Mrs Heather Sash and her dependents are to inherit the house here in California. There is also an income from a life insurance policy for her. The deceased's other properties, namely the house in England and an apartment in New York, are to be sold, and the proceeds, together with all other investments, royalty payments and incomes arising, are to be divided equally between Miss Lydia Sash, Mr Ashley Sash, Miss Pearl Sash and Master Casey Sash.' I heave a small sigh of relief. I always knew Dad was fair. A small part of me was worried that after the big row with Lydia he might have forgotten about her. Judging from her absence today, I suspect she thought the same. But I always knew he cared about her. I just always knew.

'There is, however, a problem.' Bernstein coughs importantly. A motorbike roars on the street outside his window. 'Unfortunately, the deceased's tax affairs are not in order. The Internal Revenue Service have a claim against him that I'm afraid is going to take a lot of sorting out.' Heather smiles benignly, but Ashley's face creases into concern. 'Not only that,' Bernstein continues, 'but there is a claim against the deceased's estate from Deaf Records, who advanced him monies against future royalties. There are other creditors too, who are listed on the back of the sheet I have handed to you.'

We all turn over the page in front of us, but I can't make sense of any of the figures. They seem to run into millions.

'How much money did he owe?' Ashley asks, summoning a businesslike voice. He knows this can't be too big a problem. Dad was wealthy. Surely it's just a question of paying off the debts and dividing up the rest.

'I'm afraid it's hard to make even a conservative estimate at this stage,' Bernstein replies, rubbing his chin. 'The IRS had been chasing him for years. It could run to millions and millions.'

'Does that mean he was broke?' Heather asks, the cheery veneer now disappearing from her face as the penny slowly drops.

'It means that the persons inheriting the assets will be personally liable to the creditors, the IRS and the state,' Bernstein says.

'What, we have to pay his debts?' she shrieks.

'I'm afraid so.'

'Oh my God.' She lets out a wail of despair.

'I'm afraid it means that if there is not enough money generated from the sale of the other properties, then the house in California will have to be sold too.' Heather gasps. 'We are working with the IRS—'

'But this can't be right,' Heather interrupts. She is now on her feet and pacing up and down the office. 'He was rich. He sold millions of records.'

'Surely the publishing royalties alone should cover some of this?' Ashley joins in. 'They must still be generating income.'

'You are forgetting that your father's biggest hits were not songs he wrote himself. If he had, it would have been a different story.'

'But the artist's royalties?'

'Have you ever looked at the early recording contract your father signed?' Bernstein asks. Ashley shakes his head. 'I fear his manager at the time was not a good one. It was a terrible deal he let him sign. And the manager himself took an absurd percentage. He'd never have got away with it today. Your father's split was a fraction of the record company's. Subsequent contracts were in his favour, but by then he'd had his best hits.'

'So are you telling us there's no inheritance?' I say, making sure I've completely understood.

'I'm afraid not. At least, not at the moment,' says Bernstein, just a tad too cheerfully for my liking. 'We will, of course, be working to salvage what we can. That is . . .'

He coughs. 'That is, if you would like us to stay on as your attorneys. We do, of course, need you to sign a letter of instruction, because we will need to be paid.'

The meeting continues as paperwork is signed, figures studied, strategies planned, and Ashley mercifully takes charge. Thank goodness we have a lawyer in the family. I am bewildered and confused. Is this one of those cliffhangers that you see in the movies to keep us on the edge of our seats, and Ashley will sort it all out just in time for a happy ending? I have an awful sinking feeling in my stomach that it isn't. By the time we leave the offices of Bernstein, Gottlieb and Crutcher, I'm exhausted, hungry and there's a parking ticket on the windshield of my car.

'Do you want to come and have a bite with the girls and me?' I ask Ashley despondently, as we kiss goodbye on the street. Heather has already sped away.

'No, I've got to get back to the office,' he says, looking equally dispirited. 'Do you think Dad knew he was in such a mess?' he asks. His face looks hurt, as if it's his own male pride that has been injured, not Dad's.

I think hard. 'Now you mention it, he was looking over legal letters on the last afternoon I saw him at home. He was real grouchy about them too. And . . .' My mind is now racing. 'There were all kinds of accountant's letters in his desk too. I've got them all in boxes in the car still.'

'I better go through them.' Ashley sighs wearily. 'Poor Dad.'

'But it'll all be all right, won't it?' I ask.

'I don't know,' says Ashley uncertainly. 'It doesn't exactly look good.'

'But I don't understand why Dad would have signed such a bad contract with the record company in the first place. Or given so much to his manager.'

'Desperate for success, I suppose.' Ashley sighs again. 'People will sign anything for the promise of fame.'

*

I recount the details of the meeting over a late lunch with Lizzie and Bella at Le Petit Four. It's a tiny restaurant with linen-clad tables that spill out on to Sunset Plaza. Lizzie greeted me with her usual flamboyant air-kissing and demanded to know how she looked. 'New ensemble. What do you think?' she said, twirling around in a strapless red and white spotted dress by Betsy Johnson, with a white Prada belt, bag and shoes.

'Bitchin',' I told her, forcing cheerfulness. And she really did look stunning, with her bright red lips and her mane of curly red hair tumbling over her shoulders. Bella has her blond hair tied up in a chignon and her curves accentuated in an Ella Moss, but Bella never craves the attention like Lizzie, and squirms uncomfortably when you give her compliments, so I don't.

'It'll all sort itself out in the end. You just need to veg,' Lizzie says breezily, pouring herself a glass of Perrier from a big bottle, after I've revealed the extent of Dad's debts.

One of Dad's songs comes up on the sound system in the restaurant. Over the years I've got used to hearing his songs pop up all over the place, but it's odd to hear them now that he's no longer around. I hear his gravelly voice above the clatter of restaurant dishes, and feel the pain of his departure.

'Were you relying on the inheritance?' Bella asks sensibly.

'No, Adam will take care of me,' I say. 'I'm just sad that it doesn't look like it will work out the way Dad wanted it to. He would have wanted to take care of us.' A waiter brings goat cheese and walnut salads. 'And I shall be sad if we have to sell Dad's house. It's where I grew up.'

'It'll never come to that,' says Lizzie with absurd optimism that I know is designed to make me feel better. I'm about to argue the point, but Lizzie is pointing to some writing in the wide blue sky overhead where the tiny spot of an aeroplane is painstakingly marking out the letter B, then a heart, with its vapour trail. 'Ooh look. It's a Valentine,' she trills. 'Have you seen what Cameron gave me, by the way?' She shows us a heart-shaped diamond brooch, which she has pinned to her chest. 'Isn't it rad?' she demands. It's clear she wants to talk about her big new romance, and I'm pleased for the diversion. I so want Lizzie to have her happy-ever-after.

'Well, we still haven't slept together,' she announces. 'Cameron says all good things are worth waiting for. But it's driving me nuts. I soooo need to have sex with him. Like you wouldn't believe, I need to have sex.' She screws up her face theatrically into a picture of frustration – or ecstasy, I'm not sure which. And pants. A woman from the table next to us turns to study us, which Lizzie loves, of course, so she pants some more. 'And you'll never believe this.' She puts down her fork, and takes a bite out of a bread roll. I don't think I can remember seeing her ever eat bread before. 'Dudes, I've joined the Div.'

'The what?' Bella and I say in unison.

'It's what Cameron calls his church. It's short for the Division.'

'The division of what?' Bella asks.

'I'm going to be a Quantum Spiritualist,' she tells us proudly.

'A Quantum Spiritualist!' I let out a gasp. Across Hollywood there are famous actors and actresses who have signed up with the Church of Quantum Spirituality. But everyone sane knows it's a weird cult. 'Lizzie, you're not serious.'

'I so am. Like, Cameron's introduced me to everyone. He says any woman who wants to be with him has to be part of his church. And there's a lot to it. I've been studying.' She straightens up and juts her chin proudly. 'They believe that each person is a unit of the spiritual universe, and we're all immortal.' Bella and I stare blankly, but Lizzie is reciting lines like an automaton. 'As an immortal entity, the spirit lives on in the form of fish. And guess what? I'm going to be verified.'

'Like a restaurant bill?' Bella asks. She's trying not to laugh.

'It's a special technique where I confess my deepest dreams,' Lizzie trills, unperturbed. 'I'm giving them a whole bunch of money too.'

'Oh Lizzie, you can't.'

'Just a few thousand,' she adds.

'Lizzie, please don't. It's too weird,' I plead.

'Come on, Lizzie. Everyone knows QSs are weird,' Bella adds, seeing now that Lizzie is serious about this.

'People just think they're weird. But that's only because they don't really understand,' Lizzie continues, scarcely taking a breath. 'These are decent people. And I think if I go through with it, Cameron's going to propose to me. He's a really good guy, you know? And,' she says loudly, pausing for full dramatic effect, 'he says he's going to put me in all his movies. He's shown me the script for his next one. He has a role for a girl who's overweight . . . Can you believe it? I can actually eat.'

I can't believe I'm hearing this. I thought I'd set her up for a date, not a cult membership.

'But Lizzie, if he likes you, it shouldn't matter what church you go to.'

'Blah, blah, blah,' says Lizzie, putting her hands to her ears.

'You shouldn't have to compromise who you are for a guy.'

'I'm not compromising,' she argues. 'I'm not.'

'But Lizzie . . .'

'But Pearl . . .' She mimics my voice, and I know defeat when I see it. I take a gulp of mineral water. Bella and I exchange glances like concerned parents who can't control a teenage daughter. The woman at the next table pays her bill and leaves.

'Anyway, what's going on with Brett?' Lizzie demands, now waving at the waitress. 'Can I see the dessert menu?' she calls. 'I saw the picture of you and him in the tabloids,' she adds flippantly. 'They're saying you're back together.'

I catch Bella's face – now contorted with irritation. I knew she'd be mad at me. 'Well you know not to read those rags,' I say.

'Looked pretty cosy in the pictures together, though,' Lizzie bangs on. Didn't I tell her not to say anything? I try to kick her under the table but miss, and she's too busy ogling the desserts laid out on a tray that the waitress is balancing in front of her to notice. 'Can I get the tarte aux pommes, please?' she asks. Lizzie never eats desserts.

'What were you doing with Brett?' Bella demands. Her tone is neutral, but within the vowels and consonants lurks the current of disapproval. 'I thought you agreed not to see him again.'

'He showed up at Thackeray's school. There was nothing I could do,' I tell her weakly.

'Why was he there?'

'I don't really know,' I lie, and Bella immediately senses my reluctance to give details.

'You didn't ask him what he was doing there?'

'Well . . .' She fixes me with a penetrative stare. It's no use. Like a barnacle on a sinking ship, she's not going to let it go. I fill her in on the details of the day, the story of our escape from the paparazzi siege, and how Brett masterfully took control. I realise as I'm telling the tale that I'm making him out to be something of a hero. For some reason I've always wanted Bella to see the good in him, rather than just the bad.

'So now he's the knight in shining armour.' She laughs

cruelly. 'God, he's such an arse. Next thing you're going to tell me is he took you back to his place and you fell into his arms and made mad passionate love.'

'Of course not,' I say, and find I have to look away. I grab a spoon, and take a bite of Lizzie's dessert.

'This is delicious,' I say with unnatural jollity, desperate to move the conversation on. I focus on the tarte aux pommes, but Bella knows me too well. I feel her staring at me.

'Oh. My. God. You did, didn't you?' she says slowly.

'No I didn't,' I say, and reach for another bite. It's a nice try, but I know the game is up.

'Yes you did. You couldn't keep a secret if your life depended on it.'

'You must absolutely not tell a soul,' I say desperately. 'Promise?'

'Of course I promise,' she says, still shocked.

'Me too,' Lizzie adds.

'But what now?' Bella asks, solicitude replacing reproof in her voice as the seriousness of the situation sinks in.

'I don't know. I just don't know. I feel so stupid.' I hold my head in my hands in an effort to blank out everything.

'Honey, don't beat yourself up. It was always going to happen,' Lizzie says, now licking cream off her spoon.

'No it wasn't.' I feel irritation rising. What does she know?

'Well, you always loved him.'

'No she didn't,' says Bella. 'She just thought she did.'

'Did I? Oh God. I'm so confused. It's all such a mess.' I run my hands through my hair in frustration and long to turn the clock back by a week and live it differently.

'But you do still love Adam, don't you?' Bella demands gently. I know her practical mind is working on this.

'Of course I do.'

'And have you heard from Brett since?'

'No ... Yes. He phoned to say he was going away. Urgent business that he had to attend to.'

'Good. Then you've just got to forget it ever happened. Don't see him again. Tell him you can't and move on.' Bella is brisk with her advice. It sounds so simple.

'But what if they really are meant to be together after all this time?' Lizzie interjects. 'Supposing Brett really is the big love of her life?'

'If Pearl was the big love of *Brett*'s life, he wouldn't have cheated on her,' Bella fires back.

'But he wouldn't have been waiting outside the school if he didn't have feelings for her still.'

'It's too late for that,' Bella retaliates. 'He's missed the boat.'

'Did he send you a Valentine?' Lizzie asks me.

'No,' I whisper. Not that a Valentine would make my life any easier – I've enough to worry about without hiding Valentines – but I'd half expected there might have been something. Brett knows how much I love them, and it would have been reassuring to know I wasn't just an impulsive fling.

'Maybe it was him who did the skywriting,' Lizzie suggests, but I'm barely listening now. There's too much to think about.

'Pearl, you've got to forget him,' Bella insists with all the practicality of Martha Stewart baking a cake. 'I know it's not easy. But he's unreliable. He's not to be trusted. And it would break Adam's heart if he found out. You want to jeopardise all that you have with him?'

'No, of course not.'

'Well then?'

Lizzie says nothing. After all, what can anyone say?

'I know. I'm just going to forget it ever happened.'

The waitress brings the check, and after paying, we walk through to the parking lot at the back of the restaurant. It's a bright day, and the reflection of the sun on the rows of cars makes me squint. Lizzie disappears to find her Corvette, after offering one of her special sympathy hugs.

'Has your aunt gone back, by the way?' I ask Bella, as we saunter on to find our own cars. I feel relieved to have told Bella, and I am conscious of the familiar companionship of her company. I couldn't bear there to be an untruth between us. We're too good friends for that.

'Not yet,' she says gleefully, hunting in her purse for car keys. She smiles as she does it, and I feel a twinge of envy. She looks so happy. 'I've put her up at the Beverly Hills Hotel for an extra week. I wanted to show there was no hard feeling for all that happened before.'

'That's pretty generous of you.'

'You'd do it too if you'd just found a long-lost aunt. It's been brilliant having her here, Pearl. I can't begin to tell you.'

'What about her kids?'

'Oh, they're being looked after in the UK. I've told her I'll go visit them at Christmas. And I can't wait. I really can't. Christmas in England ... with a family that's actually mine.'

Bella clasps her hands together, as if to contain her zeal. She looks like a small child again – innocent and guileless.

'And you're sure you want to give her all that money?'

'I want to help, Pearl. She's family. I know you're sceptical. But this is important to me.'

I guess I understand. I'd want to help out if it was my family, I suppose.

25

Admittedly, the following two weeks are a little odd – as if everything is slightly off kilter. I accidentally smash the other wing mirror of the car reversing out of a parking spot (honestly, I'm not that bad a driver), I leave my purse in Macy's (although someone kind hands it in), and I throw some of Stephen's unopened mail into the trash by mistake (I've yet to find out if it was anything important). But the main thing is I am a good and adoring wife, and Adam hasn't suspected a thing. You can eat your heart out, Monica Lewinsky. I have this deception thing down. We bustle along through our daily life with our late-night suppers, and power yoga on Sundays, and no one would know the difference. It's only a question of time before I will have forgotten the whole incident with Brett completely. What incident? See, I've forgotten already.

In a bid to further my mission and demonstrate to Adam how much I love him and make him feel secure, I have also booked us a surprise romantic Saturday night in a suite at the Sea Breeze Hotel in Santa Barbara, described in the guidebooks as a terracotta-tiled luxury hotel surrounded by palms and bougainvillea overlooking the beach. Babysitter is arranged.

'Are you sure you researched the hotel properly?' Adam asks as we speed up the 101 freeway in his car

232

(mine being without wing mirrors). 'Only it's always worth checking the reviews before booking anything. Did you check?'

'Yes, of course I checked.'

'And you looked at all the guidebooks for their best recommendations?'

'Sure.'

'Only you know it's always worth researching everything beforehand.'

'Honey, it's going to be lovely.'

The 101 freeway to Santa Barbara clambers over the Santa Monica mountains with its grassy hillsides that are a vivid spring green. Cattle graze scenically, letting travellers know they've left the concrete behind. Then the road drops down sharply to farmland on the Oxnard Plain, where rows of vegetables make dizzying patterns on the landscape. And beyond that it meets the ocean and clings to the rocky headlands.

We talk lazily along the way about nothing in particular, but everything that is the fabric of our lives: Adam's work, Thackeray's school, Dad's departure – funny that this is now part of my fabric. And of course, there's our usual discourse on the screenplay Adam's writing. 'So I need a romantic scene where the guy asks her to marry him. Any ideas?' he asks.

'He takes her for a night-time picnic on the beach and writes "marry me" in little tea-light candles,' I say without even thinking.

'Yeah, that's great,' Adam says merrily. 'Great idea. But how does he present the ring?'

'Well, he keeps pointing to the sky and says, "Look at that bright star, honey," and she keeps looking and looking but she can't see it. "Up there," he says, pointing all the time. And eventually she sees that on the finger he's pointing with is a diamond ring.'

'Oh, yeah. I can use that. That's great, Pearl.'

It was how Brett proposed to me. We sat in the sand and watched the sun set together on Santa Monica Beach. Brett produced a picnic with lots of salamis and cold meats – protein because I was already pregnant with Thackeray. It was a kiss-and-make-up outing. He'd been so freaked out when I first told him I was pregnant – it had come as a shock to us both. Then we made out on the sand under the mantle of darkness. Brett used to put so much thought into the things we did together. He'd wanted to do the right thing when he knew I was pregnant. It was only later when Thackeray became imminent that it changed. But we're not thinking about Brett. We're thinking about ideas for screenplays.

'Perhaps I should write my own screenplay,' I say absent-mindedly – mostly as an attempt to bring my thoughts back to the real world.

'You?' Adam almost laughs. 'It's a lot harder than you think, Pearl. It requires a lot of concentration. You have to sit down for longer than twenty seconds to write a screenplay.'

'Are you telling me I'm incapable of concentrating on something for longer than twenty seconds?'

'I'm just saying writing a script isn't quite the same as running around looking after Stephen. It takes persistence.'

Is he saying that I'm not smart enough? I'll swear that he is. I feel my hackles rise. But I'm not in the mood for a fight. This is meant to be a happy night away, and perhaps he's right anyway.

The Sea Breeze is everything it promised to be. Our room is airy, light, with whitewashed walls and a balcony with a precipitous drop, overlooking the beach and waving palms. The decor is a little uninspiring – beige furniture, bed throws, and safe pictures of fruit on the walls. But neatness and conventionality always work for Adam. We rent a cabana and laze by the pool, sipping margaritas, and I finish *Love in the Afternoon*. In the evening we eat lobster in the restaurant, drink too much wine and fall asleep in the unfamiliar bed.

But now with a pink dawn outside and the salty damp air pouring through the balcony door, Adam is awake. 'Honey,' he says, pulling me close to him in the familiar way that ensures I know what comes next. Even half asleep, I pull away. I have not had sex with Adam since that afternoon with Brett. And Adam's touch makes me uneasy. His hand loiters on my hip and makes me want to tear my skin off. I get out of bed to go to the bathroom.

'Come on,' he calls after ten minutes. 'Are you coming back?' I stare into the bathroom mirror and loathe the person who stares back. You must try, I tell the stranger. You owe it to him.

The first night Brett and I slept together was so unrestrained it frightened me. There was a ferociousness to our passion that bordered on lunacy. It was as if nothing and no one else mattered in the world. The craziness waned a little with time, but the sensations that he made me feel still haunted me for days afterwards. They haunt me now. His embrace. His confident touch. His eager advance. In a single breath, I can imagine myself back in his apartment.

When I first got to know Brett, I was distrustful of him. I mean, why would anyone this charismatic and striking be interested in someone as ordinary as me? I hadn't told him I was Gavin Sash's daughter, remember. He still thought my name was Pearl Java, and if I didn't tell people I was Gavin Sash's daughter, well, what was there about me that was special? Nothing. I wasn't even a blonde. I was a short brunette who worked as an assistant to an agent. I was nothing special in a town where everybody is a somebody.

'Beauty shines from within,' Brett said on our second date. 'And you shine inside and out.' Of course I didn't believe he could possibly mean me. I almost wanted to look behind me to see who he was really talking to.

He must have discovered who my dad was, I thought. But there were no signs that he had.

'I think you're funny,' he said on our third date. No one had ever told me that before. He must have been thinking of someone else. I looked for his angle; what was it that he wanted from me? He couldn't be genuine, surely? Especially not here in Hollywood.

'Why do you like me?' I asked him.

'Because you're cute and sexy and funny and you care about people.'

'Yes, but—'

'And you can't see it in yourself at all. That's the real trip.' It took me a long time to realise he was being sincere. He really did seem to like me for me.

And when I did eventually tell him that Pearl Java was a creation off the side of a coffee cup, he laughed uproariously at me. (It had got to be kind of embarrassing when we bumped into people I knew around town and everyone was asking how my dad was.)

'You think I'd only love you because of who your dad is?' he guffawed. 'You've got to be kidding, right?'

He looked over at me, and then when he saw that I wasn't, wrapped his arms around me and pulled me into his warm, protective chest. 'Pearl Sash, I love you,' his voice boomed. 'I love you. Although . . .' He paused a second. 'You couldn't get me your dad's autograph, could you?' Then we both laughed. He'd got it. He understood.

But that was a long time ago, and this is now. I must be real. I must be practical. I slide back into bed with Adam.

'What kept you?' he asks impatiently.

I close my eyes and my body concedes to what is required. With time, I shall forget about Brett entirely. I know I will.

*

After breakfast, we take a stroll along the beach. A group of seagulls are sitting expectantly on the sand, as if waiting for something, and the ocean water dances and sparkles in the bright morning light, eventually breaking into waves against the sand. I kick my shoes off and thrust my hand into Adam's as we set out towards the headland at the end of the beach.

'We needed this,' he says, holding my fingers tight, anchoring me to his side. 'There's never enough time for just us.'

He's right, of course. Marriage to me came with an instant family, and we've never had the unencumbered days of spontaneity and autonomy that most couples have before a child comes along.

'Perhaps we should take a proper vacation,' he continues. 'I think you could use the rest. You've been so edgy recently.'

'Have I?'

'Well . . .' He pauses. 'You've had a lot on your mind, with your dad and everything.'

He stops to pick up a shell off the beach. 'Look how perfect it is,' he says, admiring it in the palm of his hand. 'Here, a souvenir.' He hands it to me, and I put it in my jeans pocket.

I have a handful of shells at home that Adam gave me on our honeymoon. It was a small wedding in Los Angeles, and afterwards five days in Mexico, leaving Thackeray with Dad and Heather. It was a happy time, reading books, plotting out a future, not to mention several movie ideas. Adam already had one film out then, but he had ambition beyond that. He was going to conquer Hollywood, he told me. And I could see that he might.

'Would you be able to take the time off?' I ask.

'I shall make the time,' he says emphatically. 'Where shall we go?'

'Africa,' I tell him.

He lets out a loud laugh that sends a curlew flying into the air in shock. 'Africa! That's quite a ways.'

'Well, you asked.'

'I guess I did,' he says with a smile. 'Not sure I can take that much time off. Wouldn't you settle for somewhere closer to home?' he asks. 'What about Mexico again?'

'Maybe we could go after Thackeray's half-term break from school.'

We walk on in silence for a while, stepping over seaweed and watching the joggers panting along the bike path that runs parallel to the beach. There's a faint breeze rippling the water. It feels soothing on the face. And then suddenly it hits me. Didn't Bella's aunt talk about her children being on half-term break? But it was only January then. Schools don't have a half-term break in January. Not even in England. She didn't know. That was it.

'I think she's a fraud,' I say, stopping in my tracks.

'Who?' says Adam, pulling on my arm.

'Bella's aunt. She's a fraud who wants Bella's money.'

'What?' Adam looks at a loss. I fill him in on all the details as we resume our stride, walking slower now as I think it through.

'I felt uncomfortable about my conversation with her at the time. She wouldn't say where she was from, she wouldn't say how old her children were. Of course she wouldn't because she wants Bella's money . . . And didn't she have to get back because the bailiffs were knocking down her front door?'

'You can't think someone is a fraud just because they're vague about their children's ages and don't say where they're from,' Adam says matter-of-factly.

'Yes, but there was something not right about her. Bella probably wouldn't remember what her aunt looked like. And she gives interviews all the time to magazines. It's all out there – how she lost her mum and dad, how her aunt left her with foster parents, and how she arrived penniless in Los Angeles and made it. Magazines love a rags-to-riches story. It would be easy for someone to read that story and pretend to be her aunt.'

'You've been reading too many of your romance novels,' says Adam and picks up his pace, dismissing the notion.

'But it's possible, isn't it?' I race to catch up.

'I suppose it is,' he muses. 'But Bella's not stupid. She would have known.'

'Would she? She's so happy to have any kind of family connection, she's not even suspicious. And another thing, this woman didn't bring any family pictures with her.'

'So?'

'Well, she told Bella she had all these photos of her mum and dad, which Bella was just so thrilled about. So why didn't she bring them with her if she had them?' Adam stops in the sand. He looks serious. 'And she's handing over twenty thousand pounds to her! Just like that.'

'Twenty thousand!' I can see he believes me now. A big wave crashes suddenly, and sends water racing towards us.

'I must call Bella and tell her.'

'Wait, Pearl. Don't rush into this. What if you're wrong? You need to be sure you're right before you start making accusations. This is going to be a big deal for Bella.'

He's right, of course. 'But I must do something.'

Adam studies his toes, deep in thought. 'Look, do you know where her aunt is supposed to live?

'No.'

'What about her name?'

'Bella called her Livonia.'

'Last name?'

I shake my head. 'Don't know. She was married, so it's not going to be the same as Bella's. This is going to be too difficult.'

'No it's not,' says Adam confidently. 'All you need to do is find Bella's real aunt. If you're correct and this woman is a fraud, then her real aunt is going to be living somewhere in England. Call Bella and get her aunt's last name. You can think of some excuse or other to do that, can't you?' I nod. 'Find out where she's supposed to live, then find her. If you find another Livonia Whatever-her-name-is, then you tell Bella and call the police.'

'But I haven't much time. I think her aunt is back in England now, and Bella was going to wire her the money at the end of the month.'

'Well, that gives you a week. But if I know anyone who'll be able to pull it off, it'll be you.'

I smile. Adam's compliments are few and far between.

By the time we drive back down the 101, we're promising to go away more often. The change of scene has been good for me. I feel like I've turned a page. The past is behind me. And now I've got a mission.

On Monday morning, Stephen calls me into his office. I am keen to get on the phone straight away to find Bella's aunt – with the time difference, it's already the afternoon in England – but Stephen has had a phone call from New Look Pictures.

'Did you send a picture of a redhead into New Look?' he growls from behind his desk – a caricature of power, swamped by the acres of embossed leather that stretch out in front of him.

'Um, yeah,' I say sheepishly. Oh God, he's going to be furious about this.

'Your friend? Lizzie What's her name?'

'Um, yeah.' Oh, God. It will be so embarrassing if he fires me.

'Yeah. They want her to audition for *Dog Knows*, their new comedy. They say she's got just the right look.'

'They do?'

'Yeah. But I'm mad at you, Pearl. You know why I'm mad at you?'

'Er . . .'

'I'm mad because you didn't mention her to me before. We should have had her on our books years ago. I mean, she's perfect for the part. Perfect. Why didn't you tell me about her before?'

I feel the urge to protest, but what's the use?

'Get Frank to draw her up a contract, wouldchya? And by the way, I'm mad at you for something else too.'

What now?

'I found the lights left on in your office over the weekend.'

'That's because you wanted a new internet cable line put into the house. I had the guys in working on it.'

'There's always an excuse, Pearl,' Stephen berates. 'Leaving lights on is a waste of electricity. Do you think I'm made of money? You must tell the staff to turn off all electrical items after use. Send an email.'

'Yes, Stephen.'

Sometimes I wonder what I am doing here. Back in my own office, I call Lizzie to break the good news, and while she rhapsodises, I find a British telephone directory on the internet. I look up Livonia Spires, which was Bella's maiden name. I've left a message asking Bella to call me, so this is the best I've got to go on for now. There's an L. Spires in the Guildford area, which is where Bella is from. I try it once Lizzie is off the phone, but it's the wrong number. There are five L. Spireses in the London area – I leave three answerphone messages and the other two don't pick up.

This is like wading through quicksand. I don't even know if she goes by the name of Spires. But then I see an advertisement for a detective agency, Peter Dobsworth PI, promising 'Discreet personal service. Guaranteed results'. Why didn't I think of that before? A gruff northern voice answers. I explain the situation. I tell him I don't have much other information, but he seems untroubled.

'Actually, there have been quite a few cases of fraudsters targeting celebrities,' he says calmly. 'They read every interview there is about their personal life, and if there's an opening to make money, they try it on. It's not that uncommon. Do you know where your friend Bella lived?'

'Guildford, I think.'

'Do you know the names of her mum and dad? Did she ever mention the names of her cousins?'

I rack my brains for any small snippets Bella might have given me, but there's not much.

'Not to worry,' says Dobsworth cheerfully. 'I've worked with less. And your friend Bella was orphaned at age thirteen?' He speaks slowly as he writes it down. 'That'll give me a head start with the social services.' I hear him sucking on a piece of candy. 'I'll do what I can, but the minute you can get your friend to give you any more details, let me know.'

He takes my credit card details as a deposit, and as I hang up, I feel a lightness of spirit. It wasn't cheap, but I know that woman is not Bella's real aunt. I just know she isn't.

At mid-morning, a truck pulls up at the house to deliver ten sixty-inch flat-panel plasma TVs costing ten thousand dollars each. There are also speakers, DVD players and a sound system that would be at home at the Coachella music festival. I laugh quietly to myself. This from the man who is worried about his electricity bill. I think of Brett and his take on excess.

'Stephen, did you order some new TVs?' I ask through

the intercom with an impatient delivery man waiting
outside, keen to unload.

'Oh, yeah, I did,' he mutters. 'Get them to set them up
for me.'

'And what would you like me to do with the old ones?'

'Chuck 'em,' he says flatly. 'Oh, and would you call
Karlof Crase. Tell him Lilly Callaghan's going to be at the
Ivy for lunch today.'

Lilly Callaghan is one of Stephen's A-listers, whose
latest film has tanked and who needs something to keep
the public compelled. Karlof Crase is the king of the
paparazzi, a man who has grown wealthy by employing
fleets of photographers to stick to the stars like chewing
gum. Stephen's relationship with him is symbiosis at its
most rewarding. A paparazzi picture of a star is publicity.
Not always the best kind, but if you're not in the news,
then you're not in the public eye. Pap pictures can boost
a star's appeal, even their movie price tag. So Stephen
gives Crase tip-offs about his clients – anything that will
boost his own profits.

'Karlof Crase?' I ask down the phone line.

'Who wants to know?' demands a gruff voice, and I
know immediately that it's him. We've spoken many
times.

'It's Pearl, Stephen Shawe's assistant.'

'Oh, yeah?' He's interested now.

'Stephen wanted me to pass on that Lilly Callaghan
will be at the Ivy at lunchtime today.'

'Got it,' he says firmly. 'Anything else? You know
where Brangelina are?'

He always wants to know where they are.

'Can't help you,' I say, and with the task taken care of
I'm about to hang up, but it occurs to me to call in a
favour. I have, after all, just given him a tip-off that will
make him sales. 'Say, Karlof. Can I ask you something?'

'What?'

'Would you call your boys off me? They've been following me everywhere since Dad died and it's driving me nuts. You must have better people to follow than me.'

'Yeah, we have.' Karlof clearly never made it to charm school. He pauses, and I hear him light a cigarette. 'Actually, I got something here that you might be able to help with. We need a few more details. You know, you scratch my back, I'll scratch yours.'

'I can't divulge any of Stephen's clients' information, you know that.'

'Yeah, but what if it's concerning your ex?'

'My ex?'

'Yeah, we've got an interesting picture here. It's about to go out in next week's tabloids. Wondered if you knew anything about it. Would you look at it?'

'No harm in looking.'

'I'll send it over as a Jpeg file. What's your email?'

I give him the address and ponder what the picture could be. Not that I would ever give Karlof any personal details about Brett. Publicity tip-offs is one thing, but divulging personal stuff is off limits. Karlof's email pops up whilst he holds on the line. I open it and stifle a gasp. Suddenly I am unable to swallow, unable to breathe, unable to think.

'Got it?' Karlof's abrasive voice comes lumbering into my world, but I can't summon any words. 'You still there?' he asks again. I stare at the picture. 'Did you know anything about this?'

'I'm sorry, I don't know anything,' I manage to mutter, and hang up.

There in front of me is a picture of Bella and Brett together. It's a paparazzi shot, taken with a long lens. They are walking down a street together, not hand in hand, but as anyone can see and the caption points out, they look very happy together. *Brett Ellis and Bella Shawe – Hollywood's Hot New Couple*, reads the caption.

No wonder Bella didn't want me getting back together with Brett. She wanted him for herself. I let out a howl and hit the edge of the desk in fury. How could she? How could *he*? How could *they*?

'You OK?' Maria calls from another room.

'Yes, I stubbed my toe,' I lie, recovering fast. I peer at the photograph again. There's no mistake. It really is them. And they really do look happy together. Bella's got a flirtatious look in her eye, and Brett looks like he's about to wrap his arm around her shoulder.

I'm an idiot. Repeat three times. I'm an idiot, an idiot, an idiot. I've been taken in. Made a fool. Brett hasn't changed at all. Of course he hasn't changed. Men never do. He didn't want me to come back to him at all. I was just another conquest.

And Bella! She's supposed to be my friend. But it all makes sense now. There was a time when Bella messed around with a producer guy behind Jamie's back. She always made light of it and said she had never been unfaithful. But now I don't believe her. And wasn't it Bella herself who told me that leopards never change their spots? And wasn't it her who told me never to trust Brett? Wasn't it her who urged me to divorce him in the first place? Was it all so she could have him for herself? Could she really have done that to me?

My head reels. I've been so stupid. Repeat that three times. Stupid. Stupid. Stupid. I need to go home, curl up and die.

26

Unfortunately, Adam is part of the anti-gun lobby so there is no gun in the house to shoot myself with. I also have a five year old to feed and put to bed, so although a hurricane that would knock the stuffing out of Katrina is breaking loose inside my head, as far as Thackeray is concerned, it's a perfect evening for soccer in the garden. It's also a perfect evening for macaroni cheese, a Winnie-the-Pooh story, and capturing a poor unwitting house spider that made the mistake of hanging around in Thackeray's bathroom.

When Thackeray is finally in bed, I allow myself to unleash the torrent of agitation inside my head. I pace. I swear. I find the packet of cigarettes I hid inside my old Ugg boots at the back of the closet years ago, and light one, sitting amongst my shoes. I savour the charge of nicotine and find the stuffed toy Superman that Thackeray lost last week and we spent three hours looking for. He looks how I feel: lame, pathetic and totally powerless in spite of all he's cracked up to be.

I contemplate lighting a second cigarette. But instead I call Melodie May, my psychic, who can do readings over the phone. She'll tell me what to do.

'I see dark colours,' she says.

'Yes?' A storm brewing, no doubt.

'I see a small room.'

'Yes?' A jail perhaps. It's a message. If I kill him, I'll end up in jail.

'I see a woman.'

That would be Bella. 'What does she say?'

'She says would you like it in a size six or a size eight.'

'Twelve dollars and ninety-nine cents a minute, and you call yourself a psychic!'

I hang up, and am about to call Lizzie – because even she would be more helpful than Melodie May – when I hear Adam's car pulling up in the driveway. What? He's never home at this time. I race to the bathroom, hurriedly sloosh mouthwash to mask the cigarette smell and make it to the sofa before he comes through the door. I even have a copy of *Love in Paradise* in my hands, which arrived in the mail today. The book is upside down, but I don't think Adam has noticed.

'I wondered if you needed one of these?' Adam says, handing me a brown paper bag with a curiously crooked smile on his face, as he kisses me on the cheek. 'It's one of the best on the market. *Consumer Buys* magazine rates it as the most reliable.' He points at the bag.

My heart plummets. I have an awful feeling I know what this is. And it's not chocolates. The problem with a husband who is fastidious and organised is that he rarely forgets anything.

'It's been nearly three weeks,' he adds, 'and you haven't had your . . . er . . . Have you?'

I shake my head. I haven't. In fact, with everything going on, I haven't even thought about it. In the bag is a home pregnancy test.

'Well?' he says expectantly. 'Should you . . . er?'

'Yes,' I say with feigned joy, and put it down on the table next to me. 'They work best in the mornings, so we'll do it then.'

'Actually, you can use it any time. It says so on the packet. Look.' He picks it up and points to the instructions, where it says clearly that it can be used at any time of the day. I catch sight of his face. Thackeray has the same expression when he's spotted a lollipop in a shop and wants desperately for me to buy it for him.

'But I don't need to pee,' I lie.

Adam disappears to the kitchen and returns with a glass of water, and waits expectantly for me to drink it.

Our bathroom has dark blue walls on the top half and is lined with some pretty blue and white tiles on the lower. I took particular trouble choosing the decoration. Bathrooms often get overlooked in a house, but it's the room that guests always study the most. With this in mind, I chose some antique brass taps for the basin, and left candles and potpourri on a neat wooden shelf. But the room's *pièce de résistance* is a photograph on the wall, taken in the sixties, of Elvis Presley sitting in a car on our very street. I bought it at an auction and was so thrilled to find it.

I stare hard at the picture now and imagine myself sitting in the car next to Elvis. Perhaps he could just whisk me away from this situation, drive me off to a new life in a different era, perhaps to the 'Green Green Grass of Home', wherever that might be.

I pee on the pregnancy stick, pull the toilet lid down, sit on it and wait. It takes three minutes for the indicator on this pregnancy test stick to make its decision. Please don't let me be pregnant, I plead to an anonymous god, possibly Elvis himself. 'Dear Elvis, please could you help me out here,' I say quietly to the picture. Talking to a picture of Elvis in a bathroom, I realise, can only be three steps away from insanity, but I need help. 'Only I seem to have fucked up,' I tell him. 'You know all about fucking up, don't you? God, you knew about messing everything up.' Elvis says nothing. 'Yeah, I knew you'd understand. The thing is, if it turns out I'm pregnant, I won't know who the father is. And that will be Heartbreak Hotel.'

Elvis smiles silently back at me. 'You remember Heartbreak Hotel?' He looks so happy in the picture.

I stare hard at the stick, willing it to be negative. A dark line slowly forms, which I know means negative. But it's only been one minute. And I know I must wait three. Time inches slowly. If it's positive, do I lie to Adam? Or do I confess? Do I jeopardise everything between us? Or should I stay quiet and maybe he'll never know? We could have the baby, and there's a fifty per cent chance it's his anyway. But what if it isn't? And would it be right to mislead a child about its father? I'm not sure I could live with such a lie.

'Please don't let me be pregnant, Elvis. Please. Please. Please.' Elvis looks on placidly. He's still smiling. But it's no use. A plus sign is now emerging, and prayers are useless. Even to Elvis, king of the fuck-up. I will tell Adam it's negative and terminate the pregnancy later. Did I just say the word terminate? It sounds so awful. To terminate a life. Yes, but there's no time, and I must be practical. There's nothing for it. You must lie to him and then deal with it later. Yes, that is absolutely right.

'Well?' says Adam as I travel the distance across our living room, back to the comfort of the sofa, my heart pounding in panic. Stay calm. You must stay calm. Adam looks up expectantly from the newspaper he's pretending to read. I know he's desperate to know. He scrutinises my face.

'It's positive, isn't it?' he says, looking me straight in the eye before I've had a chance to say anything. 'I know it is. I can see from your face. We've done it.' He gets up and throws his arms around me. 'Baby! We've done it.'

Why must I be so transparent? I hug him back, but what with the stress of it all, tears are now falling uncontrollably. Oh God, how did I get in this mess? I must tell him the truth. 'Adam, I need to talk to you . . .' I start. But Adam is in no mood to listen.

'Oh honey, of course you do. There's lots to talk about. But I can see you're emotional. Probably hormones. Having babies is very emotional. But it's such great news. What shall we call him?' He stops himself. 'Or it might be a her. What about a daughter? A baby brother or sister for Thackeray.'

How could I have done this to him? I don't even know where to look.

After Adam departs for work the next day, taking Thackeray with him for the school drop-off, I pace the house and garden. I don't know what else to do. With a mind that needs to be quieted, I march down to the oleander bushes that border the bottom of our garden, then round the flowerbeds laden with geraniums and bird-of-paradise plants, and back to the patio. My hands tremble. My head aches. I haven't slept all night. I feel the urge to call Bella – she'll know what to do. But then I remember the photo, and I can't. I won't call her ever again. I feel the venom of betrayal and try walking around the garden once more. This time, down past the boxes containing a swing seat that Adam spent several Sunday mornings researching and still has yet to put together, down past the gardener's outhouse containing a lawnmower and tools, back up through the camellia bushes, which still have some flowers left on them. Some squirrels are squabbling with each other in a tree, chasing each other around the trunk, but I have no headspace for nature.

Pregnant! How could I be pregnant?

I pick up a flowerpot filled with a cactus and smash it on to the concrete patio floor. Dizzy and raging, I pick up another, and another. Earth spews everywhere. I've been such a fool. I storm back into the house and collapse, face down, on the sofa in tears.

*

Eventually the phone wakes me. I must have dropped off. My eye make-up has left a brown mark on the pale green silk of the sofa, and a wet patch where my face has been. I hear Stephen's voice invading the answer machine, wondering where I am. Oh, shit. What time is it? The clock on the mantelpiece chimes midday. Jesus.

'Stephen, I'm sorry, I had a flat,' I tell him, calling him back straight away. 'It's been a terrible morning, but the mechanic's here now. I'll be with you within the hour.'

At work I feel as if I'm on autopilot. The confusion in my head is so great that the regularity of mundane tasks is almost soothing. If I read enough emails, I can pretend nothing has happened at all. I sift through Stephen's list of tasks.

Maria puts her head through my office door to drop off the mail. 'You don't look too good, meesus,' she says sympathetically. I piled layers of cream on to my face before coming here. My skin was puffy from the weeping and there were dark circles under my eyes that no amount of foundation seemed to hide. 'You want some of your mint tea?'

I accept meekly and the phone rings. It's New Look Pictures wanting to know if they can courier over the *Northanger Abbey* script for Brett's perusal. I tell them it's fine. Among the mail is a copy of the *National Enquirer*. Just leave it, I tell myself. Don't even look. But I can't stop myself. Obsessively I tear through it for evidence of Bella and Brett together. There's nothing, but didn't Crase say his picture was for next week? It had only just come in. Of course there wouldn't be anything in this copy. He's still working on the story. Chill out, I tell myself. Everything's going to be fine. Get back to the emails. Breathe in. Breathe out.

But somehow I can't put the magazine down. Maybe there's a small news item about them. I peruse the pages slower now. Kate Hudson has a new guy, Jennifer Aniston has a new one too. I pause at the 'Ten Best Dressed' page, with all the stars lined up in their evening gowns. Victoria Beckham is in Balenciaga and looking rake thin. Boy, she needs to eat! I reach the adverts for home improvements and liposuction, and then I see an advertisement taking up a full quarter of the page. What the heck is this?

Gavin Sash memorabilia. Online auction of the personal effects of rock's greatest legend. Go to www.gavinsashauction.com.

Is there anything else that the cosmos can throw at me? I mean, come on, guys, give it your best shot. Hit me when I'm down, why don't you? There was no mention of any of this in my horoscope today, let me tell you. No mention of a pregnancy, an evil stepmother, a cheating ex-husband (can you have such a thing?). You've got it wrong, I want to shout. I'd like to make a complaint. All this chaos was meant for someone else. My horoscope promised love and fulfilment. Where's that, please? I'd like to change my order.

Dad hasn't even been dead two months. Would Heather really have done this already? I log on to the website and see all his belongings – clothes, guitars, shoes, sunglasses, hats, an old microphone, some of his awards, and even the train set. The train set!

I pick up the phone straight away. 'Heather, it's Pearl.' I'm in no mood for pleasantries.

'Yes, honey,' she says in a bored tone.

'I've just seen the online auction.'

'Yes, honey,' she repeats in the same tone.

'Couldn't you have asked first?'

'Asked what?'

'Asked if I wanted any of this things before you sold them. I told you I wanted to keep the train set for Thackeray.'

'Yes, honey. But that was before I knew I had a billion-dollar tax bill of your father's to pay.'

'We don't know how much we have to pay in tax yet. Some of those things are sentimental to me. He was my dad.'

'And I've told you before. He was my husband,' she says emphatically.

Silence echoes down the line.

'Couldn't I just have a few of his trinkets?'

'There are some boxes of stuff here that I'm about to throw out. You can have them if you want. But you better make it round soon, or they'll be in the trash.'

They say you never know somebody properly until you've divided an inheritance with them. Boy, is that true. I hang up.

The web page is still open on my computer. There's a minimum price of $2,000 on Dad's train set. $2,000! It was only a train set, for goodness' sake. No one else has put in a bid yet. I register and tap in $2,025. Immediately someone else bids $2,050. I bid $2,200. Someone else bids, $2,300. I bid $2,400 and close the page.

I'm just turning off the lights and switching off my computer, remembering Stephen's conservation efforts, when the phone rings again. I hesitate, because Thackeray's school charges a fine if you're late to collect the kids, but the ring on this phone is an abrasively insistent one, and I've still got five minutes to spare.

'Peter Dobsworth here,' says a voice I don't recognise.

'Yes, can I help you?' I say officiously.

'Is that Pearl Sisskind-Sash?'

'Yes.'

'Right you are then. I promised I'd get back to you,' the voice carries on. He hesitates, realising that I don't recognise the name. 'I'm the PI you put on to Livonia Spires.'

'Oh, I'm sorry.' I must be losing my mind. I'd completely forgotten.

'Yes, well I have some good information that I think you'll be interested to hear.'

'Already?' I hadn't expected him to be so fast.

'As far as I can see, Livonia Spires is now a Mrs Livonia Masters, living at 72 Bankhurst Road, Catford. I checked the marriage records, and from that it was pretty easy.' He pauses and I hear him turning the pages of a notebook. 'She had a brother, John Spires, married to Lily, both now deceased, and they had a daughter, Isabella. This Livonia Masters has three children, and as far as I can see, a husband who is also deceased. I have a couple of photos of her that I took myself from a distance that I can get over to you as a Jpeg. Perhaps you could identify them and see if it is the same woman you met.'

Already I'm switching the computer back on, and sitting down at my desk. I click on his email and then open the attachment.

The photos are perfectly clear – a short, rotund woman is leaving her house, dressed up warmly in an old sheepskin coat, hat, gloves, and a handbag scooped into the crook of her arm. In one shot she's locking her front door, in another she's walking down her garden path in front of a pre-war semi-detached house, the kind that you see so many of in Britain.

I study her closely. Her hair, visible beneath a woolly hat that is clearly worn for function not fashion, is greying, and there are a few lines on her face, but she doesn't look so old. Late forties, maybe. As she walks down the path into a hidden candid photograph, she looks weary, sad possibly. But most importantly of all, she is most definitely not the same woman I met with Bella.

'Are you sure this is her?' I ask the detective.

'I never like to say I'm a hundred per cent until I've spoken to the person myself to confirm it, but, let's say I'm ninety-nine per cent certain that this is the real Livonia Masters. The records had no gaps in them at all. Is this the woman you met?'

'No, it isn't. It absolutely isn't. She doesn't look anything like her.'

'Then may I suggest that we approach this lady for final confirmation that she is the real Livonia Spires, that was. Then we need to notify the authorities, as well as your friend, as soon as possible. Would you like me to do that?'

'No. Let me.' For some reason, I feel it's only decent to do it myself. 'Do you have her telephone number?'

'Of course.'

'This is a sensitive matter. I'd like to spare her feelings. Thank you very much for your help. I'll get back to you when I've spoken to her.'

I don't have the focus or the will to call the number in the evening. There is also the question of whether I even want to get involved any more. I am so angry with Bella that I'm tempted to leave her to be ripped off. She deserves it, I tell myself through another long sleepless night.

It's her problem, not mine. I stare at the ceiling in the dark, Adam snoring next to me with his face looking ever upward, waiting for the midnight suntan, and his inert form stretched out beneath the comforter. Once upon a time, I imagined that I'd be friends for ever with Bella. You don't feel it always with girlfriends, but Bella was always so loyal. And didn't we always have a laugh together? I remember when she first arrived in Hollywood, she was mystified by the martini I ordered for her, complete with an olive. 'Back home we eat our veg with the Sunday roast,' she chortled. She'd never even seen an olive before. But boy, she was a fast learner. Learnt all the Hollywood tricks, right down to stealing an ex-husband.

4:35 a.m. glows in red lights from the alarm clock, sending the faint shadow of a glass of water on the table next to it on to the bedroom wall. I long to sleep, and turn my head into the pillow once more, closing my eyes and forcing myself into a meditative state. I think of space, and darkness. I must clear my mind, I repeat several times. But five minutes later the clock is still glowing on the bedside table and I'm still thinking of Brett and Bella and a baby now growing in me. Not to mention the train set! The subjects whirl around my mind like a carousel.

Grabbing a dressing gown from a hook on the back of the door, I slip downstairs and into the kitchen for a glass of milk. I switch on the light. Outside, the night is black and the city eerily quiet. I shiver and wrap my gown closer around me, as I pour milk into a glass. I'm never usually fearful of the dark, but tonight I feel demons everywhere. The thought occurs to me that I could call Bella's aunt now. It would be lunchtime in England. I might catch her biting into beans on toast or fish and chips. British food is always so comforting. Daylight and busy daily life going on somewhere else, whilst it's so dark here, is strangely appealing. But do I really want to get involved now? Bella is such a vixen. The kitchen phone sits on a counter top. I'd like to know that I was right about the phoney. Carefully, I dial the number.

'Hello,' a hesitant voice answers straight away. It's an English accent, not posh, but kind of homely.

'Is that Livonia Masters?'

'Yes,' she says matter-of-factly.

'Is that Livonia Masters that used to be Livonia Spires?'

'Yes, dear. Who is this?'

'Um . . .' Now it comes down to it, I'm not really prepared for this. 'Um . . . my name is Pearl Sisskind-Sash.'

'It's what?'

'Pearl Sisskind-Sash. Yes, bit of a mouthful, I know.

Look, you don't know me, but I am a friend of Isabella, who I think is your niece.'

There's silence down the line. 'You do have a niece called Isabella?'

There's another pause. 'Yes,' she says eventually. 'Is she in trouble?'

'Well, no . . . Yes, kinda. You see, she was contacted by a woman who claimed to be her Aunt Livonia from England, and she wanted money from her, and I believe she is a fraud, pretending to be you.'

'Pretending to be who?'

'You?'

'I don't quite understand.'

I explain again. More slowly this time. 'Have you contacted Isabella at all recently?' Now there's silence down the line. Perhaps I've made a mistake doing this. 'Mrs Masters?' I hear her sniff and then blow her nose. 'Mrs Masters?'

'Yes, I'm still here, love. No. I haven't had any contact with Isabella. I haven't seen her since John's funeral.' She pauses and lets out a small sob. 'That was her dad. There were too many bills, you see. Too many kids. My husband had lost his job, and he didn't want me to take Isabella in . . .' She sniffs again. 'It wasn't right. I should have taken her in. I promised John I'd look after her, but my husband wouldn't . . .' She sobs again down the phone. 'He was a difficult man . . . He's gone now.'

She weeps some more into the phone and I feel the weight of her grief, bounced into space via a satellite dish, all the way from Catford to Los Angeles. This wasn't quite what I expected.

'But she's doing fine. Don't feel bad,' I soothe. I feel bad that I've made her cry. 'The truth is, I think she'd love to see you.'

'Why? Why on earth would she want to see me?' She seems shocked at the idea. 'I was the one who turned her away. She was only thirteen. She was an orphan and I turned her away. She must hate me.'

'I don't think she's holding any grudges. In fact I know she isn't. She's just paid for a woman who she thinks is you to stay at the Beverly Hills Hotel.'

'Why would she want to do that?'

'Because she thought she was family.' The phone goes quiet again. 'Mrs Masters, I don't think she hates you at all.'

'But I don't even know where she lives. I thought there might have been some contact after the social services took her. But I never heard anything, and . . .'

'I don't think she is angry, and she's living here in Los Angeles now.'

'Los Angeles?' I hear her gasp.

'Yup.'

'Los Angeles!' Her voice trails away. 'Is that where you're calling from?'

'Yeah.'

'Heavens above. And is she all right? Bella was always a smart girl.'

'She's fine. And she presents a TV show.'

'A TV show! Well I never.'

'Would you like her phone number? Or her address maybe?'

Livonia hesitates. 'I don't know.'

'I think she'd like to hear from you.'

'You really think so?'

I give her the details and tell her that I will pass her number on to Bella. I drink the milk after I've hung up, and reflect on the conversation a while. That was a good job done. Now I can go back to bed.

But I still can't sleep. Even after reading *Love in Paradise*, I still can't sleep.

So just before six, I throw on some clothes and leave a note for Adam telling him I've gone for a drive.

It's one of those mornings where a mist clings to every crevice of the hillsides, blurring the brightness of the street lamps, which are still on, and making everything indistinct and still. The first slivers of sunlight are grappling with the night's dimness, and I shiver briefly before getting into my car. I set the radio to Star 98, to liven my mood and feel a connection to the real world.

'There are going to be highs in the seventies and it's going to be g-r-e-a-t day,' cheers the DJ. Yes it is, I tell myself with forcefulness. Because I'm going to tell Bella exactly what I think of her. If nothing else, it will make me feel better. I may tell her the information I have about her aunt, but first I shall tell her what she can do with her dishonesty. I shall let her have it. Guns blazing.

I turn the car on to Sunset and hit the accelerator with all the fury and venom that is raging inside me. Bella's going to be so sorry she got out of bed this morning. How dare she lie to me? How dare she warn me off Brett?

By the time I reach the Pacific Coast Highway at the end of Sunset, the roads are no longer my own, and daylight has conquered the night, although not the mist. The fog is thicker down here by the beach and I am forced to slow my speed, but not my resolution. By the time I pull up outside her house, which overlooks the beach, I have a whole speech written out inside my head.

I lean on her buzzer without respite. I will catch her unawares, force her out of bed, and call her the names she deserves. I'm still running through my repertoire when I hear the locks of the door being turned.

'How could you?' I begin as the door slowly opens. 'How could you?' I repeat shrilly.

'How could I what?' asks a curious male voice. Jamie, Bella's husband, is now standing in front of me in pyjama bottoms and a T-shirt. His dark hair is messed up and there is stubble on his chin.

This is a shock. I thought Bella had said he was away

filming. And for some reason, in my blind, selfish rage, I hadn't thought about what this would mean for Jamie. How was he going to feel about his wife's affair? How would he cope? It isn't for me to tell him, I decide right there. No matter what Bella deserves, I can't be the one to tell her husband.

'How could you take so long to answer the door?' I dissemble hastily, now racking my brains for a reason why I would be standing on his doorstep at 6.45 in the morning. 'Bella in?' I ask breezily.

'Yeah, she's in bed still,' Jamie mumbles, rubbing his eyes sleepily. 'Kinda early, isn't it?'

'Early bird,' I say blithely.

'Come in.' Jamie holds the door wide. 'Want some coffee?' he asks, sliding his slippers along the hardwood floor as he disappears into the kitchen.

'Yes, please.'

Bella's house is not a big one, but its position is spectacular. Her living room opens out on to a wide terracotta-tiled balcony that is railed in by clear glass so that the view of the ocean is unobscured. I wander out on to it and contemplate the ocean crashing on to the beach. The water becomes tame on the sand once the violence of the wave has been exhausted.

'Pearl, what are you doing here so early?' Bella demands, standing in the doorway behind me and tying the cord of her silk dressing gown. Her cat, Mr Wilberforce, follows her. I allow her to kiss me on both cheeks, hiding the daggers in my heart.

'I have some news for you,' I say brightly. Fortunately, I do have the perfect excuse for being here. 'Urgent news, actually. And I wanted to tell you myself.'

'What?'

Jamie emerges on the balcony with a tray with three cups of coffee, and we settle at the table as if nothing has changed between us. 'Is that a dolphin?' he asks carelessly, casting his eyes out to the ocean. This is so not what I was intending.

'That woman who said she was your aunt . . .' I begin.

'Yes.' Bella's eyes are bright at just her mention.

'Well, she isn't your aunt. She's a fraud.'

'What do you mean?'

'She's an impostor. Have you wired her the money yet?'

'No. But—'

'Don't do it. Whatever you do, don't send her any money. Because I've found your real aunt, who's living in Catford, England.'

Bella sits perfectly still, her features frozen in astonishment. I'm not sure if she believes me.

'Your real aunt didn't want to get in contact with you because she was so ashamed of not taking you in,' I continue. 'She had a husband who wouldn't let her. She's always regretted it. She even cried when I called her.'

'You've spoken to her?' Bella asks incredulously.

'Yes.'

'But how?'

I tell her the whole story, feeling a little like a triumphant Miss Marple. I tell her about my hunch, the detective, the photographs. She and Jamie listen avidly. I let her absorb the news and feel good about telling her. It would be wrong not to pass on the information. Immoral. Bella might be a lying cheat, but she deserves to know the truth. And she looks strangely vulnerable now. Sad, possibly. I even feel sorry for her. She will mistrust her own judgement now, and I know how that feels.

'I've got to say, I was never wild about that woman,' Jamie announces. 'I just thought she was nosey, but I can see it now. She was casing the joint. We must call the police, of course.'

'Pearl, I don't know how I'm ever going to be able to thank you for this,' Bella says suddenly. She gets up and throws her arms around me with tears now forming in her eyes. 'You did this for me!'

'That's what friends are for,' I mutter and flinch at the words. I pull away from the embrace. Hugging her feels strained. Deception comes in many forms, and Bella's touch makes me uneasy.

'Well, I must go,' I say, hearing ice appear in my own voice.

'Must you? Please stay, Pearl. Stay and have some breakfast.'

'No, really.' I get up to leave.

'But the police will want to talk to you.'

'You can tell them where to find me.'

'Is everything all right?' Bella asks.

'Everything's fine,' I say curtly.

'You don't sound fine. You sound strange. Are you upset about something?'

'No, of course not. Look, I must go now. Stephen will be expecting me at work.'

27

It feels odd knocking on the front door of Dad's house. This is the house I grew up in, and the door has never been closed to me before. But I feel I ought to knock. Without Dad in it, it's not my home any more. The early-afternoon sun is hot and unyielding as I wait on the doorstep. A lizard is disturbed from its sunbathing on a rock and scuttles into a flowerbed, flicking its tail as it moves. Down at the end of the garden, where I always played as a child, some crows are cawing to each other – an argument about a titbit they're fighting over.

Still angry after failing to have my confrontation with Bella on Tuesday, I trudged through the rest of the week like a soldier on duty, forcing myself to carry on. But today is Friday, and I've skipped off work at lunchtime because Stephen's gone into his office. As I wait for Heather to answer the door, I contemplate what I shall do over the weekend to quell the resentment that still needles away at me. Thackeray needs some new shorts, so maybe a shopping trip. I have made an appointment with Dr Greenblatt, feeler and fumbler to the stars, to talk about an abortion next week. I never thought I'd be the kind to contemplate such a thing. I love kids too much. It's just to talk about it. And maybe the doctor will know about some new technology that will let me know who the father is. If it is Brett's, I'll have it terminated and tell Adam it was a miscarriage. If it's Adam's, I'll keep it. Anyway, it's just to talk. Nothing is set.

Russell Anders answers the door. I am astonished, and the sight of him strips away all the poise and demeanour I've worked on for this moment with Heather. I recognise him instantly, of course. He's the lead singer in the Stupid Lucky Dogs, who blare out on Star 98. You find celebrities everywhere in LA, but not usually opening your dad's front door. What's he doing here?

'Can I help you?' he asks me officiously.

'Um, I'm Pearl. I came to collect a few of Dad's things.'

His face breaks into a generous smile and he opens the door wide, gesturing towards a number of boxes that are lined up in the hallway, overflowing with books, hangers, tennis shoes, cricket bats, papers, sweaters, shirts, maps, all spilling on to the floor. 'Well, come on in,' he says warmly.

Lullabelle and Perdy greet me enthusiastically, wagging their tales and licking my toes affectionately as I walk in. They must be missing Dad too.

'Who is it, honey?' I hear Heather's voice from the kitchen.

Honey? She schleps out, placing her hand in the small of her back. The pregnancy is really showing now. 'Hiya, Pearl,' she says nonchalantly. 'Just help yourself to what you need.' She points at the boxes. 'I've kept the good stuff for the auction, and the thrift store will take away the rest. You met Russell, by the way?'

She leans into him and he wraps an arm around her in a way that leaves no shadow of a doubt about their relationship. It has taken her less than two months to replace Dad. She hasn't even given birth to their baby yet.

'Hi,' I say flatly and look away. I can't tolerate even facing them. Was Russell around before Dad died? They look mighty familiar with each other.

'You want me to help you out with any of this stuff?' Russell asks helpfully.

'No, I'll be fine,' I say, getting to my knees and beginning my task – combing through the flotsam and jetsam of Dad's life. I pick out a wooden pot carved in the shape of a cat. It smiles cheerfully at me, but I don't recognise it. Underneath it is an old camera. I fight a coat hanger to pull it out, but the clicker doesn't work. Next to it is a Mickey Mouse mug filled with ping pong balls. Useless junk, all of it.

At the bottom of the box there's a belt Dad used to always wear. I put it aside. At least it's something. I find some gold cuff links in a trinket box that Heather must have missed for her auction. I hide them quickly in my pocket. There's an entire box of photographs – mostly of us kids when we were small. I load that box into the trunk of my car straight away, but find the boxes I took from Dad's desk before are still sitting in there. I've forgotten to take them out, and I curse because they're taking up a lot of space.

But still, there's room for Dad's tennis racquet, and his cricket bat also gets shoved in. After half an hour I've filled four more boxes with souvenirs and mementoes. Stupid stuff – a roulette set, some CDs, an old cricket sweater, a baseball cap, some platform boots that I remember him wearing on stage – but I feel instantly better for having some keepsakes. I load them into the passenger seat of the car and call goodbye through the door. I don't want to prolong this, and leave quickly.

How can the summary of one life be reduced to four cardboard boxes of trinkets? I don't know what I'll even do with this stuff. Put it in the loft probably. Maybe Heather is right. Maybe none of it's important. It's the memories that matter.

*

Adam is waiting for me when Thackeray and I pull into the drive later in the afternoon, after I've collected him from school.

'Daddy's home. Daddy's home,' Thackeray squeals with delight. I feel a surge of joy. We'll be able to eat together for once. I have some steaks in the refrigerator, which we could barbecue in the garden. It's easily warm enough to sit out.

But Adam is not himself. He's been as buoyant as champagne all week, filling the house with baby clothes and books of baby names.

'How do you like the name Abraham?' he asked this morning, reading one of the books over breakfast. 'Or Adrian, or Adonis, or Adolf. Does anyone really call their child Adolf any more?' he laughed.

But there's no laughter this evening. He has a habit of being quiet when he is fussed by something. He often goes silent when he is gearing himself up for a pitch to a studio. He also fidgets. His hands need things to do – they smooth over his hair, rub his chin, get plunged into pockets and then withdrawn again; they drum on worktops. There are also dirty coffee cups from this morning still on a kitchen surface that he hasn't tidied away. Something's clearly up.

'Are you all right?' I ask him, as I unpack Thackeray's lunchbox in the kitchen and wash out the empty containers.

'I'm f-f-fine,' he says, and I pick up on the anger in his voice that tells me he is anything but. His hands are now drumming on the cockatiel's cage and Snowy lets out a squawk of indignation.

'Did anything happen at the studio?' I demand.

'No,' he says firmly. Thackeray puts on the TV in the living room, and I hear Curious George leap into his sunny theme tune.

'Would you like a beer?' I open the fridge and pull out

a Miller Lite. 'I thought we could barbecue some steaks for dinner.'

'Pearl . . .' Adam begins to say something, but stops himself and I hear despair in his sigh. He's finally settled in a chair at the table and stares out into the garden. The colour has gone from his face and he looks like a man who is weary with the world. I stop bustling in the kitchen and hug him, but he does not respond. My arms are wrapped around his neck, but his remain firmly by his sides.

'What is the matter?' I move round to face him.

'I was never enough for you, was I?'

'Oh, not this again. I've told you a million times that I love you.'

'But not like you loved B-B-B . . .'

'Brett.' Sometimes the urge to finish his sentences just cannot be contained.

'Yes. Brett,' he spits.

'I love you more than I ever loved Brett,' I reassure him and try to take his hand, now drumming on the table, but he pulls away.

'I think it's time to stop playing games,' he says quietly.

'What are you talking about?'

He summons intent in his voice, draws a deep breath and says, 'I think you should just take your things and g-g-g-go.'

The bombshell hits me like a cartoon-style mallet, but there is no Tom-and-Jerry-style instant recovery 'What?' I reach for the refuge of a kitchen chair, and drop into its seat.

'I know all about your sordid little afternoon with Brett. I don't know why you're even pretending.'

I say nothing. Too stunned to think of anything articulate.

'Your affair with Brett. I've heard all about it.'

Affair seems so improbable a term. People have affairs in movies and romance novels. There are clandestine meetings and secret messages. There's the promise of love. This wasn't an affair. It was a momentary lapse. A hiccup. A mistake. I look down at my shoes – they're red leather with a kitten heel. They look like the shoes of an adulterer, I realise.

'I don't know what to say.'

'I know it's true.' Adam looks severely at me, his face twisted with hurt.

'It was never an affair. Brett just caught me off guard.'

'Off guard? You end up having sex with someone because you happened to be off guard?' His voice is rising with anger.

'You weren't around. You're never around. My dad died, and I wanted someone to talk to.'

'Or someone to fuck?'

Oh God, does it have to be this ugly?

'Just because I work long hours, that's an excuse to fuck someone else, is it?' he continues.

'No!'

'And all the while I'm putting in the hours to pay for you and Thackeray.'

'Look, it's not an excuse. It shouldn't have happened. I'm just trying to explain. I . . . I . . .' I struggle to find the right words, but there are none. How do I explain how sorry I am? How do I show him that it was all an awful mistake? I see the pain in his face and long to make it go away. My heart crumples on the inside. 'I'm sorry,' I whisper. 'I'm so, so sorry.'

'You've betrayed me,' he says furiously, walking towards the kitchen sink. 'But more than that, you've betrayed Thackeray and you've betrayed yourself.'

I know he is right. Adam is not a mean man. He is absent and inattentive sometimes – a workaholic who craves success. A man who knows all about determination and ambition. But he has never been unkind, and more than anything, he is right.

'What about the baby? Do you even know whose it is?' There's meanness in his voice now. I shake my head, and fight back the tears that are threatening to fall. I deserve this. 'You would have me raise another of Brett's children, wouldn't you?' he snarls, contorting his features into a grimace that I've never seen on him before.

'No. I . . . I . . .' In Muslim countries I'd be stoned to death for adultery. What a merciful release that would be. Nothing could be as bad as this chasm that now yawns between us. Silence falls – despairing, painful, uncertain.

'I'll get my things,' I say eventually, and force myself to stand. I walk unsteadily across the room. At the door, I turn to Adam, hoping for what? I don't know. A reprieve, perhaps. Forgiveness. Instead, I see tears falling down his cheeks and realise I deserve neither. I have broken his heart.

Upstairs, I throw clothes into a bag through watery eyes. I have no idea what I am packing and I don't care. I grab Thackeray's pyjamas from beneath his pillow, a few pairs of shorts, T-shirts. What will I tell Thackeray? My head throbs and I feel suddenly dizzy and faint. I sit down on our bed and put my head between my knees for a few minutes.

'Are you OK, Mummy?' Thackeray is standing in the doorway.

'Mummy wasn't feeling too good,' I tell him. 'But I'm better now.' I head into the bathroom, throw water on my face and clean my teeth, while Thackeray watches. I pack the toothbrush in a toiletry bag.

'Why was Daddy shouting?'

'He's a little upset. Sometimes mummies and daddies get a little upset with each other, but everything's going to be fine. And you and I are going to go on a little adventure together.'

'To Disneyland?'

'No, not to Disneyland.' My mind is racing. Where? Where will we go? 'It's going to be a magical mystery tour,' I tell him.

Downstairs I heave the bag into the passenger front seat of the car because the rest of the car is full of boxes of Dad's stuff. Adam is nowhere to be seen.

'I want to say goodbye to Daddy,' Thackeray insists, so we head back into the house to search for him. How can this be happening? I look at my treasured sanctuary. The rugs, I chose. The framed photos, the books, the spring lilac I put into a vase only this week. Am I to leave all this? What have I done?

'Why aren't you coming with us?' Thackeray asks Adam. He's found him sitting on a sunlounger in the garden, staring into space.

'I don't know,' Adam says, wrapping his arms round him, and wiping away tears. 'I'll be missing you, though.'

'I'll miss you too, Daddy.'

'Should I call you?' I say cautiously.

'What for?' Adam answers coldly.

'I don't know . . .' Like Lady Macbeth, I feel guilt beckoning me to insanity. 'Oh Adam, I feel so ashamed. It really didn't mean anything,' I plead. 'It wasn't an affair. It was nothing. Nothing at all. I haven't even heard from him since.'

'Well that figures,' Adam snarls. 'But it's not my problem now.'

'I'm sorry, I really am.' Adam says nothing. 'Please believe me. Please. I can't bear that I've hurt you.' He still says nothing. His back, turned to me, says it all. 'Come on, Thackeray,' I reach for his tiny hand. 'How did you find out?' I ask from the doorway.

'Lizzie.'

'Lizzie?' I look round in shock.

'I bumped into her at a restaurant. She's becoming a Quantum Spiritualist. Did you know?'

'Yes.'

'She told me she was compelled to tell me because that's the way her church do things. They believe you've got to always tell people the truth about the things they can't see for themselves.' He pauses. 'I guess there's something to that.'

I say nothing. I knew I should never have told her. I squeeze Thackeray's hand. 'I'm sorry,' I whisper again. 'Come on, Thackeray. We'd better go.'

28

Numbed and on autopilot, I drive us to the Beverly Hills Hotel. It will do as a temporary refuge for now. As I pull into its leafy driveway on Sunset, past lush foliage with exotic flowers and palms, I wonder how often has this hotel been used as a breathing space for marital strife. Probably even more frequently than it's been used for famous celebrity liaisons. Everyone knows that Clark Gable and Carole Lombard used to secretly rendezvous in the bungalows here, Liz Taylor brought all of her husbands here at one time or another, and Barbara Streisand and Elliott Gould would frolic in the pool. But what of the break-ups? How many people have checked in here with their tails between their legs, begging for sanctuary from the turbulent travails of association? How many have hidden here with separation hanging over their heads? How many have walked through the doors fighting back the tears of despair and fearing the future, uncertain even when they might leave? The hotel doesn't advertise those. And I'm grateful.

I'm grateful also for the cheery faces of the valets in their pink polo shirts as we pull up – and for the serenity of the hotel reception with its piped music, thick carpeting, polished door handles and fragrant flower arrangements. It feels calm. I will stay here a few days and pray that Adam might forgive me in the fullness of time. There is a double room available not far from the pool, the receptionist tells me. Non-smoking. Twin beds.

'That will be fine,' I say, handing her my credit card. Anything will do. I just need to close the door on the day. I feel desperately tired suddenly. I steady myself against the reception desk and wrestle with the heat, the trauma, and the nausea that's building in my stomach. Thackeray is whining that this is not as good as Disneyland.

'I'm sorry, this card has been declined,' the receptionist says politely. 'Do you have another I can try?'

I give her another, which she runs through her machine.

'I'm afraid this one too.'

She tries all five of the cards that I carry in my purse, and as each one is declined, with the piped music cheerily playing on, the enormity of my situation thuds into place. Adam has cut off access to our accounts. I am to be punished. He is no longer paying for us.

'Can you try them again?' I plead with the receptionist. 'I'm sure one of them will work.' None of them does.

'How much is the room?' I search through my purse for cash. I have $115 in notes.

'Three hundred and eighty-five dollars,' says the receptionist, whose smile is wearing thin. She is looking at me now as one might a piece of dirt on the carpet, and that's precisely how I feel. 'Plus tax,' she spits. Wow. That's expensive. I never even knew.

'I'm sorry,' I say quietly, grabbing Thackeray's hand and racing back to the car.

Where now? Thackeray is whining more than ever because he's hungry. But no money! I can't believe I have no money! I can't even ask Dad any more. Or Heather. Reality smacks me in the face like a cold wet fish and leaves me fighting back tears on the side of the road, where I am forced to pull over. I am on my own, with less than a quarter of a tank of gas in the car, no credit cards and only $115 in my pocket until Stephen next pays me.

We find a McDonald's at Sunset and Crescent Heights and I buy Thackeray a Happy Meal, with a Batman toy that restores a smile to his face. Only $2.99! What good value. But there's no thick carpeting or serene waiting staff here. A homeless person is being shooed away, cursing, by security. Piped music tinkles here too, but it's caustic not serene.

Stay calm, I tell myself, and call Ashley. But my call is directed to voicemail. Sometimes he flies to New York on business. Did he say he was going away? I can't remember. What about Lizzie? No way. I can't call her. Nor Bella. The duplicity stabs painfully in my side still. I have other girlfriends, and there's Stephen. But the embarrassment. How can I face anyone ever again? The queasiness returns, and the urge to be sick. I race outside, leaving Thackeray alone, and vomit dramatically on the sidewalk. Everyone stares. Well of course they do.

The Happy Nites Motor Hotel is at the other end of Sunset Boulevard – the cheaper end, up near Hollywood, where concrete replaces foliage and strip malls substitute mansions. There are fast-food outlets and cheap shoe warehouses, a Ralphs supermarket and the social security administration building. A couple of girls wearing miniskirts, heels and not much else hang out on the sidewalk outside the motel. They check me over as I pull the car into the parking lot. The Mercedes looks out of place next to beaten-up trucks and tourist rentals. I never imagined ever having to stop here.

'How much is a room?' I ask a young girl in reception. She's wearing giant hoop earrings, blue eyeshadow up to her eyebrows and is chewing gum.

'Seventy-nine,' she says without looking up from the magazine she's reading.

'I'll take it,' I say.

'Plus tax,' she adds, now looking me over suspiciously.

This will be fine for now. It's even got a TV.

For a split second, there is a magical moment when I wake. I am at home in my own bed, in my own Bloomingdale sheets. Dad is still alive, I am not pregnant and everything is normal. Then I open my eyes, and as consciousness heaves me into the day, I remember. I cannot even bear to move – for if I do, I will feel the foreign nature of the bed, the cheap sheets, the nasty nylon coverlet, the unyielding foam pillows, the uncertainty of this circumstance. Thackeray found a used condom under the bed last night, and the noise coming through the thin wall from the room next door was something that might win the couple a gold in the lovemaking Olympics but was scarcely suitable for a five year old. It's a Saturday morning and I am homeless, with twenty-six dollars in my pocket. Have I reached rock bottom yet? I wonder. I close my eyes and wish for darkness to envelop me again and the day to disappear.

'Mummy, are you awake?' Thackeray slips out of the bed on the other side of the room and crawls in next to me. Pleasure courses briefly across my thoughts as I hold his body against mine. 'What are we going to do today, Mummy?'

'I don't know, sweetheart,' I say shakily. We can't stay here anyway. I don't have enough money. The dead weight in the bottom of my stomach returns, and all my senses silently scream out in alarm. I deserve this, I know I do.

'You look awful. When did you last eat?' Ashley asks when he opens his front door. Thank God, he called me back. We drove straight away to his penthouse apartment.

'Well, at least you've got a job,' he says pragmatically. The matter of money always comes first with Ashley. The two of us are seated at his polished rosewood dining table, contemplating the empty plates from the bacon and eggs he fried for us – also the debris that Thackeray has left on the table. I hear Thackeray cheering from Ashley's bedroom, where he is playing on his pinball machine.

'Yeah, but only for so long. Stephen's too tight to give me pay during maternity leave.'

'So you intend to keep the baby?' he asks cautiously. 'You don't have to, of course.'

'I know.' I shudder at the thought. It would be sad to let the baby go, especially since Adam and I tried so hard to conceive. 'Do you think there's a test they can do to find out who the father is?'

'You can only do a DNA test after the baby is born,' he tells me. Ashley has always been fascinated by science. He bought champagne when they cloned Dolly the sheep. Said it was one of mankind's biggest break-throughs. 'They haven't worked out the technology yet, I don't think. Would it make any difference anyway?'

'Maybe. If it was Adam's, he might take me back.'

'And if it were Brett's?'

'Well, he's scarcely reliable. He was fine when he first thought I was pregnant with Thackeray, but by the time I was ready to pop, he'd run. Anyway, it's not an issue. He's busy messing with Bella now.'

Ashley shakes his head and sighs. 'Well, you can stay here, of course, as long as you want.'

He holds his arms wide, gesturing at his apartment. It's on the sixth floor of an art deco tower in West Hollywood – spacious and stylish, especially with all the deco furniture that he has spent years collecting, but it only has two bedrooms, and no garden for my rambunctious, lively and very messy five year old.

'Thank you,' I say gently, and collect the plates,

scooping up the bacon pieces that Thackeray has strewn on the floor. It's a kind gesture, but I can't be dependent on my brother.

'And there's always Mum's,' Ashley suggests doubtfully.

'God, let's hope times don't get that bad.' We both force a laugh. I take the plates to his kitchen. 'Do you think we might see any money from Dad's estate?' I ask as I return. 'I know the lawyer said not to be too hopeful, but it would be so useful right now.'

Ashley takes a deep breath. 'It's not looking good,' he says gloomily. 'You know his manager really skanked him. Dad was living beyond his means for years. I think Heather is going to have to give up the house.'

It's almost impossible to imagine that house no longer belonging to our family. I somehow imagined that we'd find a way to keep it, in spite of everything. 'You know she's hanging out with Russell Anders from the Stupid Lucky Dogs now?'

'That didn't take long.' Ashley doesn't seem surprised. 'I always thought she was a gold-digger.'

'I guess she's just making sure she's taken care of,' I say, realising how smart Heather has been. Why couldn't I be that sharp? Why did I have to mess up so badly? What am I even going to live on? Despair crawls back into view. The $1,200 a week that Stephen pays me will barely even cover somewhere to live, let alone Thackeray's school fees. What am I going to do? A tear begins to roll down my cheek, followed by another, and another. Ashley reaches across the table and squeezes my arm awkwardly, but the torrent will not be stopped.

'I just feel so foolish,' I bawl. 'How could I have been so stupid?' I feel a line of snot streaming down my upper lip. 'And the worst thing is I've hurt Adam. I've been awful to him. You should have seen his face.'

Ashley disappears to find some tissues. Emotional

stuff has never been his thing, and a bawling woman is a challenge for him. He returns with a roll of toilet paper. 'Adam will get over it,' he mutters, in an effort to make me feel better.

'Will he? I feel so bad. He was so hurt.' I pull off some toilet paper and blow my nose.

'I think he always knew you still held a torch for Brett,' Ashley says gently.

'But I didn't. I really didn't.' Why does everyone keep saying I did?

Ashley frowns at me. 'Time to get real, don't you think?' he says sternly. 'Adam has always felt he wasn't as good as Brett in your eyes. Sure, most of it was probably his own insecurities, but it must have come from somewhere.'

I say nothing. For someone who doesn't like talking about emotional stuff, Ashley is quite forthcoming. And he knows Adam better than anyone.

'Look, Adam will go to work, bury his head in his next script, make his next movie probably,' he continues. 'Just give him some time. He's ambitious. That'll keep him busy. The point is, what do you really want?'

I stare at him in disbelief. 'I want him to take me back.'

'Do you?'

'Of course I do. I just want everything to be back to normal.'

'It's just . . .' Ashley pauses. 'Perhaps I shouldn't say this.'

'Go on. Just say it.' If ever there was a time for home truths, I suppose now would be it.

'Of course, it's never right to pass judgement on other people's marriages, but . . .'

'But?'

'It's just I've always wondered if you two were ever really right for each other. Adam's such a serious guy. He's kinda uptight sometimes, and so earnest. And you're . . .'

'You're telling me I'm not clever enough for him?'

'Don't be silly. Of course not. It's just that you're more light-hearted, more fun, more . . .' He sighs. 'I don't even know what I'm trying to say.' He gets up from the table and grasps the back of the chair – an attorney-style debriefing pose, as if I'm one of his clients about to sign a deal for millions of dollars. 'It's just I've always wondered what you two have in common.' He coughs sheepishly and the disclosure sits uncomfortably in the air. I never thought I'd hear this from Ashley. Adam is his friend. I thought he'd be rooting for us to get back together.

'Look, what about if I take my nephew out for the day?' he asks. 'I don't think I'm cut out to be an agony aunt.'

'Can we go to Disneyland?' Thackeray demands, standing in the doorway. How long has he been there? I wonder how much he has overheard and even understood of this.

'Yes. Let's go to Disneyland. I haven't been there in years.'

It's odd to be left alone in someone else's home. Ashley's apartment has the air of a gentlemen's club – lots of dark wood, books and masculinity. His furniture was carefully chosen, a heavy 1930s sofa with scrolling deco arms, wood-framed club chairs, jazzy zigzag curtains. It's the kind of room my grandparents might have felt right at home in. I wander on to the balcony. It's another misty morning and the view is shrouded in cloud. On a clear day, it's possible to see the Pacific from up here, but not today. Today, I can only see cars charging up and down Fairfax. I can see the post office by the traffic lights on Norton, and shoppers fighting for parking spaces in the Whole Foods lot. The jacaranda trees are about to flower along Hayworth, sending out lilac-coloured shoots that look so pretty against the grey of the rooftops.

I feel restless. I tour Ashley's bedroom, taking in the black leather headboard on his bed, the sci-fi novel on the side table, the *fin de siècle* alarm clock, and then feel guilty for snooping. I try sleeping in the guest room but there's too much disruption in my head for sleep, so I make some camomile tea, and then I remember the photos and old files in the back of my car. Ashley will enjoy seeing them, so I catch the elevator down and haul several of the boxes into his apartment.

There are dozens and dozens of photos. In the living room, I fall to my knees and pull them out, one by one. On the top are more recent ones: Ashley and me with Dad on the beach at Malibu as teenagers, Ashley as he graduated from law school, me in my English school uniform. It's funny how everyone in pictures always look so happy, their smiles frozen for ever in time. But the smiling faces never really tell the full story.

There are lots of photos from our childhood. Me on a horse, Ashley on a horse, Lydia on a horse. Mum in a bikini on a beach somewhere. Lydia and her mum in a tiny garden in England, Lydia on Dad's knee in an English front room, probably no more than Thackeray's age, Lydia with Dad around a Christmas dinner table, wearing tissue-paper hats and laughing, Lydia with her mum when she was a baby, Lydia on a potty, Lydia cooing in her cot, Lydia here, Lydia there, Lydia, Lydia, Lydia. The bottom half of the box is almost entirely made up of pictures of Lydia. How could she think she wasn't loved? What was he doing with all these if he didn't adore her?

I move on to the other boxes with some of the papers from Dad's desk. At the top are the three files I found with our names on. I open the file marked *Ashley*. Same as there was in mine, there are souvenirs of his childhood – old school reports, a certificate of merit for soccer, a lock of baby hair tied with a blue bow, some crayon

drawings and an old Father's Day card. I set the file aside.
Ashley will want to keep it, I'm sure.

I move on to the file marked *Lydia*. More school
reports, crayon drawings, an order of service from her
christening, certificates for swimming – she was always a
good swimmer – and at the bottom of it all some letters,
one scratched out in Dad's scrawly handwriting. The top
one is a copy of a typed letter to Robert Stone, who was
his first manager. It's addressed to Robert at Arden Inc.,
which strangely rings a bell with me, although I can't
think why. It's dated 1981. Lydia would have been five
years old. I wasn't even born.

> *Dear Robert,*
> *This letter is to inform you that next week I will be
> bringing my wife and daughter out to California to
> live with me. I cannot keep them secret any more.*
> *I am aware that this puts me in breach of
> contract with the record label, and goes against our
> agreement. However, they are part of my life and I
> cannot bear to be without them any more. If I am to
> be dropped from the label, and there are penalties
> to pay, then so be it. My wife and daughter matter
> more.*
> *Yours sincerely,*
> *Gavin Sash*

He did love her! He risked his record deal for her. Dad
did love you, Lydia, I want to yell out. But there is more
to read. There are some lyrics to a song, entitled simply
'Forgive Me'.

> *I didn't mean to turn my back on you,*
> *But one day we shall make it through,*
> *Lydia, I know that I have caused you pain,*
> *I wish that we could start again.*

Didn't you know I'd be coming back?
I'd never leave you just like that,
Lydia, I know that I have caused you pain,
I wish that we could start again.

Don't you know I thought of you?
Always, always, always you,
Lydia, I know that I have caused you pain,
I wish that we could start again.

I can't believe what I'm reading. Why did he never show this to her? Why didn't he let her know? Well, here's something I can do that's right. I call Lydia straight away. It'll be lunchtime in New York.

'Lydia, I've got something I want to read to you,' I say, the minute I hear her voice.

'Pearl?'

'Listen, I found this file in Dad's desk, and I want to read something to you.' I take a breath and read the letter that Dad wrote to his manager in 1981.

'I don't understand. What is this?'

'It's a letter Dad wrote telling his manager that he wouldn't keep you a secret any more and he didn't care if he lost his record deal over it.' I pause for a reaction. But Lydia says nothing. 'Don't you see, he didn't *want* to keep you a secret and you need to know this.'

'Why do I need to know this?' There's defiance in Lydia's voice still, and the bitterness I always remember about her.

'Because he loved you.'

'Why do you even care so much, Pearl?'

'Because I loved him. And I don't want to remember him being heartless like you make him out to be.' I feel my own tears welling up again, and fight them back. There have been too many already this morning. 'Because I don't want you to be right,' I find myself almost yelling.

Lydia lights a cigarette, and I hear the roar of New York traffic in the distance. Her scepticism comes in the form of silence. I take a deep breath.

'Look, it wasn't his fault,' I insist. 'It was in his contract. So the record company and his manager forced him into it. But Dad obviously didn't like it or he wouldn't have breached the contract to get you out here. He risked everything for you.'

'Well, it came too late,' Lydia fires back crossly. She inhales on her cigarette, and I try to understand. Being abandoned leaves a scar. All she ever wanted was to feel loved.

'There's more, Lydia. There's a song he wrote for you too.'

'Let me guess. Its title was "Listen to the Bullshit",' Lydia snarls, so viciously it sends a shiver down my spine.

'Actually, it's called "Forgive Me".'

From the absence of words, I guess she is shocked by this. 'Can I read it to you?' I ask gently.

'Go on then,' she says cautiously, and I sense her wanting to believe. I read her the song, and then, for the first time I can ever remember, I hear her sob. Just one. A hiccup of emotion, unleashing years of resentment and pain.

'Are you all right?' I ask quietly.

'Yes,' she sniffs.

'He really did love you, you know.'

'Yes,' she almost whispers.

I listen to the New York traffic for a while down the phone line. Manhattan traffic sounds different to anywhere else on earth. It's louder, more ferocious.

'Why didn't he ever tell me he'd risked his contract?' Lydia asks at last. 'Why didn't he ever show me his song? Why didn't he talk to me?'

'I don't know. Too ashamed perhaps. Too many drugs. Too much time gone past. Too frightened of you. You're pretty scary sometimes.' We both force a laugh.

'But now it's too late,' Lydia says sadly.

'Not completely. Look, you have a lot to forgive him for. He wasn't perfect, and he didn't do it right. But if you could find forgiveness in your heart, it might somehow help you. You might not feel so much resentment.'

I hear Lydia blow her nose.

'Anyways, I'm going to put the letter and the song in the mail for you. And I'll save the photos for when you're next over.'

'What photos?'

'Oh, didn't I tell you? There are billions and billions of photos here of you when you were little.'

'Really?' She sounds so pleased.

'Yes. Tons of them. All of you. All kept by Dad. And there are far too many to mail. So I'm leaving them at Ashley's place, and next time you're over you can collect them.'

'Thank you, Pearl,' Lydia says, weighing her words with earnest gratitude. 'Thank you.'

'It was nothing.'

'Speak soon?' she says, almost as a question.

'Yes, let's.'

Sometimes great distances between people can be shortened with only a couple of words.

It is a long morning alone in Ashley's apartment, but I feel a little better. I don't know why I needed the reassurance that Dad loved all of us, but somehow that mattered to me. By lunchtime, I have sorted all the photos into three neat piles, one for Ashley, one for Lydia and one for me. I like sorting and tidying. I always have. It's good thinking time. I've also worked my way through several of the other boxes from Dad's desk. He really was hopeless with money. There are old bank statements here, credit card bills, receipts. I even found his first ever contracts. There's the one he signed with Robert Stone, giving Arden Inc. thirty-five per cent of anything he made. Thirty-five per cent! Stephen would die to make thirty-five per cent off any of his artists. The most that managers and agents take these days is fifteen or twenty per cent. But why does Arden Inc. sound so familiar? I know I've heard that name before somewhere.

Dad's first record contract is equally painful reading. He got only two per cent of net record sales out of Deaf Records. Only two per cent! No wonder he was broke. No wonder Deaf Records, coincidentally part of New Look Pictures and Stephen's conglomerate, is doing so well. A normal record deal would give the artist fourteen per cent, and given the number of albums Dad sold, he should have made a mint. But poor old Dad must have been glad of any kind of a deal. He didn't know he was going to sell over fifty million albums back then. I doubt he even made any money over his advance.

I sift through more papers, and find the love letters that Dad and Mum wrote to each other in the year after they met. I sit back in a chair to read them because my legs have got pins and needles. There's such tenderness in these letters that I feel guilty reading them. Dad wrestled with wanting to be with another woman while Jodie, Lydia's mum, was being admitted into a psychiatric ward. She was diagnosed with early Alzheimer's and didn't even recognise Dad any more. I always knew he wrote 'Remember Me' for her, but I never understood its full meaning. Did no one ever think to explain all this to Lydia? Dad wasn't always emotionally forthcoming. It would be just like him to not explain it. I put the letters in the same envelope as the other papers I've set aside for Lydia.

By the afternoon, I've had enough of sorting boxes and staring into space with my own brooding company. So I force myself to escape to the world of *An Italian Stallion*, which fortunately is still in my handbag from yesterday.

Outside, the scorching Tuscan sun was making heat hazes of the air close to the sandy track leading to the villa. Matteo pulled Ernestina into the shade of the olive grove and laid a blanket on the stony ground. He kissed her lightly on the lips and told her he wanted to ask her something important.

'Cosa c'e?' Her Italian was not very good.

'I want to sposare.' His English was little better.

'Sposare?'

'Si'

'You want to get married?' She could barely believe what she was hearing. After all that had gone before.

'Si.'

The thing I love most about romance novels is that

there is always the predictability of a happy ending. I know it's not very avant-garde of me, but it makes me feel safe. I like it that I am assured of contentment at the end. It's what we all crave in our lives. I don't want a literary finish that leaves me feeling sad. I don't want an arty read that leaves me struggling for a conclusion. I don't want a political drama that leaves me scared of the world around me. A happy-ever-after is what we all hope for really. I just wish I could write my own. Wouldn't that be great? What would I write? Adam would call. 'Darling, I forgive you. Shall we put it behind us and start again?' he'd say.

'Oh yes, let's,' I would cry. 'Let's go and take that vacation in Mexico together,' and we'd sail off into the sunset.

And what about Brett? He would have to get his just deserts, of course. An ancient tribe of cannibals would arrive off a boat in Los Angeles, and end up in Beverly Hills, where they'd break into his apartment and eat him for breakfast. Or maybe they'd break in and just slice off his penis – a delicacy where they come from. Yes, I like that.

My cell phone rings, disturbing my dramatic licence.

'Darling!'

I recognise Brett's voice straight away. How apt that he should call now. The nemesis and great destroyer of my own happy ending.

'What do you want?' I say tersely.

'Where are you?'

'At Ashley's.'

'At Ashley's! Everything OK?'

'None of your fucking business,' I explode. 'Why are you calling me?'

'Whoa there,' he says, taken aback. 'I was just—'

'I'm not that stupid, you know,' I say, interrupting him sharply.

'Did I say you were?' He sounds confused.

'I saw the pictures of you and Bella. How could you?'

Brett lets out a howl of laughter, which is not quite the reaction I was expecting. How callous and hurtful can he be? How could he make light of such a thing as this?

'With Bella?' he bursts out. 'Darling—'

'Don't call me darling,' I interrupt. 'I'm not your darling. Don't even start to deny it, because I've seen the pictures—'

'Pearl, I'm coming round,' he announces. 'I'll be there in twenty.'

'No, don't,' I say, but he's gone.

I'm still dabbing gloss on my lips when the doorbell rings. In the face of a gladiator showdown, it's always good to look one's best.

'Hi,' he says cautiously when I open the door, perhaps waiting for me to hurl something at him. It's what he deserves. He's wearing a leather biker's jacket and carrying a helmet under his arm. Seeing me unarmed, he takes a step in. 'I want you to come with me somewhere.'

'No way.'

'It will explain everything.'

'How can it?'

'You'll find out when you get there.'

'Why should I?'

'Just come with me, and you'll see.'

'Well I can't,' I snap. 'I've got things to do.'

'Pearl, this is important,' he insists, and I see that he's serious. 'Please. I want to explain something to you. Something that's very, very important to me.'

'But I saw pictures of you and Bella.'

'Just come with me.' He sounds exasperated now. 'It won't take long, I promise.'

He always was persuasive.

Riding pillion on the back of his bike forces me to wrap my arms around Brett's chest. I feel his great frame beneath his jacket and the rise and fall of his breath. I haven't been on the back of a bike since Dad used to take me to the beach. Memories come flooding back, but we're clearly not heading for the beach now. Brett still hasn't told me where we're going, and I can't begin to imagine as we speed off along Fountain, heading east past small weatherboard houses and styleless fifties apartment blocks. Then we join the freeway. I feel the thrill of speed, and close my eyes as Brett dodges traffic. 'I'm a mother, don't kill me,' I shout above the engine roar. What on earth am I doing? The freeway concrete whizzes beneath us. God, these things are dangerous.

The 101 heads towards Downtown – Los Angeles' own mini-Manhattan, with its soaring skyscrapers and high-rise financial district. There are some fancy offices here and the Museum of Contemporary Art. Chinatown is close by, and Little Tokyo. And then there's the Garment District, where you can buy cheap designer knock-offs. But we're not stopping here.

Soon the skyscrapers are gone and the landscape becomes intimidating and utilitarian. Railway tracks, warehouses, depots, the vast hangar-like structures of industry dot the horizon. Away from the palm trees of Beverly Hills, LA is a disfigured landscape. We pull on to the 710 and head south. 'Where are we going?' I try to scream, but Brett can't hear me, and after twenty minutes or so we pull off the freeway. This is nowhere I have ever been before.

Litter lines the kerbs and telephone wires impede the skyline. Bars swathe the windows of shops and homes, barbed wire straddles fencing, and graffiti and gang tags cover everything. We pass car body shops, porn shops, thrift stores, and billboards that advertise their wares in Spanish. Brett eventually pulls up outside a large building surrounded by a breeze-block wall and heavy metal gates.

'Welcome to Compton, better known as the Hood,' he says once he's parked the bike between two trucks on the side of the road, and we've pulled our helmets off.

'The Hood!' Everyone knows that Compton is one of the most dangerous inner-city areas in the whole of the States, famous for two things – crime and gang violence. 'What are you bringing me here for?'

'You'll see,' he says with a crooked smile. 'Come on.'

He leads me to some big rusted metal gates and presses a buzzer. 'It's Brett,' he says into the intercom. Eyes appear at a peephole, and then I hear bolts being carefully drawn back on the other side. A young Latino girl, maybe twelve or thirteen years old, heaves the door open. 'Hi, Brett,' she coos, smiling as if to save her life and barely taking her eyes off him.

'Hello, Amelia. This is my friend Pearl,' he announces once we're inside a small courtyard that is filled with flowerpots and flowering plants – a sharp contrast to the harsh concrete of the street outside.

'Welcome, señora,' the little girl says, slamming the door shut after us. I notice now that her belly protrudes. She's wearing a Barbie Doll T-shirt beneath which her golden caramel skin escapes. Not pregnant, surely? She can't be. She's still got her hair in pigtails.

'Due in three months,' she says proudly, noticing where my eyes have travelled. 'Then I have my own babe.'

'But how old are you?'

'Thirteen, señora. Come on, I show you round.' She gestures to the blue front door of the building, which I realise now must once have been a school of some kind.

Immediately inside is an office, where two administrative staff stop tapping at computer keyboards to chorus greetings to Brett. Beyond is a long dark corridor at the end of which is another outside door, where sunshine blasts against the dark. Doors lead off the corridor and I am shown into the first room – an empty bedroom with three beds, each neatly made up with a yellow coverlet. It reminds me immediately of my English boarding school. Except the decor is possibly better here – the paint still smells fresh. It's white and clean. The curtains are homely, and there's a carpet on the floor.

'This is my bedroom,' Amelia says proudly. She sits down on one of the beds. 'And this is Feliz,' she says, holding up a teddy bear. 'It means happy in Spanish. This bed belongs to Beatriz and this to Dora.' She points at the other beds. 'And this is where we study.' She indicates three little desks along the wall.

'Very nice,' I say encouragingly, as we follow her out. Brett says nothing, but I am aware that he is watching me, waiting for a reaction. Amelia points out other bedrooms along the corridor, all uniformly the same. She shows me bathrooms and cupboards and then a big dining area where a handful of teenage girls, mostly African-American, are sitting around one of the tables drinking lemonade.

'Are you going to tell me why we're here?' I ask Brett, as we move on through the dining room to the outer door, where a garden is catching the sun. It's not a big garden, but it's been well taken care of. There's a giant avocado tree casting a shadow over a patio area, where some more girls are playing cards. A bush of honeysuckle fills the air with its fragrance.

'Do you like it?' Brett asks, as we stand in the doorway looking out on the garden. Amelia has disappeared to join her friends on the patio.

'What is this place?'

'It's an orphanage, kinda,' Brett says quietly. 'Every one of these girls has been abandoned, most have been abused, all have known nothing but foster care. I have places here for sixty girls. Sixty girls who will need special support to get them into college. Sixty girls who had better make it to college or their future is working at McDonald's or worse.' He pauses to let me take this in.

'And they need a lot of help. Look at Amelia. She's not the only one who's pregnant here.'

'What will happen to her?'

'We'll take care of her. We'll teach her to take care of the baby, and we'll provide childcare so she can still make it to school. It's a special programme I'm setting up.' He wanders over to a water fountain in the corner and pours water into a paper cup. 'Would you like a drink?'

I shake my head.

'This is my project, Pearl. This is what I wanted you to see. You want to know why I was in photos with Bella?' He drinks from the cup. 'Who do you know who is an orphan? Who do you know who would be the best person in the world to advise on a project such as this?' He looks carefully at me, scrutinising my face as the penny drops. 'And you of all people should know not to believe anything you read in those magazines.' He laughs.

I reach for a chair at a round patio table with an umbrella offering shade and sit down. Relief floods through me, allaying fears and redressing misjudgement. I have been a fool. 'I would have called you before, but you told me not to. I didn't want to interfere between you and Adam. I know things can't have been easy.'

I shift uncomfortably in my seat. It's the first time he's made a reference to that fateful afternoon together, and I'd so much rather forget it.

'And this was a big project,' he continues, perhaps sensing my unease. 'It's taken months to get off the ground. I've been down here every day, building stuff, dealing with the social services, employing people. This is what I was meant to do. Being in movies is OK. But this is real, Pearl.' I catch the excitement in his expression. 'This stuff makes a difference.'

I smile. He wants me to be impressed. And I am. The

old idealistic Brett with his mission to change the world has returned. I can see that.

'The point is, Pearl . . .' Brett pulls up another chair and sits next to me. 'I wanted you to see this place because I wanted you to see how I've changed. I wanted to prove to you that I'm not the same person I was. And I asked Bella not to say anything because I wanted to bring you here myself.'

I feel unexpectedly thirsty. I think I will have a drink after all. It's become quite a warm day. I walk over to the water fountain and turn on the tap, relishing the cool of the water in the paper cup. This week has been such a tornado of events. I feel almost faint thinking about them all.

'You do like it, don't you?' Brett asks.

'Yes.' I'm too overcome to be able to express anything smarter. A police siren wails close by.

'At the moment I'm pouring all my royalty cheques into the place,' Brett continues. 'And they go quite a long way.' He smiles awkwardly. 'But I'm going to have to do some fund-raising soon. There are a lot of costs.' He starts listing them, and I smile as if listening, but his words have faded, because suddenly my thoughts have lurched backwards in time to that paperwork I was looking through this morning.

I feel like I've been hit by a passing truck – a top-speed heavyweight one, capable of knocking an idea into a slow and stupid brain. Royalty cheques. That's it. I know exactly where I've heard of Arden Inc. before. How could I have been so blind? And I know what this means too. It means I have something very important to do.

'Pearl, you've gone very quiet,' Brett says, nudging me slightly. 'Are you all right?'

'Sorry?'

'You've gone very quiet.'

'Sorry. Um . . . Look, I need to get back to Ashley's.'

'Have I said the wrong thing?'

'No. I . . . er . . .'

'Did I do the wrong thing bringing you here?'

'No. But I need to go.'

'Is it Adam? I've been worried about what damage I've caused. If there's anything I can . . .'

'Oh . . . No. He threw me out, actually,' I say, and surprise myself at how casually the words come. I didn't intend to tell Brett, but there's no point keeping it a secret. And I've got some important things on my mind now.

'He threw you out?'

'Yes. He found out about our afternoon together.'

Brett closes his eyes. 'That explains the weird phone call to me.'

'What phone call?'

'Adam just told me to call you.'

'What?' I let out a laugh, for want of anything else to do. Adam called Brett! What does he think I am? Some kind of chattel to be passed from one man to another? Is that what he thinks? That I can't look after myself? That I don't know how to? How dare he call Brett! How dare he suppose that if I'm not with him, I'll go to Brett. How dare he interfere. What kind of warped man calls his wife's ex-husband after he's kicked her out and cancelled all her credit cards? I feel insulted. I don't need to be looked after. Not by Adam, not by Brett, not by anyone.

'Will you take me back to Hollywood now, please?' I ask tersely.

Brett looks perplexed. 'Are you angry with me?'

'No. Yes. No. Look, will you just take me back to Hollywood, or shall I call a cab?'

'Of course I'll take you. To Ashley's?'

'Yeah.'

'You're staying there?'

'For now.'

'And then?'

'Just take me back there, would you?'

'Pearl, would you consider . . .' He reaches across to catch my hand, but I pull away.

Consider what? Just picking up where we left off? Just pretending he never left us? Just pretending I'm not pregnant? That afternoon together was a mistake. A huge mistake, because I was caught off guard. But I'm not making it again. I don't need anyone. I will take care of myself, and my children – both of them.

'Just take me back to Hollywood, would you?'

30

Ashley and Thackeray are not back from Disneyland by the time Brett drops me off. 'Thanks,' I say, waving him away dismissively.

'Can't I come in?' he asks.

'No.'

'Will you let me see you again?'

'I don't know,' I say, and run inside, fumbling for Ashley's front-door key. In truth, I don't know what to think about Brett any more. But one thing, at least, is clear. I have to take care of Thackeray and me, and the new baby, all by myself. No longer will I be dependent on a man. I don't need one. Dad always said we had to be self-reliant, and now, for the first time perhaps, I realise why it's so important. I shall have my baby – and I shall do it in style, and on my own terms. I know how to do it now.

First I pull out several of the papers that were in the boxes. I check them over carefully. Then I scour Ashley's bookshelves for a book on entertainment law and look up a chapter on talent agents and illegal practices. It's all here, clear as day. This is going to be easier than I thought. I put the papers in my handbag, and smile briefly to myself. There's going to be satisfaction in this.

On the dresser in Ashley's bedroom is an old Apple laptop I've seen before gathering dust. I place it on his dining-room table, dust it down, and it considerately bleeps into life. I open up a new document, draw a deep breath, and start.

Even at sixty-three words per minute, I can't write fast enough. Words pour out of me. Words I didn't realise were in me. Words that reach the page in surprising order and effectiveness. Why didn't I ever think to do this before? Thackeray and Ashley return, demanding attention, with tales of rides in teacups and encounters with Mickey. I tell them I'm busy. I've simply got to write.

'Can you let us stay a month?' I ask Ashley, after he's put Thackeray to bed for me.

'Sure. Take as long as you want.'

'It won't be more than a month, I promise.'

'It's fine if it isn't. But then what?'

'I can't tell you.'

'Why?'

'I've got a plan.'

'Yeah?'

'Yes, but I can't tell you yet. I don't want to jinx it.'

'OK. Then I won't ask.' Bless him. Ashley always was so understanding. 'Want something to eat?'

'No, I've got to write.'

I write all evening, until my eyes can focus on the screen no more, and then I'm up at five writing again on Sunday morning. Ashley offers to take Thackeray to the beach for me, and I accept readily.

'You don't mind?' I ask.

'No, it'll be fun. But will you tell me what you're doing?'

'You promised you wouldn't ask.'

'Oh, come on, tell me,' he persists.

'I'm writing my own happy ending,' I say confidently.

'Is it one of your stories, like you used to do when you were at school?' he asks, peering over my shoulder.

'Kinda,' I say, closing the computer quickly.

'I used to enjoy them.'

'You did?'

'Yeah. I always wondered why you didn't do more.'

See, I knew it was a good plan.

The next day I take Thackeray to school and then I resume my position at Ashley's dining-room table. I write, and I write, and I write some more.

Stephen calls. 'I've got measles,' I tell him. 'Doctor says I'm highly contagious. Got to stay in isolation for a month.'

'But—'

'Sorry, you'll have to get a temp,' I say, and hang up.

And then I carry on. Monday rolls into Tuesday, rolls into Wednesday, and still my fingers fly over the keyboard. Lizzie calls.

'I don't want to talk to you,' I say crossly.

'Why not?' she trills.

'You know very well why not.'

'I was trying to help, Pearl.'

'Like hell you were.'

'Oh, don't be like that, Pearl. Can I come over and explain?'

'No.'

'Please.'

'I'm busy.'

'Doing what?'

'Why would I want to tell you anything ever again?' And then I hang up. The former me might have listened to Lizzie. But I haven't the time. For the first time in ages, I can see a clear way ahead. Besides, it'll do Lizzie no harm to be left to simmer and fret.

Bella calls. Brett calls. Stephen calls again. Even Adam calls. 'I can't talk,' I tell them all. 'I'm busy.'

And I am. Writing becomes an obsession. I stop to take Thackeray to school and fetch him, and for a few hours in the evening we play together. But once he's in bed, I'm back at the computer. Sometimes even until dawn. There aren't enough hours to get it all down.

Sometimes I stop in the long, dark evenings. Only for five minutes, to think, stretch, to add another coffee cup to the many littered around me. And I look at Thackeray fast asleep in his bed. 'We're going to be OK,' I tell him. 'We are, we really are. It's going to be you, me and the baby, and we're going to be fine.'

At the end of the month, I read through what I've written, clean up the spelling mistakes, adjust a bit of dialogue, hone the description and borrow Ashley's printer to print out all hundred and fifty pages, finishing with the title page. Now for some bright red lipstick, and a change of clothes from these jeans and the T-shirt I've been living in. Living out of a holdall hasn't been easy. But at least I remembered to pack my bright red Donna Karan suit on that miserable day when I left Adam behind.

Now a quick call-in at Stephen's house to collect some papers that are vital to my plan, and I drive to Shawe Towers in Beverly Hills.

It's a Wednesday morning and Stephen's always here on Wednesday. I park my car in the parking lot and catch the elevator to the ninth floor. Frank, his office PA, greets me with a puzzled look as the elevator doors open. His desk is squeezed into a small area right outside the elevator, while Stephen's oversized, overdecorated office takes up the rest of the floor.

'Pearl, what a surprise. I thought you had measles,' Frank says, as I march past him on the thick carpet. Beautifully, confidently, intelligently. 'Stephen's in a meeting right now. Shall I . . . ?'

'Don't bother,' I say, as I reach the glass door of Stephen's office and walk straight in.

'Hey, can't you see I'm in a meeting?' Stephen barks at me.

'Not any more,' I tell him. 'Sorry, gentlemen, I'm afraid I'm going to have to ask you to leave. This meeting's over,' I say to the two men in dark suits who are sitting in the chairs in front of Stephen's desk. They look a little startled, but obligingly stand up. Stephen is outraged.

'No it's not. Sit down,' he barks at them. They obligingly sit. 'Whatchyou think you're doing, Pearl?' he bellows.

'Gentlemen, I think it's best if you *do* leave, or you might find yourself witnessing scenes that may need more than an R rating.' They stand again, looking uncertainly at Stephen. 'This way please.' I usher them towards the door, where Frank is standing looking bemused.

'How dare you?' Stephen yells at me, as I close the office door behind me. He's gone quite red in the face. 'Aren't you supposed to be contagious?'

'Yes. Very.' I smile cruelly. 'Now sit down!' I order, surprising even myself with the Nazi commandant that seems to have entered my tone. Stephen's mouth drops open in surprise and he falls back into his chair. I could quite get used to this.

'Now you and I have got something to discuss,' I say, walking round to his side of the desk, swinging his chair towards me and bringing my face within inches of his. I look him straight in the eyes. I'm a wolf going in for the kill, I tell myself, resisting the urge to snarl, but only just. 'I want you to cast your mind back thirty-odd years. Arden Inc. was one of yours, wasn't it?'

'What are you talking about?' says Stephen, looking annoyed. There's a mark on his shirt, I notice, where he's spilt something, and his breath smells. God, he's disgusting.

'I know it was one of your management companies. So don't even try to deny it.'

'OK, so I won't try to deny it,' Stephen says

defensively. I like that. It's good to see him defensive. 'What's Arden Inc. got to do with anything anyways?'

'Arden Inc. was the management company that signed my dad to Deaf Records. Thirty years ago, Robert Stone was your partner, wasn't he?'

'Er . . .'

'Wasn't he?' I say fiercely, and lean right into his face again.

'Yes,' says Stephen quietly. 'But Robert's dead now. Long gone.'

'Doesn't matter. He was your business partner. And Deaf Records is one of your companies too. A subsidiary of New Look Pictures. Right?'

'What is this? Twenty questions?'

'Not twenty questions. Just one very important one.' I pause for full dramatic effect, and lean back, resting against the desk. 'If Arden Inc. were my dad's managers, and they were signing him to their own record label, then it was a case of double-dipping, was it not? You took your commission as managers – thirty-five per cent. Daylight robbery in itself. Thievery from a talented guy who was just desperate for fame. And then you took the profits on the record too.'

Stephen says nothing, but fidgets uneasily in his seat. He knows I've got him.

'Two per cent! Two lousy per cent was all you gave him!' I struggle to contain the anguish in my voice. Stephen runs his hands over his bald patch with a look of disquiet. 'If you'd given him fourteen per cent, like most decent human agents, he'd have cleared seventy, eighty, maybe even a hundred million after his advance. Instead he got nothing. Nothing, Stephen, nothing!' I say angrily. 'My poor dad was ripped off by the very person I end up working for.' Stephen looks anxious.

'But you didn't declare your interest in Deaf Records at the time, did you?' My collected demeanour is back now. I'm Hannibal Lecter on the scent of flesh. 'Did you know that's illegal, Stephen? Not to mention unethical, immoral and greedy.' I stare at him intensely and watch him squirm. 'Of course you know it's illegal. But I wonder if you know that makes your management contract with my father null and void.'

Stephen still says nothing, and coughs uncomfortably.

'By my calculations, taking in accrued interest and the artist's royalties that should have been his, that means that you owe my father's estate some forty to fifty million dollars. You can see the calculations here.' I hand him a piece of paper.

Stephen takes the paper and without reading it, crumples it into a ball and throws it at a trash can by the door. He misses. But his confidence appears to have returned. 'You think I'm just going to write you a cheque?' he says with a venomous laugh. 'Honey, you are kidding yourself. You'll have to take me to court.' He gets to his feet. 'There's no way I'm paying you anything.'

'What a shame. Then I'll have to expose your interest in New Look Pictures, and let all your clients see how you've been ripping all of them off too.'

Stephen sits back down again. 'You wouldn't dare,' he says, and I watch the look of alarm spread.

'Let me see. I counted over fifty separate contracts – all your clients, all sent to New Look Pictures, and none of whom knew your interest in the company. That's an awful lot of double-dipping. An awful lot of lawsuits. An a-w-f-u-l lot of money.' I linger over the words, watching Stephen squirm. 'Might cost you billions. And who would trust you ever again? It would be enough to put you out of business, wouldn't you think?'

'You haven't the proof.'

'Let me think. I have all the contracts. I wonder what else I would need,' I say smugly. I'm really quite enjoying this.

'You took the contracts?'

'Well, you do keep them in my office. It wasn't exactly hard.'

Stephen lets out a deflated sigh. At least he has the decency to know when he's beat.

'How much do you want?' he says unhappily.

'I had a feeling you'd come round to my way of thinking,' I snarl. 'I'll take fifty million.'

'What?'

'And that's being generous. That's still leaving you with a cut. But I also want—'

'This is blackmail,' Stephen interrupts, now looking really quite shaken. It's funny, I don't think I can ever remember him looking fearful before. Ugly, yes. Fearful, no. 'I'm not paying you any more,' he warns.

'You.' I prod him hard with one finger in his shoulder, pushing him back in his seat. 'You will do exactly what I tell you.' The latent Nazi commandant really is going great guns. Who knew I had it in me?

'First of all you're going write me out a letter, with a copy to your bank instructing them to pay Gavin Sash fifty million dollars.'

'Right now?' Stephen splutters.

'No time like the present,' I say, pulling open the drawer in his desk where I know he keeps paper. 'I will forward Frank some bank details and you will have the money in Dad's account before the end of the week.'

'The end of the week?' Stephen is aghast.

'Or I spill the beans.'

'But your dad's dead,' Stephen says. 'You don't want me to give the money to you?'

'That would make me no better than you,' I bite back. Lydia and Ashley deserve their share. Even Heather. 'Dad's estate will take care of it,' I tell him and hand him a pen.

Stephen writes the letter and hands it to me with a nervous look in his eye.

'Next, you're going to take a script into New Look Pictures for me.'

'What script?'

'This script.' I walk over to the bag I've left on one of the chairs, pull out my script, and thump it on his desktop with a loud, definitive bang.

Stephen peers at it cautiously, like it's a bomb that might explode, and reads aloud, '*Twenty-Two Hours*, by Pearl Sash.' Then suddenly he lets out a raucous laugh. 'What, you?' He can hardly contain himself.

'Yes, me.'

'You've written a script? You!' He guffaws so hard, there is a small tear emerging from his piggy little eye. 'But you're just a secretary.'

'Oh yes, so I am.' I mimic his voice. 'Want to read it?'

'Sure. This should be hilarious.' He contains the laughter, turns the title page and reads the pitch. 'Not bad,' he mumbles. Then he turns the next page, and reads the first scene. Then he's on to the next page, and the next. I stand over by the window, looking out on to Beverly Hills. I can see Stephen's mansion from here, over the tops of the palms. His wealth is obscene.

'OK. You can read it later,' I say, now that I can see it's got his attention.

'This is good,' he announces, turning another page. 'I actually like it.'

'I thought you would,' I say confidently. I don't know why I feel so confident, but I do. 'I want you to offer it to Barry Finemann. He'll pay me what he thinks it's worth. If it's not worth anything, that's fine. But I want you to get him to look at it.'

Stephen stares at me, dumbfounded. 'Does this mean you quit?' he asks. Even after I've blackmailed him, he still wants me to work for him? He's extraordinary. 'You

304

know, you're quite impressive when you're angry,' he offers.

'Yes, it means I quit,' I tell him. 'And you better make a doctor's appointment quick, in case you've got the measles.'

31

Ashley was almost tearful when Thackeray and I moved out of his skyrise apartment. To be honest, it bothered me being up so high in a town that rests on the San Andreas fault line.

'You really don't have to go,' he pleaded. 'I'm going to miss having the little guy around the place.'

'I said we'd only stay a month, and you've been too good to us already,' I told him, kissing him lightly on the cheek. 'And you'll never get a girlfriend if you've got your sister living with you.'

We ended up staying longer than a month, because after banking my million dollars – let me just say that again, it sounds so good. Because after banking my million dollars, it took me a while to find us a place to live. As it turned out, Barry Finneman loved the script. I mean, l-o-v-e-d it! He paid a million up front for it immediately – and there will be another million at the back end, after the movie comes out. And thanks to Stephen's little deposit, there'll be money coming from Dad's estate eventually too.

I've found us the perfect little house, tucked away in one of the tiny leafy streets of West Hollywood. Three bedrooms, a small garden for the children to play in (because there will be two of them soon enough), a beautiful wraparound porch, and a guest house that I am converting into an office, to work on my next script. It's not as grand as our old house. And its zip is 90069 – not nearly as prestigious – but I'm done with trying to keep up with the rest of Hollywood. Moderation is the new excess, I tell myself. Brett was right about that. I'm only renting it, but I have an option to buy, and as time goes on, I think I might. I like the neighbourhood – many of its inhabitants are gay, and many of them have children. There are kids with two dads, or two mums, or one mum or one dad. The twenty-first-century family unit is different to what it was in the last century. We fit in here – no questions asked.

And my new autonomous, man-free life has a simplicity about it that I'm relishing. No dramas, more bed space. Didn't Ginger Rogers do everything Fred Astaire did, except backwards and in heels? I've been too dependent on men in the past. I realise this. I find myself thinking of one of Lizzie's jokes all the time: What's a woman's best rule of thumb? If it comes with bumpers or balls, you're going to have trouble with it sooner or later. My life had become so steamrollered by guilt, confusion and anxiety, all I craved was space – and that space couldn't include Brett. I needed to look after my kids, look after me and devote some time to my new career. I needed to learn how to be an independent woman.

But feminism is all very well, until you have a kid who misses his dad. Thackeray misses Adam terribly, and that situation needs to be addressed. There are other matters to be discussed too. Important ones. So this afternoon, much as I'm dreading it, we're heading back to our old house for the first time to see him. When I called Adam on the phone, he was surprisingly agreeable. It's been nearly seven weeks since we last saw him.

'Daddy.' Thackeray runs into Adam's arms the minute we pull up in the drive and he escapes his car seat. 'Daddy, I've missed you.'

'I've missed you too,' Adam says, closing his eyes and holding him tight.

'Shall we go play?' Thackeray asks him expectantly. I love the way children always cut straight to the chase. No preamble or wasted words. This is the purpose of the visit as far as Thackeray is concerned. Adam looks across at me as if to ask if he should, and I gesture to go ahead.

While they play chase in the garden, I look around our house. Nothing has changed since we left it. Everything is still meticulously in its place – cushions neatly plumped, kitchen surfaces clean and clear, potted plants still green and watered. And not a coffee cup out of place, of course. But the house feels different now. It feels unlived in and no longer mine. I feel different too, I realise. Hard to explain, but I feel somehow more confident about being me.

I settle on a patio chair and sort though my mail, which I found neatly stacked by the front door. There are some catalogues and out-of-date social invitations, but nothing important. So I watch Adam and Thackeray play. Thackeray tears around like a wild cat. How did he get so big so suddenly? I hadn't even noticed. Adam tries to keep up with him.

Eventually they are both sweating and panting. 'Now, I'm gonna find my toys in my bedroom,' Thackeray announces after downing water, and Adam collapses in the chair next to me.

'Why don't you see which ones you want to take to our new house?' I suggest.

For a while, neither Adam or I speak. We just stare out at the garden. The orange trees have blossomed since I left. I've prepared a million speeches inside my head, but I can't remember a word now.

'The hedges need trimming,' I venture.

'Yes, I should tell the gardener,' he agrees.

More awkward silence. Then we both speak at the same time and feel silly.

'You first,' I say.

'No, you.'

'I just want to say I'm sorry,' I say quietly.

'I know. I'm sorry too.'

'But you have nothing to be sorry for.'

'I do really. I was possessive and obsessive.' Adam lets out a sigh of resignation.

'No you weren't. You were kind and sweet, a lovely dad, and I behaved badly. You were the perfect husband.'

'But not the perfect husband for you. Our marriage was never quite right, was it?'

He's right, of course. It never was quite right. Even I know it in my heart. But I'm not sure that I have the guts to say it out loud. I've given up all notions of Adam taking me back. I know that's not going to happen. But to admit that our marriage was fundamentally unsound is too awful.

'It was never the big passionate union I thought it was going to be,' Adam continues, looking at me now.

'Was I such a let-down?'

'No, but being together wasn't how I expected it would be. I'd always loved you from afar . . .'

'And I was that horrible up close?'

'No, not at all.' Adam shakes his head. 'That's not what I mean.'

I stare down at the patio tiles. There are some weeds working their way through the cracks between them.

'The truth is, I was your rebound relationship. I know that, and in your heart, you know that too. You leapt into it, hurt and wounded from what had gone before. I was convenient. You needed someone to help raise Thackeray. But it was too soon. I was glad of your attention. If I was guilty of anything, it was idolising you. But you never loved me. We were friends. It's why the sex never sent us to the rafters. It's probably why we never conceived a child. The chemistry wasn't there.' He sighs deeply. 'The chemistry was never there. Deep down, I probably always knew it. I was just clinging on.'

'Oh, Adam.' I reach across to grab both his hands, and find myself kneeling at his feet. I didn't expect this. A shouting match and vile name-calling would have felt better than this. I want to fling my arms around Adam's neck and make everything better for him. I can't bear the pain I've caused. 'You must feel so used,' I mutter. 'It was never what I intended.'

'I know.' Adam smiles at me calmly and wipes away the tears that seem to be running down my cheeks. He always was so gentle.

'You know I do still love you,' I say quietly.

'I know you do. But not in the way that a wife should love her husband. In the way that a friend loves a friend. You know, the ancient Greeks had five different words for love, because they felt the one word didn't cover all its different forms.'

Our hands are still entwined, with fingers knotted together as they have been so often in the last few years, but I know he's right.

'Whether Brett showed up or not, our marriage was always going to flounder at some point,' Adam carries on. 'I thought having a kid together might put us on a firmer footing, but a kid is the wrong prop. It was wrong of me to push that.'

'Oh, Adam.' It's all I seem able to say.

'The point is, I have to find someone who really does love me and isn't just trying to convince herself that she does.'

'Is it that obvious?'

'I know you wanted to love me. But it was never the big love like in those romance books you read. It was never that. And the time has come to stop papering over the cracks and call it what it is. In many ways I'm grateful to Brett.'

'But I can't bear to hurt you.'

'I know. But we're grown-ups. I wanted you to love me the way you loved Brett, and I don't think you ever could. I see you straining at the leash to be with him. I see it in your eyes. I see it in your heart. How could real love flourish between us in the shadow of another that has never been forgotten? You want Thackeray to know his father? So let him. I can't fight the tide. It is what it is.'

'But Brett doesn't mean anything to me any more.' Adam looks unconvinced. 'No, really. He doesn't.'

'Only you can work that out,' he says with another deep sigh.

'I want to forget about that awful afternoon. I want to obliterate it from my memory. It was a terrible, terrible mistake. Not just because I was unfaithful, but for a million other reasons too. But I've decided I want to have the baby. You don't have to support me. I'm going to have it on my own. I've rented a little house. I've sold a script. I'm going to be an independent woman.'

'Hold on a second. You did what?' Adam looks astonished, like I've just told him I've been to the moon.

'I'm going to be an independent woman.'

'No, the bit before that. What did you say?'

'I said I sold a script. Two million.'

'You wrote and sold a script in s-s-s-six weeks?'

'A month, actually.'

'B-b-b-but that's incredible.'

'Why is that so incredible? You do it.'

'Yes, but . . .'

'What, you didn't think I had the focus?'

'No . . . I . . . I . . .'

'Go on, you didn't think I was smart enough, did you?'

'No. I . . . I'm j-j-j-just shocked. And you sold it for two million?'

'Two million.'

'T-t-t-two million.' The stutter is back. Adam must really be shocked.

'Yes. You see, I had a rather interesting meeting with Stephen.'

'With Stephen?'

'Yes, with Stephen. Are you going to repeat everything I say?'

'No.'

'Well . . .' I heave myself back into the patio chair next to him – my knees are starting to fall asleep – and tell him all about my big deal with Stephen. Adam listens attentively, relishing every detail. And I realise that he and I really were just good friends, and suddenly I can see that we always will be too. Whether the baby turns out to be Adam's or not, he will want to be involved. He will always be involved in my life.

'So what's the screenplay?' he asks.

'It's about a rock star who meets a beautiful model on a plane heading for Australia, and they end up having a twenty-two-hour stopover in Hawaii. But he's married, and so they try to forget each other, but they end up writing to each other for a whole year.'

'And then?'

'Then they get married, of course. It had to have a happy ending. You know how I feel about happy endings. It's called *Twenty-Two Hours*.'

'Awesome, Pearl. Awesome. And New Look have green-lighted it?'

'Not only have they green-lighted it, they've commissioned me to write another.' I feel the rush of adrenaline, just telling the story.

'I can't believe it!' Adam is blown away. 'I just can't believe it. Of course you've always had such a great imagination.'

'Well, I didn't exactly dream it up. It's Mum and

Dad's story. You know that, don't you?'

Adam's face is blank a second, and then realisation dawns. 'Of course it is. How stupid of me.' He pauses a second. 'But you really want to make it so public?'

'No one else will know it was their story. A few people might guess. But it was very cathartic writing it. And I wanted to show that Dad was a romantic, loving man who tried to do the best he could. Lydia has always made him out to be a calculating womaniser, but I always knew there was more to him.'

'No, you're right.' Adam pauses, and rubs his chin thoughtfully. 'Although . . .' He stops himself.

'What?'

'No, it would be wrong of me to say.'

'Go on.'

'Well . . . your mum and dad's marriage didn't exactly turn out to have a happy ending in the end.'

'Not in the traditional sense, I suppose. But we still muddled through as a family. An odd, dysfunctional one. Dysfunctional isn't always so bad. And anyway, the movie stops at their wedding.'

The thought of losing Dad makes me sad again. I wish he was around still. He'd have been proud of me. Adam reaches out and squeezes my shoulder.

'I better go,' I say, suddenly realising how late it has got. The sky has turned to gold and the sun has disappeared beneath the horizon. It feels awkward to say goodbye.

'But we've still got stuff to talk through,' Adam insists with a serious expression. 'Practical stuff.'

'I don't need anything. I told you, I'm an independent woman,' I say, getting up and pulling the strap of my bag over my shoulder. 'You don't have to support me any which way.' It feels good to say it.

'What about stuff from the house? A lot of this is yours.'

'I don't think I can face dividing everything into two. It would be too awful. Besides, I'm not into having lots of possessions any more.' I turn to leave. 'Though maybe I'll take some of my clothes. These ones are looking kind of old. And I think Thackeray would love some of his toys.'

'But Thackeray and I will still see each other, won't we?' Adam is suddenly fearful.

'You think I'd take him from you?' I smile and watch Adam's relief. 'Are you crazy? And what about this little guy?' I point to my belly. 'He may be yours.'

'I doubt it. We never conceived in four years of trying. Why would we suddenly conceive now? It's sure to be Brett's.' The pain in his face makes me flinch.

'Well, no matter what, we'll be our very own dysfunctional family. I'm an expert. Remember, I come from a dysfunctional family.'

It's dark by the time we've loaded three crates of Lego, a Fisher-Price playhouse, four Buzz Lightyears, a sack of cuddly toys and a Hot Wheels race track into the trunk of my car. My clothes are going to have to wait for another trip; there isn't the space. After Thackeray is strapped into his car seat, I hug Adam goodbye and resist the urge to cry. It wouldn't do Thackeray any good. He's confused enough as it is.

'Friends?' says Adam as we part.

'Always.'

'Will you come and see our new house soon?' Thackeray calls to Adam through the open car window.

'You betchya, buddy,' Adam calls back.

I get into the car and buzz my window down.

'Have you told Brett you're pregnant?' Adam asks, as I start the engine.

'No.'

'Why not?'

'You saw how he took off just before Thackeray was born.'

'So you're too frightened he'll do it again to even tell him?' He lets out a laugh. 'Well, that makes no sense whatsoever. If you're never going to let go of him, it's time to give him another chance.'

'But I have let go of him. I'm an independent woman, remember.'

'Just tell him, Pearl,' Adam sighs. 'If he abandons you again, then you'll know what a loser he is.'

'And then?'

'Then you make your plans accordingly. You're an independent woman.'

In the following months, spring gets swallowed up by
the heat of a long summer. Even by October it's still
ninety degrees, melting sidewalks but not my resolve for
self-reliance, which over time has only gained in appeal.
Adam visits us. We visit him. Thackeray and I see more of
him now than when we were living in the same house. I
think he's even seeing someone. I've also hired a
Guatemalan nanny called Carolina, who relieves me of
the after-school pick-up, allowing me to squeeze just a
few more hours of the day to work in.

I'm working on a new script now. This one's pitch is
the Great Gatsby meets the Seven-Year Itch, set in
modern-day Los Angeles. I've called it *Indecision*. And so
far it's going well. But I've got to deliver *it* before I
deliver the baby. Which is growing so fast, my body
should carry a wide-vehicle warning. The alien, as
Thackeray has so promisingly christened my bump, is at
thirty-seven weeks. That means it's about seventeen
inches long and weighs six pounds.

'Can it hear me if I talk to it?' I asked Dr Greenblatt
when I went for an ultrasound.

'Probably. And no need to call it *it* any more. Do you
want to know its sex?'

'Sure.'

'Of course, an ultrasound isn't always a hundred per

cent accurate,' he muttered away at my belly. 'But I would say that is a penis, right there.'

And there it was on the monitor. A beating heart, a head, and a whole bunch of strange shapes, one of which was apparently a penis. And oh my goodness, the pregnancy suddenly seemed very real. Two boys! Two boys to raise, all on my own. I had a moment of panic about it right there on the doctor's table. Singledom is all very well, but every mother knows that having kids is a lot easier to get into than out of. But then I reminded myself that five million in the bank can buy you a whole lot of help. Let me say that again. Five million! All of which I've earned myself. And that does more for a girl's confidence than any amount of therapy. The studio liked the first script so much, they paid me up front for the second. Imagine that. I'm actually good at this.

Writing the script has been a good fixation for me too. With a cup of mint tea in hand (no caffeine any more because of the baby), I lock myself away in the guest house every day. I close the yellow drapes I've installed, lean back in the 'E Z High Back Executive Leather Chair' I bought myself, turn on my Apple and write. It's absorbing, consuming, and a relief not to have to think about anything else. In particular, anything like Brett.

Thackeray sees Brelt every couple of weeks. I had to explain to him that he was a very lucky boy because he had two daddies. I wasn't sure how the news would go down that Brett was his other one, but Thackeray didn't even blink. 'Cool,' was all he had to say. That, and 'Can I watch *Spider-Man* now?'

So I get Carolina to drop him off at Brett's place for a few hours and collect him later. I don't want to see Brett. He has been persistent in asking me to come back to him. But I can't. Life is too messy and complicated when he's around. I haven't told him I'm pregnant. This is perhaps irrational. I won't be able to hide a baby away for ever.

But I can't bring myself to tell him. I'm too scared he'll run away again, just when Thackeray's got to know him.

'You've got to tell him,' the girls urge me, like they always do, as we meet in the café at Fred Segal for some late-night shopping. It's a little treat I'm allowing myself. There hasn't been time for any fun recently, and I've sworn to buy only one new maternity shirt. Moderation is the new excess, I remind myself. Thankfully normal relations have resumed with both Bella and Lizzie. The wall of attrition was always going to be worn down at some stage by Lizzie. She who never misses a chance for drama turned up on my new doorstep in West Hollywood with spa gift certificates and an expression of contrition.

'I shouldn't have said what I said. It was totally wrong . . . and I'm, like, totally sorry,' she warbled, choosing words that I know she must have rehearsed in the car. Her face had lost its customary joy. Even her curly hair looked limp. 'I know you must hate me.'

'I don't hate you,' I said, and invited her in.

'Will you ever forgive me?'

'Eventually,' I teased with a smile. 'Depends how much that spa certificate is worth.'

Lizzie threw her arms around me. 'I am really, really sorry.'

'I know you are.'

'Although you should know it wasn't really me,' she added, sending my eyes rolling to the ceiling.

'What do you mean, it wasn't you?' I felt annoyed again. 'Of course it was you.'

'Well, yes it was me. But it wasn't me, not the real me, if you know what I mean.'

'Not really.'

'It was the Quantum Spiritualists.'

'What, they made you do it?'

'Yes. Well, no. Well, kinda. They took me over. It was weird. They told me all this stuff. They told me I should right the wrongs and speak the truth. Look, it probably doesn't make much sense, but I kind of got sucked into it all. I fell for it.'

'But that's terrible.' I hadn't realised the extent of their influence. 'And are you still involved with them?'

'No. I got desperate.'

'Desperate?' What had they been doing to her? I felt suddenly guilty that I hadn't been watching out for her.

'Yes. Desperate for sex. Cameron Valentin wouldn't know his way to a girl's G-spot if she gave him a tour map. None of them believe in sex before marriage. Can you imagine?'

I laughed until my belly ached, glad to have Lizzie back on side. It was one thing to part from a husband, but to lose a girlfriend! That's when life can get really lonely. And to think I nearly lost Bella too.

Now, perversely, having spent years telling me what an asshole Brett is, Bella is surrounded by shopping bags in the Fred Segal café, convincing me that I should tell him I'm pregnant.

'Doesn't he have a right to know, if he's the father?' she demands.

'But you're the one who said he had no rights.'

'Ah yes, but I've seen how much he's changed.'

'So only assholes have no rights.'

'I just think he'd do the right thing by you.'

'But I don't want anyone to do the right thing by me.' The girls look unconvinced. 'I'm fine on my own.'

'But Pearl, wouldn't it be great if you and Brett got back together again.' Lizzie joins in. 'You've always loved him. And obviously he loves you. What about all that skywriting?'

'What skywriting?'

'For sure you remember. On Valentine's Day.'

'What skywriting on Valentine's Day?'

'Remember I showed you? B heart P? Brett loves Pearl. Romantic, huh?'

I think back and remember it only vaguely what seems like a lifetime ago.

'It was a B, then a heart, then a P,' Lizzie repeats. 'I watched it.'

'I only remember a B . . . Anyway, it could have been anyone. Ben loves Penny. Brad loves Patsy. Babycakes loves Princess.'

'But it coulda bin Brett loves Pearl.' Lizzie smiles cheekily.

'It makes no difference. I don't need a man. I don't want a man.'

'Course you need a man,' says Lizzie, checking out one who is hanging around the café looking lost. 'Well, I know what I'm getting you for Christmas.'

'What?'

'It comes with a battery and starts with the letter V,' she shrieks loudly. 'Now, do you want to hear about *Dog Knows* or not?'

'Not,' Bella and I tease, knowing that we have little choice. Shooting has just started on the film I sent Lizzie on the audition for back in the spring. She got the part, and consequently there is a lot of drama, both in front of and behind the camera, that we simply *have* to hear. The stage is Lizzie's natural home – and as she wallows in the glory of finding it again, I see her years of homesickness for it recede into distant memories. She could do well in this film and have a career back on track.

But I want to hear Bella's news too. After the police were called and the hoaxer finally found and arrested, Bella spoke to her real aunt in England and went to visit her last month for the first time.

'How was England?' I ask her, when we can listen to Lizzie's tales no more.

'Rainy,' Bella answers flatly. She doesn't look as

euphoric as I hoped she'd be. I get the sense that she is disappointed.

'And . . .'

'Well, it was awkward, if you want to know the truth. My aunt invited me to her house for the afternoon. She was perfectly nice. I mean, she shook my hand, made me tea. But it was all very reserved. I don't know what I was expecting, but we were like strangers.'

'It'll take time to get to know each other,' I say gently.

'Yes, I suppose.'

'But she *did* want to get to know you?'

'Yes. She spent a long time telling me how sorry she was about not taking me in. She told me the whole story. And it wasn't her fault. It was her husband who wouldn't have me. Anyway, I told her we had to put it behind us now.'

'I expect she was relieved about that.'

'Yes, it's just . . .' Bella looks doubtful. 'I don't know. It's all so confusing. I think I expected to feel more between us. I wanted there to be more of a connection. Strangely, I think I felt more of a connection with that woman who was pretending to be my aunt.'

'But don't you see that was because she was acting out what you and she thought a reunion ought to be? She was acting out a Hollywood fantasy. And it was fake. Real life takes longer to develop than celluloid. It's awkward and messy. But it will come, and it'll be better for it because it will be genuine.'

Bella nods her head. It's nothing she doesn't know herself, but sometimes it's helpful to have someone else say it out loud.

'Did you get some pictures of your mum and dad?' Lizzie asks.

'Yes,' Bella says, looking happier. She rummages in her bag and produces a collection of photos, which I pore over, taking in the happy expressions of the two people in front of me, who I feel I have come to know.

'It'll be all right, Bella. Give it time.' I squeeze Bella's arm. She smiles.

'And just think, you're twenty thousand pounds better off,' adds Lizzie brightly. 'That ought to make you happy. You could pay for my designer vagina.' We laugh and I relish the moment. I can manage without a man, but not without Bella and Lizzie.

This house has really come to feel like home, I realise, as I park my car in the garage and walk up the garden path. The tree right outside the front always seems so welcoming, and the wide veranda where I've placed a swing seat tempts me to linger there. It's pretty, and with the lights on inside reflecting on the hardwood floors, and its creamy drapes and cottage-style furniture, it has a warmth to it that I never quite managed to achieve with our old house. A real-estate agent would describe it as 'an enchanting hideaway with a cosy atmosphere, decorated with warmth and attention to detail'. It's small, and I like that.

I'm just pulling on my PJs and crawling under my quilt, having said goodbye to Carolina and put sixty dollars into her hand for the night's babysitting, when my cell phone bursts into activity. I really must change the ring tone. I have Elton John singing 'Rocket Man' every time someone rings.

'Pearl, it's Heather.'

'Er ... hi,' I say. Apart from phone conversations about Dad's estate and the explanation that she wouldn't have to sell Dad's house, I've barely heard anything from her since she decided to sell every last sweater and pair of underpants that Dad owned. What's she doing calling me now? It's gone ten p.m.

'Pearl, I need your help.' There's the same urgency to her voice that she used when Dad was in hospital.

'What is it?'

'I'm in labour.' She starts panting down the phone.

'What, now?'

'Yes, now. Please, Pearl, I need your help. There's no one else.'

'But what about the Stupid Lucky Dog guy.'

'We broke up. Actually he ... Aaagggghhhhh ...' More panting and heavy breathing. 'Actually he dumped me. Aaaagghhhh! Please ... Aaaaggghhh ...'

'Where are you?'

'I'm in a cab. Joely's taking care of Casey. I'm heading for ... aaaggghhhhhh ... Cedars.'

'OK, I'll meet you there. Just hang in there. Breathe. Remember, breathe. In, two, three, four, out, two, three, four, in, two, three, four, out, two, three, four.' Funny how it all comes back to you.

'You'll really meet me?'

'I'll meet you.'

'Only I'm on my own ... and. ...' Heather starts to whimper. 'Pearl, I'm scared.'

'It's OK. I'll be there. Where are you now?'

'Um. We're on Melrose and ... and ... Where are we?' I hear her asking the cab driver.

'Doheny,' I hear him shout.

'You got that? Melrose and Doheny. Aaagghhhhh!'

'You're nearly there. Just breathe. I'll be as quick as I can.'

I hang up and call Carolina straight away. She probably hasn't even got home yet.

'Carolina, my stepmother is in labour. She's having a baby. I've got to go to Cedars. Can you come back?'

'Si, meesus. Right now?'

'Si. Now. I might be a while. Can you stay with Thackeray all night? I'll pay you double.'

'No problem, meesus.'

Carolina is there within ten minutes, and in less time

I'm at Cedars. I had to come. Heather might be the stepmother from hell, but she's family. I'm told she's already in triage when I arrive. The room is sectioned off into separate cubicles, each with a green curtain drawn closed around the bed, but I know instantly where Heather is. I'd recognise that wailing anywhere.

'Aaaaaaaaggghhhhhhhh!' she screams. 'Will someone get me a fuckin' epidural?'

I find her behind the curtain. There's an IV tube going into her arm and a black belt wrapped around her middle with wires disappearing into a computer. Overhead on a black-and-white monitor are the peaks and troughs of a graph showing both the baby's heartbeat and the strength of Heather's contractions – a new life fighting to get into the world.

'Oh Pearl, thank you for coming. Thank you,' she cries. Tears begin to trickle down her cheeks, leaving black streaks of mascara.

'It's OK. Everything's going to be fine. You've done this before.' I hold her hand tightly and she looks pathetically grateful. 'Nothing to it.'

'It's just I wanted your dad to be here,' she says, now crying harder. I squeeze her hand, and we listen to the groans of the other women in labour in beds all around us.

'Aaaaagggghhhhh!' Heather suddenly screams again. 'This is so fucking painful. Why isn't your dad here? I'm so mad at him for dying. I'm so fucking mad at him.'

'I know,' I say soothingly. 'But he wouldn't have been any use anyway. You know that Dad's best joke about childbirth was that he liked his kids to be born at home so he wouldn't have to miss anything on the TV. Now, we've got to concentrate on you. Breathe. In, two, three, four, out, two, three, four . . .'

Heather breathes. 'I don't know why we couldn't just have had another dog,' she laments.

'In, two, three, four, out, two, three, four . . .'

'Where's the fucking anaesthetist anyway? I want an epidural,' she yells at the top of her lungs. I may be deaf for the rest of my life.

Eventually a Latino nurse appears through the curtain. 'What's all this noise? Too much noise,' she tuts, as she studies the monitor and the sheet of paper it spews out with its scratchy graph. 'OK, darlin', let's see how far along you are.'

She pulls back the bedsheets and Heather is examined. I hold her hand and we both stare at the monitor as the baby's heartbeat beeps its tune.

'Oh, you've got a long while to go yet, you're only five centimetres dilated,' announces the nurse.

'A while?' says Heather, scarcely able to believe her ears. 'With all this pain?'

'You've got to get to ten centimetres,' the nurse explains.

'How long will that take?'

'How long is a piece of string?'

'But what about my fucking epidural?' asks Heather angrily.

'I'll see what I can do,' says the nurse huffily.

'Aaaaaggghhhhhh!' Heather is on to another contraction.

It's another seven hours before Heather's cervix is ten centimetres dilated and her bed is finally whizzed through automatic doors and down sterile white corridors to her own labour room, where Dr Greenblatt is waiting, wearing a mask over his face. He has nice eyes. I haven't noticed before.

'Dr Greenblatt's your doctor?' I ask Heather. I never knew.

'Fuck, fuck, fuck!' she screams.

Heather did eventually get her epidural, but it has to

be removed for the final stages of labour in order that she can push.

'Fuck, fuck, fuck . . .' she screams again.

'How are you, Pearl?' says Dr Greenblatt, ignoring the profanity, as Heather's feet are placed in stirrups and she's wired up to a new monitor by a team of nurses. He must get lots of it in his job.

'Fuck, fuck, fuck . . .' Heather screams.

'I'm good,' I say, wiping Heather's forehead with a cool flannel.

'Fuck, fuck, fuck . . .' she continues.

'Yourself?'

'Fuck, fuck, fuck . . .' says Heather.

'Just dandy,' he says, now peering between Heather's legs. 'And how's the next screenplay?'

'Fuck, fuck, fuck . . .' says Heather.

'It's coming on.' I wipe the flannel on Heather's hot red cheeks and erase the mascara streaks.

'Fuck, fuck, fuck . . .'

'OK, you're doing good here,' Dr Greenblatt tells Heather. 'The baby's in a good position. His head is engaged. This is going to be real easy. But when the contractions come, you've got to push. Really push. Do you feel the urge to push?'

'Fuck, fuck, fuck . . .'

'Yes, but do you feel the urge to push?'

'Yes!' she yells.

'OK, I see a contraction coming now,' he says, watching the monitor. 'I want you to push.'

'Push, Heather. Push. You can do it,' I say encouragingly.

Heather pushes, screams, and squeezes my hand so hard it may take until next year before the feeling returns to it.

'OK, I see the head now. It's coming, Heather,' says Dr Greenblatt. 'Stop pushing now. We need to wait for the next contraction. You're doing great.'

'Fuck, fuck, fuck,' says Heather.

'You're doing great,' I repeat to Heather. And wipe her face again.

'Fuck, fuck, fuck . . .'

Seconds later there is another contraction. There is more pushing. More cursing, and then suddenly, as if by magic, which it couldn't possibly be, because it wouldn't hurt so much if it was, a small, perfect, dark-haired baby boy shoots out into the world. He's covered in blood, gunk and all kinds of oozy liquids, so he doesn't necessarily look cute yet. But he will, and suddenly I find tears spilling down my face.

A new brother. Another child. He even looks like Dad. Oh God, how I wish Dad was here. My whole body aches at the thought of how much he would enjoy this moment.

'Alreet, our kid,' he'd say to it.

He'd hold the baby in his arms, wrapping himself protectively around him as he always used to with me. He'd take him over to the window and show him the view of the city.

'Now this is a weird place called Los Angeles,' he would say in his strange northern accent. 'But I come from a place called Newcastle in a country called England, where people speak properly, and one day, son, I'll take you there. And you'll learn how to play soccer like a reet good'un.'

I smile to myself, and realise for the first time that I'm not as sad as I was about him being gone. Of course I'm sad. But not *as* sad. Maybe I've moved on, like Heather told me I should.

Dr Greenblatt eventually says farewell, after declaring Heather fit but likely to be sore for a while. He departs with the nurses, leaving us alone.

'Would you like to hold the baby?' she asks me, much calmer now, and looking surprisingly beautiful for someone who's just been through labour. She hands me the bundle – all pink and smelling of freshness.

'What are you going to call him?' I ask.

'Gavin, after your dad, of course.'

I smile. He'd have liked that.

'Pearl, I owe you an apology,' Heather says quietly. 'I behaved badly after your dad died.'

'It's OK.'

'No it isn't. I know I was mean.'

'It was tough for you.'

'Yes, but that was no excuse. I'm sorry.' She pauses, but I can see she wants to say more. 'The truth is, I was jealous of you.'

'Of me?'

'Yeah. You and your dad were always such big buddies. I felt threatened.'

'There was never any need to feel that.'

'I know. And you've been so good to me too. You even sorted out keeping the house. I don't really deserve it.'

'Don't be silly.'

'But we're friends now, right?'

'Of course we are.'

'I want us always to be friends, and I don't want you to ever feel a stranger in your dad's home. He would never have wanted that.'

I feel a sudden wave of relief. Perhaps I hadn't even realised how much that meant to me.

'Thanks,' I say.

For a while we say nothing to each other. Heather closes her eyes, and I sit in the rocking chair by her bed, taking in the tiny features of this new person in my arms. He's so exquisite. I put him back in the bassinet and stroke his little face. Outside it's light already. I can hear the rumble of the morning traffic and the bustle of the day begin. Where did the night disappear to? I ought to go home. But a wave of tiredness sweeps over me, and I feel momentarily giddy.

'You OK, miss?' asks a nurse who has appeared from nowhere and is removing the IV from Heather's arm. 'You look a bit pale.'

'I feel a bit dizzy. But I'll be fine. I'll just sit down a minute.'

The nurse wraps several blankets around me on the rocking chair and I close my eyes a while. It feels good to close my eyes.

Some time later I'm woken by Heather, asking me if I want some breakfast.

'What time is it?'

'I don't know, but I'm so hungry I could eat at McDonald's. Shall I go find us something?' She pushes back the covers and starts to get out of bed.

'Are you crazy? You've just given birth. Let me go.'

'No, I'm fine. I want to get up. I want to stretch.'

'You do?' First woman I ever knew who wanted to go disco dancing after labour. I watch her ease herself gently to her feet. 'Are you sure about this? Why don't you let me go?'

'No, you look too comfortable, all snuggled up in that blanket. My turn to take care of you.'

'I don't think the nurses would approve. You might hurt yourself. Rupture something.'

'Get outta here. You watch the baby. I'll find the breakfast,' she insists, producing a dressing gown from her overnight bag and hobbling out of the door.

Boy, she's a force to reckon with. I lean back into the rocking chair next to the bassinet and peer through its glass sides. Gavin has gone to sleep with his tiny fingers curled into a fist. He'll certainly be a fighter with parents like his. I wonder what my new baby will be like. Will he be gentle and studious – a mini Adam? Or will he be charismatic and handsome like Brett? I stroke my tummy and find myself praying for an easy delivery no matter what. A knock at the door disturbs the daydreaming.

'Come,' I call, imagining it must be a nurse looking for Heather, but when the door opens, I can only think I must still be daydreaming. It's Brett. 'What are you doing here?'

'I came as quickly as I could.' He looks flustered. There's sweat on his face, like he's been running. 'Are you all right?'

'Bit tired, but I'm fine.'

'And the baby?'

'The baby's doing great. Look.' I point towards the bassinet. 'But what are you doing here?' Brett peers over its edge and I watch his eyes fill with tears. 'How did you know I was here?'

'It's beautiful. Beautiful.' Brett can't take his eyes off the baby. A tear rolls down one cheek, reminding me how sexy it is to see a man cry. 'Boy or girl?' he whispers.

'A boy.'

'A boy!' Emotion makes his voice crack. I never thought Brett would get so choked about babies.

'Has he got a name yet?'

'Gavin.'

'Of course. After your dad. And you're all right? You're really all right?'

'Of course.' Why's he going on about it so much?

'Pearl, why didn't you tell me you were having a baby?'

'Who told you I was having a baby?'

'The nanny. When she was dropping Thackeray off this morning.'

Oh goodness, I'd forgotten that it was Brett's morning with Thackeray.

'She said you were having a baby. You'd gone to Cedars. Pearl, why didn't you tell me?'

'I don't know.' I feel stupid now for not telling him. 'I was scared of you running out on me again after Thackeray had just got to know you. Scared of falling for you again. Scared of ending up the wreck I was after I had Thackeray.' Brett holds on to the side of the bassinet and hangs his head in shame. 'I've only just pieced myself back together. I couldn't risk going there again.'

'Pearl, if you only knew how I wish I could push the clock back. I do. I really do.' His face is buckling with concern. I think he really means it. 'Remember when we had sex that afternoon?'

'That was you?'

'Don't joke with me, Pearl. I'm serious.' His eyes peer at me defiantly. 'I haven't been able to get you out of my head. I've thought about you all the time. I don't know what I can do to convince you that I want you back. I'd do anything. Anything. And I don't mind waiting. But it's hard when you're groping in the dark. I don't even know if you saw my Valentine.'

'What Valentine?'

'It was in the sky. I didn't want to make it too obvious, but I was sure you of all people, you, my big romantic girl, would surely have known it was for you.'

'So it *was* you.'

'Of course it was me. I wanted you to know I was thinking of you. But I didn't want to rock the boat for you with Adam. It wouldn't have been right. I thought the best thing I could do was just let you know I was thinking of you and wait. I told myself, if I have to wait for ever for you, well, it will be worth it.'

I say nothing. I mean, how romantic could he be? But this is Brett. Do I trust him?

'Oh . . . and I meant to tell you, I bought Thackeray the train set.'

'What train set?'

'Your dad's train set. The one you said you wanted. It

was up for auction back in the spring. It's taken ages for it to arrive.'

I let out a burst of laughter.

'What are you laughing about?'

'Because I tried bidding on it too.'

Brett laughs, but then his face is serious again. 'I can't believe Adam would throw you out when you were pregnant. How could he do such a thing?'

'Well,' I smile awkwardly, 'he actually had good reason to. But it's OK, we're friends now.'

'And what will you do?'

'Raise the baby on my own, just like I did Thackeray. What did you think I'd do? Give it away?'

'Pearl, won't you let me take care of you?' Brett is staring at me closely now, his dark eyes filled with sentiment. 'I want to take care of you. I want to make up for abandoning you.' He suddenly falls to his knees, right by me in the rocking chair. He grabs my hands and looks up at me pleadingly.

'Get up. A nurse will think you're proposing to me,' I tell him jokingly.

'Well, maybe I am. If I asked you to marry me, what would you say?'

'I'd say what kind of question is that?' And suddenly we're both laughing again.

'But would you?' He coughs and rearranges his tall, lean body so that there's only one knee on the floor. 'Pearl, I know I've been an idiot, but I want to take care of you. I don't care that the baby isn't mine. I just care about you. Please, will you marry me?' He gazes at me with the look that always used to make my heart do gymnastics, and suddenly it's leaping energetically again in a way that might win it a gold in the Olympics. Easy does it, I tell it. Don't rush into anything.

'But I'm already married,' I tell him. 'I'm scarcely in a position.'

'A trifling detail,' he says, still staring at me with those big, expressive eyes. I feel the warmth of his hand. Just its touch sends an electric current through to my heart. 'Would you think about it?' he asks.

'I'll think about it,' I say, failing to sound as nonchalant as I would like. Brett always had a way of making me feel protected. Suddenly the urge to curl up in his arms is too hard to resist any more. I close my eyes and lean forward, for the kiss that I now know is inevitable.

Brett moves closer too. 'You see, the thing is . . .' he whispers. His lips are so close to mine, I can feel his breath. 'The thing is, I love little Gavin's mummy.'

'What?' I shriek, opening my eyes wide. 'You what?' I push him hard, so that he loses his balance and falls on to the floor.

I get to my feet angrily. How could he? How could he ask me to marry him, but tell me he loves Heather in the next breath? What is this, swingers? I march furiously towards the door to show him the exit. How dare he? But halfway across the room – very, very slowly, because obviously I've been very stupid here – I realise what's happened, and I start to laugh. I laugh so hard it's difficult to stop.

Brett looks confused. Not least because without the blankets covering me, he's suddenly able to see my huge, very pregnant belly.

'You thought that was my baby, didn't you?' I manage to spit out, gasping for breath.

'Carolina told you I was having a baby and I'd gone to Cedars. You think that's mine.'

'Isn't it?' says Brett uncertainly, still on the floor.

'No, this is Heather's baby.'

'Heather?'

'Dad's Heather. She went into labour last night and asked me to be with her. She's gone to find some breakfast. This,' I grasp my swollen tummy with both hands, 'this is my baby. Not due for another month.'

I watch his face. It is a picture of perplexity.

'This isn't your baby?' he says slowly, pointing at the bassinet and pulling himself to his feet. I shake my head. 'But you are having a baby?' I nod. 'In a month's time?' I nod again.

Brett sits down on the rocking chair to take in the news. He leans forward, knotting his hands together, brow furrowed in concentration. I wonder briefly if he is in tune enough to make the calculation. Not all men are. But Brett is on to it.

'In a month's time, you say?' He looks up at me, with hope replacing confusion in his expression. I smile knowingly. 'Which will make it exactly nine months after that wonderful, spectacular, mind-blowing afternoon we spent together?'

'Yes.'

'Which means the baby is mine?'

'Not necessarily. It could be Adam's.' My smile falters. It's such an awful admission to not know who a baby's father is.

'But it could be mine?'

'Yes, it could be yours.'

Brett springs suddenly to his feet, bouncing across the room to grab my hands and spin me in a circle. 'Then you've *got* to marry me. You've simply got to.'

'But it might be Adam's.'

'Doesn't matter. Will you marry me?'

'I told you I'd think about it.' I pull my hands away. This is too fast. My head is still spinning, but Brett will not be turned away. He pulls me close to him and kisses me. A long, slow kiss. So long that the baby starts kicking, so long that I know my future is certain, and so long that I don't even notice that breakfast has arrived and we have an audience.

*

'Bravo,' says Heather, clapping her hands. She's back in her bed, with two breakfast trays, alongside Joely and Casey, who have come to see the baby. 'We were all waiting for you two to get back together.'

'You were?'

'Sure. Your dad always said you and Brett were the perfect match.'

'He did?'

'Yeah. Brett just needed to grow up a bit first.' She plants a kiss on Casey's forehead. 'Anyways, what do you think of little Gavin?' she asks him.

The kids crowd around the bassinet, and while they're cooing over Gavin's perfect features, there's another knock at the door. This time it's Carolina with Thackeray.

'Sorry, meesus, but ee wanted to come find 'is mummy,' she explains as Thackeray hurls himself at me. 'I try call you, but you no answer your phone, so I came to the hospital.'

'Mummy, where were you?' Thackeray asks pointedly. 'You weren't there when I woke up.'

'I'm sorry, honey. I came to help with Heather's baby in the night. Would you like to see the baby?'

I lift Thackeray so he can see into the bassinet, where the baby is sleeping on regardless of the hullabaloo around him. 'If I cut it open, would there be blood?' he asks.

Definitely going to be a doctor. And I'm just musing over setting up a college fund when there's another knock at the door. Now it's Ashley with Lydia.

'I came to pick up those photos,' Lydia explains, hugging me tight. 'I couldn't wait. And then Heather called, told me I had a new baby brother.'

'You did?' I glance across at Heather, who's looking a little sheepish. 'How did you get to be so forgiving?'

'Dr Phil. On TV.'

And we all laugh, because here we all are – my own

dysfunctional, odd, crazy family, acting like we're a real one. Ashley produces a bottle of champagne, and for a while nobody fights. And if Gavin Sash's family can manage to do that, then I know my own stands a chance too.

'You really think it's going to work second time round?' I whisper to Brett.

'Have I ever let you down?' asks Brett with a smirk.

'You really want me to answer that?'

'Not just now,' he says, and squeezes my hand. 'We've got things to do together first.'

Epilogue

Lizzie's movie *Dog Knows* was so successful, she is now making a sequel, even though it turns out she's allergic to dogs and they bring her out in a rash. She married and divorced the director within three weeks, and with the settlement money she's paying for a designer vagina.

Bella went back to England a second time, for Christmas with her family. It rained non-stop and she says next time they're coming to her, because you can never get a decent hot shower in Britain and the price of eating out is extortionate.

Stephen made a public declaration of his interest in New Look Pictures in order to preserve his reputation as an honest and reputable agent. Three weeks later he was arrested for picking up a transvestite prostitute.

Ashley recently began dating another lawyer, in the rights department of his firm, and I held my breath. But they broke up after a month, after she turned out to be a Quantum Spiritualist. They seem to be everywhere.

Lydia has opened a shop here in LA. Her jewellery was in *Vogue* last month, and Angelina Jolie wore her earrings to the Oscars.

Heather married Chad Sucker of the Red Hot Mystics the year after little Gavin was born. Video footage of their sex life is currently available on the internet.

Adam is dating Jasmin Lee, the script-reader I tried to set Ashley up with at the charity ball. I think they are a good match, although she could still use a makeover. I've offered to take her shopping.

My mother is still living in Hawaii, but planning to marry her personal trainer. It will be a church wedding.

I had my baby at Cedars. We've never had a DNA test done, because there was no need. He's a carbon copy of Thackeray, who remains a carbon copy of Brett. Brett moved in with me and the kids. He tells me every day that he loves me, and I'm almost ready to believe him.

little black dress

brings you fantastic new books like these
every month - find out more at
www.littleblackdressbooks.com

Why not link up with other devoted Little Black
Dress fans on our Facebook group? Simply type
Little Black Dress Books into Facebook to join up.

And if you want to be the first
to hear the latest news on all things
Little Black Dress, just send the details below to
littleblackdressmarketing@headline.co.uk
and we'll sign you up to our lovely email
newsletter (and we promise that we won't share
your information with anybody else!).*

Name: ─────────────────────────

Email Address: ────────────────────

Date of Birth: ─────────────────────

Region/Country: ────────────────────

What's your favourite Little Black Dress book?

─────────────────────────────

How many Little Black Dress books have you read?──────

*You can be removed from the mailing list at any time

Pick up a *little black dress* – it's a girl thing.

978 0 7553 4715 5

THE FARMER NEEDS A WIFE
Janet Gover
PBO £5.99

Rural romances become all the rage when editor Helen Woodley starts a new magazine column profiling Australia's lovelorn farmers. But a lot of people (and Helen herself) are about to find out that the course of true love ain't ever smooth . . .

It's not all haystacks and pitchforks, ladies – get ready for a scorching outback read!

HIDE YOUR EYES
Alison Gaylin
PBO £5.99

Samantha Leiffer's in big trouble: the chest she saw a sinister man dumping into the Hudson river contained a deady body, meaning she's now a witness in a murder case. It's just as well hot, hard-line detective John Krull is by her side . . .

978 0 7553 4802 2

'Alison Gaylin is my new must-read' Harlen Coben

Pick up a *little black dress* – it's a girl thing.

978 0 7553 4334 8

IT SHOULD HAVE BEEN ME
Phillipa Ashley
PBO £5.99

When Carrie Brownhill's fiancé Huw calls off their wedding, running away from it all in a VW camper-van seems an excellent idea to her. But when Huw's old friend Matt takes the driver's seat, could fate be taking Carrie on a different journey?

'Fulfils all the best fantasies, including a gorgeous, humanitarian hero and a camper van!' Katie Fforde

TODAY'S SPECIAL
Alan Goldsher
PBO £4.99

When chef Anna Rowan and boyfriend Byron Smith are asked to star in a reality-TV show about their restaurant, TART, they find themselves – and their relationship – under the hot glare of the TV cameras. Do they have the right recipe for love?

A.M. Goldsher serves up another deliciously quirky and original romance.

978 0 7553 3996 9

Pick up a *little black dress* – it's a girl thing.

978 0 7553 4731 5

HANDBAGS AND HOMICIDE
Dorothy Howell
PBO £4.99

Haley didn't actually mean *murder* when she said she'd 'kill for' the latest fashions. But when her department store boss is discovered dead in the store room, fingers are pointed firmly at her! Will gorgeous Ty Cameron believe in her innocence?

A sharp, comic debut combining mystery, romance and shopping – what more could a girl want!

TRULY MADLY YOURS
Rachel Gibson
PBO £4.99

Delaney Shaw has to stay put in the town of Truly, Idaho for an entire year to claim her three-million-dollar inheritance ... At least the other condition of her stepfather's will, that she has nothing to do with sexy bad-boy Nick Allegrezza, sounds more manageable ... doesn't it?

Fall in love with Rachel Gibson and her fabulous, sexy romantic reads!

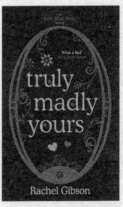

978 0 7553 3744 6

Pick up a *little black dress* – it's a girl thing.

ANIMAL INSTINCTS
Nell Dixon
PBO £5.99

Clodagh Martin's celebrity sister Imogen couldn't have turned up at a worse time: Clodagh's beloved animal sanctuary is under threat. Facing ruin, can Clodagh figure out whether property magnate and bad-luck Jack Thatcher's interest is in her, or her assets?

978 0 7553 4520 5

Lose yourself in this gorgeous tale of romance, mystery and a foul-mouthed parrot!

SEE JANE SCORE
Rachel Gibson
PBO £5.99

Journalist Jane Alcott's big chance finally arrives when she lands a job reporting on ice-hockey team the Seattle Chinooks – and on their star player, Luc Martineau. Hot-shot Luc has no time for dirt-digging reporters, but he's about to discover there's more to Jane than meets the eye . . .

978 0 7553 4634 9

Cold ice meets red-hot tempers – grab ring-side seats for another brilliant romance from Rachel Gibson.

Pick up a *little black dress* – it's a girl thing.

978 0 7553 4743 8

ITALIAN FOR BEGINNERS
Kristin Harmel
PBO £5.99

Despairing of finding love, Cat Connelly takes up an invitation to go to Italy, where an unexpected friendship, a whirlwind tour of the Eternal City and a surprise encounter show her that the best things in life (and love) are always unexpected . . .

Say 'arrivederci, lonely hearts' with another fabulous page-turner from Kristin Harmel.

THE GIRL MOST LIKELY TO . . .
Susan Donovan
PBO £5.99

Years after walking out of her small town in West Virginia, Kat Cavanaugh's back and looking for apologies – especially from Riley Bohland, the man who broke her heart. But soon Kat's questioning everything she thought she knew about her past . . . and about her future.

978 0 7553 5144 2

A red-hot tale of getting mad, getting even – and getting everything you want!

Pick up a *little black dress* – it's a girl thing.

978 0 7553 4801 5

TRASHED
Alison Gaylin
PBO £5.99

Take two suspicious, Tinseltown deaths and add them to the blood-stained stiletto of a beautiful actress who's just committed suicide... Journalist Simone Glass is finally on to the story of her life – but is she about to meet a terrifying deadline?

Hollywood meets homicide in Alison Gaylin's fabulous killer-thriller.

SUGAR AND SPICE
Jules Stanbridge
PBO £5.99

After the initial panic of losing her high-flying job, Maddy Brown launches Sugar and Spice, making delicious, mouth-wateringly irresistible cakes. Can she find the secret ingredient for the perfect chocolate cake – and the perfect man?

A rich, indulgent treat of a novel – love, life ... and chocolate cake.

978 0 7553 4712 4

Pick up a *little black dress* – it's a girl thing.

IT MUST BE LOVE
Rachel Gibson
PB £4.99

Gabrielle Breedlove is the sexiest suspect that undercover cop Joe Shanahan has ever had the pleasure of tailing. But when he's assigned to pose as her boyfriend things start to get complicated.

978 0 7553 3746 0

She thinks he's stalking her. He thinks she's a crook. Surely, it must be love?

ONE NIGHT STAND
Julie Cohen
PB £4.99

When popular novelist Estelle Connor finds herself pregnant after an uncharacteristic one-night stand, she enlists the help of sexy neighbour Hugh to help look for the father. But will she find what she really needs?

One of the freshest and funniest voices in romantic fiction

978 0 7553 3483 4

You can buy any of these other
Little Black Dress titles from your
bookshop or *direct from the publisher*.

FREE P&P AND UK DELIVERY
(Overseas and Ireland £3.50 per book)

I Do, I Do, I Do	Samantha Scott-Jeffries	£5.99
A Most Lamentable Comedy	Janet Mullany	£5.99
Purses and Poison	Dorothy Howell	£5.99
Perfect Image	Marisa Heath	£5.99
Girl From Mars	Julie Cohen	£5.99
True Love and Other Disasters	Rachel Gibson	£5.99
The Hen Night Prophecies: The One That Got Away	Jessica Fox	£5.99
You Kill Me	Alison Gaylin	£5.99
The Fidelity Project	Susan Conley	£5.99
Leopard Rock	Tarras Wilding	£5.99
Smart Casual	Niamh Shaw	£5.99
Animal Instincts	Nell Dixon	£5.99
It Should Have Been Me	Phillipa Ashley	£5.99
Dogs and Goddesses	Jennifer Crusie, Anne Stuart, Lani Diane Rich	£5.99
Sugar and Spice	Jules Stanbridge	£5.99
Italian for Beginners	Kristin Harmel	£5.99
The Girl Most Likely To . . .	Susan Donovan	£5.99
The Farmer Needs a Wife	Janet Gover	£5.99
Hide Your Eyes	Alison Gaylin	£5.99
Living Next Door to Alice	Marisa Mackle	£4.99

TO ORDER SIMPLY CALL THIS NUMBER

01235 400 414

or visit our website: www.headline.co.uk

Prices and availability subject to change without notice.